William Lithgow

The Poetical Remains of William Lithgow the Scottish Traveller

Now First Collected

William Lithgow

The Poetical Remains of William Lithgow the Scottish Traveller
Now First Collected

ISBN/EAN: 9783337203023

Printed in Europe, USA, Canada, Australia, Japan

Cover: Foto ©Andreas Hilbeck / pixelio.de

More available books at **www.hansebooks.com**

THE

POETICAL REMAINS

OF

WILLIAM LITHGOW,

THE SCOTISH TRAVELLER.

M.DC.XVIII.—M.DC.LX.

NOW FIRST COLLECTED.

EDINBURGH :

THOMAS GEORGE STEVENSON,

22 SOUTH FREDERICK STREET.

M.DCCC.LXIII.

IMPRESSION:

LIMITED TO ONE HUNDRED COPIES,

CHIEFLY FOR SUBSCRIBERS.

Colston & Son, Printers, Edinburgh.

CONTENTS.

—∞8∞—

PREFATORY REMARKS.

MONGST the remarkable characters that figured during the reign of the first James and his unfortunate son, WILLIAM LITHGOW occupies a prominent position. He was the first Scotsman who has left a record of his travels in foreign lands, and his adventures are so varied and romantic, that his personal narratives still possess attraction to those readers, who, despite of his inflated and obscure style, have the courage and perseverance to peruse them. He has been compared to Tom Coryate, whose " Crudities" are deservedly still held in esteem by the curious, and undoubtedly there is a considerable resemblance between the two Worthies ;— but although the English traveller is decidedly the most amusing, his Scotish contemporary has the advantage of recounting more startling adventures, and more hair-breadth escapes. His apprehension, detention, and torture by the Inquisitors in Malaga ; and the narrow chance he had of not figuring in an *auto da fe*—a favourite pastime of the holy fathers in those days of fiery zeal, and one much patronized by Spanish Royalty—would afford a fitting subject for a romance, which would eclipse the horrors of Mrs Radcliffe, and leave her *"Italián,"* with all its inquisitorial terrors, far behind.

Mr Brockett, in the preface to his reprint of Lithgow's " *Siege of Newcastle*," * asserts that the Author was originally bred a " Tailor,"

---

* Newcastle, 1820.

A

and if this be correct, the fact is remarkable, for Lithgow had received
an excellent education, was well versed in classical literature, and
was much esteemed by persons in high places both in England and
Scotland.   That he was a native of Lanark is known from his own
statement, and that his father was a Burgess of that ancient town is
proved by the retoûrs, where, on the 29th May 1623, there is this
entry :—" Wilhelmus Lythgow, heres Jacobi Lythgow Burgensis de
Lanark."

There was a small estate in the parish of Lanark, which, for a very
considerable period owned the Lithgows as proprietors.   It was held
in feu of the Carmichael family, and was called Boathaugh.   This
property was alienated to the Bonnington family about the middle of
last century, by the grandfather of William Lithgow, Esq. of Stanmore,
who still possesses the burial place of the family, and the tradition is
that William was of the Lithgows of Boathaugh.

In the beginning of the travels, Lithgow condescends to inform the
readers of the causes which induced him to go abroad.   This, however,
he does in a very obscure and mysterious manner.   He writes :—

The reason
why the
Author begun
his Travels.
" To satisfie the world in my behalfe as touching my travells, I sin-
cerely protest, that neither ambition, too much curiosity, nor any reputation I ever sought from the bubling breath of breathlesse man
(whose defective censure inclineth, as instigation or partiality, moveth
his weake and variable opinion) did expose me to such long peregrinations and dangerous adventures past, But the proceeding whereof,
thousands conjecture the cause, as many the manner ; Ten thousand
thousands the effect ; The condition reserved, I partly forbeare, to
penetrate in that undeserved Dalida wrong ; and reconciled times
pleading desistance, moderate discretion inserteth silent patience."

In another passage Lithgow more fully, but almost as unintelligibly,
refers to the original cause of his peregrinations :—" And thus have I
in the late days of my younger years beene grievously afflicted !   Ah,
yea, and will more, than disastrous injuries over-clowded, O heavy

underpropd wrongs. But hath not the like accident befalne to man before? Yea, but never the like condition of murther: Nay, but then preponderate seriously this consequence. May not the scelerate hands of foure blood-shedding wolves, fairly devoure, and shake in pieces one silly stragling lamb! Yea, and most certaine, that unawares, the harmless innocent unexpecting evill may suddenly bee surprized by the ambushment of life-betraying foes: All this I acknowledge, but whereupon grew this thy voluntary wandering and unconstrained code? I answere, that being young and within minority in that occurrent time, I was not only inveigled, but by sedusements inforced, even by the greatest powers then living in my country to submit myselfe to arbitrement satisfaction and reconciliation. But afterwards growing in yeares, and understanding better the nature of such unallowable re-dresses and the heinousnesse of the offence, I chosed rather, *voti causa* to seclude myselfe from the soyle and exclude my relenting sorrows to be entertained with strangers than to have a *quotidian* ocular in-spection in any obvious object of disastrous misfortune; or perhaps any vindicable action might from an unsettled rancour bee conceived. O! a plaine demonstrate cause and good resolution: for true it is, that flying—the flying from evill, is a flying to grace; and a godly patience is a victorious freedome, and an undaunted conquerour over all our wrongs. Vengeance is mine saith the Lord, and I will repay it. To this I answere, mine eyes have seen the revenging hand of God upon mine adversaries, and these night-gaping foes are trampled under foot; while I from strength to strength, doe safely goe through the firey tryall of calamities."

The author of a critique on Lithgow's Travels, in the *"Retrospective* Vol. XI., *Review,"* commenting on this passage, which he characterises as very p. 343. obscure, infers that the traveller " would give us to understand that political reasons induced him to fly from evil at home to seek grace abroad." This assumption is not supported by the text, and it is not easy to see how the onslaught of four blood-shedding wolves on one

"silly stragling lamb" can be converted into a political squabble.
The reviewer overlooked, too, the remarkable words " that undeserved
Dalida wrong," which would lead to a somewhat different conclusion,
if the word Dalida be read as Dalila, which we suspect it must be ;
for Lithgow had a very strange way of dealing with words, so much so,
that his volume of travels, which otherwise would be, even in this
critical age, a very amusing book, is so much disfigured by his repulsive
style, that it requires more patience to wade through it than falls to the
lot of most readers. Now the term "Delilah" was used to designate a
deceitful wanton. Minshew, in his very valuable folio published in
1628, includes the word in his dictionary,—thus, "Delilah or Dalilah
nomen meretricis quam Samson deperiit, dicta* a Dalal, i. exhausit, ex-
haustus fuit, sunt enim meretrices lupæ, voragines, abyssi, putei, foueæ,
Scyllæ, Charybdes, mare, lues adolescentium, quorum loculos exhauriunt
ipsumque adeo sanguinem." Minshew then refers to Judges xvi.,
4 to 21.

The natural interpretation to be put upon the preceding quotations
is, that the author, when in minority, had been victimized by some
Dalilah, and had been assaulted to the effusion of blood by some of
her admirers or relatives. The tradition in the Lithgow family countenances this supposition, if not to the full, at least to a great extent.
The present representative of the Lithgows of Boathaugh, and grandson of the gentleman who sold the lands, states that the traveller was
understood to have been of that stock. According to the understanding of his predecessors, the traveller had contracted an intimacy
with a daughter of the Laird of Bonnington, and the lovers having
been caught by the young lady's brothers, they were so indignant that
they used the unfortunate youth in the most barbarous manner, and
cut off his ears. As he could apparently in those times get no redress
—for the female is represented to have been of a powerful family—he

---

* From the Hebrew.

left Scotland for years. The vexation was increased by the outrage having become public, and the people so far from sympathising with him, ridiculed him as " Cut lugged Willie."

In further evidence of the tradition, Mr Lithgow of Stanmore, informed the writer of these observations, that the grandfather of Dr. Newbigging, the eminent Edinburgh physician, when mentioning this story, stated that the house where this abominable act was perpetrated had become his property, and was well known by reason of the outrage committed in it. Generally speaking, family repute is to a certain extent evidence, and it has been admitted, at least, " *de bene esse*," as the English lawyers have it, in many cases of pedigree, even by that most suspicious of all tribunals, the House of Lords. The only material difficulty is, to apply the epithet of Dalilah to a respectable woman. Giving due weight to the natural and just anger of the injured youth against the brothers, there can be no excuse for maligning the sister, and calling her by the name of the deceitful mistress of Samson.

Taking Lithgow's own statement in connection with the tradition, the truth probably is, that having had the misfortune to form a connection with a female of higher position than his own, whether pure or impure cannot now be ascertained—the liason had been disclosed in some way or other to her brothers, who caught the two offenders in the house in Lanark where they were accustomed to meet. That their victim believed, at least in after years, he had been betrayed by her, may explain why he applied the offensive epithet to his lady love.

The exact period of Lithgow's birth has not been ascertained, but as the outrage upon his person was perpetrated when he was a minor, and as he left the place of his birth shortly afterwards, there are reasonable grounds for presuming that it took place between 1580 and 1590. On the 7th of March 1609 Lithgow left Paris for Italy, having previously, as he informs us, taken two voyages to the Orcades and Shetland Isles, and after surveying, "in the stripling age of his

B

adolescence," Germany, Bohemia, Switzerland, and the low countries. Supposing he was twenty-four years of age in 1609, the time of his nativity may be fixed in 1585.

Upon Lithgow's return to Great Britain he gave to the world the first fruits of his travels. This very rare edition, in small 4to, was printed in London in 1614, and the only copy that has been traced is the one formerly in the library of the late George Chalmers (No. 695), which was purchased by Mr Thorpe for the late William Henry Miller of Craigintinny. In the Sale Catalogue the following note was appended to the entry:—" This edition is not mentioned by Lowndes. Ben Jonson assisted Lithgow with money for his travels, and S. Grahame, author of ' *The Anatomie of Humors,*' prefixed verses to his book."

The "second impression" was printed at London in 1616, with the following commendatory Poems prefixed :—

1. To my deere friend, Countriman and Condisciple,
WILLIAM LITHGOVV.

Rest Noble Spirits in your Native Soiles,
Whose high-bred thoughts on deare-bought sights are bent ;
Renowned LITHGOVV by his brave attempt
Hath eas'd your bodies of a world of toyles.

Nor like to some, who wrongfully retaine
Gods rarest gifts within themselues ingrost,
But what thou hast attain'd with care and cost,
Thou yieldst it *gratis* to the world againe.

Vpon the Bankes of wonder-bending *Clide,*
To these designes thy heart did first assent ;
One way, indeed, to give thy selfe content,
But more to satisfie a world beside.

Thy first attempt in excellence of worth,
Beyond the reach of my conceits confinde,
But this thy second pilgrimage of minde,
Where all thy pains are to the world set forth
 In Subject, Frame, in Methode, Phrase, and Stile,
 May match the most vnmatched in this Ile ;
 But this renownes thee most, t'have still possest
 A constant heart within a wandring brest.

ROBERT ALLEN.

2. *To his most affectionate friend,* W. Lithgow.

No *Arabs, Turkes, Moores, Sarazens,* nor strangers,
Woods, Wildernesse, and darke vmbrag'ous caues,
No Serpents, Beasts, nor cruell fatall dangers,
Nor sad regrates of ghostly growing graues,
 Could thee affright, disswade, disturbe, annoy
 To venture life to winne a world of ioy.
 This Worke, which pompe-expecting eyes may feed,
 To vs, and Thee, shall perfect pleasure breed.

W. A.

The verses by Robert Allen are graceful enough. The lines signed
W. A. are of a magniloquent character, and somewhat resemble the
productions of Sir William Alexander, afterwards Earl of Stirling. Of
this edition, which is almost as rare as the preceding one, there is a
copy in the Library of the Faculty of Advocates.

In 1618 there issued from the press of Andro Hart, at Edinburgh,
" *The Pilgrimes Farewell, to his Natiue Countrey of Scotland.*" This
interesting tract in verse has now been for the first time reprinted
from a copy in the Library of the Faculty of Advocates. The wood-

cut of the author on the back of the title, we believe, is the earliest portrait of the eccentric " Pilgrim." It was unknown to Granger,* who was aware only of the one which occurs in the first complete edition of his travels, published at London in 1632, and represents Lithgow in his Turkish dress, with his staff in his hand.

Allusion has already been made to the seizure of Lithgow by the Inquisition at Malaga, and to the deeply painful but exciting account of his subsequent sufferings, and ultimate escape. A separate account has been reprinted in Morgan's *"Phœnix Britannicus,"* and is given at length in the edition of his travels, to be immediately noticed. Upon returning to England in his mangled state he was naturally the object of great commiseration, and by the order of the " sapient " monarch, he was ordered to be carried to Theobald's, that his Majesty might be an eye witness of his " martyred anatomy." The Court crowded to see him, and his Majesty sent him at his own expense twice to Bath. Gondomar promised to obtain suitable reparation, but without the slightest intention of redeeming his promise. When the clever but unprincipled ambassador was about to leave England, Lithgow encountered him in the presence chamber, and was not sparing of his reproaches. This war of words was followed by blows, and as the traveller has it, the ambassador " had his fistula contrabanded with his fist."† For this offence Lithgow was sent to the Marshalsea, where he continued a prisoner for nine months. In the next reign Lithgow brought his case before the Upper House, but there is no evidence that his application was successful.

It is probable that, after the termination of his imprisonment, Lithgow returned to Scotland, as in 1623 he was served heir to his father. His opinion of the state of his native country, or perhaps it would be

---

* Vol. II., p. 153, 5th Edition, 8vo, London 1824.

† Gondomar was suffering from fistula, which occasioned his using a perforated chair, as exhibited in one of his prints.

more proper to say, its " lamentable and desolate condition," which he was courageous enough to address to his Sovereign, in the able and patriotic sketch, which we venture to think is the chief attraction of the present volume. But of this afterwards. Meanwhile he was engaged in arranging and collecting into one volume his three voyages, during which " his painfull feet have traced over, besides passages of seas and rivers, thirty-six thousand and odd miles, which draweth near to twice the circumference of the whole earth." This has been asserted to be "incredible." Yet—although there may be some exageration—when we remember that Lithgow had been almost continually travelling one way or the other from his youth for twenty years, perhaps more,—his assertion is not quite so marvellous as at first sight it might appear.

In 1632 the first collected edition of Lithgow's Travels appeared, with numerous recommendatory verses prefixed. They commence with a poetical address by Patrick Hannay :—

(1.) To his Singular Friend
Maister *Lithgow.*

The double trauell (*Lithgow*) thou hast tane,
One of thy Feete, the other of thy Brane,
Thee, with thy selfe, doe make for to contend,
Whether the earth, thou'st better pac'd or pend.
Would *Malagaes* sweet liquor had thee crownd,
And not its treechery, made thy ioynts vnsound,
For Christ, King, Countrey, what thou there indur'd
Not them alone, but therein all iniur'd :
Their tort'ring Rack, arresting of thy pace
Hath barr'd our hope, of the world's other face :
Who is it sees this side so well exprest,
That with desire, doth not long for the rest.

C

Thy trauell'd Countreyes so described be,
As Readers thinke, they doe each Region see,
Thy well compacted matter, ornat stile,
Doth them oft, in quicke sliding Time beguile,
Like as a Mayde, wandering in *Floraes* Boures
Confind to small time, of few flitting houres,
Rapt with delight, of her eye pleasing treasure,
Now culling this, now that Flower, takes such pleasure
That the strict time, whereto she was confin'd
Is all expir'd; whiles she thought halfe behind,
Or more remayn'd: So each attracting line
Makes them forget the time, they doe not tyne:
But since sweet future trauell, is cut short,
Yet loose no time, now with the *Muses* sport;
That reading of thee, after times may tell,
In Trauell, Prose, and verse, thou didst excell.

                                   Patrick Hannay.

Hannay was a Scotsman, and a favourable specimen of his poetical powers will be found in Ellis' collections.[*]

In Longman's " *Bibliotheca Anglo Poetica* " (No. 46), there occurs the following article :—

" A Happy Husband, or Directions for a Maid to chuse her Muse, Together with a Wives Behaviour after Marriage, by Patrick Hannay, Gent., London.—Printed by John Harland, 1619, pp. 26."

See also " *The Censura Literaria,*" by Brydges, Vol. 5, p. 365-369. He was also the author of " Two Elegies on the late Death of our Soveraigne Queene Anne, with Epitaph's written by Patrick Hannay,

---

[*] *Vide* Specimens of the Early English Poets, vol. 3, p. 135.

M. of Arts, London.—Printed by Nicholas Okes, 1619. Dedicated
to Prince Charles."

It may be noticed that Okes was the printer of the "*Total Discourse*" of Lithgow's "*Rare Adventures,*" the work just mentioned.
Perhaps Hannay recommended his friend the traveller to his own
printer.

(2.) *To his dearly respected friend*
William Lithgow.

Shall *Homer* sing of stray'd *Vlysses* toyle?
From *Greece* to *Memphis,* in parch'd *Ægypts* soyle:
Flank'd with old *Piramedes,* and melting *Nyle,*
Which was the furthest, he attayn'd the while:
A length of no such course, by ten to one,
Which thou thy selfe pedestrially hast gone:
Then may thy latter dayes out-strip old times,
That now hast seene, Earths circulary climes:
And far beyond *Vlysses,* reach'd without him,
Both East and West, yea, North and South about him:
Which here exactly, thou hast sweetly sung
In ornat style, in our quick flowing tongue;
Of Lawes, Religion, customes, manners, rites
Of Kings and people: life sublimest sprits,
In policies and gouernment: Earths spaces
From soyle to soyle, in thy long wandring traces.
But what my soule applaudes! and must admire
Which eu'ry zealous Christian, should desire
To learne and know; is this, *Spaines* tortring Racke
And torments sharpe, which for the Gospells sake
Thou constantly didst beare: O ioyfull payne!
Whilst *Grace* in those sad pangs, did thee sustaine,

With loue and patience : O blest liuely faith !
That for Christ's cause, condemned was to death.
Liue then (O liuing Martyr !) still renown'd
Mongst Gods elect ; whose constancy hath crown'd
Reformd Religion : And let *heauens* thy mind
Blesse with moe ioyes, than thou didst torments find.

> *Walter Lyndesay.*

Allen's verses, already given, are here inserted, but those signed
W. A. are omitted. This curious circumstance countenances the supposition, that as the writer had become a very great a man, he was
apprehensive the praise he originally gave as William Alexander could
not safely be bestowed upon one who had the boldness to point out to
his liege Lord the wretched state of his native country.

(3.) To his kind friend and countreyman *W. Lithgow.*

Thy well adventur'd Pilgrimage I prayse,
Although perform'd with perrill and with paine,
Which thou hast pen'd, in more than vulgar phrase
So curiously, so sweetly, smooth, and plaine,
Yet whilst I wondring call to minde againe.
That thou durst goe, like no man else that liues ;
By sea, and land, alone, in cold and raine,
Through Bandits, Pirats, and Arabian Thieues,
I doe admire thee ; yet a good euent
Absolues a rash designe : So hardest things,
(When humane reason cannot giue consent
T' attempt) attain'd, the greater glory brings.
  Then Friend, though praise and paines rest both with thee,
  The vse redounds vnto the world, and me.

> JOHN MURRAY.

(4.) *In commendation of the Author*

William Lithgow.

Come curious eyes, that pierce the highest scopes
Of sublime stiles: come satisfie your hopes
And best desires; in this prompe Pilgrimes paines
Whose deepe experience, all this worke sustaines
With solid substance, of a subject deare
And pregnant method; laid before you heare
In open bonds: come take your hearts delight
In all the colours of the worlds great sight.
Come thanke his trauells; praise his painfull Pen
That sends this light to liue, 'mongst liuing men;
To teach your children, when he, and you are laid
As low as dust; how sceptered Crownes are swaid;
Most Kingdomes gouernment: How rul'd with Lawes
The South world is: their rites, Religious sawes:
Townes Topographick view, and Riuers courses,
Fonts, Forts, and Cittadalis; scorch'd Asiacs sources:
All you may see, and much more than I name
Seal'd in the Authors, neuer-dying fame.

Eleazar Robertson.

(5.) In Commendations of this History.

Thou art not hatch'd, forth from anothers traine,
Nor yet Collect'd, from others toiles thy sight,
The selfe same man, that bred thee beares the paine
Of thy long birth; O weary wandring Wight!
Its carefull he, by knowledge giues the light,
And deeupe experience to adorne thy name;

D

Both Pilgrime, Pen-man, so thy maister right ;
Who best can iudge, in what concernes the same :
Then free-borne toile, flee forth with winged Fame
Thy Countries Virgin, thou the first penn'd Booke
That in his Soile, did euer Pilgrime frame
Of curious Trauailes ; whereon the Learned looke :
    Then knit thy maiden brow, with Garlands greene,
    The first of times, the last this Age hath Scene.

                                        Alexander Boyde.

The eulogies terminate with an address by—

                The *Author* to his Booke.

Go painfull Booke, go plead thy owne defence,
Walke with undaunted Courage, stop the Breath
Of carping tongues ; who count it small offence
To bulge Thee up, within the iawes of Death :
Go liuely charg'd, with stout Historian Faith,
And trample, downe, base Crittickes in the Dust :
Make Trueth thy sword, to batter down their wrath
So shall thy graue discourse, triumph as iust :
Who yeeld Thee credite, and deseruing trust,
There prostrate fal, giue them their hearts content :
Point forth the Wise, and court them as thou must,
Giue them insight, as I giue Argument :
    Instruct the curious, inlarge the serville mind,
    Illuminate, misunderstandings blinde ;
    Sound knowledge in their eares, deigne to approue me,
    Since Friends and Foes, the World and I, must loue thee.

                                        L.

The travels were again reprinted in small 4to, in 1640, without any alteration. This was perhaps the previous book with a new title. There was an edition printed on Lòndon Bridge, 4to, 1682, of which a copy occurs in a late catalogue of Willis and Sotheran; and again, in Scotland, in the following century [1770], with a tolerable copy of the Portrait from the edition of 1632. A later edition, not very accurate, emanated from Leith in 1814, in 8vo.

Lithgow's veracity has been impeached, and it is asserted that, in narrating his travels, he has drawn very much upon his imagination. We are not disposed to admit the accusation to any material extent. Lithgow had a strangely constituted mind, indulged in the most fantastic notions, used the most inflated language, and entertained a high notion of his talents as a poet—a sad mistake, as we presume most readers will think if they have courage to peruse that most dull and prosaic production of his entitled "*The Gushing Tears of Godly Sorrow.*" He may, perchance, from his poetical temperament, have coloured his pictures, but that he traded in fiction we cannot bring ourselves to believe. His seizure at Malaga, his strange and wonderful escape from the Inquisition, and his marvellous recovery from the tortures inflicted on him, however incredible, are distinctly proved. Had the story rested upon his own declaration it would have been discredited without hesitation. Yet his public exhibition satisfied the most sceptical, and, at the King's own charge, he was sent to Bath for recovery of his health. That he could extract nothing from Gondomar is only an additional instance of the Spanish influence which predominated, for ridiculing which, Middleton, the dramatic writer, suffered smartly.

The inveterate and bitterly expressed hatred of Lithgow to Popery naturally exposed him to the hostility of the Papists, and formed an essential element in determining the Catholic Monarch and his subtle Ambassador to withhold reparation; for, not unlike a certain illustrious indivdiual of the present century, it was a state axiom, then as now, to reverse the old rule, " parcere subjectis et debellare superbos." The candour of our traveller, notwithstanding what has been said of his disregard to truth, is shown in some instances where the revelations are not particularly creditable to himself. For instance; the following adventure, recorded by him, affords direct proof of this assertion ; and, lax as the morals of the time undoubtedly were, places our author in an equivocal position. Whilst traversing Sicily, he determined to visit " Trapendie," with the intention of crossing over to Africa. He took up his abode in the " Bourge of Saramutza," belonging to a young Sicilian Baron. Our traveller rose early one morning with the intention of visiting the young Baron of Castello Franco, at a distance of eight miles. He had got about half way, when to his astonishment he beheld the youthful Lords of Saramutza and Castello Franco lying dead in a field, and their horses tied to trees in the vicinity adjoining the road. It seems that they had quarrelled about the love of a noble Dame of the country, and had settled their differences by slaying each other. Hence, as Lithgow has it, " Troppo amore " turned " Presto dolore." " Upon which sight," continues the peripatetic Scotchman, " to speak the truth, I searched both their pockets, and found their two silken purses full loaden with Spanish pistoles; whereat my heart sprung for joy; and taking five rings off their four hands, I hid them and the two purses in the ground half a mile beyond this place, and returning again, leaped upon one of their horses, and came galloping back to Saramutza." This, it must be confessed, was a trick worthy of Don Raphael, or his friend Ambrose Lamela; of course, he informed the family of the disastrous occurrence, and having done so without hesitation, took his speedy way to Castello Franco, where he repeated the same story. He left both families in a distracted state, and, having repossessed himself of his hidden treasure, fled from the spot as fast as he could. The gold in the purses consisted of " three hundred and odd double pistoles, and the rings, being set with diamonds, and valued at one hundred chezqueens of Malth (eight shillings the piece), he "dispatched" for less. "But the gold was my best second, which, like Homer's *Illiades* under Alexander's pillow, was my continual *vade mecum.*"

The palliation of this nice bit of theft shall be given in the author's own words :—"Well, in the mutability of time there is aye some fortune falleth by accident, whether lawful or not, I will not question; it was now mine that was last theirs; and to save the thing that was not lost, I travailed that day thirty miles to Terra Noua, where, the next morning, being early embarked for Malta, and there safely landed, I met with a ship of London called 'The Mathew.'"* Trapendie is evidently Trapani. In the time of the Carthagenians it was the scene of a celebrated sea fight between them and the Romans (B. C. 249.) It was then called Drepanum. From its being immediately opposite the African coast, there is still a considerable traffic in salt, coral, and such like articles.

For a young man, the job was certainly very ingeniously and judiciously managed. To prevent any suspicion falling upon himself, the plunder was carefully secreted, then the friends were informed of the melancholy event;—meanwhile, the traveller quietly removed from the scene of the tragedy, and securing his prize, got off before any question arose either as to the loss of the money or the diamonds. The latter commodity was disposed of under their value on the earliest opportunity, and as to any identification of the doubloons, that was out of the question. One remarkable feature of the case is his subsequent disclosure to the public of an act which was certainly little better than a positive robbery. He must have viewed the matter in a very different light from what it would be considered in this enlightened age, in which deeds equally discreditable daily occur, but which the perpetrators contrive to keep to themselves if they can, and not publish to mankind.

---

* The Nineteen Years' Travels of William Lithgow, p. 355, edition 1632.

E

Lithgow had intended to visit Russia, and, as he tells us, left, on the 16th of May 1637, " the truly noble and magnanimous Lord Alexander, Earle of Galloway," mounted upon a " Gallowedian nagge," and passing into Cumberland he paid his court to " Docter Potter, that Painfull Preacher and religious prelate the Lord Bishop of Carleisle." He next visited Doctor Morton, Lord Bishop of Durham, and entering Yorkshire, " made homage unto Docter Niell, my singular good Lord and friend the Archbishop of York, where leaving his Grace in the fulnesse of his deserved dignity I arrived in London and so to Court." These Church dignitaries were men of learning and virtue, and we have purposely referred to them as proving that Lithgow must have been considered by them as a man entitled to notice. Is it likely that they would countenance for one moment a person of equivocal character ?

" Divers weeks being spent," continues our author, " in beholding the changes and viscissitudes of time and fortune, whereof I was both a *testator* and *probator*, I left the new-begun Progresse, and stepped down to Gravesend ; where staying for my Russian voyage and shipping fayling, the Summer being also gone I resolved to goe see Breda." The vessel he embarked in was commanded by a skipper, who was unhappily both " fearful and ignorant," so much so, that he and the other passengers were much put about, and were landed sixty miles from Rotterdam, the place of their destination, by which means it cost the " passengers above 200 English Crownes."

Upon his return, Lithgow gave the fruits of his travels to his countrymen in the following work :—" A True and Experimentall Discourse, upon the beginning, proceeding, and Victorious event of this last siege of Breda, with the Antiquity and Annexing of it to the House of Nassau, and the many alterations it hath suffered by Armes, and Armies within these threescore yeares. Together with the prudent Plots, Projects, and Policies of Warre : The Assailants and Defendants matchlesse man-hood, in managing Martiall Affaires :

The misery and manner of Souldiers living, their pinching, want, and fatall accidents: Strange weapons and Instruments used by both parties in Seuerall Conflicts. Lastly, their Concluded Articles, with the Circumstances and ordering of the Siege and Victory. Being pleasant to peruse and profitable to observe. Written by him who was an Eye-witnesse of the siege—William Lithgow. London: Printed by J. Okes for J. Rothwel, and are to be Sold at his Shop in Paul's Chnrch-Yard at the Signe of the Sunne. 1637."

To this work was prefixed the following commendatory verses:—

(1.) To his Singular Friend and Renowned Travailer, Mr Lithgow.

Can not this Ile, thy wandring minde contayne,
When age hath crown'd thy Forrain toiles & sight,
But now that Belgia must thy stepps sustaine,
To prie where Mars involves his awfull might:
Thy former Travailes lend the World great light,
And after times thy memory shall praise:
But now Breda claimes in thy paines a right
To rouze her worth, her strength, her change, her strayes:
Thou bringst remotest toiles, to home-bred waies,
And turnes thy tune, to sing a Tragick song.
It's done, and wel, each work thy merits raise,
Patron of Pilgrims, Poët, Pen-man long.
    A Souldier's phrase thy curious stile affords,
    To fit the subject, with their deeds and words.
    Soare then (brave Spark) on flying wings of Fame,
    That in this taske, reuives thy living name.

ALEXANDER GRAHAME.

(2.) To his Peculiar Associate, and Pilgrimagious Brother,
William Lithgow.

From Paris once to Rome with thee I went,
But further off thy brave designe was bent,
Which thou atchieved, in two-fold Asia twice,
And compass'd Europe, courted Affricke thrice.
O curious toile! expos'd in soiles remote,
But rarer for that rare discourse thou wrot
To light the world: and now thy Quil the while,
Shuts up Breda, within this Tragicke stile.

JAMES ARTHUR.

This tractate is perhaps the best specimen of Lithgow's prose composition that we have, excepting perhaps, his amusing " *Survey
of London.*" From his strong national feeling, he loses no opportunity of commending the valour of his countrymen, and recording
with a laudable enthusiasm many gallant acts performed by them.
The enumeration of names is exceedingly interesting. Amongst other
worthies, he mentions " that hardy and redoubted gentleman, Colonel
Cunninghame, a sonne of the house of Bonnington upon the river
Clyde, and one of my condisciples in Lanerk." We notice this particular entry only, because, according to the traditionary account, Lithgow
had been indebted to the Bonnington family for the injuries he had
sustained in his youth. It is very unlikely that he would have had
sufficient charity to eulogise one of a family which had acted so
cruelly towards him. Tradition has given the name of Lockhart,
and as that family subsequently acquired the Bonnington estates it
may have been some of their predecessors who were perpetrators of
the outrage.

Lithgow's next production was occasioned by the sad accident that occurred in the blowing up of the Castle at Dunglasse, which will be found in the present collection of his pieces. It is of very rare occurrence, not more than two, or perhaps three, copies being in existence. This disastrous event was, according to Scotstarvit, in his "*Scandalous Chronicle*," brought about by an indiscreet jest of the second Earl of Haddington, uttered in presence of his page, an English lad of the name of Edward Paris. His Lordship had been ridiculing the English, and calling them a pack of cowards for suffering themselves to be beaten at Newburn. This so nettled the youth, that he took a red hot poker, and thrust it into one of the powder barrels, blowing himself up with the rest. Lithgow confirms the statement, and asserts that Ned took the kitchen poker, and proceeding to the magazine, where there was eighteen hundred weight of powder, blew it up. He says not a word, however, as to the provocation, but contents himself with abusing the unhappy being, whose revenge was the cause of it, in no measured terms,—so much so, that in the annals of cursing there can hardly be found anything to exceed his maledictions.

Amongst those who suffered was Colonel Erskine, the third son of John seventh Earl of Mar, who was the subject of the beautiful Scottish ballad "*Lady Anne Bothwell's Lament*," which was erroneously supposed by some to refer to a divorced Countess of Bothwell, whereas the real party was the aunt of the first Lord Holyroodhouse, and a daughter of Bishop Bothwell, who, as Father Hay asserts, "fell with child to a son of the Earl of Marre." One of the verses has peculiar reference to his final catastrophe, and would lead to the inference that the poem was composed after the event :—

> " I wish I were unto the bounds
> Where he lays smothered in his wounds,
> Repeating, as he pants for air,
> The name of her he once called fair.

F

No woman yet so fiercely set,
But she'll forgive, but not forget."

The same year in which Lithgow versifies the disaster at Dunglasse
he printed, as he informs us, " at his own expense," the " *Gushing
Teares of Godly Sorrow.*" Perhaps we judge erroneously in pronounc-
ing this to be a most unreadable and unsatisfactory production, so
much so, that we would have excluded it from the present volume,
had our publisher not been of opinion that its non-insertion would
have been injurious to a collection represented as containing the poetical
remains of the Traveller. That there was only one edition is not
surprising, and the author was fortunate if the sale paid the cost of
printing. The only interesting portion is the Dedication to the gallant and noble Montrose, one of the few noblemen of whom the Scottish nation has cause to be proud, and whose reputation has recently
been so thoroughly vindicated by his accomplished biographer. We
need hardly mention that the " *Gushing Teares*" have at least one
merit, namely, that of rarity; for it is not supposed that more than
half-a-dozen perfect copies exist.

Lithgow left Scotland, as he informs us, on the 24th of August
1643, embarking at Prestonpans in a coasting ship for London. His
voyage was dreary enough, as, between " Forth and Gravesend," he
saw only three vessels " two Scotsmen, and one Norwegian."

On his arrival at the metropolis, his *cacaothes scribendi* again seized
him, and he speedily put to the press, for the instruction of his countrymen, " The Present Surveigh of London and England's Estate ;
containing a Topographical Description of all the particular Forts,
Redoubts, Breast-works, and Trenches, newly erected round about the
Citie, on both sides of the River, with the several Fortifications
thereof; and a perfect Relation of some fatall Accidents, and other
Disasters, which fell out in the City and Country, during the Author's
abode there ; Intermingled also with certaine severall Observations,

worthy of Light and Memorie.   By William Lithgow.   London, Printed by J. O.   1643."

When the Author left Scotland, he tells his readers that, at the period of his departure from his native soil, he was past threescore years,—a statement confirmatory of what the writer of these observations hazarded at the outset.   Sir Walter Scott has inserted this piece in his edition of Lord Somer's Tracts,* and has prefixed a few lines, in which, after noticing the dispute with Gondomar, and Lithgow's imprisonment for assaulting him, he remarks, " This circumstance did not increase Lithgow's reverence for the House of Stuart, which was, moreover, diminished by his zeal for Presbytery.   It grieves me to say, that his countrymen adopted the opinion of the Spaniard; and the lower ranks, with whom, notwithstanding, his book was long a favourite, distinguished him by the epithet of 'Lying Lithgow.'"   "*Aliquando dormitat bonnus Homerus* ;" and we suspect that our immortal countryman had been slumbering when he dreamt of any popular feeling in favour of Gondomar to the prejudice of the sufferer by the Inquisition at Malaga.   The Spanish preponderance was notoriously unpopular. It would, therefore, have been desirable that some sort of evidence should have been brought forward instructing that his own countrymen, with whom Presbytery was pre-eminent, and to whom Popery was abhorrent, ever designated him as " lying Lithgow."

We have only space to give the concluding paragraph of this very curious pamphlet, which deserves to be disinterred from the vast collection in which it is bound :—" Neither may I here obumbrate the memorie of this late designe framed for the overthrow of Parliament and London, the discoverie and deliverie whereof was wonderfull, and yet the purpose far more cruel, if it had taken effect : I will not further insist herein, since the oracle of the lower house hath twice already most largely manifested the same, both under print and power.

---

* Vol. iv., p. 545.

But this much I may avouch, that if that unnatural attempt had prevailed, then and there had I doubtless suffered with the rest, for now
as I live to Malaga a living martyr, so then they had sacrificed me with
London, a dying martyre.   Yea, and the like designe, and that same
time, was contrived against Bristol, whereupon there were two of the
villaines hanged for their paines.   There was a solemn thanksgiving
to God through London June 15th, and the country about, for that
happie day of their deliverance, and fourty-six of their adversaries taken,
and under tryall of the martiall law.   And although every man
wisheth and speaketh as he affects, yet have I indifferently (like to the
passenger sayling betweene Scylla and Charibdis) carryed myself to
neither hand, but in a just way keeping a right course, least I should
have offended the truth, and so have slaine the honesty of my good intention ; for though it is impossible to give all parties content, yet I
had rather please many as to offend any.   And now to close: Almighty God preserve aright and sanctifie the royall heart of our dread
liege and governour.   And now, good Lord, either in thy mercy convert the Papists, else in thy furie confound them, and turne their
bloudy swords back in their own bosomes, that their devilish designes
may never henceforth prevaile any more against thy saints and choicelings ; and send us, and all true believers, the life and light of peace
and truth.   Amen."

   This distinct avowal of Lithgow of his anxiety to keep well with
both sides is characteristic of the man, and qualifies the observations of
Sir Walter Scott, that his great zeal for Presbytery had weakened his
attachment to the Stuart Dynasty.   He purposely pointed out, when
recording his departure from Galloway for the English metropolis,
the kind manner in which he had been received by the Ecclesiastical
Peers he visited during his progress south—a circumstance assuredly
establishing that his zeal for the followers of Calvin was not so great as
to preclude his paying court to Episcopal dignitaries.   The truth is,
Popery was his bugbear, and he was not likely ever to forget the cruel

usage he received at Malaga. It was consequently a natural result, that in his productions he should take every opportunity of exposing, in the bitterest language, his feelings of hatred and detestation towards Popery.

The last acknowledged production of our indefatigable traveller was—" An Experimental and Exact Relation upon that famous and renowned Siege of Newcastle, the diverse conflicts and occurrances fell out there during the time of ten weeks and odde days ; and of that mghtie and marveilous storming thereof, with power, policie, and prudent plots of warre : Together with a succinct commentarie upon the battle of Bowden Hill, and that victorious battell of York or Marston Moor, never to bee forgotten. By him who was an Eye Witnesse to the siege of Newcastle, William Lithgow. Edinburgh : Printed by Robert Bryson, 1645." There are copies of this tract—which, like his " Siege of Breda," is full of notices of his countrymen, many of them deeply interesting—in the Library of the Faculty of Advocates, and in the Abbotsford Library. From the latter the late Mr Brockett made his reprint at Newcastle in 1820. At the outset, Lithgow, after a few observations in his ordinary magniloquent style, commences with the following lines :—

> " This long-crossed labour, now it comes to light,
>   And I, and my discourse set in my right,
>   Which reason craved ; for where can truth prevaile
>   But where sound judgment may it countervaile.
>   For what seek I ? in what these times afford,
>   But of my Countrie's praise a just record,
>   Which God allows ; and what can contraires bring,
>   But man for men the light of truth may sing,
>   Else after ages would be borne as blinde,
>   As though our time had come their time behinde :
>   For curious Penman and the Paper Scroule,
>   They are of memorie the life and soule."

G

Lithgow's account of the beleaguering of the town is interesting from its minuteness. We have only room for one extract, giving an amusing, but no doubt prejudiced account of its inmates :—"As for the Inhabitants resyding within, the richest or better sort of them, as seven or eight Common Knights, Aldermen, Coale Merchants, Pudlers, and the like creatures, are altogether Malignants, most of them being Papists, and the greater part of all I say, irreligious Atheists. The vulgar condition being a Masse of silly Ignorants, live rather like to the Berdoans in Lybia, (wanting knowledge, conscience, and honesty), than like to well disposed Christians, plyable to Religion, civill order, or Church discipline. And why? because their brutish desires being onely for libertinous ends; Avarice, and Voluptousnesse; they have a greater sensualitye, in a pretended formalitye, than the savage Sabuncks, with whom I leave them here engrossed."

From this period we lose sight of our restless worthy, whose activity, old age had probably lessened to a great extent. Indeed, it is astonishing how, after his sufferings at Malaga twenty-five years previously, he continued so vigorously to battle with the world. It was once believed that Lithgow survived the Restoration; but we question this, as the supposition is based on evidence of a very slight description. It arose in this way: in the volume containing the remarkable address to King Charles I., there follows a " Parænesis " to Charles II., in which the writer refers, in a side-note, to " the author's poeme intituled ' Scotland's Welcome to King Charles,' in anno 1633." Hence it was conjectured that as Lithgow had written an address to the unhappy Charles in 1633, he necessarily was the author. This idea was to a certain degree countenanced by the fact that the volume had belonged to Robert Mylne, a well-known book-collector and enthusiastic antiquary, who having survived for above one hundred years, must have been a young man of more than twenty years of age when the " Parænesis " appeared in 1660; and, as he had arranged the contents of the volume in the order in which it at present remains, it might be taken for granted that he did so in the belief that it was a supplement to the poem that preceded it. *

As the publisher has included the " *Parænesis*" in this collection the reader can easily judge for himself; but the Editor, who, in general does not consider internal evidence usually very conclusive, is disposed to think, that in this instance it is so,—for it presents the most striking contrast to the euphonistic style of Lithgow that possibly can be conceived. Independent of this it so happens that there was a somewhat obscure rhymester who had also addressed Charles I. on his visit to Scotland in 1633, to whom with more probability the authorship may be attributed.

In 1646 Lithgow must have been approaching seventy years of age, and if he survived the Restoration. which we doubt much, he must have been very nearly ninety. By the kindness of David Laing, Esq., whose extensive knowledge on all subjects connected with the history and literature of Scotland is well known to every one who has had occasion to consult him, the attention of the Editor has been called to a document of singular interest as connected with the fortunes of the traveller. It is the last will of a lady, whom we have every reason for regarding as his mother. The following is an abstract of its material portions :—

" Testament Testamentar of Alesoun Grahame, sumtyme spous to James Lytgow, merchand burges of Lanark—the time of her deceis quta deceisiut upon the xvi. day of Aprile the zeir of God dmvj " foure zeiris."

(The Inventory is long, and not worth copying.)

---

* " 21 *Dec.* 1747.—Robert Myln, writer, aged 103. He enjoyed his sight and the exercise of his understanding, till a little before his death, and was buried on his birth-day."—*Britisb Magazine,* or *London and Edinburgh Intilligencer.*

" Summa of the Inventar,	-	-	L.389 1	8
„ „ Dettis awing to the deid,	-		703 5	0
			L.1092 6	8
„ „ Dettis awn be the deid,	-		12 10	0
		Frie Geir, -	L.1079 16	8

It commences thus:—"Wpoun the xvj day of Aprile 1603, I,
Alesone Grahame seik in body and haill in mynd, makis my legacie
and latter will in maner following,—In the first I nominat and con-
stitutas James Lytgow my husband onlie executr and introt wt my
guidis geir and dettis. Item, I leif of my part of geir xls. to be dis-
tribut to the pure be the Session. Item, I leif to Marionn Grahame
my sister xls. Item, I leif to Wm. Lytgow my sone twa hundret
merkis. Item, I lief to James Lytgow my zoungest sone thrie hundret
merkis with foure zowis and lambes. Item, I leif to Marionn Lytgow
my dochter fyve hundret merkis with quhat funds her fader thinkis
expedient to wair upon her quhen scho gettis ane honest mariage.
Item, mair I leif to the said Marionn, sex pair of new scheittis, two
pair small and four pair round, twa new coueringis, twa kistis, four
cuscheonnis, ane brass pott, ane pan, four peuder plaittis, the zoung
kow, foure aulde scheip, with my haill lynning and wowin clayth.
I ordaine my husband to infeft Wm. my eldest sone in the house and
zairdiss barne, and twa half aikeris of land, Reservand his awn lifrent
yr of. I leif ourseiris to my bairnes Johne Weir, baillie, Wm. Wakin,
and James Lytgow, tailzour, to sie my husband fulfill this my legacie,
and sua scillis vp my latter will, day, place, and befoire the witnesses
aboue written. In witness quhairof I have causit the Notar vnder
written subscrybe these presentis at my command becaus I could not
wryte myselff. Sic subscribitur *Jta est Gedioun Weir notarius publ. et
testis in Premisis manu propria testant.*

" We Mr Johne Nicolson, &c., and gevis and committis the intromission with the samyn to the said James Lytgow, onlie execu^r test^r to the said umquhile Alesone Grahame, his spous;—Reservand compt, &c., quha being sworne, &c., and Oliver Kay, merchand, burges of Ed^r is become cautioner." *

The will throws important light on the position of the Traveller. We learn from it that Lithgow's parents occupied a respectable station in Lanark, the usual winter abode of the County proprietors.   His father certainly was not a laird, in the proper sense of the word, but his moveable estate, for the period, was considerable.   Few of his higher-born neighbours could boast of the possession of half his personal wealth.   He was resident in a Royal burgh, where he owned in his own right a house, garden, and at least " twa half acres of land." He was in all likelihood what used of old to be called in Scotland " a merchant,"—a designation indiscriminately applied in that country, till recently, to all persons in trade, without respect to its being wholesale or retail.   Indeed, in the year 1604 and later, a merchant, in the English sense of the word, was not known on this side of the Tweed.

The old gentleman, moreover, was a Burgess of Lanark; and it is not unworthy of remark that members of most of the influential families in the neighbourhood did not think it beneath their dignity to be also so denominated.   Thus the Carmichaels, originally Lords of Parliament as Barons, and latterly as Earls, were, at least many of them, Burgesses of Lanark.   So were the Chancellors of Shieldhill, an ancient race,—the Johnstons of Westraw,—and many other individuals of noble and gentle blood.   These persons usually possessed houses, gardens, and acres in Lanark, which they continued to occupy, until fashion, that inflexible despot, transferred their habitations to the Scotish metropolis.

Neither, in that part of Scotland, did the exercise of a trade exclude intercourse with the landowners.   Whilst searching the Register of

---

* Edinburgh Commissary Record, Vol. xxxix.

H

Sasines for the Upper Ward of the county of Lanark, the editor was amused with an entry [last day February 1623] of an infeftment in which various parties of different stations are brought together. Thus James Hamilton, tailzeour, is joined with Hugh Carmichael, a son of the deceased Thomas Carmichael, in Eastend, as attorneys for John Carmichael. Next comes James, the lawful son of James Chancellor, " callit lang James," in overtown of Quodquen, as attorney for Walter, a brother of Hugh Carmichael. Then James Muir, whose designation is not given, acts as the attorney of William, another brother, for the purpose of feudally vesting the three brothers in " all and haill the lands of Craiglands, extending to four oxengait of land, now occupied by James Chancellor,·called meikle James," and by John Wardlaw.

The legacy of Lithgow's mother may have been the means of enabling him to prosecute his violent desire for travel, and as he was desirous of quitting a place where he had been so basely used, her bequest would put it in his power to gratify this desire. The lady bore the honourable and ancient name of Grahame, and perhaps was remotely connected with that noble gentleman the first Marquis, who was, notwithstanding the attacks upon his memory by Puritans, one who was entitled, as the Scotish Bayard, to bear as a motto, " *Sans peur et sans reproche.*" This belief is strengthened by the circumstance, that although Lithgow latterly inclined to the party opposed to his monarch, he nevertheless on every occasion speak of the Montrose family with the greatest respect and affection.

We may here, as again referring to the travels, notice a fact which only recently came under our notice, and for which we are indebted to the obliging and learned Librarian of the Society of Writers to Her Majesty's Signet. Lithgow's adventures were not likely to be tolerated in Roman Catholic countries, but in Protestant Holland they attracted notice. They were translated into Dutch, and published in Amsterdam by Jacob Benjamin in the year 1652, in small quarto. The engraved frontispiece preceding the title is by Christian de Pas, and represents, it is presumed, Lithgow on horseback, receiving the stirrup-cup from one hand of a fair lady, and clasping the other in the act of bidding farewell, whilst Fame, flying above his head, is proclaiming his wonderful acts with the aid of no less than *two* trumpets, displaying at same time a scrolled banner, containing a map of his travels. On one side, in front, " Hispania " is placed on a pedestal, and immediately opposite, " Vrancryck " [France]. The former is pourtrayed as an elderly gentlewoman, at least the figure very much resembles one. Of the gender of the other there can be no mistake. The body is somewhat plump, and has a slight look of the portraits of that very injudicious lady, Henrietta Maria, whose bad advice had no small effect in bringing about the calamitous event that made her a widow. Several well-executed engravings occur at various places, and at page 77 of the concluding portion of the volume will be found a remarkably striking representation of the torturing of Lithgow at Malaga. The Dutch translator evidently knew nothing of his author's parentage, or of his existence at the time, if, in point of fact he was then alive. He designates him as an Englishman, perhaps thinking he was safe in so doing, as Cromwell had in a manner extinguished Scotland as a separate and independent nation. It may hardly be necessary to state that this Dutch edition is of great rarity, at least in this country, and the only copy that has fallen under the editor's notice is one in very fine condition in the library of David Laing, Esq.

Nothing has hitherto been discovered in relation to the brother and sister mentioned in the will of Mrs Alison Grahame or Lithgow, although it may be conjectured that the considerable dowry bequeathed by her mother, to say nothing as to what might have been gifted by her father, would afford a great attraction even to the landed proprietors in the vicinity, to whom five hundred merks would have been a very handsome marriage portion, irrespective of the household plenishing, not to mention the young cow and " the foure auld scheip." We can hardly imagine that a young lady with such seductive attractions could be allowed to remain by some of the Chancellors, or the Johnstons, the Lockharts, or even the lordly Carmichaels, in a state of single blessedness.

There is one remarkable injunction, or rather command, in the testament, which would induce a belief that Mrs Lithgow not only expected to get, but actually got, after the usual fashion, very much of her own way, for she *ordains* her husband to infeft William in the house, yard, and half-acres in Lanark. It is hardly necessary to observe, that as the house, &c., belonged to the husband in fee-simple, the wife had no legal right whatever to control him in any way as to its ultimate destination. She does not merely express a wish that the elder son should succeed, but she " ordaines " the father to put his son in possession, subject to his own liferent. Perhaps the hot blood of the gallant Grahame's, which flowed in Mrs Alison's veins warranted her in issuing this imperative requisition.

Of Walter we can learn nothing. He may have been the progenitor of one or other of the races of Lithgows which flourished subsequently in various parts of Scotland. There was a Thomas Lithgow, who owned a tenement of land in the burgh of Pittenweem in Fife, whose daughter Margaret was served heir to him 29th December 1647. She also, of the same date, was served heir to her uncle David in another tenement in the same burgh. This lady married a man of the name of Anderson, by whom she had three daughters, Margaret, Mortoun, and Christian, who on the 10th November 1652 were served heirs-portioners to their mother in the above-mentioned subjects.

There was another family of the name, who were burgesses of Edinburgh. One of them, Gideon, was a printer of some note. In the index to the retours (26th February 1663) there is this entry :— " Joannes Lithgow, mercator, burgensis de Edin., hæres Gideonis Lithgow, topographi, burgensis de Edinburgh, fratris immediate junioris, in tenementis in Edinburgh."

But the chief family of the name were the Lithgows of Drygrange.

' "Lithgow of Drygrange in Teviotdale" (says Nisbet) "carries *argent*, a demi otter *sable*, issuing out of a loch, in base, proper."

"William Lithgow, son and heir to David Lithgow of Drygrange, gets a new charter from the abbot and convent of Melrose of the lands of Drygrange, for his special service in resisting, to the hazard of his life, depredators and robbers of the dominion of Melrose, as the charter bears (which I have seen in the custody of Drygrange), of the date 18th January 1539, which charter is confirmed by King James V. the same year; and from William is lineally descended the present Lithgow of Drygrange."

When the Lithgows originally became church vassals of the monastery of Melrose is uncertain. From the collection of charters presented to the Bannatyne Club by His Grace of Buccleuch, it appears that there was a James Lithgow in the convent of Melrose, who, with Andro, the abbot and the " hail consent and assent " of the convent, at a chapter held for that purpose, granted to " Elene Lawsoun, ye relyct of umquhill Thomas Wod in Edmenston Grange, and to Thomas Wod, her son," their heirs, executors, and assignees, " beand of no greter degre na ther sellfis," all and haill the forty shilling land pertaining "till our malt myll of the said Grange," &c. This document is dated 12th August 1534.*

Drygrange has now passed into other hands. When the Lithgows ceased to have connexion with it is uncertain, but it must have been prior to 1748. The Reverend Adam Milne, minister of the gospel at Melrose, who published the "second edition corrected " of his description of the parish, therein informs his readers that the Lithgows got that estate in James the Fifth's time, from the abbot and convent of Melrose, for resisting at the hazard of life the depredators and robbers of the dominions of Melrose. What follows is not so clear as could be

---

* The name of Robert de Lythgow, notary public in the reign of James II., occurs in three instances in the Liber de Melros, 561.

wished : " That family was forfeited, and one of the name and family purchased these lands from John Earl of Haddington, as they were lately acquired by Thomas Paterson, and are now the heritage of Mr Colin Maclaurin, professor of Mathematics in the University of Edinburgh."

When the alleged forfeiture took place, and for what cause, is not explained. John was the fourth Earl of Haddington. He was served heir to his father on the 10th April 1645, and he died on the 1st September 1669. He was grandson of " Tam o' the Cowgait," the founder of the family, President of the Court of Session, who was created Earl of Melros, a title he subsequently exchanged for that of Haddington. We may be wrong, but we suspect the noble lord was merely overlord of Drygrange, as coming in place of his grandfather, who had a grant of all that belonged to the convent, consisting for the most part of the superiorities of various lands possessed in property by the church vassals.*

The modern historian of the county of Roxburghe has transferred Mylne's account to the pages of his book, in such a way as to induce his reader to imagine that he was treating of a recent alienation of property, instead of one made more than a hundred years before.

In the month of February 1730, there was laid before the kirk-session of Lanark a letter in Latin thus addressed, ' Summe Reverendo Ecclesiæ Lauricencis in Scotia Ministerio Domino, Seniori, cæterisque laudati Ministerij assessoribus.—Pateant Landerick." The object of this epistle was to obtain information as to the genealogy of a James Lithgow, and the writer was George Marcus Knock, bookseller, who offers to pay the expense of the inquiry. He says : " Vixit aliquando apud vos Jacobus Lithgow, utrum civis an ex ordine militari fuerit, de eo certe quid affirmare non possum. Loci et temporis, ubi et quando vixit longinquitas hujus rei memoriam ex animo meo delerunt. Vobis

---

* The will of William Lithgow of Drygrange occurs in the Commissary record under date of 1st November 1574.

autem nihil erit facilius quam ex genuinis documentis me ejus rei facere certiorem. Sigillatim scire desidero, an Willielmus Lithgow qui in oppido Scotiæ Landrick tamquam civis floruit, Jacobi Lithgow frater, an vero pater fuerit."

Marcus Knock then assures the reverend gentlemen that his principal temporal felicity is dependent on the knowledge of the fact. Wherefore, " per Deum eaque qua possum animi demissione, vos oro, ut quanta fieri potest celeritate desiderio meo satisfaciatis, literisque ad me datis omnes quas invenire potestis genealogiæ hujus cirumstantias mihi exponatis."

The kirk-session reported that inquiries into the Lithgow genealogy had been made. That they had been successful in procuring what they supposed would satisfy the anxious inquiries of their Dantzic applicant. This was obtained, not in Lanark, but in the adjoining county of Linlithgow, where two individuals named John and Daniel Lithgow were discovered. These persons gave originally a certificate, but on reconsideration they wrote a letter to the session, dated 27th December 1729, in which they enclosed their joint deposition on oath, taken at Linlithgow on the 25th December preceding, before Sir David Cunningham of Miln-Craig and James Carmichael of Pottyshaw, two of His Majesty's Justices of Peace within the shire of West Lothian. It is so curious that we cannot refrain from inserting it entire :—

"John Lithgow, solemnly sworn and interrogated upon oath, depones, that his grandfather John Lithgow of Botehaugh, near Lanark, in Scotland, had two sons of different marriages. The eldest son, Thomas, succeeded his father ; the youngest son, William, father to the deponent, went abroad. That the said Thomas, uncle to the deponent, had of sons William, his successor, and Daniel, gardener to the said Sir James Cunningham, both still alive in Scotland, and a younger son, James, who went abroad about the time of Bothwell Bridge, which was about the year of our Lord 1685, and till the dear years, which was about the year 1699, never returned, at which time he brought along with him to Scotland a wife whom he said he married abroad, called Mary Crawfurd, of Scottish parents, come of the family of Crawfurd of Jordanhill in Scotland, giving out that in the course of his travels, he had for some time resided in the Duke of Brandenburgh's dominions, and for three or four years after his return to Scotland practised the trade of a tallow chandler in the town of Lanark; that he and his wife again returned to their travels, and since that time has never been heard of by the deponent till now that a letter from Dantzic to the magistrates and kirk-session of Lanark gives an account of one of that name. That the said James, cousin to the deponent, being bred a merchant traveller, went with the pack into England about the Revolution, which was in the year of our Lord 1688, but since that time has never been heard of till now, that the foresaid letter gives also an account of one of the name, and whether he and the said William, the deponent's father be dead or alive the deponent cannot tell, which is the truth, as he shall answer to God."

As the kirk-session had been addressed in Latin, in transmitting the declaration it was thought expedient to send an answer in the same language, " Eximio viro Georgeo Marco Knock, bibliopolæ apud Gadenses celeberrimo." As we do not suppose our readers will care much for a specimen of the latinity of the reverend gentlemen who assisted in the composition of the epistle, we shall merely observe that after some circumlocution, the authenticity of the mode of proof was verified; and it is to be hoped that the celebrated bookseller of Dantzic was relieved of the anxiety which led him to institute the inquiry.

It is evident from this document that the branch of the Lithgow family of which the traveller was so remarkable and distinguished an ornament, had either a very remote relationship to the Boathaugh family, or had ceased to be much known in Lanark. Indeed, it would have been a feather in the cap of the Dantzic worthy if he could have been identified as a descendant of the traveller, and through him have inherited a portion of the " blue blood," as the Spaniards have it, of the gallant Grahams. But there was no proof of anything of the kind, and although the Bibliopole pointed in his letter at a knightly origin, his hopes on this head must have experienced a sad downfall when the answer came to hand.

In the *"Picture of Scotland"* it has been remarked, that after his sufferings, Lithgow settled down in his native town, married, had a family, died, and was interred in the churchyard there. The first of these assertions is disproved by evidence adduced by himself in his account of the *"Siege of Breda,"* in 1637; his *"Survey of London,"* 1643; and his *"Siege of Newcastle,"* 1645.* Of the second and third, the writer of these remarks has not seen the slightest evidence; and of the fourth, it would be most desirable that something like proof should be adduced. It would no doubt, in ordinary circumstances, be a fair inference that a person living in a particular burgh permanently, and dying there, would be buried in its churchyard; but with so very erratic a person as the Traveller, the presumption can hardly be accepted.

Whether Lithgow was originally destined to follow the calling of a tailor is questionable. The belief may have arisen out of the circumstance that, in his mother's settlement, one of his "overseers" or trustees bearing the same name is described as one. There can be little doubt, whatever the prejudices in the more barbarous portion of Scotland may have been, that in 1600 there were no such paltry feelings on the subject of trade in the Lowlands. An honest dealer was regarded as a person who, by probity, perseverance, and economy, had earned for himself a respectable position in the world.

Latterly a change came over the dream; but this proceeded entirely from that pride, which, as the ballad has it, "dings a' the kintry doun." The shopkeeper's helpmate was foolish enough to attempt to rival the lady of the adjoining laird,—hence arose discords,

---

* It is remarkable that Lowndes, in enumerating Lithgow's works, should not have noticed his poetical account of the disaster at Dunglasse. Its rarity, probably, was the cause of this omission.

K

heart-burnings, and every sort of disagreeableness, all which ultimately tended to create an almost impassable barrier between "town folk" and "country folk," a separation which exists at the present date in too many localities.

If Lithgow, when a lad, had been brought up a tailor, it ought to raise him considerably in the estimation of posterity; but we have not found the slightest adminicle of evidence of a contemporary date of such a fact, and we are inclined to consider the allegation as the fiction of a comparatively recent date. In his time, and very long afterwards, there existed in Lanark an excellent school, at which we have little doubt Lithgow was educated. It may be inferred that he was there when his mother died, and we do not imagine that this energetic lady, when she named a tailor as a trustee, intended to make her eldest son his apprentice. If she had wished anything of the kind, she would have set it down in her will. In the bond granted by him, which is printed in the Appendix, Lithgow is styled "Generosus."

The Traveller has been accused of disloyalty to his sovereign, Charles the First, or at least of something very like it. To this allegation we respectfully demur. In the Appeal to his royal master in 1633, on the state of Scotland, there is an honest exposition of opinion, and a disclosure of painful truths; but nothing which can justly be pointed out as disrespectful to his Majesty, or inconsistent with the author's reiterated protestations of veneration and love.* Unquestionably the tortures he suffered in the Inquisition at Malaga,

---

* Charles had a fine taste for books, as well as for paintings. Occasionally some of the volumes composing his library turn up, and when exposed to public competition, produce enormous prices. Thus, in the sale catalogue of Bindley's Library, part II., 2504, there is a copy of Lithgow's Travels. This is the edition 1632, on large paper. It is " bound in morocco, and formerly in possession of King Charles I." It is characterized as unique, and was bought for the large sum of £29, 8s. 6d. It was purchased by Henry Jadis, Esq., and was resold at his sale at the enormous price of £42. Lowndes, our authority, does not mention the name of the purchaser.

made him a bitter enemy of Romanism, and influenced him in passing over to the ranks of the Covenanters; yet it is worthy of note that the dignitaries of the Church of England were inclined to think well of him, which would never have been the case had he been a Puritanical fanatick.

As we have noticed, with one exception, the various poetical lucubrations contained in this volume, we have little to add, excepting to call the reader's attention in particular to the " *Pilgrime's Farewell,*" as affording a somewhat favourable specimen of the writer's poetical talents. There is in it much energy and vigour, and in some instances considerable poetical beauty. The Address to Charles, on the other hand, although deficient in most of the essentials of verse, is, as a picture of the state of Scotland in 1633, of the greatest value, and we cannot sufficiently esteem the manliness of a writer, who in those dangerous times, exposed the nakedness of the land and the profligacy of its nobility to the eye of its monarch. His description of Edinburgh is curious, and the peculiar habits and customs of its inmates are remarkably interesting. His notice of the plaid and its uses, is strange enough in all conscience.

The exception we alluded to, are the funeral verses to the memory of King James, which appeared for the first time in a volume of Transactions published by the Antiquarian Society of Perth. It is not stated there where they were found, but there seems no doubt of their being perfectly genuine.

Of the pecuniary value of the original editions, it is not necessary to say more than that they are all of very rare occurrence, and realise large prices whenever they occur for sale. Indeed, of some of them, " *The Dreadfull Disaster at Dunglasse* " for instance, not more than three copies are known to exist. With the exception of the Travels, of which, when enlarged, there have been several editions, the same may be said of all Lithgow's prose productions.

We take this opportunity of noticing three errata occurring in pages 29, 30 of these prefatory remarks. By some strange oversight, the printer has converted " bonus " into " bonnus," a new reading assuredly, but one which we suspect will not be accepted even in these days of progress. Then, a little below, the word " buried " is metamorphosed into " bound." On the other side, on the seventh line from the bottom, the word " he " has been used in place of " we." There may be other errors which have escaped notice, and the only apology we can offer, if it should turn out that such is the case, is the almost impossibility, with every desire to be accurate, to avoid clerical errors,—an excuse which most editors will readily admit. .

We have still one other duty to perform: that is, to return our thanks to those gentlemen who have given us their assistance in collecting these materials for a life of Lithgow. In particular, we have to offer our best thanks to William Lithgow, Esq. of Stanmore, whose communications have been of the greatest use ; to G. R. Kinloch, Esq., of the General Register House, for access to his valuable collection of extracts from the Kirk Session Records of Scotland ; and to David Laing, Esq., Librarian of the Society of Writers to Her Majesty's Signet, a gentleman always ready to supply, from his inexhaustible stores, invaluable information not elsewhere to be procured.

J. M.

25 ROYAL CIRCUS,
July 1863.

APPENDIX.

———o··o———

I.—Extract from Letter.—Locke to Carleton.*

"The Spanish Ambr. Gondomar is upon going there, is an other
at hand for Sr. Lewis Lewknor hath warrant to goe meete him. I
thinke he cometh this day. The Lo. Gondomar is growne verie
colereck, he beate a Scottish man the other day openly with his fists,
in the presence of the E. of Gwartzenberg and others, for saying that
such a great man in Spayne (of whom the Sp. Ambr. and the Scott
who had bin in the inquisition in Spayne were speaking) had not
used him like a christian : though the Scottish man tooke his blowes
patientlie, yet he was after committed to prison, where he yet
remayneth."

———

II.—Mr Lithgowe's Bill of Charges in the Marshalsey.†

Itt. for IX. weeks dyet and lodgeinge, at XXs. per wecke,	£9	o	o
Itt. delivered since in mony in the time of his sicknes, and to discharge his nessessaries, - -	2	15	o
His comittment fecis, and other charges, -	1	16	8
	£13	11	8

---

* State Papers.—Domestic, April 25, 1622, vol. 129, No. 50.
† State Papers.—Domestic, June 19, 1622, vol. 131, No. 47.

L

III.—Supplication of Aquila Wykes.*

To the Right Honourable the Lordes and Others of Her Maiestie's
Most Honourable Privie Counsaile.

May it please yor honors. According to yor Lo^{ps} command by yor
ho. letter, I humblie pray yor Lo^{ps} to take informacion of all such prisoners which remayne under my custodie, by his Mat^{ies} and yor ho^{rs}
comandes. But because yor ho^{rs} warrants seldome or never express
anie cause of their comyttments, I cannot certifie yor ho^r of their offences.

Patrick Moreton, an old Scotts gent, a servant to his Mat^{ie}, was
comytted uppon great accions of debt, eight yeares past, and hath been
allowed on his Mat^{ies} charge by his Mat^{ies} directions from tyme to
tyme.

John Baynard, gent, comytted 6 yeares past, by warrant from the
Lo. Verulam, then Lo. Keeper of the Great Seale of England, for matter tending to treason against his Mat^{ies} person. And hath bene by
yor ho^{rs} allowed to bee on his Mat^{ies} charge.

Edward Halley, gent, commytted by his Mat^{ie} close prisoner, Aprill
16, 1622, ffor whom yor supplicant hath had no allowance nor pay-
ment.

John Knight, clark, comited by yor ho^{rs} warrant, 21 Aprill 1622.
The cause not expressed in yor ho^{rs} warrant, on his Mat^{ias} charge.

Thomas Whittgifte, commytted by the Right Ho. Mr Secretarie
Calvart, Decemb^r 12, 1621, and allowed by yor ho^r to bee on his
Mat^{ies} charge.

William Lithgowe, committed by the Right Ho. Mr Secretarie
Calvart close prisoner, 2 Febr. 1622, and allowed by yor ho^r to bee
on his Mat^{ies} charge.

Thomas Russell, committed close prisoner by order from the Right
Ho. the Lo. Keeper of the Great Seale of England, Julie 8, 1623, for
words spoken against the kinges Mat^{ie}.

---

* State Papers.—Domestic, Oct. 9, 1623, vol. 153, No. 26.

John Sweet, a Romish priest, committed by warrant from yor ho^r, December 21, 1621, not allowed to be on his Maties charge.

For all which his Maties said prisoners and divers others, sithence Christmas 1619, discharged by yor ho^{rs}, there remayneth due to yor suppt neere 2000l., as by billes signed by yor ho^{rs} and others to bee signed by yor ho^{rs} at yor good pleasures may appear. The disburse-m^{ts} and long forbearance whereof, yor ho^{rs} suppt, sitting at a great rent for the prison, and having but a small allowance from his Matie, and being inforced to take up money at interest, hath utterlie undone hym. Whereof his moste excellent Matie being informed, hath bene gratiouslie pleased to signifie his pleasure to the Right Ho^{ble} Lo. Trea-surer that yor poore suppt should bee pay'd his said debt. And yor poore suppt. by his Maties writt of Privie Seale, being to bee quarter-lie payd as heretofore (till of late yeares) he ever hath bene.

Hee most humblie beseecheth yor ho^{ble} commiseracion and media-tion to the Right Ho. Lord Treasurer, that yor suppt may bee payd his sayd debt, and be preserved from utter ruyne, who hath most faithfullie to his uttermost power, according to the duties of his place, performed yor ho^{rs} comandes therein.

AQUILA WYKES.

IV.—Bond of Wm. Lithgow in £200, for good be-haviour and appearance before the Council when required, &c.*

Noverint universi per præsentes me Gulielmum Lithgow gene-rosum, teneri et firmiter obligari Serenissimo Domino Regi in ducentis libris bonæ et legalis monetæ Angliæ solvendis eidem Domino Regi heredibus et successoribus suis. Ad quamquidem solutionem bene et fideliter faciendam obligo me heredes et administratores meos firmiter

---

* State Papers.—Domestic. Jan. 21, 1624, vol. 158, No. 39.

per præsentes sigillo meo sigillatas. Datum 21o Januarii anno regni
Serenissimi Domini nostri Jacobi, Dei gratia, Angliæ, Scotiæ, Franciæ et
Hiberniæ, Regis fidei defensoris, Angliæ quidem Franciæ et Hiberniæ
vicesimo primo, Scotiæ vero quinquagesimo septimo.

[The signature has been cut out,]

Signatum et sigillatum et deliberatum
  in præsentia Georgii More, Georgii Guggin, servientum J. Dicken-
  son, Clerici Consilii.

Indorsed.—The condicion of this obligation is such that if the wthin
bound Willyam Lithgowe doe hereafter behave himself honestly and
dutifully, and tender his apparence whensoever the Lords of his Mast
most honble Privie Counsell shall thinke fit to call for him, then this
present obligation shalbe voide and of none effect, or els stande, remaine, and abide in full strength and force.

V.—WILLIAM DOUGLAS, the Scotish Poet.

The Editor is very much inclined to suspect that the real
author of the "*Parænesis to Charles II.*," was one William Douglas,
author of a poem entitled "*Grampius' Gratulation to his High
and Mightie Monarch, King Charles,*" which will be found at the end
of a volume of "*Addresses by the Muses of Edinburgh to his Majesty,*"
printed in small 4to by the heirs of Andro Hart, 1630.

As the volume is one of considerable rarity, it was thought that a
specimen of Douglas's juvenile muse might not be unacceptable. It
is taken from the end, and refers to the departure of royalty from the
kingdom of Scotland. The title is—

GRAMPIUS' REGRATE AT THE DEPARTURE OF HIS MAJESTIE.

Ah Reader! pause a while, and with the eyes of pittie,
  Behold how soon my songs of joy turn in a tragick dittie,

Heere I lament the lose of what I newly gain'd,
  The presence of my loving Prince, which hath not long re-
    main'd.
Hei mee, why have I beene thus paradiz'd in joy?
  To be so soone plung'd in the maine deludge of all annoy;
Not so the posting spheres out-drive the flowrie Spring,
  But by a slow serpenting pace the gray hair'd winter bring.
But scarce had I well view'd whom long I wished to see,
  When like a lightning hee did passe in twinckling of an eye;
So doth a poore man dreame hee fangs the Indian treasure,
  But when hee doth awake, his dreame is past, so is his pleasure;
So to the love sick Nymph, her dreames of love bring harmes,
  When she awakes, and finds him gone lay dalying in her arms,
If this my soone spent joy may not be cald a dreame,
  Yet of a true realitie 'tis but a glance or gleame,
The drudging clown by use can swallow all annoyes,
  Not capable of divine mirth or heroick joyes.
But they who on small glance of Tabors joyes did gaine,
  Wished that they never might descend into the noysome
    plaine;
Had I the nectar of his presence never tasted,
  I could have well the used gall of absence now digested;
But I of late who triumph'd on suns flamming chaire,
  Am cast down in Eridanus; cold water quenches fire.
Yet what? Not mee alone this palenesse doth appall,
  But even a change is in the face of all within this all;
The Heavens begins to weepe, the imber months appeare,
  The very senslesse things themselves do change their wonted
    cheere;
The sea doth rore amaine, the sun doth lose his heate,
  The pleasant groves and arbors shake their pompe among their
    feete,
And who within short tyme list to behold my face,
  Shall see a snow whyt winding sheete me round about imbrace.

Whilst I did view those courts of late minaced the skie,
  Which now like silent Hermit halls alone deserted ly,

M

I did my sad complaint this elegie begin,
   But loe mine eyes did drown in tears, sighs, boistered so within
That from my trembling hand the quivering pen did fall
   At my Parnasaus *Ochells* feete where all the muses dwell;
Whair *Helicon* is turned in *Dovens* lively spring,
   And where Apollo with more skill this dittie may foorth
   bring.*

The ensuing note from the "*Catalogues of Scotish Writers,*"† in all probability refers to the Panegyrist of the Two Charles,—"William Douglasse, Professor of Theology at old Aberdeen.   He wrote a Treatise on Psalmedia, 4to; Item Academiarum Vindicias, 4to; Item, Orationem Panegyricam de Carolo Secundo, 4to; Item, Stable Truth, 4to, 1660.   He dyed towards the year 1670.   Item, Vindicias Veritatis, 4to, 1655."

We have not been able to find any of the above works in the Library of the Faculty of Advocates, with exception of the panegyrical address to Charles, which, as we have previously mentioned, Robert Mylne has placed in the volume of tracts, immediately after Lithgow's poem.

VI.—PATRICK HANNAY.

To the small amount of information contained in the Preface (p. xv.) as to this Scotish Poet may be added the fact that he wrote a volume of verses under the title of "Poems, viz., Philomela; The Nightingale; Sheretine, and Mariana; A Happy Husband; Elegies on the Death of Queen Anne, with Epitaphs; and Songs and Sonnets," 8vo.   London, 1622.

---

* This, it is presumed, is intended as a compliment to Sir William Alexander, the poetical Earl of Stirling, whose Barony of Menstrie was situated at the foot of the Ochills, and where he had an occasional residence.   One of his titles was Earl of Dovan or Devon.

† Edinburgh, Stevenson, 1833, 8vo, p. 50.

There was a copy of the work described as above in the possession of Mr Bindley, which brought, at the sale of his library, £35, 14s., and having been purchased for the Sledmere Library, was, at the dispersion of that magnificent collection of books, sold for £42, 10s. 6d. Perry's copy brought £38, 6s., and Wrangham's copy, £40.

The " Songs and Sonnets," which have a separate title, were reprinted by E. V. Utterson, Esq., at his private press at Beldornie, Isle of Wight, M.DCCC.XXI. As twelve copies only were thrown off for private circulation, the reprint is very nearly as rare as the original.

" Hannay," observes Mr Utterson, " was one of those heroic spirits who, in the latest age of expiring chivalry, drew their swords in the cause of the unfortunate but high-minded daughter of James I., the wife of the Elector Palatine and titular King of Bohemia."

As a specimen of his talents, perhaps the reader may not be disinclined to accept the following Sonnet (p. 15) :—

> Once early as the ruddy bashful morne
> Did leave Dan Phœbus purple streaming bed,
> And did with scarlet streames east heav'n adorne,
> I to my fairest Coelias chamber sped :
> She Goddesse-like, stood combing of her haire
> Which like a sable veile did cloath her rounde,
> Her ivorie combe was white, her hand more faire ;
> She straight and tall, her tresses trail'd to ground ;
> Amaz'd I stood, thinking my deare had beene
> Turned Goddesse, every sense to fight was gone,
> With bashfull blush my blisse fled, I once seene,
> Left me transformed (as it were) to a stone,
>   Yet did I wish so euer t' haue remained
>   Had she but stay'd, and I my sight retain'd.

In a work to which few persons would think of resorting, and which has been overlooked by Mr Utterson, will be found these particulars of the poet, showing his descent from an old Gallovidian family :—" Ahannay of old, now writ Hannay. The principal family of the name was Ahannay of Sorbie, an old family in Galloway ; carried, as in Pont's MS., argent, *three roebucks heads couped*, azure ; *collared*, or ; with a *bell* pendent thereat, gules. But on the frontispiece of a book of curious poems, printed in anno 1622, and written by Mr *Patrick Hannay*, grandson of *Donald Hannay* of *Sorbie*, are his arms in tali-duce, with his picture, being—argent, *three roe-bucks' heads couped*, azure ; with a *mollet* in the collar-point, for his difference, his father being a younger son of Hannay of Sorbie, with a cross-croislet fitched, issuing out of a *crescent* sable for crest ; and motto relative thereto, *Per ardua ad alta.*" *

Nisbet next mentions that Sorbie has past from the family, but that the representative is Robert Hannay of Kingsmuir in Fife.   He also records the existence of another family of the name, "still in Gallo-way, descended of Sorbie," viz., Hannay of Kirkdale.

---

* Nisbet's Heraldry, original edition, 1722-42.   Dr Murray has a brief notice of Hannay in his excellent, but not properly appreciated, Literary History of Galloway, second edition, Edinburgh, 1832, 8vo, p. 268.

THE PILGRIMES FAREWELL,

To his Natiue Countrey of

SCOTLAND:

Wherein is contained, in way of Dia-
logue, *The Joyes and Miseries*
OF PEREGRINATION.

With his LAMENTADO in his second Trauels, his PASSIO-
NADO *on the Rhyne, Diuerse other Insertings, and Fare-*
wels, to Noble Personages, And, THE HEREMITES
WELCOME *to his third Pilgrimage, &c., Worthie*
to be seene and read of all gallant Spirits,
and Pompe-expecting eyes.

By WILLIAM LITHGOW, the BONAVENTVRE of
EVROPE, ASIA, and AFRICA, &c.

Patriam meam transire non possum, omnium una est, extra hanc nemo
projici potest. Non patria mihi interdicitur sed locus. In quamcunque
terram venio, in meam venio, nulla exilium est sed altera patria est. Patria est ubicunque bene est. Si enim sapiens est peregrinatur, si stultus
exulat. *Senec. de re. for.*

Imprinted at *Edinburgh*, by *Andro Hart.*
ANNO DOMINI 1618.
At the Expences of the Author.

THE EPISTLE DEDICATORIE,

To the nine Pernassian *Sisters,*

The Conseruers of HELICON.

Ou sacred *Nymphes*, which haunt *Pernassus* Hill,
Where *Soron* flowes, and *Demthis* run at will:
Out from your two-topt Valley shew me grace
And on the lower Listes meete mee apace.
Infuse in me the Veine, I gladli craue,
To sing the sadde FAREWELS my SOYLE must haue.
And yee Supreames of this poore MUSE of mine,
As Iudges justlie censure this Propine:
I bring no Stones from *Pactole*, Orient Gemmes,
Nor Bragges of *Tagus*, signes of Golden Stemmes:
I search not *Iris*, square-spread clowdie VVinges,
Nor of the strange *Herculian Hydra* singes,
These Franticke Fansies, I account as vaine,
In Vulgare Verse, my FAREVVELS I explaine.
If I debord in Stropiate Lines, or then
In Methode faile, attache my wandring Pen.
This Veine of Nature, and a Mother VVit,
Is more than haughtie Schollers well can hit.
So this small Fondling, borne of your nine VVombes,
Turnes backe, and in your Bosome her intombes.
Then nurse your Youngling, and repurge her Veines,
And sende her backe in haste, to yeelde mee Gaines.
In doing this, to you, and to your Fame,
I consecrate my Loue, and her new Name.

Yours, longing to bee drunke of Helicon.

WILLIAM LITHGOW.

To the courteous peruser of these my sad
FAREWELS.

DEare Gentle READER, graunt mee this small suite,
Reade this ou'r kindlie, and no fault impute:
I cannot please the VVorlde, and my selfe too,
For that is more, than brauest Sprites can doe.
Heere I am plaine, and yet the plainest way,
Is fittest for the Diuine *Muses* aye.
A greater VVorke, I meane to put in Light,
But *LONDON* claimes it of a former Right.
And if thou knewst how quicke, and in small time,
This VVorke I wrote, thou wouldst admire my Rime.
Though mightst demaund the Reason why I sing :
And done ; this Answere, I would to thee bring :
There's some that sweare, I cannot reade, nor write,
And hath no judgement, for to frame or dite.
And to confound their blinde absurd conceat,
My *Muse* breakes foorth, to shew their Errour great.
These Calumnies, enuious VVormes spue foorth :
They grieue to see mee set at anie VVorth.
The Cause is this, These Giftes I haue, they lacke,
And from my Merite, they their Malice take.
O ! if I might their Names in *Print* foorth set,
A just Reuenge, their just Desert should get.
But to the VVise, the Learned and the Kinde,
The Noble Heart, and to the Vertuous Minde,
I humblie prostrate mee, my *Muse*, my Paines,
If I can win your Loue, there's all my Gaines.

To the Courteous, still humble,
And to the Knaue as hee deserues,

WILLIAM LITHGOW.

Some Extemporaneall Lines,

Written at the verie view of this *Poeme* going to the Presse,
in comendation of the Author his Trauels and Poesies.

PRAYSE-*worthie* Pilgrime, *whose so spiring Sprite,*
  Rests not content, incentred in one Soyle :
Thy Trauels *past, though alwayes exquisite,*
Diuertes thee not, from well-intended Toyle.
  Two Voyages, of Wonder-breeding Worth,
  And can they not enough thy Fame set foorth ?

In thy first Course, thy restlesse Paines ou'r past,
The Rockie Alpes, *and Mountaines* Pyrhenees,
High Atlas, Ætna, *and* Olympus *wast,*
With all those Yles, of Mediterrane *Seas.*
  Olde Athens, Rome, Troy, Byzans, *and* Iudæa,
  Ægypt, *both* Arabs, *Desart, and* Petræa.

Then chiefest thinges, of South, *by thee were seene,*
Both in the Yles, and in the Continent :
What rare in Europe, Africke, Asia, *beene,*
But few they are, therewith so well acquaint,
  With Iordane, Nylus, *and* Euphrates *strand,*
  And all the Rareties, of that Holie Land.

Thy Iourney next, did subject to thy sight,
The Emprours Boundes, and Germane *States of Worth.*
Braue Boheme, Transyluania, Hungar *wight,*
And all the Nations, to the furthest North :
  Great Rhyne, *and* Volg, *from* Danubie *declynde,*
  The Hans Towns, Dans, Swenes, *and Prouinces combynde.*

What restes then, for thy restlesse minde to doe ?
What Iourney next, then shalt thou undertake ?

  Where

Where shall thy neare way-weari'd Legges nowe goe ?
And whither mindst thou nowe this voyage make ?
  All vnder Artike Pole, *since thou not cares,*
  For Antipodes *thy passage thou prepares.*

And since nought can thy Sprite from Trauelles seuer,
Guiana *marke,* Virginia *by the way,*
And Terra de la Feugo *eeke consider.*
In fortunate Ylandes, pray thee make no stay,
  Least thou, allur'd, by sweetnesse of that Soyle,
  By Birth, that's due, thou so thy Countrey spoyle.

But what in thee most (LITHGOW) *I admire,*
Tis flowing Veine, of thy Patheticke *Quill,*
Fullie infus'd, with Acedalian *fire,*
Whilst to thy Soyle, thou singst thy last Farewell.
  As Trauelles strange, doth Pilgrime, *thee decore,*
  So Poemes rare, shall thee aduance farre more.

As deepest Daungers can thee not affray,
No Lyon, Tiger, nor stupendious thing,
No Barbar, Turke, *nor* Tartar *can thee stay :*
By Trauelles to thy Minde, Contentment bring :
  Cease not to sing, what thou doest see by sight,
  That Countrey Praise, and Ignorants, get light.   Ignoto.

To his singular Friend, WILLIAM LITHGOW.

WHiles I admire, thy first and second wayes,
  Long tenne yeeres wandring, in the Worlde-wide Boundes :
I rest amaz'd, to thinke on these Assayes,
That thy first Trauaile, to the Worlde foorth-soundes :
  In brauest sense, compendious, ornate Stile,
  Didst show most rare aduentures to this Yle.

And nowe thy seconde Pilgrimage I see,
At LONDON thou resolu'st, to put in light :
Thy LYRIAN wayes, so fearefull to the eye,
And GARAMONTS their strange amazing sight.
  Meane while, this Worke, affordes a three-folde Gaine
  In furie of thy fierce CASTALIAN Veine.
  As thou for Trauelles, brook'st the greatest Name,
  So voyage on, increase, maintaine the same.
               W. R.

To the Kinges most excellent Majestie.

MOST Mightie *Monarch*, of Great *Britanes* Yle,
Vouchsafe to looke on this small Mite I bring ;
VVhich prostrate comes, cled in a barren style,
To Thee, O Kinglie *Poet !* *Poets* King.
    And if one gracious looke, fall from thy face,
    O then my *Muse*, and I, finde life, and grace.

Euen as the Sunne-shine, of the new-borne Day,
From *Thétis* watrie trembling Caue appeares,
To decke the lowring Leaues in fresh Array,
VVhich sable Night, inuolues in frozen Feares :
    And *Elitropian*-like, display their Beautie,
    Unto their Soueraigne *Phœbe*, as bound by duetie.

So Thou th' *Aurore*, of my prodigious Night,
Lendes Breath vnto my long-worne wearie Strife :
And from thy Beames, my Darknesse borrowes light,
To cheare the Day, of my desired Life.
    So Great *Apollo*, as thou shin'st, so fauour,
    That I, mongst thousands, may Thy Goodnesse sauour.

Great Pious Paterne, Patrone of Thine owne,
This rauisht Age, admires Thy Vertuous VVayes :
VVhose Princelie Actes, Remotest partes haue knowne,
And wee liue happie, in Thine happie Dayes,
    Thy VVisdome, Learning, Gouernment, and Care,
    None can expresse, their Merites as they are.
    Long mayst Thou raigne, and long may GOD aboue,
    Confirme Thine Heart, in thy Great Kinglie Loue.

        The most Humble and Ingenochiat
        Farewell of WILLIAM LITHGOW.

To the High and Mightie Prince,

CHARLES,

Prince of Great Britane. &c.

Loe heere (braue Prince) I striue thy Worth to prayse,
But cannot touch, the least of thy Desertes ;
I showe good-will, let brauer Spirits rayse,
Thy Name, thy Worth, thy Greatnesse, and good partes :
Late famous *Henry*, did not leaue the earth,
(The Heauens esteem'd the Earth too base for him)
Till thou his second selfe, in blood, in birth,
Hadst strength to his mast Princely parts to clim :
Sweet youth, in whome, thy Grandsires worth reuiues,
And noble vertues, are renew'd againe,
In Thee, the hope, of that Succession liues :
VVhose braue beginning, cannot ende in vaine.
Most hopefull Image, of thy vertuous Sire,
And greatest Hope, of that renouned Race,
These Unite Kingdomes, limite thy desire,
From seeking Conquest, in a Forraine place.
This Noble Yle yeeldes matter in such store,
For thy braue Sprite, to gaine a glorious Name :
And rayse thy State, all *Europe* yeeldes no more,
Heere stay, and striue, to match thy Fathers Fame.
   VVho knowes, but thou, resembling him in face,
   Mayst one day liue, to equall him in Place ?
   So euer Happie Prince, I humblie bring,
   This Eccho of Farewell, Farewell I sing.

Your Highnesse most prostrate
and Obsequious Oratour,

WILLIAM LITHGOW.

To the most *Reuerende* Fathers in *G O D,*
My Lordes Archbishops of Sainct Andrewes and Glas-
gow, &c. And to the rest of the Reuered L. Bishops of Scotland.

Scorne to flatter, and yee Reuerende Lords,
I know, as much abhorre a flattring name ;
What in my power, this simple meane affords
I heere submit before your eyes the same.
I haue small Learning, yet I learne to frame
My VVill agreeing to my wandring Mind ;
And yee graue Pillars of Religious fame,
The onlie Paternes of Pietie wee find :
How well is plant our Church, and what a kind,
Of Ciuill Order, Policie, and Peace,
VVee haue, since Heauens, your Office haue assign'd,
That Loue aboundes, and bloodie jarres they cease :
Mechanicke Artes, and Vertues doe increase :
The Crowne made stronger, by your Spirituall care ;
Yee liue as Oracles, in our learned Greece,
And shine as Lampes, throughout this Land all where :
The stiffe-neck'd Rebelles, of Religion are
By you press'd downe, with vigilance but rueth ;
So liue great Lightes, and of false VVolues beware,
Yee sound the Trumpets of Eternall Trueth :
 And justlie are yee call'd to such an hight,
 To helpe the VVeake, defend the poore mans Right :
 So sacred Columnes of our chiefest VVeale,
 I humblie heere bid your great VVorths farewell.

Your Lo-euer deuouted Oratour to his death,

WILLIAM LITHGOW.

B

To his euer-honoured Lords, the right noble
Lords, A L E X A N D E R, Earle of Dvmfermeling,
Lord Fyuy, Great Chanceller of S cotland, *&c.*
THOMAS, Lord BINNIE, Lord President of the Col-
ledge of Iustice, and his Maiesties Secretarie for *Scotland*, &c.
And to the rest of the most Iudicious and honourable Lords,the Judges
and Senatours of the high Court and Senate of this Kingdome, &c.

AS thou art first (great Lord) in thy great worth,
So thou dost liue a Loadstarre to this North :
Next to our Prince, in all supreme affaires,
Art chiefest Iudge, and greatest wrong repairs.
A second *Solon*, on the Arch of Fame,
Makes Equitie and Iustice seale thy name.
And art indued with Faculties diuine,
From whose sage Breast, true beames of Vertue shine.
Out of thy fauour, then true Noble Lord,
To this my Orphane Muse, one looke afford.

AND PRESIDENT, lest flattrie should bee deem'd,
I scarce may sing the height, Thou art esteem'd :
Euen from thy Birth, auspicuous Starres fore-tolde,
That mongst the Best, thy name should bee enrolde.
The source of Vertue, who procures true peace.
A third *Licurgus*, in this well-rul'd Greece :
VVhom Learning doth endeare, and wisdome more,
That *Atlas*-like, supportes our Senate glore :
Then as thine honours, in thy merit shine,
Vouchsafe (graue Lord) to fauour this propine.

AND yee the rest, Sage SENATOURS, who swey
The course of Iustice, whome all doth obey.
VVhose wisest censures, vindicates vnright,
To you I bring this Mite, scarce worthie sight.
Yee doe the cause, the person not respect,
And simple Ones, from Proudlinges doe protect.

The VViddow findes her Right, the Orphane sort,
And VVeaklinges yee with Iustice doe comfort.
Yee with euen handes *Astræas* Ballance holde,
Iudges of Right, and Lampes of Trueth enrolde,
Long may yee liue, and flourish in that Seate,
Patrones of Poore, and Pillars of the State :
That Iustice, Law, Religion, Loue, and Peace,
By your great meanes may in this Land encrease.

Your Lo. most Afold and quotidian Oratour,
WILLIAM LITHGOW.

To the truely noble and honourable Lord,
IOHN, EARLE OF MARRE, &c.
Lord high Thesaurer of SCOTLAND, &c.

A Mongst these VVorthies of my worthlesse paines,
I craue thy VVorth would Patronize my Quill :
VVhich granted, then, O there's my greatest gaines,
If that your Honour doth affect good-will.
    And whiles I striue, to praise thy condigne parts,
    Thy selfe, the same, more to the VVorlde impartes.

Though noblie borne, thy vertue addes thy fame,
And greater credite is't, when man by merit,
Attaines the title of True Honoures Name,
Than when voide cyphers, doe the same inherit,
    For Fortune frownes, when Clownes beginne to craue,
    And Honour scornes to stoupe vnto a slaue.

Euen as the shade, the substance cannot flee,
And Honour from true Vertue not degrade :
Though thou fleest Fame, yet Fame shall follow thee :
For Power is lesse than VVorth, VVorth Power made.
    And I, I wish, GOD may thy Race preserue,
    So long as Sunne and Moone their Course conserue.

Your L. low prostrate Oratour,
WILLIAM LITHGOW.

To the Magnanimous, Renowned, and
most Valourous Lorde, IOHN Earle of MONTROSE,
LORD GRAHAME, &c.

G Rant this (graue Lord) to patronize my paines,
This my Conflict, before thine eyes I bring:
If thou affect good will, O there's my gaines.
I show my best, though plaine, the trueth I sing:
A two-folde debt mee bindes, Thy Worth, Thy Name,
That still protectes all them that heght a GRAHAME.
  So (Noble Earle) accept these small Effectes,
  Thy Vertue may draw Vales ou'r my Defectes.

To lift thy worth, on admirations eye,
It farre exceedes, the reach of my engine:
But this (great Lord) I dare attest to thee,
While breath indures, this wandring breast is thine:
And that great loue, I found in thy late Sire,
I wish the Heauens the same in thee inspire:
  And as his late renowne, reuiues his name,
  So imitate his life, increase his fame.

That thou when dead, thy Race the same may doe,
As thou, I hope, shalt once excell thy Father;
That time to time, thy long successours too,
May each exceede the former, yea, or rather,
The one ingraft, the other stampe it more,
That who succeedes, may adde anothers glore.
  So shall thy selfe liue famous, and thy race,
  Shall long enjoye the earth, then Heauenlie grace.

Your Lo. most seruile seruitour
on his low bended Knees,

WILLIAM LITHGOW.

A CONFLICT,

Betweene the Pilgrime and his Muse:

Dedicate to my Lorde Grahame,

EARLE MONTROSE, &c.

Muse.

F this small sparke of thy great flame had sight
O happie I, but more if thou suruay mee ;
Thy dying Muse, bewailing comes to light,
And thus begins, halfe forc'd for to obey thee :
O restles man ! thy wandring I lament,
Ah, ah, I mourn, thou canst not liue cōtent.

Pilgrime.

To liue below my minde, I cannot bow,
To loue a priuate life, O there I smart ;
To mount beyonde my meanes, I know not how,
To stay at home still cross'd, I breake mine heart.
And Muse take heede, I finde such loue in Strangers,
Makes mee affect all Heathnicke tortring dangers.

Muse.

But, O deare Soule, that life is full of cares,
Great heat, great colde, great want, great feare, great paine,
A passionate toyle, with anxious despaires,
Where plagues and pestes, and murders grow amaine :
Thy Pilgrimage, a tragicke stadge of sorrow,
May spende at night, and nothing on the morrow.

A CONFLICT,

Pilgrime.

No; Pilgrimage, the VVell-spring is of Wit,
The clearest Fountaine, whence graue VVisdome springs:
The Seate of Knowledge, where Science still doth sit,
A breathing Iudgement, deckt with prudent things.
  This, thou call'st Sorrow, great Ioye is, and Pleasure:
  If I bee rich in Minde, no VVealth I measure.

Muse.

But, O, recorde, how manie times I know,
VVith bitter Teares, thou long'dst to see this Soyle:
And come, thou weariest, and wouldst make a show,
There is no pleasure, but in Forraine Toyle.
  And so forgetst the Sowre, and loath'st the Sweete,
  To wracke thy Bodie, and to bruise thy Feete:

Pilgrime.

All Rares are deare, Contentment followes Paine,
No Heathnicke partes, can bee surucighed, but feare,
And dangers too: But heere's a glorious gaine,
I see those thinges, which others haue by care:
  They reade, they heare, they dreame, reportes affect,
  But by experience, I trie the effect.

Muse.

In Cabines, they on Mappes. and Globes, finde out,
The wayes, the lengths, the breadth, the heights, the Pole:
And they can wander all the VVorlde about,
And lie in Bedde, and all thy sightes controle.
  Though by experience, thou hast nat'rall sight,
  They haue by learning, supernat'rall light.

Pilgrime.

Thou knowst Muse, I had rather see one Land,
Be true eye-sight, than all the VVorlde by Cairt:
Two Birdes in flight, and one fast in mine hand,
VVhich of them both, belonges most to my pairt:
  One eye-witnesse is more, than ten which heare,
  I dare affirme the Trueth, when they forbeare.

Muse.

Heere thou preuail'st, with Mis'ries I must daunt,
Thy Braines: Recall the house-bred Scorpion sting,
The hissing Serpent, in thy way that haunts,
The crawling Snakes, which dammage often bring:
   The byting Viper, and the Quadraxe spred,
   That serue for Courtaines, to thy Campane Bedde.

Pilgrime.

I know the VVorld-wide Fieldes my Lodging is,
And ven'mous thinges, attende my fearefull sleepe:
But in this Case, my Comfort is oft this,
The Watchfull Lizard, my bare Face doeth keepe.
   By day, I feede her, she saues mee by night,
   And so to trauaile, I haue more than right.

Muse.

The cracking Thunder, of the stormie Nightes.
The fierie burning, of the parching Day,
The Sauage dealing, of those Barbrous VVightes,
The Turkish Tributes, and Arabian Pay,
   May bee strong meanes, to stoppe thy swift returne,
   To make thee liue in rest, and heere sojourne.

Pilgrime.

All these Extreames, can neuer make mee shrinke,
Though Earth-quakes mooue mee, more than all the rest,
And I rejoyce, when sometimes I doe thinke
On what is past, what comes the LORD knowes best.
   I can attempt no plotte, and then attaine,
   Vnlesse I suffer losse, in reaping gaine.

Muse.

The Seas and Floods, where fatall perills lie,
The rau'nous Beastes, that liue in VVildernesse:
The irkesome VVoods, the sandie Desarts drie,
The drouth thou thol'st, in thy deare-bought distresse:
   I doe conjure these Feares to make thee stay,
   Since I, nor Reason, can not mooue delay.

A CONFLICT,

Pilgrime.

Though scorching Sunne, and scarce of raine I bide,
These plagues thou sing'st, and else what can befall :
My minde is firme, my standart cannot slide,
The light of Nature, I must trauell call :
   The more I see, the more I learne to know,
   Since I reape gaine thereby, what canst thou show?

Muse.

The losse of Friendes, their counsell, and their sight,
The tender loue, in their rancountringes oft ;
In this, thy brightest day, turnes darkest night,
When thou must court harde heartes, and leaue the soft.
   What greater pleasure, can maintaine thy mirth,
   Than liue amongst thine ownc, of blood and birth ?

Pilgrime.

The fremdest man, the truest friend to me,
A stranger is the Sainct, whome I adore :
For manie friendes, from faithfull friendship flee,
Law-bound affection failes than framelinges more.
   What alienes show, it lastes, and comes of loue,
   But consanguin'tie dies, so I remouc.

Muse.

A rolling stone, can neuer gather mosse :
Age will consume, what painefull youth vpliftes :
Bee carefull, bee, and scrape some mundane drosse,
And in thy prime, lay out thy wittie shiftes.
   When thou grow'st old, & want'st both means & health,
   O what a kinsman then is worldlie Wealth !

Pilgrime.

The Sea-man and the Souldiour, had they feare,
Of what ensues, might flee their fatall sorrow :
Who cloathes the lillies, that so faire appeare,
Prouides for mee to day, and eke to morrow :
   Liue where I will GODS prouidence is there,
   So I triumph in minde, a figge for care.

Muse.

If (deare to mee) thou wouldst resolue to stay,
Our Noble Peares, they would maintaine thy state :
If not, I should finde out another way,
To moue the worlde to succour thine hard fate :
  And I shall cloathe, and lende, and feede thee too :
  Affect my veine, and all this I will doe.

Pilgrime.

To feede mee (Slaue) thou knowst I am thy Lord,
And can command thee, when I please myselfe :
VVouldst thou to rest, my restlesse minde accorde,
And ballance deare-bought Fame, with terrene Pelfe ?
  No, as the Earth, helde but one *Alexander*,
  So, onelie I, auow, All where to wander.

Muse.

VVhat hast thou wonne, when thou hast gotte thy will ?
A momentrie shaddowe of strange sightes :
Though with content, thou thy conceite doest fill,
Thou canst not lende the worlde these true delightes :
  Though thyselfe loue, to these attemptes contract thee,
  VVhere ten thee praise, there's fiue that will detract thee,

Pilgrime.

It's for mine owne mindes sake, thou knowst I wander,
Not I, nor none, the worldes great voyce can make :
Thinkst thou mee bound, to them a compt to render,
And would vaine fooles, I trauell'd for their sake :
  No, I well know, there is no gallant spirit,
  (Vnlesse a knaue) but will yeelde mee my merit.

Muse.

Thou trauel'st aye, but where's thy meanes to doe it ?
Thou hast no landes, no exchange, nor no rent,
There's no familiare sprite doeth helpe thee to it,
And yet I maruell how thy time is spent.
  This shifting of thy wittes, should breede thee loathing.
  To liue at so great rate, when friendes helpe nothing,

C

A CONFLICT,

Pilgrime.

The VVorlde is wide, GODS Prouidence is more,
And Cloysters are but Foote-stooles to my Bellie:
Great Dukes and Princes, oint my Palme with Ore,
And *Romane*-Clergie Golde, with griede I swellie.
   It comes as VVinde, and slides away like Water:
   These meritorious men, I daylie flatter.

Muse.

Mak'st thou no conscience, to deale with Church-men so?
VVhen they for *Limbus*, these giftes giue I know:
They freelie giue, thou prodigall letst goe:
And done, derid'st, the Charitie they show.
   But friend, they binde thee, to thine holie Beades,
   To *Pater nosters, Mariaes,* and to *Creedes.*

Pilgrime.

Forbeare in time, I dare not heere insist,
An Eele can hardlie well bee grip'd that's quicke:
From duetie and desert, I now desist,
It's no great fault, ten thousand Friers to tricke,
   And Iesuites too, which Papall harme fore-sees,
   These Ghostlie Fathers, I oft blinde their eyes.

Muse.

Desist, and I forbeare, so leaue this point,
Fear'st thou not Sicknesse, Dangers of the Pest?
The Fluxes, Feuers, Agues that disjoint,
Thy vitall powers, and spoyle thee of thy best:
   If thou fall'st sicke, where bee thine Helpers then?
   Then miserable Thou, forlorne of Men.

Pilgrime.

But, *O my Loue*, remarke what I must say,
The greatest men in trauaile that fall sicke,
In Hospitalles, for health, are forc'd to stay.
The circumstance I neede not now to speake:
   Doctors they haue, good Linnen, and good Fare,
   And giues it *Gratis*, Medicine, and VVare.

BETWEENE THE PILGRIME, &c.

Muse.

Thou here borne North, vnder a Climate colde,
I thinke farre South, with heat should not agree:
And in my minde, I this opinion holde,
These vigrous heats, at last thy death shall bee:
  I know these *Nigroes*, of the Austriale Sunne,
  Haue not endur'd, such heat, as thou hast done.

Pilgrime.

For to conserue mine health, I eate not much:
When I drinke Wine, it's mixt with VVater aye:
They are but Gluttones, Riote doeth auouch,
I trauaile in the Night, and sleepe all Day.
  My disposition and complexion gree,
  I am not sanguine, nor too pale, you see.

Muse.

A murthrer judg'd, set on a wheele aboue,
How many pinnes, for murther hast thou tolde?
No lesse than twentythree, I will approue,
And dar'st thou in these dead mens wayes bee bolde?
  Think'st thou thy fortune, better still than theirs?
  The Foxe runnes long, at last entrapp'd in snares.

Pilgrime.

All that haue breath must die, and man much more,
Some here, some there, his *Horoscope* is so,
Bewee are borne, our weirds they poste before,
None can his dest'ny shunne, nor from it goe,
  Nothing than death more sure, vncertaine too,
  Who aymes at fame, all hazards must allowe.

Muse.

But swollen man in thy conceat, take heed,
What great distresse, of hunger has thou tholde?
That often times, for one poore Loaue of bread,
Thou wouldst (if poss'ble) giuen a worlde of gold:
  Remember of thy sterile Lybian wayes,
  Where thou didst fast, but meate or drinke nyne dayes.

A CONFLICT,

Pilgrime.

Dispeopled desartes, bred that deare-bought griefe,
No state but change, no sweete without some gall :
Yet in *Tobacco*, I found great reliefe,
The smoake whereof expell'd that pinching thrall :
    And for that time, I graunt, I drunke the water
    That through my bodie came, insteade of better.

Muse.

The vaprous *Serene*, of the humide night,
VVhich sprinkled oft, with foggie dew thy face,
Gaue to thy bodie, and thine head such weight,
VVhen thou awak'd, couldst scarce aduance thy pace :
    And scarce of Springes, did so thy thirst increase,
    Thy Skinne growne lumpie, made thy strength decrease.

Pilgrime.

I yeelde, thou knowst these thinges as well as I,
But when I slept, great care I had to couer
My naked face, and kept my bodie drie,
The manner how, I neede it not discouer.
    Though thou object these mistes, the clouds forth-spew.
    All thy *Brauadoes* cannot make mee rew.

Muse.

The Galley-threatning death, where slaues are whipt,
Each banke holdes foure, foure chaines ty'd in one ring :
VVhere twise a day, poore they are naked stript,
And bath'd in blood, their woefull handes they wring :
    They roll still scourg'd, on bread and water feede,
    Twise this thou scap'd, the third time now take heede.

Pilgrime.

At *Cephalone*, and *Nigroponte* I know,
And *Lystra* too, three Slaueries I escap'd ;
And tenne times Galleotes, made a cruell show,
At *Little Iles*, to haue mee there intrapp'd :
    But their attemptes still failde, I thanke my God,
    Yet I no way can liue, if not abrode.

BETWEENE THE PILGRIME, &c.

Muse.

But ah recall, the Hearbes, rawe Rootes yee eate,
White Snails, greene Frogs, gray streams, hard beds derayd :
And if this austiere life, seeme to thee meete,
I yeelde to thine experience long assayd.
   Then stay, O stay, succeeding times agree,
   To reconcile thy minde, thy meanes, and thee.

Pilgrime.

To stay at home, thou knowst I cannot liue :
To liue abroade I know, the worlde maintaines mee :
To bee beholden to a Churle, I grieue :
And if I want, my dearest friende disdaines mee.
   And so the forraine face to mee is best,
   I lacke no meanes, although I lacke my rest.

Muse.

I graunt it's true, and more esteem'd abroade,
But zeale growes colde, and thou forgetst the way :
Better it were at home to serue thy GOD,
Than wandring still, to wander quite astray :
   Thou canst not trauaile, keepe thy conscience too,
   For that is more, than Pilgrimes well can doe.

Pilgrime.

I wonder Muse, thou knowst to heare a Messe,
I make no breach of Law, but for to learne.
And if not curious, then the worlde might gesse.
I hardlie could twixt good and ill discearne :
   I enter not their Kirkes, as vpon doubt
   Of faith ; but their strange erroures to finde out.

Muse.

O well replyde, but yet a greater spotte,
Thou bowst thy knees, before their Altars hie :
And when comes the Leuation, there's the blotte :
Thou knockst thy breast, and wallowst with thine eye :
   And when the little Bell, ringes through the streete,
   Thou prostrate fall'st, their Sacrament to greete.

A CONFLICT,

Pilgrime.

Thou fail'st therein, I still fledde Superstition :
But I confesse, I got the holie Blessing :
And vnder colour of a rare Contrition,
The Papall Panton heele, I fell a kissing.
But they that mee mistake, are base-borne Clownes :
I did it not for Loue, but for the Crownes.

Muse.

O ! There's Religion, Dissimulation,
Vtrunque is thy Stile, I feare no lesse :
And from a borrow'd Æquiuocation,
Would'st frame thy Will, and then thy VVill redresse,
No, Pilgrime, no, That's not the VVay to Heauen,
To make the Euen to glee, the Gleede looke euen.

Pilgrime.

Away vaine Foole : I scorne thy pratling Braine :
When I confesse the Trueth, thou mee accuses.
I never solde my Soule for anie Gaine,
Nor yet abus'd my Minde, with Forraine Uses,
As manie home-bred heere Domestickes doe,
In changing State, can change their Conscience too.

Muse.

I grant there's some for Gaine, their Soules doe sell :
But learne the good, and soone forget the ill :
A Vale at home ou'r-drawne, I plainlie tell,
Is fit for thee, though not fit for thy Will.
And bee aduis'd, Repentance comes too late,
He mournes in vaine, that spends both Time and State.

Pilgrime.

I loathe to liue, long in a priuate place :
My Soyle I loue, but I am borne to wander.
And I am glad, when I Extreames imbrace.
Sweete Sowre Delightes, must my Contentment rander.
So, so, I walke, to view Hilles, Townes, and Plaines,
Each day new Sightes, new Sightes consume all Paines.

BET'VVEENE THE PILGRIME, &c.

Muse.

Liue aye in Paines, ambitious Pilgrime then,
Since thy proude Breast, disdaines thy Mindes surrandring :
It's thou who striu'st to ouer-match all men,
In Perrill, Paines, in Trauaile, and in VVandring.
  Striue still, I feare that some Desasters grow,
  Long swimme the Fish, so long as VVaters flow.

Pilgrime.

Leaue off, and boast no more, no more I sing :
I rest resolu'd, holde thou thy peace the while :
And to the EARLE MONTROSE, I humblie bring,
Our mutuall CONFLICT, in this barren Stile.
  And so Illustrious Lord, approue my saying,
  Conuict my Muse, and let mee goe astraying :
  To this small Suite, if that your Honour yeeldes,
  Shee shall perforce with mee affront the Fieldes.

Heere endeth the Conflict, betweene
the Pilgrime, and his Muse.

To the *Right honourable and Noble Lord,*
ALEXANDER, Earle Home, Lord Dunglasse, &c.

THese meane abortiue lines, of my Lament,
On my low-bended knees I sacrifice them
To thee, on whome my greatest loue is bent :
They gladlie come, and I doe authorize them.
 And so this simple mite with loue receaue,
 If thou affect good will, no more I craue.

To paye the debt I owe of my great duetie,
Which in large bondes, lies bound to thy great worth,
Is more than I can doe, vnlesse by fewtie,
I striue (though weake) thy vertues to set foorth :
 Yet for my debt, my duetie, and my prayer,
 I'me bound on earth, and GOD will bee thy payer.

Thy noble feasting of our gracious King,
And kindlie wellcome, to the *ENGLISH* Kinde ;
O ! had I time, the trueth that I might sing,
Thy great desert, a just reward should finde :
 But my Farewelles mee poste, yet by the way,
 Thy Vertue, in thy Worth, triumphes each day.

Compendious workes, on high stupendious thinges,
Which brauest wittes, wring from inuentions braine,
No knowledge yeeldes, but admiration bringes,
To vulgare sortes, and to the wisest pane :
 I sing but plainlie in Domesticke verse,
 The watrie accents, of a pilgrimes herse.
 So (worthy earle) protect my *Lamentado,*
 And done, I scorne the wretched worlds *Brauado.*

     Your Lo, most incessant Oratour,

       WILLIAM LITHGOW.

THE PILGRIMES
LAMENTADO,

In his second Pilgrimage.

Ut of the showrie shade of Sorrowes Teares,
VVhere in the darkest Pit of Griefe I lay,
I trembling come, astonisht with these Feares,
Of stormie Fortune, frowning on mee aye :
For in her fatall frownes my wracke appeares.
  And from the concaue of my watrie Plaintes,
  I powre abroade, a VVorlde of Discontentes.

Shall I, like *Lemphos*, mourne to lengthen life ?
O ! I must mourne, or else this Breath dissolues :
No greater paine, than mine in-cloystred Strife,
VVhich Sea-waue-like, to tosse mee still resolues,
For so the Passions of my Minde are rife :
  There's none like mee, nor I like vnto none :
  None but my selfe, in mee my selfe must grone.

These joyes that I possess'd, are backward fled,
My sweete Contentes, to sowre Displeasure turnes :
My quiet Rest, Ambition captiue led.
And where I dwell the *Pagane* there sojournes.
My Sommer Smiles, on VVinter Blastes are spred.
  All Loue-sicke Dreames, of VVorldlie Ioyes are gone.
  Mine Hopes are fled, and I am left alone.

D   Alone

Alone I mourne in solitarie Songes,
And oft bewaile mine infranchized lotte :
The Heauens beare witnesse of my long past Wronges,
Which best can judge, how this blinde Worlde doth dote.
This pondred so, my bleeding heart it longes,
   To bee dissolu'd, made free, or ty'd more fast,
   Vnto the Substance, of a Shaddow past.

I wish, and yet I cannot haue my will,
It's onlie I, must helplesse spende my Mones :
With out-run Teares, mine out-worne Bedde I fill :
And Sighes disbende, whiles I retaine sadde Grones,
Which both constrain'd, conuert a sobbing ill.
   So when my Malecontentes to Sorrow grew,
   These pale Complaintes, from my wanne Visage flew :

Ah haplesse I ! vnmatch'd in matchlesse Woe,
Plagu'd with the terrour of horrendious strokes,
Am *Cretane*-like, transported to and froe,
Twixt Sandie *Scylla*, and *Charibdin* Rockes :
Ship-wracke I finde, where euer that I goe.
   Though once I scalde, the scope of my desire,
   No sooner vp, but all was set on fire.

Like *Pha'ton* young, too fast my Sorrowes bred,
And bridle gaue, when I should haue holde fast :
On the *Pegasian* winges poore I was led,
VVith course so swift, made all my Pow'rs agast,
Till at the last I found that Fawnes mee fed :
   Then tooke I breath, and saw how I was reft,
   The poorest man, that in the worlde was left.

Meane-while I stroue against the strongest Streames,
VVhilst my small strength, waxt weaker than a Stroe :
                        The

In his second Pilgrimage.

The Sunne dissolu'd in darke declining Beames,
And I in Moone-shine colde was tortred so,
That all my look'd-for Ioyes, became but Dreames.
  Still driuen backe, from my transported Hope,
  I rang'd the Hill, could neuer reach the toppe.

Yet once I sat vpon the fatall VVheele,
Whiles that the second Round, came round about:
Then fell I backward, hanging by the Heele,
Astonisht of my Change, I stoode in doubt,
If I should mount, then fall, more turninges feele.
  VVhich when conceiu'd, I euer swore to mount,
  Ten thousand falles, should neu'r my Breast confront.

I cannot fall no lower than the Earth,
From which I came, and to the which must goe:
This borrowd Breath, is but a glaunce of Mirth,
No constant life, this trustlesse Worlde doth show,
The surest man, the meanest stile in Birth,
  Great Falles, attende great Persons, and their Glore,
  For when they fall, they cannot rise no more.

Care I for Golde ? I scorne that filthy Drosse :
It's VVorldlinges God, so Mundanes loue his sight,
Shall I despaire ? Or care I for my losse ?
Although I want, which once was mine by right,
No double on you waues, still crosse on crosse :
  I, *Camele*-like, beare all vpon my Backe,
  And liue content, and there's the thought I take.

Yet fragile flesh, is friuolous and proude,
Some sad disgust, gaue mee this second toyle :
I sing but low, I may not sing too lowde,
VVho winnes the Fielde, may triumph in the Spoyle.

D 2

I, van-

I, vanquisht I, must liue vnder the Shrowde,
  Of farre-fled Fortune, scattred to a Ragge :
  Mine Haire-cloath Gowne, my *Burdon*, and my Bagge.

All *Her'mite*-like, my Face ou'r-cled with Haire.
Once my faire Fielde, is now turn'd VVildernesse :
I harbour'd Beautie, within my full Moone Share,
VVhere nought restes now, but VVrinckles of Distresse.
Europiane Sorrow, and *Asiaticke* Care :
  The *Africke* Threatninges, and *Arabiane* Terrour,
  Makes my pale Face, become a bloodlesse Mirrour.

I Pennance make, if Pennance could suffice :
I forward wrestle, gainst all Forraine Care.
I still contende, this wandring Breast to please :
I trauaile aye, and yet I know not where,
Led with the VVhirle-winde, and Furie of Unease.
  And when I hauc considered all my strife,
  O happie hee, who neuer knew this life !

A life of sadnesse, still to liue estranging :
A life of griefe, turmoylinges, and displeasure :
A life fastidious, aye to run a ranging.
A life in bounding, bondlesse Will no measure :
A life of tormentes, subject to all changing.
  A life of paine, where fearfull Danger dwelles,
  A life, whose passions counter-match the Helles.

My Sommer Cloathing, is my VVinters VVeede :
Times change, and I, I cannot change Apparrell :
The Spring's my loathing, and the Haru'st my neede :
Each Seasons course, by monthlie fittes mee quarrell,
And in their Threatninges, threaten to exceede.
  From VVeeke to Day, from Day to hourelie minute,
  Still I opprest, must pay my Passions tribute.

From tortring toyles, to tortring feares amaine,
Poore I, distrest, am tost with great extreames :
VVhen I looke backe, to see the VVorlde againe,
O what a clowdie show of eclips'd Beames
I doe beholde ! and seene, I them disdaine.
 Heere mournes the Poore, there foame the rich & great :
 From *Swane* to *Prince*, I see no quiet state.

VVhat art thou VVorlde ? O VVorld, a VVorlde of woes,
A momentarie shaddow of vaine thinges.
The *Acheron* of paine, so I suppose,
A transitorie helper of Hirelinges,
VVhich nought but sorrowes to mine eyes disclose :
 Opinion rules thy state, selfe-loue thy lord,
 To him who merites least, doth most afford.

Thou traitour VVorlde, art fraught with bitter cares,
Pride, Spite, Deceite, Greede, Lust, ambitious Glore :
Thy dearest Ioyes, depende vpon Despaires,
And still betrayes them most, most thee implore,
Thy bound-slaues wrestle, hurling in thy Snares.
 VVhose course as VVinde, instable is and reaues,
 In crossing brauest Sprites, aduancing Slaues.

I smile to see thy VVorldling puft in pride,
Though meanlie borne, and no desert, if rich,
Hee liues, as if his mansion could not slide.
Such proude conceites, deceiue thy sillie VVretch,
VVhiles in his blinde-folde humoures hee would bide.
 And so they loue, and I abhorre thy sight :
 They dwell in darknesse, and I liue in light.

Thou lead'st thy Captiues, headlong into traines,
And in thy trustlesse show, beguiles thy Louer :
D 3

VVho

VVho most affectes thee, greatest are his paines,
Thy verded face, contaminates thy proouer,
And with false showes, besottes his braine-sicke braines.
  So whilst thy mundane liues, his gaines are losses,
  And dead, for loue of thee, eternall crosses.
    :

Thou seem'st without, more brighter than the Golde,
Ten thousand vales, of glistring showes decore thee :
But hee whose eyes, once saw thine inward mould,
VVould loathe to liue, so vainelie to adore thee,
VVhose counterfeit contentes are bought and solde.
  A painted VVhore, the Maske of deadlie sinne,
  Sweete faire without, and stinking foule within.

VVho puts trust in thee, whome thou deceiu'st not ?
VVho loues thy sight, but thou conuerts 't in death ?
VVho sets his joyes on thee, and him bereaues not ?
VVho most is thine, findes shortest time to breathe ?
VVho cleaues most to thy loue, and then him leaues not ?
  VVho would thee longest see, what trouble choaks him ?
  VVho thee imbrace, Enuie to wrath prouokes him.

Thy pleasures I compare vnto the flight
Of a swift Birde, which by a window glides :
A glaunce, a twinckling, a variable sight,
As dreames euanish, so thy glorie slides,
VVhose thornie cares, thy joyes downe-sway, with weight :
  And could thy wretch, but learne to know the trueth,
  Hee would contemne thee, both in Age and Youth.

I see the changing course, of thy selfe-gaine,
There one buyes, the other buildes, the thirde selles,
The fourth hee begges, and the fifth againe,
Beginnes to seeke the path, the first fore-telles :
                                      For

For in thy fickle force, thy craft showes plaine :
  Thus restlesse man doth change, and changing so,
  If rich, findes friendes : if poore, his friend turnes foe.

To sing of Honour, and Preferment too,
I know, thou knowst, what I haue seene abroade :
Meane Lads made Lordes, and Lordes to Lads must bow :
Such Fauourites on Noble Breastes haue trode,
As what Kinges doe, the Heauens the same allow.
  But heere's the plague ; if dead, ere they bee rotten,
  Their Stiles, their Names, and Honoures are forgotten.

The Duke of *Vrbine*, Count *Octauious* Lord,
Preferd this Youth (though base in birth) for beautie :
And vvas his *Bardasse*, so the *Tuscane* word
Doth beare : and farre beyonde all Princelie duetie,
Aduancing him, his Nobles did discord.
  And when growne great, his friendes began to hate him,
  And at the last, a Ponyarde did defate him.

So VVorlde beholde thy late Marshall of *France*,
Whom *Mons. du Vitres*, pistolde through the head :
That Queene for priuate thinges did him aduance,
But in the ende, his Honoures now lie dead.
VVho mountes without desert, findes oft such chance.
  O hee vvas great ! now gone, vvhere liues his Fame ?
  Now, neither Race, nor Stile, nor Rent, nor Name.

I could recite an hundreth Upstartes moe,
VVhose meanest VVorth, on greatest Glore was set :
Meane-while mine eyes, admire their greatnesse so,
A suddaine change, these blowne-vp Mineons get,
Time doth betray, what Fortune oft lets goe.
  Soone ripe, soone rotte, when free, liues most in thrall :
  A suddaine rising, hath a suddaine fall.

This worthlesse Honour, that desert not reares,
Is but as fruitlesse showes, which bloome, then perish :
VVhere Merite buildes not, that Foundation teares.
There's nought but Trueth, that can mans standing cherish :
This great Experience, dayly now appeares ;
    VVhat one vpholdes, another he downe casts,
    This gentle-blood, doth suffer many Blasts.

I smyle to see, some bragging Gentle-men,
That clayme their discent, from King *Arthur* great ;
And they will drinke, and sweare, and roare, what then
Would make their betters, foote-stooles to their feet ;
And stryue to be applaus'd with Print and pen :
    And were hee but a Farmer, if hee can
    But keepe an Hound, *O there's a Gentle-man.*

But foolish thou, looke to the Graue, and learne,
How man lies there deform'd, consum'd in dust :
And in that Mappe, thy judgement may discearne,
How little thou in Birth and Blood shouldst trust.
Such sightes are good, they doe thy Soule concerne.
    VVer'st thou a Kinglie Sonne, and Vertue want,
    Thou art more brute, than Beastes, which Desarts hant.

And more, vaine VVorlde, I see thy great transgression,
Each day new Murther, Blood-shed, Craft, and Thift :
Thy louelesse Law, and lawlesse proude Oppression :
Thy stiffeneckt Crew, their heads ou'r Saincts they lift,
And misregarding GOD, fall in degression.
    The VViddow mournes, the Proude the Poore oppresse
    The Rich contemne, the silly Fatherlesse.

And rich men gape, and not content, seeke more,
By Sea and Land, for gaine, run manie miles :

                                                    The

In his second Pilgrimage.

The Noblest striue for State, ambitious Glore,
To haue Preferment, Landes, and greatest Stiles,
Yet neu'r content of all, when they haue store :
- And from the Sheepheard, to the King I see,
  There's no contentment, for a VVorldlie Eye.

O ! is hee poore, then faine hee would bee rich :
And rich, what tormentes his great griede doth feele :
And is hee gentle, hee striues moe Hightes t' touch :
If hee vnthriues, hee hates anothers weele :
His Eyes pull home, what his Handes dare not fetch.
  A quiet minde, who can attaine that hight,
  But either slaine, by Griede, or Enuies spight ?

Man's naked borne, and naked hee returnes,
Yet whiles he liues, G O D S Prouidence mistrustes :
Hee gapes for Pelfe, and still in Auarice burnes,
And hauing all, hath nothing, but his Lustes.
Insatiate still, backe to his Vomite turnes.
  Vilde Dust and Earth, belieu'st thou in a Shadow ?
  VVhose high-tun'd Prime, falles like a new mowne Me-
                                                    (dow.

I grieue te see the VVorld, and VVorldling playing,
The VVretch puft vp, is swell'd with Hellish griede :
The Worlde deceiues him, with a swift assaying.
And as hee standes, hee cannot take good heede,
But for small Trash, must yeelde eternall paying :
  And dead, another enjoyes what hee got,
  And spendes vp all, whiles hee in Graue doeth rot.

To see thy Plagues, false Worlde, I breake mine heart :
I'me tost, he crost, another lost, and most,

                    E   To see

To see a wretch for gaine his Soule decart;
Men in themselues such blyndnes haue ingrost;
To flee their good, and follow fast their smart:
   Away vaine world, blest I, disdaines thy sight,
   VVhose sugred snares, breed everlasting night.

And when I haue seene most part of thy glore,
Great Kingdomes, Ylandes, statelie Courtes, and Townes,
Herbagious Fieldes, the *Pelage*-beating Shore,
And georgeous showes, of glorious renownes,
Faire Floods, strong Forts, greene VVoods, and *Arabe* Ore:
   I crie out from my griefe, with watrie eyes,
   All is but vaine, and vaine of vanities.

So welcome Heauen, with thine eternall Ioyes,
VVhere perfect pleasure is, and aye hath beene:
This Masse below, is lode with sad annoyes:
No rest for mee, till I thy glore haue seene,
So put a period to my toyles and toyes.
   I loathe to liue, I long to see my death:
   I die to liue, Sweete I E S U S haue my Breath.

Ah, whither am I carry'd, thus to mourne?
To breake with griefe, the powers of my Breast,
There where I ende, to that ende I returne,
And still renew the Accentes of vnrest,
VVhiles in my selfe, mine onelie selfe I burne.
   VVhiles frozen colde, whiles fierie hote I grow,
   I come, I flee, I stay, I sinke, I flow.

No, no, poore heart, my spirit sadlie spoke,
Leaue off these Passions, of extreame conceate:

                       And

And learne to beare with patience this thy Yoke,
VVhich from aboue is sent, not from thy fate :
For the Creator, hath the Creature stroke.
 Bee steadfast still, despaire not for annoyes,
 They are the tryall, of thy future joyes.

So VVorlde farewell, I haue no more to say,
 . Tort mee, and tosse mee, as thou wilt, I care not :
I hope that once, I shall triumph for aye :
And so to plague mee heere, O VVorlde, then spare not :
My Night's neare worne, and fast appeares my Day.
 O Ioye of chiefest Ioyes, receiue my Soule,
 And in thy Bookes of Life, my Name enroule.

Heere endeth the Pilgrimes Lamentado,
In his second Pilgrimage.

A.   H.

To the Right Honourable Ladie,

LADIE MARIE,

Countesse of Home, &c.

M Y seruile Muse low prostrate spreads her Rayes,
To $\frac{c}{p}$ great Dames, *HOMES* quintessence of fame :
The Noble *Merse*, admire thy vertuous wayes,
And as amaz'd, yeeld homage to the same.
The Vestall Maides, in honour of a Dame,
Are saide to feast *Minerva*, and great *Ioue*.
But Thou beyonde great Dames deseru'st a Name :
VVhose Breast is fraught witth nought but loyall loue.
O strange ! a Dame should from her Soyle remoue,
And though franchizd, a Stranger in some kinde.
In this Thy Course, the Heauens thy VVorth approue,
To show these matchlesse Fruites, of thy chaste Minde.
So, Countesse, so, All *HOMES* in Thee finde light :
Thou doest reuiue the Day, seem'd once their Night.
Then blest art Thou, in Thy fiue Babes : or rather,
More blest Thy Lord, in Thee, and them a Father.

Your La, most humble seruant,

WILLIAM LITHGOW.

To the Right Honorable Lord,

MY LORD SHEFFIELD,

President of Yorke, &c.

 F not ingrate, I must recall thy VVorth,
Which binds my brest to memorize thy name:
And if I could (doubtlesse) I would set foorth
Thy great desert, to liue in endlesse fame.
In passing by at *Yorke*, cras'd I, halfe lame,
Had hap to finde thy noble heart so kinde.
Great thankes (Braue Lord) I yeelde thee for the same :
First, to thy Gen'rous ; then, judicious Minde.
Thy Breast well read in Histories I finde,
But more Religious, in a Godlie course,
To Vertue and to Humane workes inclin'd :
Thou bound to them, they finde in the secourse.
   So as thou worthie liu'st, of thy good partes,
   Thine Honour growes, in conquering of Heartes.
   Long mayst thou liue, a *Loade starre* to the North,
   That brauest Wittes, may still thy prayse sing foorth.

Your Lo. euer, &c.

WILLIAM LITHGOW.

The Pilgrimes Farewell to Edinburgh,

DEDICATE

To the Right VVorshipfull, Sir VVILLIAM NISBET of
Deane, Knight : Lord Prouost, &c. And to the rest, The
right worthie Baylies and graue Magistrates of *Edinburgh.*

Hen *Albions* gēme, great *Britanes* greatest glore
Did leaue the South, this Articke Soyle to see,
Entred thy Gates, whole *Miriads* him before,
Glistring in Golde, most glorious to the eye :
First, Prouost, Bailies, Counsel, Senate graue,
Stood plac'd in rāks, their King for to receaue.

In richest Veluet Gownes, they did salute him,
VVhere from his face, appear'd, true Princelie loue :
And in the midst of Noble Troupes about him,
In name of All, Graue *Haye,* a Speach did moue.
    And being horst, the Prouost rode along,
    VVith our *Apollo,* in that splendant Throng.

What joyfull signes, foorth from thy Bosome sprang,
On thy faire Streetes, when shin'd his glorious Beames,
Shrill Trumpets sound, Drummes beat, & Bells lowd rang :
The people shout, VVelcome our Royall I A M E S :
    And when drawne neare, vnto thy Freedomes Right,
    His *Highnesse* stayde, and made thy Prouost Knight.

At last arriu'd at his great Pallace gate,
There facond NISBET, enuiron'd with throng,
Made in behalfe of Citie, Countrey, State,
A learned Speach in Ornate Latine Tongue :
    And thy strong Maiden-Forte, impregnate Boundes,
    Gaue out a world of Shottes, strange thundring sounds.

The Mustring-day drawne on, there came thy Glore,
To see thy gallant *Youthes,* so rich arrayde,

                      In

In *Pandedalian* Showes, did shine like Ore.
And statelie they their Martiall fittes displayde.
 VVith Fethers, Skarfs, loud Drummes, & Colours fleeing
 First in the Front, King I A M E S they goe a seeing.

Their Salutations rent the Aire a sunder.
And next to them, the Merchantes went in Order :
VVhose fire-flying Volleyes, crackt like Thunder :
And well conveigh'd, with Seargeantes on each border.
 So rul'd, so decent, and so arm'd a sight,
 Gave great contentment, to their greatest Light.

The vvorthie Trades, in rich approued Rankes,
In comelie Show, vvith them they march'd along :
VVhose deafning Shottes, resounded clowdie thankes,
For our Kinges VVelcome, in their greatest Throng.
 And in that noyse, mee thought, their honour'd Fates,
 Proclaim'd, That Trades, maintain both Crowns & States.

And more, sweet Citie, thou didst feast thy Prince,
Within a *Glasen* house, vvith such delightes,
And rare conceites, that few before, or since,
Did see it paraleld, in Forraine sightes.
 And those Fire-workes, on his Birth-day at night,
 Gaue to thy *Youthes* more prayse, thy selfe more light.

All these Triumphes, and moe, encrease thy Fame :
Which briefelie toucht, prolixitie I shunne.
And for my part, Great *Metrapole*, thy Name,
All-where I'le prayse; as twise past I haue done.
 And now I bidde with teares, with eyes which swell,
 Thee (SCOTLANDS Seate) deare EDINBVRGH, Farewell.

 Your Wor. neuer failing, &c.

 WILLIAM LITHGOW.

The Pilgrims Farewell to Northberwicke

Lawe. Dedicate to Sir I O H N H O M E of Northberwicke, *Knight, &c.*

Thou steepie Hill, so circling piramiz'd,
  That for a Prospect, serues East *Louthiane* Landes:
Where Ouile Flockes doe feede halfe enamiz'd:
And for a Trophee, to *Northberwicke* standes,
So mongst the Marine Hilles growes diademiz'd,
VVhich curling Plaines, and pastring Vales commaundes:
   Out from thy *Poleme* Eye, some sadnesse borrow,
   And decke thy Listes, with Streames of sliding sorrow.

And from thy cloudie toppe, some mistes dissolue,
To thicke the Planure, with a foggie Dew:
And on the Manure, moystie droppes reuolue,
To change colde *Hyeme*, in a *Cerene* Hew.
And let the *Ecchoes*, of thy Rockes resolue,
To mourne for mee, in gracing them was true.
   So Mount, powre out, thy showrie pale complaintes,
   For mee, and my Fare-well, my Malecontentes.

And now round Hight, whiles *Phœbus* warmes thy bounds,
Some glad reflexe, disbende downe to thy Knight:
And shew him, how thy Loue to him aboundes.
Since hee is Patrone, of thy Stile by right.
For from his VVorth, a double Fame redoundes,
To rayse his Vertue, farre aboue thine hight,
   Yet bow thine Head, and greet him as hee goes,
   Since hee, and his, deserue to weare thy Rose.
   And I, I wish, his Name, and Race, may stand,
   So long as thou art seene, by Sea, or Land.

Your Wor. &c.

WILLIAM LITHGOW.

A SONNET,

Made by the Author, being vpon Mount Ætna, in Sicilia, AN. 1615. *And on the second day thereafter arriuing at Mes-sina, he found two of his Countrey Gentlemen,* Dauid Seton, *of the House of* Perbroith, *and* Matthew Dowglas, *now presentlie at* Court: *to whome hee presented the same, they beeing at that instant time some* 40. *miles from thence.*

High standes thy toppe, but higher lookes mine eye,
High soares thy smoake, but higher my desire:
High are thy roundes, steepe, circled, as I see,
But higher farre this breast, whiles I aspire:
High mountes the furie, of thy burning fire,
But higher farre mine aymes transcende aboue:
High bendes thy force, through midst of *Vulcanes* ire,
But higher flies my sprite, with winges of loue:
High preasse thy flames, the chrystall aire to moue,
But higher farre, the scope of mine engine:
High lies the snow, on thy proude toppes, I proue,
But higher vp ascendes my braue designe.
   Thine height cannot surpasse this clowdie frame,
   But my poore Soule, the highest Heauens doth claime.
   Meane-while with paine, I climbe to view thy toppes,
   Thine hight makes fall from me, ten thousand droppes.

Yours affectionate, William Lithgow.

The Pilgrimes *Passionado, on the* Rhyne, *when he was robbed by fiue Souldiours,* French & Valloune, *aboue* Rhynberg, *in* Cleue, *being assosiated by a young Gentleman,* Dauid Bruce *of* Clakmanene house, ANNO 1614. Octob. 28. *And afterwarde dedicate to the most mightie Dutchesse,* ELIZABETH, *Princesse* Palatine, *of the* Rhyne, &c.

Giue life, sad Muse, vnto my watrie VVoes,
And let my windie sighes, ou'r-match despaire:
Striue in my sorrow sadlie to disclose

My

My Tormentes, Troubles, Crosses, Griefe, and Care :
  Paint mee out so, my Pourtraicture to bee,
  The matchlesse Mappe, of vnmatcht Miserie.

Euen as a Birde, caught in an vnseene Snare,
So was I fangd in lawlesse Souldiours handes :
My Cloathes, my Money, and my Goods they share,
Before mine eyes, whiles helplesse I still standes.
  I once Possessour, now Spectatour turnes,
  To see mee from my selfe, mine heart it burnes.

Nowe must I begge, or steale, else starue, and die,
For lacke of Foode : so am I Harbourlesse :
Sighes are my Speach, and Grones my Silence bee :
Bare-foote I am, and bare-legd, in distresse.
  My lookes craue helpe, mine eyes pierce euerie doore :
  I stretch mine handes, my voyce cries, Helpe the Poore.

Howe woefull-like I hing my mourning Face,
And downewarde looke vpon the sable ground :
Mine outwarde show, from Stones might beg some grace,
Though neither life, nor loue, on earth were found.
  Nowe, hungrie, naked, colde, and wette with Raine,
  Poore I, am crost, with Pouertie quite slaine.

Can Pouertie, that of it selfe's so light,
As beeing vveigh'd, in Ballance with the VVinde,
Doth hang aloft, yet seeme so hudge a weight :
To sit so sadde vpon a soaring Minde :
  No, no, poore Breast, it is thine owne base thought,
  That holdes the downe, for Pouertie is nought.

Or

On the Rhyne.

Or can the restlesse VVheele of Fortunes pride,
Turne vp-side downe ? mine euer-changing state.
Ah yea, for I, on *Regno* once did ride,
Though nowe throwne downe, to desolate debate.
    Thus am I chang'd, and this the VVorlde shall finde,
    Fortune, that Foole, is false, deafe, dumbe, and blinde.

Shall swift-wing'd Time, thus triumph in my VVronges ?
VVhiles I am left, a Mirrour of Despaire ?
Shall I vnfolde my plaintes, and heauie songes,
To grieue the VVorlde, and to molest the aire ?
    I, I, I mourne, but for to ease my griefe,
    Soone gettes hee helpe, at last who findes reliefe.

Once robd, and robd againe, and wounded too,
O what aduentures, ouer-sweigh my fate ?
Pilgrime, thou mourn'st, mourne not, let worldlinges doe,
Thinges past, recalde, they euer come too late :
    I wish, I had, is daylie full of woe :
    And had I wist, I would, is so, and so.

Well then, on lower Vales, the Shades doe lie,
And mistes doe lurke, on euerie watrie plaine.
The toppes of Mountaines, are both cleare and drie,
And nearest to all Sunne-shine joyes remaine.
    Mount then, braue Minde, to that admired hight,
    VVhere neither mist, nor shade, can hurt thy sight.
    So I'le defie Time, Fortune, *Mars*, and *Rhyne*,
    Who all at once, conspir'd my last ruine.

In his second Trauels, after his departure
from ENGLAND, arriuing at OSTEND: the sight
whereof gaue the Pilgrime this Subject.

TO view the ruines, of thy wasted VValles,
   Loe, I am come, bewailing thy disgrace:
Art thou this Bourge, *Bellona* so installes?
To bee a Mirrour, for a Martiall face:
   I sure it's thou, whose bloodie bathing boundes,
   Gaue death to thousandes, and to thousandes woundes.

VVhat Hostile force, besieg'd thee, poore OSTEND?
VVith all engine, that euer VVarre deuis'd.
VVhat Martiall Troupes, did valiantlie defende,
Thine Earthen Strengthes, and Sconses vnsurpris'd:
   By cruell assaultes, and desperate defence,
   Thine vndeseruing name, wonne honour thence.

Some deepe interr'd, within thy bosome lie:
Some rotte, some rent, some torne in pieces small,
Some VVarre-like maim'd, some lame, some halting crie,
Some blowne through clouds, some brought to deadly thrall
   VVhose dire defectes, renew'd with Ghostlie mones,
   May match the *Thebane,* or the *Trojane* grones.

Base Fisher Towne, that fang'd thy Nettes before,
And drencht into the Deepes, thy Foode to winne:
Art thou become a Tragicke Stage? and more,
VVhence brauest VVittes, braue Stories may beginne:
   To show the World, more than the World would craue,
   How all thine in-trencht ground, became one Graue.

Thy digged Ditches, turn'd a Gulfe of Blood,
Thy Walles defeate, were rearde, with fatall bones:
Thine Houses equall, with the Streetes they stoode:

Thy Limites come, a Sepulchre of Grones.
   VVhence Canons roar'd, from fieric cracking smoake,
   T'wixt two Extreames, thy Desolation broke.

Thou God of VVarre, whose thundring soundes doe feare,
This circled space, plac'd heere below the roundes :
Thou, in obliuion, hast sepulchriz'd heere,
Earthes dearest life : for now what else redoundes,
   But Sighes, and Sobbes, when Treason, Sword and Fire,
   Haue throwne all downe, when all thought to aspire ?

Foorth from thy Marches, and Frontiers about,
In sanguine hew, thou dy'd the fragrant Fieldes.
The camped Trenches of thy Foes without,
VVere turn'd to blood : for valour neuer yeeldes.
   So bred Ambition, Honour, Courage, Hate,
   Long three yeeres Siedge, to ouer-throw thy State.

At last from threatning terrour of despaire,
Thine hemb'de Defendantes, with diuided VValles,
VVere forc'd to render : Then came mourning care
Of mutuall Foes, for Friendes vntimelie falles :
   Thus lost, and gotte, by wrong and lawlesse Right,
   My judgment thinkes thee, scarcelie worth the sight.
   But there's the question, VVhen my Muse hath done,
   VVhether the Victor, or the Vanquisht wonne ?

To the Worshipfull Gentleman,
THOMAS EDMOND:
Now resident in the LOWE COVNTREYES.

Youth, thou mayst see (though brief) my great goodwill :
  It's not for flattrie, nor rewarde, I prayse :
VVee are farre distant, yet my flying Quill,
Perhaps may come, within thine home-bred wayes.

             I striue

I striue from Dust, thy Fathers Fame to raise,
For *Scotlandes* sake, and for his Martiall Skill,
VVhose fearelesse Courage, following VVarlike Frayes,
Did there surpasse, the worthiest of his dayes.
 And as his matchlesse Valour, Honour wonne,
 His death resign'd, the same, to thee his Sonne.

Yours, to his vttermost,

WILLIAM LITHGOW.

The Complaint of the late LORD,
CORONALL EDMOND his Ghoste.

OUT of the Ioyes, of sweete Eternall Rest,
I must compeare, as forc'd for to remoue,
Here to complaine, how I am dispossest,
Of Christian Battelles, Captaines, Souldiers loue.

Oft with the Pensile, of a bloodie Pen,
I wrote my val'rous fortunate assayes ;
Though I be gone, my worth is prais'd of men ;
The *Netherlandes* admyrd my warlike dayes.

And *Counte du Buckoye*, twyse my captiue was,
In cruell fight, at *Emricke* I him tooke ;
(The stoutest Earle the Spanish armie has)
Who till my death, his armes hee quyte forsooke.

At *New-port* fight, that same day, ah, I lost,
The worthiest *Scots*, that life the world affords ;
Men, a Regiment, like Gyantes seemde to boast,
A worlde of *Spaniardes*, and their bloodie Swordes.

And I escap'd so neare, was twise vnhorst :
Yea, manie other bloodie Fieldes I stroke.

My

My Foes strange plottes, was neu'r so strong secourst,
But eft-soones I, their Force, and Terrour broke.

Scotland I thanke, for mine vndaunted Breath,
Shee brought mee foorth, for to vnsheath my Sworde:
The STATES they found mee true vnto my death,
And neuer shrunke from them in deede or worde.

At *Rhynsberg* Sconce, I gottee my fatall blow,
A faint-heart *French-man* baselie was refute:
And I went on, the *Pultrone* for to show,
VVhere in a *Demi-Lune* that hee should shoote.

But ah! a Musket, twinde mee and my life,
VVhich made my Foe, euen *Spineola*, to grieue,
Although my death, did ende, his doubtfull strife,
His worthie Breast, oft wisht, that I might liue.

   Thus STATES farewell, Count MAURICE, souldiers
The most aduentrous, nearest to his fall: (all,
This *Pilgrime* passing by, where I was slaine,
In sorrow of his heart, raisde mee againe.

The author in his second Trauels beeing at
PRAGE, in BOHEMIA, did sute the Emperour for
some affaires, which being granted, a young vp-start Courtier
ouer-threw him therein, giuing him this Subiect to expresse,
after long attendance at Court, &c.

THou carelesse Court, commixt with colours strange,
  Carefull to catch, but carelesse to reward;
Thy care doth carrie, a sad *Cymerian* change,
To starue the best, and still the worst regard:
For in thy greatnesse, greatly am I snar'd.
   Ah wretched I, on thy vnhappie shelfe,
   Grounded my hopes, and cast away my selfe.

On the Court of Bohemia.

From stormes to calme, from calme to stormes amaine,
Poore I am tost, in dyuing boundlesse deepes ;
There where I perish'd Loues to fall againe,
And that which hath me lost, my losse still keepes,
In dark oblivion, my designes now sleepes :
   Cancelling thus, the aymes of my aspyring,
   Still crosse, on crosse, haue crost my just desiring.

Had thy vnhappie smyles, shrunke to betray me,
Worthie had beene, the worth of my deseruing ;
Blush if thou canst, for shame can not affray thee,
Since fame declines, and bountie is in swerving,
And leaues thee clog'd in pryde, for purenesse staruing :
   Ah court, thou mappe, of all dissimulation,
   Turnes Faith to flattrie, Loue to emulation.

Happie liu'd I, whilst I sought nothing more,
But what my trauailes, by great paines obtained ;
Now being Ship-wrackt, on thy marble shore,
By Tauernes wrackt, goods spent, gifts farre restrained,
Am forc'd to flee, by miserie constrained :
   Whose ruthles frowns, my modest thoughts haue scatterd
   The swelling sailes of hope, in pieces shatterd.

Some by the rise of small desert so hie,
That on their height, the VVorlde is forc'd to gaze :
Their Fortunes, riper than their yeeres to bee,
May fill the VVorlde with wonder, wonders rayse.
As though there were none ende to smoake their prayse.
   VVell Court, aduance, thy mineons neu'r so much,
   Doe what thou canst, I'le neuer honour such.

Iustlie I know my sad lamenting Muse,
May claime reuenge of thine inconstant state :

                    Thou

On the Court of Bohemia.

Thou fedst mee with faire showes, then didst abuse,
All, I expect'd, sprung from an heart ingrate.
Whom fortune once hath raisde, may turne his fate.
   In Court whose pride, ambition makes him All,
   In ende shall pride, ambition, breede his fall,

VVhen swift-wing'd Time, discloser of all thinges,
Shall trie the future euents of mens rising,
VVhat admiration to the VVorlde it bringes,
To see who made their State, their State surprising,
Whome they with Flattrie stoode, and false entising.
   And when they fall, mee thinke I heare these Songes,
   The world proclaims, There's them that nurst my wrongs.

Thou must not thinke, thy fame shall alwayes flourish,
VVhose Birth once meane, made great by Princelie fauour :
Flowres in their prime, the season sweetlie nourish,
Then in disgrace, they wither, loose their sauour :
So all haue course, whome fortune so will honour.
   Looke to thy selfe, and know within, without thee :
   Thou rose with flattrie, flattrie dwelles about thee.

Thou cunning Court, cledde in a curious cace,
Seemst to bee that, which thou art not indeed :
Thou maskst thy wordes, with eloquence, no grace,
Hatcht in the craft of thy dissembling head,
And poore Attendantes, with vaine showes doest feede.
   Thou promist faire, performing nought at all :
   Thy Smiles, are Wrath ; thine Honey, bitter Gall.

Curst bee the man, that trustes in thine assuring,
For then himselfe, himselfe shall vndermine :
Griefes are soone gotte, but painefull in induring,
Hopes vnobtaind, make but the hoper pine :

G   Hopes

On the Court of Bohemia.

Hopes are like beames, which through dark clouds do shine.
　VVhich moue the eyes to looke, the thoughts to swell,
　Bring sudden Ioye, then turnes that Ioye, an Hell.

Thrise happie hee, who liues a quiet life,
Hee needes not care, thine Enuie, Pride, nor Treason :
His wayes are plaine, his actions voyde of strife,
Sweetelie hee toyles, though painefull in the season,
And makes his Conscience, both his Law and Reason.
　Hee sleepes securelie, needes not feare no danger,
　Supportes the Poore, and intertaines the Stranger.

And who liues more content, than Sheepheardes doe ?
VVhome haughtie heads account but Countrey Swanes :
Leaue off, they mount you farre, and scorne you too,
And liue more sweetelie, on Valleyes, Hilles, and Plaines,
Than yee, proude Fooles, for all your puft-vp braines :
　VVhose heartes contend, to flatter, swell, and gaine,
　Ambition choakes your Breasts, Hell breeds your paine.

VVhat art thou COURT ? If I can censure duelie,
A masked Playe, where nought appeares but glancing :
And in an homelier sense, to sing more truelie,
A stage, where Fooles, are daylie in aduancing :
I'le sing no more, for feare of sudden lancing.
　For if a *Germane* gape, then I am gone,
　Hee drinkes mee at a draught, it's ten to one.

Farewell thou BOHEME Court, thy smallest Traine :
Farewell the meanenesse, of thine highest Stile :
Farewell the Fruites, of my long lookt-for Gaine :
Farewell the Time, that did mine Hopes beguile :
And happie I, if I saw BRITANES Ile.
　And whilst I see, my Natiue Soyle, I sweare,
　I thinke each Houre, a Daye ; each Daye, a Yeere.

To his vnknowne, knowne ; and knowne, vnknowne Loue,
These now knowne Lines, an vnknowne Breast shall moue,

SElfe-flattring I, deceiuer of my selfe,
Opinions Slaue, rul'd by a base Conceate :
VVhome eu'rie winde, naufragiates on the shelfe,
Of Apprehension, jealous of my State,
    VVho guides mee most, that guide I most misknow,
    Suspectes the Shaddow, for a substant Show.

I still receiue, the thing I vomite out,
Conceiues againe imaginarie wracke :
I stable stand, and yet I stand in doubt,
Giues place to one, when two repulles mee backe.
    I kindle Fire, and that same Fire I quench,
    And swim the deepes, but dare not downwarde drench.

I grieue at this, prolong'd in my desire,
And I rejoyce, that my delay is such :
I trie, and knowes, my tryall may aspire,
But flees the place, that should this time auouh.
    In stinging smartes, my sweete conuertes in sowre,
    I builde the Hiue, but dare not sucke the Flowre.

Well Honney Combe, since I am so faint hearted,
That I flee backe, when thou vnmaskst thy face :
Thou shalt bee gone, and I must bee decarted,
Such doubtfull stayes enhaunce, when wee embrace.
    Farewell, wee two, diuided are for euer,
    Yet vndiuided, whilst our Soules disseuer.

            Thine, as I am mine,

            WILLIAM LITHGOW.

A SONNET,

*Made by the Pilgrime, when hee was almost ship-wracked,
betwixt the Iles Arrane and Rossay, anno 1617. Sebtemb. 9.*

WHat foaming Seas, in restlesse hatefull rage,
Striue to surmatch, the neuer-matched Skies?
Can bounded Reason, boundlesse VVill not swadge?
Nor spitefull *Neptune*, pittie my poore cries?
Now downe to Hell, now vp to Heauen I rise,
Twixt two Extreames, extreamly make debate,
Heauens thundring winds, my halfe harm'd heart denyes
All hop'd-for helpe, to my hurt haplesse state,
I am content, Let fortune rule my fate,
Tymes alt'ring turnes, may change in joye my griefe,
Roare foorth yee Stormes, rebell, and bee ingrate,
I scorne to begge, from *Borean* blastes, reliefe.
　　Long-winged Boate, quicke-shake thy trembling oares,
　　And correspond these waues, with demi-roares.

The Pilgrime Entring into the Mouth of
CLYDE, from ROSSAY, to view DUNBARTANE
Castle, and LOCHLOWMOND, anno 1617. *Sebtemb.* 18,
Hee saluted his natiue Riuer with these Verses.

HOw sweetelie slide the Streames of silent CLYDE,
And smoothlie runne, betweene two bordring Banks:
Redoubling oft his Course, seemes to abyde,
To greete my Trauelles, with tenne thousand thankes,
　　That I, whose eyes, had view'd so manie Floodes,
　　Deign'd to suruey, his deepes, and neighb'ring woods.

Thrise famous *Clyde*, I thanke thee for thy greeting,
Oft haue thy Brethren, easde mee of my paine:
Two contrarie extreames, wee haue in meeting,

　　　　　　　　　　　　　　　　　I vp-

His Farewell to Clyde.

I vpward climbe, and thou fall'st downe amaine.
  I search thy Spring, and thou the Westerne Sea :
  So farewell Flood, yet stay, and mourne with mee.

Goe steale along with speede, the *Hyberne* shore,
And meete the *Thames*, vpon the *Albion* coast :
Ioyne your two Armes, then sighing both, deplore
The Fortunes, which in *Britane* I haue lost.
  And let the VVater-Nymphes, and *Neptune* too,
  Refraine their mirth, and mourne, as Riuers doe.

To thee great *Clyde*, if I disclose my wronges,
I feare to loade thee, with excesse of griefe :
Then may the Ocean, bereaue thee of my Songes,
And swallow vp thy Plaintes, and my reliefe.
  Tell onelie *Isis*, So, and so, and so :
  Conceale the trueth, but thunder foorth my woe.

My Bloode, sweete *Clyde*, claimes intrest in thy worth,
Thou in my Birth, I in thy vaprous Beames :
Thy breadth surmountes, the *Tweede*, the *Tay*, the *Forth*,
In pleasures thou excell'st, in glistring Streames :
  Seeke *Scotland* for a Fort, O then *Dunbertaine !*
  That for a Trophee standes, at thy Mouth certaine.

Ten miles more vp, thy well-built *Glasgow* standes,
Our second Metrapole, of Spirituall Glore :
A Citie deckt with people, fertile Landes :
VVhere our great King, gotte Welcome, welcomes store :
  VVhose Cathedrall, and Steeple, threat the Skies,
  And nine archt Bridge, out ou'r thy bosome lies.

And higher vp, there dwelles thy greatest wonder,
Thy chiefest Patrone, glorie of thy Boundes :
           A Noble

His Farewell to Clyde.

A Noble Marques, whose great Vertues thunder,
An æquiuox backe to thy Pleasant Soundes.
   VVhose Greatnesse may command thine head to foote,
   From *Aricke* stone, vnto the Ile of *Boote*.

As thou alongst his Palace slides, in haste,
Stay, and salute, his *Marquesadiane Dame:*
That matchlesse Matrone, Mirrour of the VVest,
Deignes to protect, the Honour of thy Name.
   So euer famous Flood, yeelde them their duetie,
   They are the onelie, Lampes, of thy great Beautie.

Aud now, faire-bounded Streame, I yet ascende,
To our olde LANERKE, situate on thy Bankes :
And for my sake, let *Corhouse Lin* disbende,
Some thundring noyse, to greete that Towne with thanks,
   There was I borne : Then *Clyde*, for this my loue,
   As thou runnes by, her auncient VVorth approue.

And higher vp, to climbe to *Tinto* Hill,
(The greatest Mountaine, that thy Boundes can see:)
There stand to circuite, and striue t' runne thy fill,
And smile vpon that Barron dwelles by thee.
   Carmichell thy great Friende, whose famous Sire,
   In dying, left not, *Scotland*, such a squire.

In doing these Requestes, I shall commende thee,
To fertile *Nyle*, and to the sandie *Iore*,
And I recorde, The *Danube*, latelie sende thee.
A thousand Greetinges, from his statelie Shore.
   Thus, for thy paines, I shall augment thy Glorie,
   And write thy Name, in Times Eternall Storie.
   So, euer-pleasant Flood, thy losse I feele,
   In breathing foorth this worde, Deare *Clyde*, Fareweele.

The Heremites Welcome,

To the Pilgrimes thirde Pilgrimage,

NOW long-worne Pilgrime, in this Vale of Teares,
  Thrise welcome, to thy thrise austiere Assayes :
In thee, my second selfe, it well appeares,
For in thy Mappe, I see my pensiue Wayes.
  I liue alone, vpon this desart Mount,
  And thou comst foorth alone, as thou wast wont.

Mee thinkes thou seem'st a solitarie man,
That, for some sorrowe, hadst forsooke thy Soyle :
Or else, some long-made Vowe, which makes thee than
To vnder-take this miserie of Toyle.
  Faine would I aske, the cause, why thou dost wander ?
  But thy sadde showe, doth seeme, no count to rander.

Yet in thine heauie Face, I see thy paine,
Thine hollow Eyes, deepe sunken in thine Head :
VVhose pale clapt Cheekes, and wrinckled Browes againe,
Show mee what griefe, disasters, in the breede.
  Thy sight, poore wretch, telles me thou hast no pleasure,
  In Rest, in Toyle, in Life, nor worldlic treasure.

So happie thou, sit downe heere by my side,
And rest thy selfe, thy paine is wondrous sore :
For I, I still, in this one place do bide,
But thou all-where, thy Pennance dost explore.
  Thou neuer supst, nor dynst, into one parte.
  Nor ly'st two nightes, vnchanging of thine airte.

Thy life is harde, I must confesse, deare Brother,
For where I liue, my Friendes dwell heere about mee :
                                                But

But in thy chaunge, thou seest now one, now other,
And all are Strangers, that each day may doubt thee.
   I judge the cause of this, good GOD reliue thee :
   To see a Soule so vext, it quite doth grieue mee.

My solitarie life, is harde indeede,
And I chastize my selfe with hungrie Fare :
On Hearbes, raw Rootes, on Snailes, and Frogges I feede :
And what GOD giues mee, freelie I it share.
   Three dayes in eight, I fast, for my Soules better.
   And in this time, I feede on Bread and VVater.

All this is nought to thine, with mine I rest :
For thou must toyle, and fast against thy will.
If it fall late, then thou must runne in haste,
To seeke thy Lodging, fortunate, but Skill.
   I haue the shelter of this Her'mitage,
   But vniuersall is thy Pilgrimage,

Alace, deare Sonne ! I mourne to see thy life,
Though in the passions of thy paines thou joyes :
VVouldst thou turne Hermite, thou mightst end thy strife,
My Fare is rude, but Prayer mee imployes.
   Rest, rest, and rest, the Heauens as soone they wonne,
   That rest with mee, as they all-where that runne.

Yet I confesse, thy Pennance doth exceede,
My merite farre, wonne by these austiere meanes :
For thou with *Turkes*, and *Paganes*, eat'st thy Bread,
Hast feare of death, when thou none other weanes.
   They plague thy Purse, and Hunger plagues thy Bellie,
   VVhiles in this Cottage, I contentment swellie.

I see no stormie Seas, vvhere Pirates liue :
No Murthrer dare encroach vpon my State :

I feare no Thiefe, nor at wilde Beastes doe grieue :
I neede not buy, nor spende, nor lende, nor frate.
 All these, and manie moe, attende thy wayes :
 Ah, poore slaine *Pilgrime*, so the *Hermite* sayes.

Thou seemst to bee, of some farre Northerne Nation,
And I doe maruell, that thou walkst alone :
Good Companie, should bee thy chiefe Solation,
For thou hast Plaines, and Hilles, to wander on :
 Long VVoods, and Desartes, eu'rie where must finde :
 Hadst thou a second, thou hadst a quiet minde.

But wandring Sonne, these thinges no more I touch,
I must refresh thee, with some Hermites cheare :
For I, poore I, can heere afforde but such,
As Hearbes, raw Rootes, browne Bread, and VVater cleare.
 Yet, if thou wilt conceale this gift of mine,
 I haue good Flesh, good Fish, good Bread, good Wine.

Although to common Pilgrimes I not show it,
Yet for *Ierusalem*, which thou hast seene.
Thou shalt haue part, although the VVorld should know it,
Thou art as holie, as euer I haue beene.
 So welcome, Sonne, welcome to mee, I sweare :
 Thou shalt finde more with mee, than Tauerne cheare.

Heere on this greene growne Hill, I spreade my Table,
VVell couerd ou'r, with Leaues of diuerse sortes :
VVho say that *Hermites* fast, is but a fable,
VVee haue the best, the Peasantes haue the Ortes.
 And *Pilgrime* holde thy peace, wee shall bee merrie.
 For heere's good VVine, which tastes of the true Berrie.

Fill, and content, thy long desires apace,
And bee not shamefast, *Pilgrimes* must bee forthie :
VVee *Hermites* seldome vse to say a Grace :
To pray too much at Meate, that's vnworthie.
 And what thou leau'st, thy *Budget* shall possesse,
 I cannot want, when thou mayst finde distresse.

H

And

And there a Carrouse, of the sweetest Wyne,
That growes twixt *Piemont*, and *Callabrian* shore ;
Hast thou enough ? nowe tell me, all is thine,
When this is done, I'le finde another Bore :
   And giue me out thy *Callabast* to fill,
    That thou mayst drinke, when thou discends this hill.

Thus pensiue Pilgrime, thy humble Hermite greetes thee,
And yet me thinkes, thou lookes not like a *Frater*,
If thou be Catholike, my Soule shee treats thee,
For this good worke of mine, to say a *Pater :*
   Thou seemes to smyle, and will not fall a Prayer,
    I lay my life, thou art a meere betrayer.

O Pilgrimagious sonne, now faith, I knowe thee,
At *Mount Serata*, nyne yeares past and more ;
I askd at thee, VVhat wast thou ? VVho did owe thee ?
And thou reply'd, A stranger seeking Ore.
   I answer'd, Hermits, neuer keepe no Golde,
    O Pilgrime now, on faith, now you are solde.

How dar'st thou man, within our bounds repare ?
An Hereticke, would make a Christian show :
Hast thou no conscience, for thy Soule to care ?
There is but one way, to the Heauens wee know.
   And wilt thou liue a Schismatike or Atheist ?
    No rather Pilgrime, turne with mee a Papist.

Our ghostly father, Christes Vicare on earth,
Is highly with thy old done deeds displeased :
And I doe knowe, for all thy showe of mirth,
If thou be found, these trickes can not be meased :
   A suddaine blast, will blow thee in the aire,
    Therefore when free, to saue thy life beware.

And yet it seemes, thou car'st not what I speake,
But thinkes me damn'd, for all my poore profession ;
I stand in doubt my selfe, the trueth I seeke,

To his third Pilgrimage.

And of my life, there is my true confession :
  When I was young, luxurious vice I lou'd,
  Libidinous, abhominablely mou'd.

I know, thou knowst, what Priests doe, with young boyes,
It is a common sinne, in young and old ;
O strange, gainst Nature, man his lust employes !
They seeme as Saincts, and Hell-hounds are enrold :
  Their filthie deeds, make my poore conscience tremble,
  And with Religion, gainst my heart dissemble.

I will be plaine, I am thy Countrey man,
And father *Thomson* is my Christiane name ;
In *Angus* was I borne, but after when
I left the Schooles, to *Italy* I came :
  And first turn'd Frier, of great Sainct *Francis* Order,
  But loathing that, turn'd Hermite on·this Border.

Know'st thou Father *Mophet*, that Iesuit Priest ?
As I heare say, hee lay in Prison long :
It's saide, that once hee should haue thee confest :
If not, the VVorldes wide voyce, doth thee wrong.
  And Father *Crichton*, is hee yet aliue ?
  For Lecherie, they say, hee could not thriue.

And I heare say, that Father *Gray* is dead,
And Father *Gordon*, drawes neare to his Graue,
And Father *White*, at *Rhynsberg* hath great neede,
And Father *Browne*, would seeme to play the Knaue :
  And Father *Hebron*, wee call *Bonauenture*,
  Hee studies more than his Wittes well may venture.

They say, Father *Anderson* hath left *Rome*,
For strife, which in our *Scots* Colledge fell out,
And Father *Leslie*, hee doth brooke his Roome :
There none of them, dealt honestlie, I doubt.
  Our young *Scots* Studentes, they hunger to the heart,
  The Pope allowes good meanes, and they it part.

That Icsuit *Greene*, in *Wolmets* is come rich,
And Father *Cumming*, in *Venice'* s gone madde:
And *Lylle*, at *Bridges*, is become a VVretch.
For *Ogelbie*, alace, I must bee sadde:
    They say at *Glasgow*, he was hanged there:
    Heè's now a Martyr, so *Romane* VVrits declare.

That *Veizon* Bishop, of the *Chissome* Blood,
Hath Noble Partes, and worthie of his Breath:
Hee is benigne, and kinde, and still doth good
To Passengers, vnasking of their Faith.
    And Curate *Wallace*, is a louing Priest:
    But Father *Rob*, at *Antwerpe*, playes the Beast.

Thou canst not tell, how Signior *Ferrier* grees,
VVith *Dauid Chambers*, where in *Rome* they dwell:
Ferrier is false, and takes the Pilgrimes Fees,
And *Chambers* makes a show the Pope to tell.
    They say in *Rome*, as manie *Scots* they bee,
    The one high hanged, would the other see.

Alace, if I might safelie Home returne, ·
My Conscience knowes, the time that I haue spent,
And if they would accept mee, I should mourne,
In publicke show, and priuate to repent.
    Alace, alace, wee're Hypocrites each one,
    VVee make a Show, Religion we haue none.

So, to bee briefe, deare Friende, my Counsell take,
Treade not in *Italie*, *Portugall*, or *Spaine*:
These Hellish Priestes, of whom I mention make,
VVill striue to catch thee, to thy deare-bought paine.
    Goe all-where else, but not within those Boundēs.
    These Gospellers, are blooddie hunting Houndes,
    So farewel sonne, GOD guide thee where thou wanders,
    And saue thy Soule from harme, thy Life from slanders,

To the Noble, Illustrious, and Honou-
rable *LORDES,*

LODOWICKE, *DVKE OF LENNOXE,* &c.
IAMES, *MARQVES OF HAMMILTON,* &c.
GEORGE, *MARQVES OF HVNTLEY,* &c.

TO you great three, three greatest next our Crowne,
This smallest mite (though weake in meane) I bring:
Three *Noble Peeres,* true Objects of Renowne,
Strong Columnes, still to whom the *Muses* sing.
    Two in the *West,* diuided by a Flood,
    The other Patrone in the *North* for good.

First thou, braue Duke, on *Clydes* North-coasted Bankes,
(The *Lennoxe* Landes, thy chiefest Stile, their Glore,)
Dost there illustrate, all inferiour Rankes,
Foorth from thy loue, their standinges, settle more:
    Thrise happie *Duke,* in whome the Heauens enshrine,
    True humane Vertues, Faculties diuine.

And now, bright Pole, of our Antarticke *Clyde,*
Mirrour of Vertue, Glorie of these Boundes:
In thee, the Worths of thine Ancestors byde,
VVhose Greatnesse, Honour, to this Land redoundes.
    So as thou liu'st, great Marques, great in Might,
    This *Albions* Orbe, admire, adore, thy sight.

And thou, Chiefe Marques, in the Noble *North,*
(Their Articke-Splending Light, their Hemi-spheare)
VVhat shines in thee? But wonders of great worth?

For

For from thy selfe, true Chrystall Giftes appeare.
   The glorious GORDONS, Guerdon of thy Name,
   Thou art their *Trophee*, they maintaine thy Fame.

Thus in you three, three matchlesse Subjectes great,
I humblie heere, intombe, my *Muse*, my Paines :
Next to our triple Lampes, your triple Stafe,
Is plac'd, in which true honourd VVorth remaines.
   So from your Greatnesse, let some fauour shine,
   To shaddow my Farewels, my rude Engine.

Your Lo. most Obsequious, &c.

William Lithgow.

AN ELEGIE,

Containing the Pilgrimes most humble
Farewell to his Natiue and neuer
conquered Kingdome of SCOTLAND.

Tu vero, O mea Tellus, & Genitorum Patria
Vale : Nam viro licet plurimum malis obruatur
Nullum est suavius solum, quam quod nutriuit eum.

TO thee, O dearest Soyle, these mourning Lines I bring,
And with a broken bleeding Breast, my sad Farewell I sing,
Nowe melting Eyes dissolue, O windie Sighes disclose,
The airie Vapoures of my griefe, sprung from my watrie woes :
And let my Dying-day, no sorrow vncontrole,
Since on the Planets of my Plaintes, I moue about the Pole.
Shall I, O restlesse I, still thwarting, runne this round ?
Whiles resting Mortalles restlesse Mount, I mouldarize the ground
And in my wandring long, in pleasure, paine, and greife,
Begges mercie of the mercielesse of sorrow, sorrowes chiefe.

Sith

The Pilgrimes Farewell to Scotland.

Sith after two Returnes, my merites are forgot,
The third shall ende, or else repaire, my long estranging Lot.
Then kindlie come distresse, a Figge for Forraine care,
I gladlie in Extreames must walke, whiles on this masse I fare.
The Moorish *frowning face, the* Turkish *awfull brow,*
The Sarasene and Arabe *blowes, poore I, must to them bow.*
These Articles of Woe, my Monster-breeding paine,
As Pendicles on my poore state, vnwisht for, shall remaine.
Thus fraught with bitter Cares, I close my Malcontentes,
Within this Kalendar of Griefe, to memorize my Plaintes.
And to that VVesterne *Soyle, where* Gallus *once did dwell,*
To Gallowedian *Barrons I, impart this my Farewell.*
A Forraine Debt I owe, braue Garlees, *to thy worth,*
And to my Genrous Kenmure *Knight, more than I can sing forth*
To Bombee *I assigne, lowe Homage for his loue :*
And to Barnebarough *kinde & wise, a breast whiles breath may*
Vnto the worthy Boyde, *in* Scotland, *first in* France, (moue.
I owe effectes of true good-will, a low-laide countenance.
And thou graue Lowdon *Lord, I honour with the best,*
And on the Noble Eglinton, *my strong affections rest.*
Kilmaers *I admire, for quicke and readie wit :*
And graue Glencarne, *his Father deare, on honours top doth sit :*
And to thee gallant Rosse, *well seene in Forraine partes,*
I sacrifice a Pilgrimes *loue, amongst these Noble heartes.*
From Carlile *vnto* Clyde, *that* Southwest *shore I know :*
And by the way, Lord Harreis *I, remembrance duelie owe.*
In that small progresse I, surueying all the VVest,
Euen to your Houses, one by one, my Lodging I adrest :
Your kindnesse I imbrac'd, as not ingrate, The same
I memorize to future times, in eternized fame.
Amongst these long Goodnightes, farewell yee Poets *deare,*
Graue Menstrie *true* Castalian *fire, quicke* Drummond *in his*
Braue Murray *ah is dead,* Aiton *supplies his place,* (spheare.
And Alens *high* Pernassian *veine, rare Poems doth embrace.*

There's

The Pilgrimes Farewell to Scotland.

There's manie moe well knowne, whome I cannot explaine,
And Gordon, Semple, Maxwell too, haue the Pernassian veine
And yee Colledgians all, the fruites of Learning graue
To you I consecrate my Loue, enstalde amongst the leaue.
First to you Rectors, I, and Regentes, homage make,
Then from your spiring Breasts, braue Youths, my leaue I humbly
And, Scotland, I attest, my Witnesse reignes aboue,   (take.
In all my worlde-wide wandring wayes, I kept to thee my loue :
To manie Forraine Breastes, in these exyling Dayes,
In sympathizing Harmonies, I sung thine endlesse Prayse.
And where thou wast not knowne, I registerd thy Name,
Within their Annalles of Renowne, to eternize thy Fame.
And this twise haue I done, in my twise long Assayes,
And now the third time thrise I wil, thy Name vnconquerd raise.
Yea, I will stampe thy Badge, and seale it with my Blood :
And if I die in thy Defence, I thinke mine Ende is good.
So dearest Soyle, O deare, I sacrifice now see,
Euen on the Altar of mine Heart, a spotlesse Loue to thee.
And Scotland now farewell, farewell for manie Yeares :
This Eccho of Farewell bringes out, from mee, a world of teares.

Magnum virtutis principium est, ut dixit paulatim exercitatus
animus visibilia & transitoria primum commurare, ut post-
modum possit derelinquere. Delicatus ille est adhuc, cui
patria dulcis est; fortis autem jam, cui omne solum patria
est : perfectus vero, cui mundus exilium est.

F I N I S.

Lithgow, to his noble Mecenas.

If thou accepost of my panes, my goodwill
is also a sacrifice: though the style be plane
the matter is good: If any fault be conceaved
impute it, to my present sicknes, e bodely deseass.
Vive, Vale.

By

Williame Lithgow
in
his Countreys behalf

Go prostrat Lynes; greet thyne Appolloes herse,
Weep, whylst alyes, Lykd, Lovd and read, my Verse.

SCOTLAND'S TEARES,

BY

WILLIAME LITHGOW,

IN

HIS COUNTREYES BEHALF.

1625.

LITHGOW, TO HIS NOBLE MECENAS.

IF THOU ACCEPTEST OF MY PANES, MY GOODWILL
SHALL BE A SACRIFICE; THOUGH THE STYLE BE PLANE
THE MATTER IS GOOD : IF ANY FAULT BE COMMITTED,
IMPUTE IT TO MY PRESENT SICKNES AND BODELY DESEASE.

Vive, Vale.

SCOTLAND'S TEARES.

Thow quelling Bird, that courts Meanders brooks,
Where silver swans, accoast six hundreth crooks ;
Out of thy dyeing wing, send me a quill,
Dip'd in Penneian springs, from Pindus rill ;
To moyst my sun-scorched veyne, with liquid drops,
Which flow from Soron, twixt the forked tops ;
The Nymphs I cite to ayde, let them infuse,
Sweet Demthen rills, their Heliconean Muse ;
I sing the saddest verse ere Poet wrot,
Since that my Virgin wombe, first bred a Scot :   10
Now launch I forth, now gush my watery plaints,
And shiv'ring come, as one through grief that faints :
Loade with the spoyles of sorrow, I complayne
All other woes, compar'd with myne, seeme vane ;
Onely salt teares, which from my bowells flow
Shall restles runne, and let the Occean know
My dyre distresse : Such clouddy accents wold
Have larger scope, than hembd-in Regiones hold.
Me thinks a murmuring noyse, drawes from the South,
Post, post, he comes, the horn roynds in his mouth ;   20
The spurres are prest, the horse bends o're my bounds,
The boyes lips do quiver ; Death, Death, he sounds
The sound strikes through my heart. O dysmall day !
That waxd so proud, of such a Princely prey ;
Death, packet-seald, my cheeffest City entered,
The Lords it ope, wsd Liberty so venterd :
Grim Death's disclosed, they weeping close their eyes,
Their greefs dividuat, seeme but one desease :

He flat downe falles, the other speechles stands,
One tears-strick blynd, another wrings his hands;   30
The rest distracted, all passion-rent bewry
In deep-drawne sighs, Man's fate, King's destiny;
One warbling voyce chirps out, one playnes how Death
Had robd great JAMES his high imperiall breath:
This Eccho smote the hills, the hilles rebounded
Back on the vayles: the Rivers deadly wounded
Fled to the Belgick deeps: The Seas retourne
Their sinking loade, and swore the Land should
        mourne.
Then groveling on the ground, half dead, I rose
And clos'd within myne armes, these bosome woes: 40
Thus sighing sayd I, is my Sov'raigne dead,
Or shall I want, my Ruler, and my head
My Sone, my Father, and my Lord, was he,
That crownd my fortunes, I, his Pedegree:
MY VALOUR WAS HIS STRENGTH, HIS LAW, MY LOVE,
MY DEEDS, HIS RIGHT, MY LOYALL FAITH, HIS DOVE:
Betweene a King, and Kingdome, never Nation
Had such respondence, nor such immutation.
But now I listen, whence the Message comes,
That Me, unto eternall mourning doomes;   50
England's two Deaths, hath robd me twyse, one Prince,
The last, as worst, for ever, takes him thence.
What! shall I censure? that my Sister's sin,
This judgement did procure; the lyke hath bin,
That Kings for subjects suffer: Tymes allow,
That people for their Prince, are punished too:
Or can I cleare my self, and guiltless be,
Of this desaster; Heavens best judge, and see;

But how soe're, we both are cause, or either,
That we have lost, so just, so good, a Father,   60
Myne intrest, in my right, exceeds far more,
All others losse, than milleons can deplore :
I from a never-conquer'd Race, forth brought him,
And kept him long, till other Kingdomes sought him :
I plac'd the glory, on his Diademe,
Which his Ancestors, wore, and wonne, with fame.
Who from One hundreth six of noble Kings,
His Pedegree, unviolat, he brings ;
What Countreye, in this Universe can boast ?
Of such a Stock, though now my Prince, seems lost ;   70
And yet not lost, but changeth Earth, for Heaven,
The oddes are his, my fortunes left uneven :
And yet Heavens Verdict, wele foresaw, allone,
He should not fare, to that triumphant Throne :
Three best belov'd, with Loves entire I knoe,
Did challenge Death, they dye, away they go ;
As Harbingers to Heaven : They sute as freends,
The Court Hierchall ; done, their journey ends.
Two Lennox Dukes, kynd brother, after brother
Made way before ; each gloryeing in another ;   80
As if they had contended, to make haist,
To welcome there, their owne IMPERIALL Guest.
Than Hamilton fell next, my second Sone,
Prickd with desyre, his course, he quickly runne :
Lyke to the Star, that leads the Moone, so he,
Did post before, made way for Majestie.
Last came their King, the King of Mercy, met him,
And by his throne of glory, downe he set him :
High Alleluhiaes sung, the Angells joyed,
To see his sp'rit, from hence, so wele convoyed ;   90

For they had saved him, in all fearefull seasons,
From Powder-plots, Conspiracies, and Treasons;
STILL LOVD HE PEACE, AND SO HE PEACE POSESST,
HE LIVD IN PEACE, IN PEACE, HIS SOUL, DOTH REST.
His Subjects, that the Orient Coasts have trode,
Who livd secure at home, as safe abroade;
Their PEACE, he fastned, to the furthest INDE,
Where travayles reachd, or ships could sayle by wynd:
What mighty discords, jarres, and forrane broyle,
Did he appease, and spard, no cost, nor toyle;   100
He father-lyke, still quenched all Kingly ire,
And made his aged yeares, old EUROPES Syre:
Since Salomon, a wyser King ne'er raigned,
Nor whom the Learnd, and Learning more sustaynd:
In Memory unsurpassed, in Airts excelld,
In Oratrie, a Prince unparalelld;
Whose sacred temples, knit with Delphian bayes,
Gaynd him, a Kingly Poet, Poets prayse.
His Justice, fraught with Mercy, bless'd his spirit,
And liberall, he was, beyond man's merit: 110
The widdowes, orphanes, and poore men opprest,
In him fund ayde, and in his justice rest;
This long devyded Ile, he joynd in One,
And made this Britaine orbe, one Albion:
In him, surceased, the Irish warres, and THEY,
By him, wer taught, a Sovraigne, to obey:
And for to setle, that Estate the better,
Made large plantations, thousands came his debtor.
Of late, my second Scotia he erected,
And Collonies t' America directed.   120
What gift, or grace, did Nature e're adorne,
To which my mighty monarch was not borne.

But now prodigious signes, portend my losse,
See how the surges ryse, the waters tosse
The seas presage a fall, their swelling streams
Do threat my coast : now violent extremes
Turne rage in madness : and tho waves at hand
Seeme weary, and would rest them, on the land :
They swallow up my works, and lyke to theves,
Are seldome quyet, when their nyghbour grieves ;   130
I runne, and I adjurd them to recite
The cause of their dissorder ; they hurling sit
On trembling tops, and by a tumbling show,
Presag'd, that Death had stroke the fatall blow.
The clyme, the season fits, the tyme, was one
Their fury, in, my Sou'raignes Death, is gone.
O day of darkness, covert of my woes,
Whence melancholy floods, of sorrow flowes,
My wracks erected ; The clouds profoundly wept
Fyve dayes and nights : The Sunne as clossely kept   140
His course obscure : The thundering wynds forth broke
As if they meant to shake some mighty oak :
Mens harts were loade with greef, their eyes with teares,
Are gushing spoyled ; their mynds o'recome with fears,
These elementall sygnes, foretold what losses
Death would produce, fraught with desastruous crosses :
My Darling dyes, my State declynes, and I,
My grievous plaints, in darker kynds, must dy ;
A dolefull widdow, wrapd in sable vales
I must remane, true mourning there bewayles :   150
But see my Nobles post, looke how they tracd,
To Isis banks, where his sad herse is placd ;
There to attend the corps, which they so tender ;
More, due, and duty, Death, they could not render ;

Nor is he dead, whose better parts remane,
The Sunnes ne'er set, but for to ryse agane;
He did not so, assume, to leave the earth
Voyd of his Vertues, spoyld of royall birth;
But in his Phenix ashes, there should spring
Another PHENIX, for to be a KING;   160
Lyke to old Phebus, drawing to the west,
Seemd weary of his journey sought for rest;
And left his second self, agane to ryse,
In morning majestie, to face the skyes,
And cheare the Elitropian leaves, that close
Their mourning eyes, till Titan's glory rose;
And now my spotless faith, I plight thy Sonne,
That never yet was staynd, nor never wonne
My Mayden Crowne, thy image, he shall beare,
Thou left him for to sweye thy Scepters here;   170
PEACE, LOVE, and PITTY were thy guerdons three,
With THEM, thou raignst, now raignes eternally.
Farewele Monarchick SAINCT, let Legions tend Thee,
As thou had Milleones, here for to defend THEE,

FINIS,

By WILLIAM LITHGOW.

In his Countreyes behalf.

Go prostrat Lynes, greet thyne Appolloes herse,
Who, whylst alyve, lykd, lovd, and read my verse.

SCOTLANDS
WELCOME TO
HER NATIVE SONNE,
AND SOVERAIGNE LORD,
KING
CHARLES

Wherein is also contained, the manner of His *Coronation,* and
Convocation of PARLIAMENT; *The whole Grievances,*
and abuses of the Common-wealth of this *Kingdome,* with
diverse other relations, never heretofore published.

Worthy to be by all the Nobles and Gentry perused; and to
be layd vp in the hearts, and chests of the whole Commouns,
whose interests may best claime it, either in meane, or maner,
from which their Priuiledges, and fortunes are drawne, as
from the Loadstar of true direction.

By WILLIAM LITHGOVV, the BONAVENTVRE
of *EVROPE, ASIA,* and *AFRICA.*

De REGE *Vaticinium.*

Pace datâ terris, animum ad civilia vertet
Iura suum, legesque feret justissimus auctor ;
Exemploque suo mores reget, inque futuri
Temporis ætatem, venturorumque nepotum
Prospiciens, prolem sanctâ de conjuge natam
Ferre simul nomenque suum, curasque jubebit. Ovid. Met. 15.

EDINBVRGH
Printed by IOHN WREITTOVN.
Cum Privilegio.

THE PROLOGVE TO THE READER.

Hilst SCOTLANDS *Welcome,* sends its substant show
To Mighty CHARLES, as bund duetie owe ;
To whom sweet songs, and heavie plaints it brings,
Mixt so, and framd, discovring serious things :
Yet some blind judgments may condemne my *Muse,*
For touching that, which they them selues abuse :
But if it gall, their stinking sores, long wounded,
A tush for base despight, from such hate grounded :
Whose guilt may plead, and tell their conscience thus,
Shrewd faults find eyes, and *Tyme* must punish vs ;
Which if one age ago, this *Land* had beene
Check'd of such faults, might now haue been fund cleane.
    As for the *Critick,* or the carping Slaue,
Goe hang himselfe, I care not for a knaue :
Whilst for the *Commoun-wealth,* I stand to plead,
To show Oppressours tyranny and greed :
And eu'ry grievous vyce, this Land affords,
Where I affect more matter, than coynd words,
Brayne-wrested straines, *Ænigmatick* stile,
Or epitomizd *Epilogues* the while :
Although I dyving could, and soaring fetch.
My top-winged flight, too high, for vulgar reach :
Whilst I meanwhile, haue more paynes to be plaine,
Than to be curious, in the highest strayne.
    For what this worke affoords, lyf-burning *Taper !*
I had no *Bookes* to read, when pennd, but Paper :
With *Ink,* and *Pen,* my *Chamber*-garnish bare,
Warme *Bed,* and *Boord,* none other *Book* was there :
But *Memory, Invention, Experience* great,
Whereon my labours, build their solid Seat :
Which if it bee not well done, goe and mend it,
For with the same condition, I Thee send it :
But stop, O stay ! its harder to invent,
Then adding invention, to whats here meant.
This *Web* then see, of welcome I it Warp,
Whiles playne and prolixe, sometymes breef, and sharp ;

A

Sad-

Sadled, vnsadled, spurring on I goe,
And neither spares my friend, nor hurtes my foe,
But smoothly twixt two strugling shoares I runne.
Flat-sandy *Scilla*, *Charibdin* rocks to shunne :
For twixt like two, the golden meane may rest,
Nether too bitter, nor too sweet is best :
Which justly I set downe, and purpose lyke,
Vpon the *Annill*, of the Trueth I stryke :
And if I erre in one jote, I requyre,
Let mee goe headlong to deaths fatall fyre.

    Say, if he come this yeare, say he come not,
Yet tyme shall praise mee, for a louing SCOT.
Which being doubtfull, precisely, how, and when,
I reddy made this worke, form *Presse*, from *Pen :*
Yet not to vent my Bookes, nor haue them sould,
Before myne eyes, his comming in behould :
To whome the first I owe, to be presented,
For onely, to him onely, its invented :
Which when it is devulgd, I dare expect,
From the judicious *Lector*, kynd respect.

    Then read, misconster not, but wysely looke,
If reason be, the *Mistrisse* of my *Booke*,
And if I finger, what thou fayne wouldst touch,
O ! thank mee, and be pleasd ; whylst I avouch,
The commoun sorrowes, of this groaning Land,
Which I lay open, to thyne open hand :
Then ponder, and peruse it, thou shalst fynd,
The *Sole Idea*, of thy Countreyes Mynd.

                        Thyne, as Thou art Æyne,

                          WILLIAM LITHGOVV.

*Non vita hæc ducenda est, quæ corpore & spiritu continetur,
illa inquam, illa vita est, quæ viget memoriâ sæculorum
omnium, quam posteritas alit, quam ipsa æter-
nitas semper intuetur.*

TO HIS KYND FRIEND, AND RENOWNED
TRAVELLER, WILLIAM LITHGOVV.

WHILST thyne adventures past, and Travells rare,
    In hotest *Clymes*, of vigour-parching *Sunne :*
Through *Europe, Asia, Africk* thryse thy share,
O're which brunt face, thy scorched Body runne :
Still clogd with dangers, fortunat to shunne.
Lyf-fatall hazards ; which attempts procurd,
From curious drifts ; and which thy worth begunne,
To knit thy fame, in memory immurd ;
Renownd, admyrd, applausd, for aye assurd,
To soare on wings, of never-dyeing Toyles,
And in thy paynes, thy *Countreyes* name securd,
Into the *Annales*, of remotest *Soyles :*
But what I now admyre, are these thy spoyles,
Thou bringst from *Pindus* Tops ; O rare bred straine !
And pregnant style, which thyne engyne recoyles ;
To show these greefs, which SCOTLAND, do'th sustayne :
A worke, where Trueth, most justly do'th complayne,
On the abuse, and grievance of this Land,
Which thou breks vp, from thy *Patheticque* veyne,
To show thy *Sou'raigne*, how her cace doth stand :
    Then *Royall Sir*, but listen to puruse,
    The sweet-sad songs of *Lithgows* matchles *Muse*,
    And *Thou* shalst see, what never yet was showne,
    To Scottish *Kings ;* since *Scotland* first was knowne.

                     I. W.

VIRG.

Tu ne cede malis, sed contra audentior ito.

TO HIS LOVING PILGRIMAGIOVS POET,

WILLIAM LITHGOW.

CAN not thy Travells, blaze abroad thy worth?
Which never yet did SCOT, the lyke set forth,
Nor one in *Europe*, can with *Thee* compare,
For thyne adventures, excellent, and rare,
But that thou must, in adding fame, to fame,
Thy matchles merits, in thy *Muse* proclayme :
I can not call it Pryde, but vertue showne,
From *Thee*, to vs, through this wyde *Ile* well knowne :
But more an obligation, which thou ought.
Vnto thy natiue *Soyle ;* so headlong brought,
In deep distresses, grieuances, and losse,
Whilst sorrow, on sorrow, addes crosse, to crosse,
Which thou rippst vp, vnto the very roote,
Whence all these evills come, and springing sprout :
Besydes this jouiall welcome, to our King,
Which quicke *Invention*, now to light do'th bring :
O ! rare relations ! worthy of regard !
And from thy *Prince*, and *Soyle*, deserve reward :
But more for what, thou sufferd into *Spaine*,
For CHRIST and Countrey, and thy late *Sou'raigne :*
Which if it be not weighd, in time I feare,
That late repentance, shall buy pennance deare.
Tymes haue their turnes, and ev'ry turne a Tyme.
Men could not shift, without some changing *Clyme ;*
For where neglect, claps merit on the face,
The errour, not the object, reaps disgrace :
Then pregnant *Pilgrime*, rest thou yet content,
Hope still that Tyme, shall crowne thy braue intent,
KINGS haue their mynds, and reason just demands,
For Merit, can not fall, where judgment stands.

I. A.

Virtus repulsæ nescia sordidæ
Intaminatis fulget honoribus.   Horat.

SCOTLANDS
WELCOME TO
HER NATIVE SONNE,

AND SOVERAIGNE LORD,

KING
CHARLES.

Hat dark-drawne shads, haue my sad face ore'spred?
Since *Iames*, the just, my peacefull *King*, hath fled
To court the King of *Kings*; and *Hierarchies*
Of glorious *Angels*; the sweet harmonies
Of *Saincts* and *Martyrs*; environing round
The old *Eternall*; with the joyfull sound
Of *Alleluhiaes*; singing fore the *Throne*,
Holy, Holy, Lord, to *Heavens, Holy One;*
The Lamb of GOD, hembd in, with burning glore
Praise, Might, Dominion, Majestie, and *Power;*
Where my *Monarchick Sainct*, for ever blest,
Is crownd, and raignes, in long eternall rest.
    I, I, I find, my griefe, and chiefest care,
Proceeds from wanting, of his *Sonne*, and heyre,
So long vnuiewing *Mee*, and my sad bounds;
Whose absence, prick'd *Mee*, with ten thousand wounds
Of doubts, and apprehensions, if, or not,
My lawfull *King*, would haue his Lawfull lot:

A   Whilst

SCOTLANDS *Welcome to her Natiue* SONNE,

Whilst diverse yeares and months I am refute,
A mourning *Widow*, left in sable Sute.
   True, and most true it is, the Proverbe proues,
That age is still injurd, by younger loues:
And so am I, thine eldest *Region* made,
A preye to darke obliuions winter-shade,
Even as young *Nuptialls*, make olde *Widowes* stay,
Wnwedded, till some lingring *Husbands* day,
Where, when advyce, makes resolution fast,
The cords of *Reason*, bynds him at the last.
   So now, O now hee comes! O happy, *Tyme!*
To warme the bowells of my northern *Clyme*,
Aud to revciwe that *Loue*, my *Sire* left.
Plight in my bosome, when the *Heavens* him rest:
For which I'le make him welcome, Play the part,
Of a kind *Mother*, with a chearefull *Heart*.
   What meanes this goodly sight? these trouping traines?
Which trace the *Marine:* trade the curling plaines?
Crossing neare *Tweed*, my border-bounding *Rod*,
Would enter on my Lists, a *Demi-God:*
Second'd with *Meteors*, glistring him about,
And met with *Miriads*, of my noble rout.
O some rare noveltie! some *Heros* deare!
Who with his Prime, brings in my Springtyde here,
The *Load-star* of my *Fortunes*, and the *Cime*,
Of my best *Scopes*, most pure, and most sublime,
My flowre of *Albion*, O! the solide way!
And center of my *Hopes*, my *Lyfe*, my *Stay:*
Even *CHARLES* the first, that ev'r brookd that Name,
And *Regall* title, of my *Diademe*.
   Than welcome *Sonne*, my *Husband*, and my *Father*.
All these to *Mee*, thou art, each one, or either,
My *Sonne*, and why? *Dumfermling* beares record,
I am thy *Patrian* Mother in a word:
My *Husband* too, by right from *Parents* bred,
When with my *Crowne*, thou hast my freedome wed:

                                        And

And Soueraigne *LORD*, King Charles.

And last my *Syre*, so can thy Scepter swey,
Whilst thou beares rule, I'me bund for to obey :
  And now to welcome *Thee*, what *Lesbian* layes?
With *Lyrick*-tripping songs ; what *Roundelayes* ?
In *Saphick*-seasond mirth burst from the *Muses*,
And *Cataphalion* Creeks : where *Triton* vses,
To make the *Sea-Nymphs* daunce, O ! shrill tund notes,
Sprung from *Invention ;* thundring, through sweet throates
Of euer springing joyes : *Rome* nere had
In all her Triumphs past, one day more glad ;
Than thou auspicious *Prince*, shall now imbrace
From *Millions* of kynd *Soules ;* the passing grace,
Of *Loues* extreamest force, lyke as on Earth,
Seven Town-set Loues, Heart-swelld for *Homers* birth.
  Then what dark clowds dissolue ? what showry shades ?
Dissolue in Sun-shyne clearenes? what sparkling wades ?
In thy transplendant rayes? what parching beames?
My worlds eye-sight imparts ? what glistring gleames ?
From *Heavens* star-spangled *Roabe ?* what joyes abound ?
Within my *Bowells ?* O ! what pleasant sound ?
Loues harmony affords ? O ! what rare *Fleece ?*
Acoast, myne *Arathusean* Springs from *Greece,*
With *Acedalian* Triumphes ; O ! what a blis ?
And happynes, of *Iubile* is this ?
To see my *Monarch*, enter in my bounds
To heale the sores, of my long bleeding wounds :
Whilst I, an *Virgine*, haue contingd my trueth,
Vnspotted to my all redouted *Youth.*
  Lyke to that floure, *Panthoas* into *Creet,*
That scornes the Sun-shyne day? and loues to greet.
The siluer *Moone*, in opning golden leaues,
But to the day-tyme none, then onely grieues ;
And will not with none other hearbs cohere,
But with it selfe, and from it *Cynthia* deare,
So thou the *Aurore*, of my long worne night
Reverts to giue, thy chast *Panthoas* light !

Then

Then welcome *Soveraigne*, welcome to my Soyle,
Where thou shalst pleasure, and content recoyle ;
Here water *Nymphs* exult, here *Zephire* blowes
A *Pandedalian* luster to my *Rose :*
The aire resounds thy welcome, winds their part,
And all good Subjects, one true voice, one heart :
Two *Marines* closing, clasp *Thee*, in their armes
Where clouddy *Silvan* tip-toed, stately charmes
With sweet allurements, shaddy pyping *Pan*,
Whilst worlds of voyces, seeme one singing *Man*.
  So ecchoing Birds, from sweet redoubling notes,
Sing soaring welcomes, though through diverse throates,
Ingraft from fragrant Springs. *Font*-gushing streames
Melting through *Meeds*, to welcome *Thee* from *Thames :*
Three floods sprung from one Hill, *East*, *West*, and *South*,
Clyde, *Tweed*, and *Annan*, each with gaping mouth,
Doth bellowing roare, and kyndly tumbling slyde,
To greet thy gratefull *Loue*, as they divide :
So *Don*, and *Nith*, swift *Dee*, and head-strong *Tay*
Lake-linking *Levin*, *Meandring Forth*, and *Spay ;*
Would melting murmure, rusling on fish'd Pearles,
This sweet, sweet *Eccho*, welcome, welcome *Charles*.
The *Hills* rebound, *Bellowmound* threats the *Skies*,
And piramized *Tinto* would surprise
Earths high *Æthereall* Seat ; whilst *Goatfield* hill,
In *Arrane* greets the *Mayne*, with ecchoes shrill
Of Heart-growne joyes, whiles that her snow-whyte Tops
Stoup downe, and kindly thin affection lops.
The *Vayles* exhale deep cryes, the whistling rounds,
Of Earths seven-*Æol'd* Towres, performe like sounds ;
All bid *Thee* welcome, Lithgovv bids *Thee* too ;
For what in meane hee wants, goodwill shall doe

E D I N-
BVRGHS
welcome. Let *Edinburgh*, my *Metropole*, perfite
The rest, with *Pageants*, of admird delite :
Where *Mercury* shall speake, with syde-hung wings,
And *Iuno* kisse soft *Pallas ; Venus* brings

                                               Her

Her golden Apple; *Loue* and *Riches* carp,
Gainst *Wisedome,* on, their God *Appolloes* Harp :
There shall shrill Trumpets sound, lowd thundring Drummes,
With roaring Cannons, cry, Hee comes, Hee comes :
Where, when receau'd, by that illustrious *Towne,*
Along thou rydst to *Church,* grac'd in renowne :
Where thou shalst heare, flow from a zealous heat
Divine drawne doctrine, mixt with welcomes great :
Besides rare speeches, at each *Pageant* made,
To cherish thine arrivall ; make the glad
With lovely sights and prayses ; Poets straine,
Sprung from quick DRVMMONDS fierce *Castalian* veine.
    The Sermon done, their *Provost* shall conduct
Thy sacred Person, the way, which they construct
Straight to their Banquet-house, and feasting place ;
Where rarest dainties shall present thy face :
There *Ceres* joynes with *Bacchus; Hymen* trowes,
To tye to them thy *Loue,* by solemne vowes ;
For to maintaine, their libertie and right,
Being their comfort, when they want thy sight.
And ah ! too much it is, for that kind *Towne,*
To want thy *Court* and *Presence ;* what pulles downe
Best *Citties* now on *Earth ?* But want of trade,
And Courtly Commerce ; O ! *a Soveraigne head :*
Where now I leaue them, to giue *Thee* content,
For I'le debord no more from mine intent.
    That fright-fled wandring *Prince,* from *Ilions* fire,
Neu'r coasted *Carthage,* with more glad desire ;
And the *Barbarian* shoare ; to find the grace,
Of loving *Dido,* and her pittying face ;
Than thou from this, *Numidia* of thine,
Gets meeting, greeting, treating to bee myne :
And gladder far, to see thy safe returne,
Than *Africks* soile, could in affection burne,
Vnto a Stranger ; for thou comes not so,
As if promiscuous, neither friend nor foe.

Nor comes thou with sterne bloody collours flying,

repugnant Or with a doubtfull mynd, as one a dying :
coparisons. Nor lyke these *Turkish* fyre-brands of Hell,
The race of *Ottoman ;* that loue to quell,
All sorts of People ; *Persian, Greeke,* and *Iew,*
Arabian, Moore, and *Christian,* would subdew,
The *Universe* to bee, but one *Dominion,*
Wherein, the *Spanyard* too, would bee his *Minion :*

Nay ; thou comes better, so the *Heavens* appoynted,
Euen, in the name of GOD, the LORDS anoynted :
So, I receaue *Thee,* as the righteous *Heyre,*
Of *Mee,* and myne inheritance, moſt fayre,
Which shall not crowne *Thee,* lyke these groaning bounds,
Hemb'd in about, with the *Hircanian* rounds :
Nor comes thou to encroach, on *Indian Soyles,*
To pillage *Peru ;* and to cast the spoyles
Of minrall *Mettalls,* on sterne bloody *Mars,*
Wherewith sad *Epitaphs,* bedeck *Mens Herse :*
Nor, as the *Worlds* Vsurper *Philip* did,
When hee betrayd *Navarre,* vnder plots hid :
Nor as hee seazd, on *Portugale,* and tooke,
From lost *Emanuell,* the golden Booke :
Nor like to *Petro,* basely murthring downe,
The *French,* at *Vespers,* for the *Sicile* Crowne :

Lyke instances, I many could afford,
But *Tyme,* it traitours *Mee,* and in a word,
O ! thou comes well ! and with a Conscience just ;
Of right indubitable ; *Reason* must,
On *Thee,* confer my neuer-conquerd Crowne,
Which now shall Crowne *Thee,* with the old renowne,
Of thine *Auncestors ;* and which birth *Thee* brings,
Scotlands Descended from one hundreth, and seuen *Kings :*
Crowne Which they by worth, and I by valour kept,
never con- Whilst myne encroaching foes, with *Irne* I whipt.
querd.
But by thy leaue, (Sir,) I must let *Thee* see,
What kynd of Crowne, I now present to *Thee ;*

A

And Sovaraigne LORD, King Charles.

A Mayden Crowne, vnconquerd, neuer wone,
Since *Fergus*, my first *Monarch* it begunne :
And so from him, to *Kenneth* who subdued,
The *Pights*, and in their blood his hands imbrewd :
Whence bloody battells, and braue chivalrye,
From race, to race, kept and maintaynd it free :
Whilst neither *Danes*, nor *English*, *Saxons* could,
With awfull *Romans*, this Crowne, get, or hould,
Such were my forces, in my *Champions* strong,
That still keept, it and *Mee* from forraine wrong,
    What should I speake of *Wallace, Bruce,* and *Grahame* ?
The *Dowglasses*, and *Stewarts*, of great fame ?

With thousands moe, of much renowned worth,
Which my true *Chronicle*, vively sets foorth,
But leaue *Thee* there to reade, what deeds were wrought,
And for thy matchles *Auncients*, stoutly fought,
    How many hundreth thowsand Lyves were lost ?
Which from my bowells sprung ; nay ; I dare boast,
Of *Millions* which to saue, this Crowne for *Thee*,
And purchase freedome, car'd not for to dye.
So lyke I sweare, if lyke were to invade,
My Crowne, their fates, in fields of blood, should wade :
Than let not evill Counsell, *Thee* invest,
Nor trechrous *Sicophant*, thy peace molest :
For I haue none, which burrow, of *Mee* breath,
But rather far, will spend their lives on death ;
Than suffer this, myne auncient right to goe,
To moderne friendship, ones my cruell foe,
    And now to saue, this *Virgin* Crowne for *Thee*,
There is no foe, can fright *Mee*, make mee flee,
From right, from field, from battell, force, or fight,
So long as I haue Lyfe, blood, Lungs, or might :
Whilst now ; what *Kingdome* can their *Prince* renowned
With lyke invinced, freedome of a Crowne :
Looke to my valour Past ? and thou mayst spy,
Where diuerse Nations, got of *Mee* supply.
                      France

Fraunce can approue my *Manhood*, I relieu'd
Their State from thraldome, when it was surgrieu'd :
Witnesse, our mutuall *League*, witnesse their guard
And myne their naturaliz'd, for my reward.
　Like *Belgians* sweare, their strength, their stoutest hand,
And *Warriours* best, are bred within my Land :
The *Almaynes* too record, what I haue done
And what my *Souldiers*, aunciently there wone :
Looke to my Sister *Swethland*, and behold !
What birth I send them, desp'rate, stout, and bold :
For *Polland* shee's my Nurse, brings vp my *Youth*,
Full thritty thousands, yearely, of a trueth ;
Than londes them with, the fatnesse of her *Soyle*,
Which, I, in their due tyme, doe still recoyle :
Than look to *Denmark*, where twelue thousands ly,
Serving thine *Vncle*, sharpest fortunes try.

*Some cer-
taine num-
bers of va-
liant Scots.*
　Last, step I o're to *Ireland*, and doe see,
Full Fourty thousand *Scots*, arm'd Men, there bee :
Besides, at home, one hundreth thousands moe,
Young, stout, and strong, well arm'd for *Thee*, to goe ;
To challenge *Destinie*, and cruell *Fate*,
And all *Vsurpers*, dare menace my *State* :
Then slight mee not (Dread Sir) since I, and Myne,
Still vow, to serue *Thee*, as wee haue done Thyne :
For by this count, and much more, thou mayst see,
What forces great, my bounds, reserue for *Thee*.
　The *World*, *Mans Theater*, and commoun *Stage*,
Wherein, each acts his part, in youth or age ;
Can not, nor could, produce, a Manlyer kynd
(Of *Hearts* invincible, of constant mynd ;
Stout, *strong*, and *Durable*, *Couragious* too,
Ever still, formost, where, there's most adoe)
Than those my *Martiall* Sonnes ; whose *Hearts* now yeeld,
Their hands, their swords, to fight for *Thee*, in field :
Being *Buffles* in cold, *Elephants* in rayne,
Camels in hunger, *Lyons* after gaine.

　　　　　　　　　　　　　　　　　　And

And now obsequious to thy new-reard *Crowne*,
Would lay their goods and liues before *Thee* downe :
Then bee thou jocund ; and redound them thankes.
In private and in publict, by their rauks :
Thy great *Grand-father*, O ! *King Iames* the fift,
Was *merry, stout,* and *wise, Henrie vnwift ;*
The flower of *Princes,* mirrour of his tyme,
Made *Christendome* admire his *Manly* pryme :
So *Thou* his second self, by worth succeeds,
And Nature too, to all his vertuous deeds :
Then let thy chearefull face, with joviall rayes
Illuminat thy Peoples loue and praise :
Thus, thy late *Syre, Salomon ;* my *King,*
When hee surveighd mee last, did comforts bring,
And joyes abundant to this *Albion* land ;
Which hee by death did seaze into thy hand.

  So, so, I come to crown *Thee,* whilst the *Heavens*
O'reshaddow *Thee* with *Seraph'd Cherubins :*
Whence, glorious *Angels* flee with joyfull wings
Of *Peace* and *gladnes* from the *King of Kings ;*
To blesse this sacred work, and happy vnion,
Twixt *Prince* and *People ;* O ! thryse blest communion !
The Springs *Pœneian* flow, sweet *Demthen* Rills,
Swell from steep *Pindus ; Permessis,* gushing fills
The *Sorean*-fonted *Meeds ;* the forked *Tops,*
Dissolue, and melt in *Heliconean* drops.

  From whence the *Nymphall* nyne take flight, and come,
Crownd with *Rose garlands, Delphian bayes,* and some
With *Laurell Mantles* of the *Oliue,* hew,
To grace this *Coronation,* Sir ; of You :
And leaue the *ceremoniall* rest to bee
Done by the Bishop of *Sainct-Andrewes ;* Hee
Shall blesse *Thee,* anoynt *Thee,* in word, in deed,
Then set my golden *Crowne* on thy blest *Head :*
Whilst thou in Purple *Roabes* of *State* shall stand,
To blesse thy *People,* with thy tongue and hand :

*The coro-
nation.*

B

Which

Which done, their *Hearts* and *voices* shall cry thus,
GOD saue and keepe King Charles *long for vs.*
O *Hellespont !* now groanes to beare the lode !
Of Kynd *Leanders* loue to *Hieroes* God.
Whilst both my *Sword,* and *Scepter* downe are layd
Before thy Face, in signe I am a *Mayd :*
Which *Guerdo-knot,* none can vnty, nor twist,
Till thou my *Phillipides,* lyke and list :
Now thou art crownd, and since I crownd thy *Syre,*
Iust, threescore two yeares presently expyre :
Though *Crownes* bee *Crownes* of Care ; God grant my *Crowne,*
May *Health, Wealth, Loue,* and *Peace* to Thee redoune :
Which long may thou enjoy, and thy *Race,*
So long as *Sunne,* or *Moone,* keep course or place.

The Parli-
ament.

Now comes my *Parliament,* now comes these tymes,
Where thou and they should vindicate grosse crymes :
Sit then in *Iudgement,* and bee carefull too,
For to performe what thy great charge should doe :
First then confirme both wholesome Lawes and good,
And stablish *justice ;* let thy *Grace* conclude
A finall resolution, for my *State*
In *Counsell* and in *Session :* ah ! of late
A foggy mist dissolu'd, and broke asunder ;
My *Pillars* from the *Marble* pauement vnder :
   As Iudges should bee just, so should they bee
As prompt, for to doe justice speedily ;
And not with long delayes, to wring the lyfe
Of poore Mens causes, to a doubtfull strife :
Which often blinds the right, and turnes the wrong,
Victorious over reason ; O ! sad song !
When equity is curbd ; and squink respect
Involues the trueth into a base neglect ;
Els in *Buccardo,* sealing misregard
For *fauour, friendship flattry,* or *reward :*
So thus too oft is justice wrung and wounded,
And wholesome lawes for private ends confounded.

But

And Soveraigne LORD, King Charles.

But meanewhile, I thy greatest *Care* recall,
To settle true *Religion*, and enstall
Good godly Men and sound, in *Prelats* function,
Mou'd by devoution, and conscious compunction:
So shall the *Gospell* floorish, and thy lyfe
Made peacefull, happy, from seditious stryfe.
   As for my *Clergie*, I affirming vow,
The solid trueth to God, and then to You;
There are no People, nor no Land so blest,
With Godly Preachers, and Gods word profest
With more sinceritie, taught, showne, and preach'd,
Than in my *Kingdome*, there was never teach'd
Profounder doctrine; more divine résounds
In Christs reformed *Church*, than in my bounds:
Which to persite, an vniformall mynd,
God grant his *Sacrament* may passage find:
And scruplous stops may bee hewne downe, and made
As plaine, as *Christ* Himselfe; vs taught and sayd.
   Now I'le degresse, and leaue this vpper part
Of *Church* and *State* to God, and thy just Heart:
I haue no lower house of *Parliament*,
To punish or represse each detriment;
Prest greivance, or abuse of *Commonweale*,
But what my suffrings must to *Thee* reveale;
Then heere they are, and ponder them, I pray *Thee*,
And let not these my just complaints dismay *Thee*;
But rather cause amend them, and redresse
These grosse enormities, which I'le expresse.
   True and most true it is, my chiefest health
Consists (Dread Sir) most in the *Commonwealth*:
Which ah *allace!* hath never heeretofore
Beene soundly pitch'd, lesse grounded, and far more
Disdainefully cast off, for who are they
That ever stroue a Commonn course to swey?
There is no *Providence*, nor publick good
Graft in my bosome, my *Townes* are denude

The abuse of the commounwealth.

B 2

Of

Of *Policie* and *Venters ;* Men please themselues,
And care not though my fortune split on Shelues :
Haue I not *Floods* and *Seas,* good *Ships* and *Ports ?*
Braue *Sea-men, Pilots, Skippers,* and *Consorts ;*
But where's the *Merchand* that will freely enter,
To put these *Men* to work ; and byde the venter
Of doubtfull successe ; nay ; there's none I see,
That now dare hazard further than his eye :
Yet *Mans* not borne to please himselfe alone,
That were *idolatrizing* loue to one :
But totally for GOD, partly for friends,
Partly for Countrey, last for his owne ends.

 As for my *Trades,* they're ruind with decay,
There few or none imployd : My *Nobles* play
The curious *Courtizan ;* that will not bee
But in strange fashions ; O ! what Noveltie
Is this ? that *London,* robbes Mee of my gaine :
Whilst both my *Trades* and *Merchands* suffer paine.
Nay ; I must stay, there is no courtly guyse,
Nor frivole toyes thou frenchifyed thryse,
Bee't in or out of fashion, Myne must haue it ;
Though neither meanes nor honesty would craue it.
But since they will proue fooles, yet why should Strangers
Enjoy the profit from fantastick *Rangers,*
And not myne owne ? There is no Nation can,
Compare with my best *Trades ;* match man for man.

*Superflu-
ous posting
to Court.* Besides my *Nobles,* see my *Gentry* too
Post vp, post downe ; their states for to vndoe :
Nay, they will morgadge all ; and to bee breefe,
Ryde vp with gold, and turne againe with greefe :
Who better far might stay at home, and liue,
And not their meanes to lonelesse labour giue.
It grieues Mee, I should yeeld them yeerely rent,
Whilst vainely it in Neighbour Lands is spent :
But *ecce homo,* and behold the end,
My Lands change *Land-Lords,* whilst my *Youngsters* spend.

          Nay

Nay there's a gen'rall ruyne through my bounds,
Which makes my sydes to shiver : O ! what wounds
By *Prodigals* I get ? There's not a stroake
These *Spend-thrifts* thrust, but brings Mee in some yoke :
And thus they take my money all away
To spend abroad ; whilst it should rather stay,
For to enrich my *Bowels ;* and to barter,
For Cornes and Merchandise in every quarter.
   Then Post and Post againe, Post altogether
To *Bag-shot*, then to beggrie ; nay, and whether ?
Too roote from *Earth* their memorie and Name,
Stamping themselues on *Hippodromes* of shame :
I care not for their falls, their lands ly still,
Though changd from hand to hand, from ill to ill :
And like the *Weather-Cock*, from Airt to Airts,
Their locall grounds are changd from pairt to pairts :
Now heere's a wedset, there's a flying off,
And heere's the prison, there's a *Iaylours* scoff :
In comes *Thom Tumbler* with his bags and bellie,
To alter *Tackes* and *Rentals ;* I must tell *Thee*,
I pitty my poore *Commouns*, and their toile,
Made to new Vpstarts and their greed a spoile,
   How can my *Tennants* liue ? How can they thriue ?
How can they growing stand ? When dead aliue,
Slane by oppression, extortion, debate,
From Laird to Laird, in their *Camelion* State :
The *Tennants* suffer all, allace poore Soules !
Still preyd vpon, by *Bankerouts* and *Fooles :*
Then it's no wonder, though my land bee poore,
When now most *Land Lords* play the errand whoore,
In shifting *Rents* and *Styles*, as many tymes,
As *Lais, Corinths* Strumpet did of crymes.
   Beleeue Mee Sir, I feare this revocation,
Make many one revoke both state and station ;
My *Lords* they post vp dayly to thy *Court*,
And ly there Months and Yeares ; and doe resort

Revoca-
tion.

To

To *London*, as their Livings lay and Land,
In midst of *Cheapsyde, Kingstreete,* or the *Strand :*
My *Gentry* too and *Knights*, and oft *Commissioners,*
In this repenting excesse turne *Practitioners :*
Still vp and downe they make a play of Posting,
And laugh at lavish expence ; fall a boasting
Who oftest courts thy *Court*, whilst here at home
Their *Wiues* and *Children* cry, when will they come ?
Yea, yea, they come, but with an empty hand,
And to turne back, morgadging heere more land :
Wherein I vow, that *England* turnes a curse
To mee, and my spent *Gentry*, and their Purse.
I graunt their *Tongues* can make my *Gallants* spend,
And suck them dry, till all come to an end :
And why ? cause in a *Rodomunto*, they
Play the *Orlando Furioso* aye :
As well in humours, as in lavish charges,
Which makes most femals weare such skar-clift *Targes*,
Where deepest strokes in strugling force are given,
Till both Mens Ribs and Rigs are backward driven :
Whilst the Defendants swallow vp such meanes,
As Reapers doe, that both cut downe and gleanes :
Then in a word, its gluttonie and lust,
That brings so many headlong to the dust.
  For now at eu'ry startling peevish thing,
Iack, Thome, and *Robin* post vp to the *King :*
And will not to thy *Counsels judgement* stand,
Plac'd heere as *Lights*, the Sword of thy right hand,
To judge, if *Iudges*, judge aright or not,
And may declare on each sinistruous Spot :
Which by thyselfe was done, and set a sunder,
The *Counsell* plac'd aboue, the *Iudges* vnder :
But (Sir) I humbly beg, it were well done
To punish these distractions out of tune,
And send them back, to censurd be, and stand,
Submissiue to the justice of this Land :

Els

Els they will vexe *Thee*, and such custome bring,
That *Woemen* too will post vp to the *King*.
Then let an Act bee made, in my regard,
That neither *Lord*, nor *Earle*, *Knight*, nor *Laird*,
Shall post more vp to *London*, but remayne
At home, and spend their rents, where growes their graine :
And to succumbe themselues, and their debate,
Vnto the *Lords* and *Pillars* of my State :
For which, as duety owe, they being bund,
Posting shall cease, and Iustice here bee fund :
Nay I dare say, since thy late *Fathers* death,
His buriall, and his Funerall, in Faith,
There Millions two of gold from Mee transported,
And spent at *London*, where my *Gallants* sported ;
And leaue at home (God knowes) a threed bare count,
Which far beyond their yearelie rents surmount.
Then deare and tender Sir, let this bee stopt,
Thine absence is enough, should I bee lopt
From *Top* and *Middle*, to the naked root ;
Whilst from my *Commouns* all these moneys sprout :
The *Merchand* hee complaines, the *Trads-man* mournes
The *Tennant* sore oppressd, in sorrow turnes,
His helplese plaints ; and I mongst all must tremble,
To see myne owne bred brood with mee dissemble.
Where are these late past dayes ? when *Mars* surviu'd ;
And *Nobles* keept good houses, Servands liu'd,
Well horsd, well arm'd, well lou'd, well clothd, well fed,
And when my Lords with such lyke troupes were cled :
O ! there was plenty, and abundance too
Of eu'ry thing that Nature had to doe :
Then Lairds keept Courts, and eu'ry Lord at home
Liu'd lyke a *Prince*, or *Cardinall* of *Rome* ;
Yea, and contract'd no debt, morgagd no land,
But wore the cloth their wiues wrought with their hand,
And now where Kitchins smoakd, good cheure hath beene,
There's cold and hunger, and bare walls now scene :

The decay of good house kee-ping.

The

The reason why? their sinnes procur'd GODS wrath,
And brought destruction on themselues with death.
How many ruind *Towers*, and wast falne walls
Stand namelesse now, few know their stiles, and calls:
Heere stands *Castle blood*, and their *Castle pryde ;*
Yonder *Castle oppression*, and *lust* beside ;
Heere *Castle Gluttonie ;* there *Castle Oathes ;*
Heere *Castle Falshood*, *Incest* that neu'r loathes
Of *Castle Perjurie ;* and lower downe
Stands *Desolation* in a threed bare *gowne :*
And now, though most stand namelesse and vnknowne,
Yet by these *Verdicts* may their stiles bee showne :
All which, though *Moderne*, some I haue as fast,
Ryde post to *Nothing*, and can roaring wast.

The vanitie of prodigals.   Now *Coatches*, *Cuntbotches*, *Lust*, and *Play*,
And vaine *Apparell*, rot their rents away :
In stead of serving Men, they now keep Lads,
To fetch them brow-lac'd *whoores*, wrapt vp in Plads :
Els Boy-posting newes, to goe prepare
Roome ; for his Master, shortly will bee there :
Where, when abroad this gallant rydes alone,
With *Iack* his *Lacquey* neare him, trotting on :
Either to *Limbo* in the *Brothell-house*,
Els to the *Taverne* for a deep Carrouse :
Where straight to *Cards* and *Dyce* hee fly'th amayne,
And for advantage, leaues the house his gaine.

   So, so, their sorces of *Chaulders* and their *Bolles*
Are brought from *Mountaines* downe to litle *Moles :*
They haue no deadly fead, that's gone of late,
But they're at deadly fead with their owne state :
And care not for *Allyes*, blood, *wiues*, nor *friends*,
Kinred nor *bairnes*, saue their owne wasting ends :
Whose *Riggs* speake *English*, and their falted *furres*,
Forgetting *Scots*, can speek with gilded Spurres.

Lawyers.   So *Lawyers* seaze on part, and right it stands
For lawlesse *Lairds* to haue Law-byding Lands :

And would the *Wrytters* too, could find lyke flashes,
But now the *Pen*, on *Paper* seldome dashes:
I'ts strange the *Tongue*, should gaine more than the *Pen* ?
And pleading better payd, then paynefull *Men :*
There's here, a *Labyrinth*, I'le not come in,
And for to bee obsequious, were a sin :
But here I vow, they're happy thryse and blest,
Who least frequents them, liues at home in rest :
Then *Lairds*, and *Lawyers*, *Scriuners* flock together,
They're blind that runne, a course they know not whether ;
 Ah ! what makes now, my *Countrey* looke so bare ?
Thus voyd of planting, *Woods* and *Forrests* fayre :
Hedges, and *Ditches*, *Parks*, and closed grounds,
Trees, *Strips*, and *Shaws* in many fertile bounds :
But onely that the *Land-Lords*, set their Land,
From yeare, to yeare, and so from hand to hand ;
They change and flit their *Tennants* as they please,
And will not giue them *Leasse*, *Taks*, *Tymes*, nor ease,
To prosper and to thryve ; for if they should,
As soone they thrust them, out of house and hould :
And hee who bids most farme, still gets the Roome,
Whilst one aboue anothers head do'th come :
Or els to rayse his rent, or kisse the Doore,
This is the cause, my *Commons*, liue so poore,
And so the *Peasants*, can not set nor plant
Woods, *Trees*, and *Orchards*, which my *Valleyes* want,
But leaue *Mee* halfe deformd, so they're distressd :
And by their greedy *Masters*, still oppressd :
 Then now to succour this, the onely way,
Is, that their farmes were brought, to penny pay,
And leasses let at large, for yeares or lyves,
Failling the *Husbands*, to their liuing Wyves :
To *Heyers* or *Friends*, and when the Tackes declyne,
To bee renewd againe ; paying their Fyne,
And yearely moneyes : then the *Lord* or *Laird*,
Hee needes not of a doubtfull yeere regard :

*the want
of plant-
ing.*

     C   So

So *England*, and *Ireland*, all *Europe's* brought,
To lease and penny-rent, but victuall nought,
Then might poore *Tennants* thryve, set, build, and plant,
And bee relieu'd with that, which now they want,
And till such tyme, this land can never bee,
Brought from the jawes, of willfull povertie,
    As for my *Tythes*, which nobles most recoyle,

The wrong- It is another grieuance, to my *Soyle*,
full vse of
Tythes. Should *Tythes* belond to *Laicks*? should Church rent?
Bee giv'n to temp'rall *Lords*; by *Gods* intent,
Tythes were for *Leuits*; not for *Haulks* nor *Hounds*;
Nor no reward, of *Sycophanting* sounds.
Tythes may bee calld *Gods* rent, and they pertaine
Still to his *Priests*, his service to maintaine,
The very *Turkes* and *Mahometan* leyes,
Allot their *Daruishes*, religious feyes,
Yea, sauage *Sabuncks*, of *Lybia*, the odde,
As *Tythes* they dote, to serue their *Garlick God*:
Then how much more, should *Trueth* to meanes bee placd,
When brutish *Ignorants*, are so imbracd:
    Nay more then *Clergy*, *Tythes* should too sustaine,
My *Seminary Schooles* with yeerely grayne:
My *Colledges* decay, they haue no rent,
More then the *Schollers* bring, for boording meant:
Thus *Learning* goes to ruyne, Books grow skant,
Meanes they haue none, and maintenance they want,
There is no gayne, nor no preferment neither,
Now following learning, nor desert, but rather,
The greatest *Dunsse*, if rich, is soonest plac'd,
And rarest *Schollers*, lacking meanes defac'd,
Thus *Airts* grow *Airtles*, wit repyning wit,
When *Asses* must in *Lyons Cabines* sit.
    Tythes too should build blest *Hospitals*, and doe
Erect *Schooles*, *Bridges*, and sustaine them too:
But where they should doe good, they doe most ill,
Being abus'd by vse, and corrupt will,

                                                            For

For (Sir,) take heed, what greef is this and crosse?
To my poore *Commouns*, and a yearely losse ;
That when their *Cornes* are shorne, stoukd, dead, and dry,
They can not get them teinded ; Nay ; and why ?
Some grudge or malice, moves despight to wound,
The hopefull *Haru'st*, and rot their *Cornes* on ground,
This is no rare thing, on their *Stowks* thats seene,
Snow-coverd *Tops*, below they're grass-growne greene,
Which often breeds great famyne, and great skant,
And plagues my *Commouns*, with a Heart-broke want.
For which they grieue, in this long deformation,
And hope to haue from *Thee*, a reformation :
Which GOD may grant, and blesse thy judgment too,
For to considder, what *Oppressours* doe.
  So, so, reclayme them, deale them at thy pleasure,
For GOD and godlynesse and for thy Treasure,
Which being in thine hand, and then to farme
Them back on *Lords ;* will bread a double harme,
For worse, and worse, my *Commouns* shall bee crost,
And all thy good intentions, therein lost :
Then let my *Tythes*, be brought to money rent,
For *Thee*, from *Land-Lord*, and the poore *Tennent* :
So may they sheare, and lead, and stakke their *Corne*,
At Mid-night, Midday, afternoone, or Morne,
Which shall bee their advantage and my gayne,
When *Barnes*, and *Yards*, are fill'd with tymely grayne,
  I haue some *Sycophants* ly at thy *Court*,
Disturbers of my peace, and there resort,
Still hatching of mischiefe ; projecting ends,
Which to my *Countreyes* ruine onely tends :
And though they burrowd, *Lyfe*, *Lands*, *Birth*, and *Blood*,
Of *Mee*, they're still repaying ill for good ;
For having spent their meanes, so now their braynes,
They spend in forging of seditious straynes :
Still this, or that devysing, runne such courses,
That for their crosses, they're repayd, with curses.

C 2

Nay ;

Nay; I must call them, *Bandits*, *Rebells* bred,
And *Fugitiues*, from *jure Pœna* fled :
Then, then (dread Sir) take heed, such *Snakes* may sting,
And wound the judgment of a prudent *King*.

Valuation.   As for this *Valuation* who can tell?
Whats meant thereby? or can my *Preachers* well,
With one out of each *Parish* ; lay the ground,
What euery Land is worth, or may be found :
No; no, its labour lost, and I pray *God*,
Wee be not scourgd for it, by his just rod :
A lesser fault, then this made *Israell* quake,
When *David* of his *People* count would make,
But value, stock, and brock, Tythes, fruites and all,
God must giue encrease, or the reckning fall.

the vicissi-
tude of
tymes.   So *Tymes* vntymely haue their tyme mispent,
On base *Ingratitude*, and bounty shent :
Whats worth, without wealth? merit without Loue?
Birth without Vertue? greatnes without *Ioue?*
Bairnes without duetye, Parents, without care?
Friends without Credit? Towne without repayre?
Lyfe without Learning? Servants without paynes?
Faith without good works? Comerce without gaynes?
Hope without repentance? Wit without Reason?
Greefe without Patience? Mirth out of season?
Command without Pow'r? *Prince* without People?
State without gouernment? Church without Steeple?
Preachers without rent? Poets but reward?
Rich Men without rueth? Honour but regard?
Iudges without Iustice? Agents but fees,
Clarks without decreets? *Lawyers* without pleas?
Tillage without soyle? Trafficque without peace?
Grace without godlynes? Sheep without fleece?
Pryde without puissance? Loue vnles acquent?
Wyves without Children? wealth without Content?
All which are toyles, lost labour, lost in vayne,
And drudging care, for profit without gayne.

                                      Discordant

And *Soueraigne LORD*, KING CHARLES.

Discordant things still contrare ends oppose,
The cause not the effect, wee should suppose:
So *Fates* agree; so accidents and *Clymes*,
Conclude, this age, must see such woefull *Tymes*
   So *Grammer Schooles* are ruynd, Learning rare,
Boords are so deare, and Stipends waxe so bare;
That good house-houlders, Country-men I spy,
Can hardly boord their *Bairnes* abroad, and why?
Broughs are so fingring; *Schoo'e-Masters* so needy;
Lore at such rate, and *Victuallers* so greedy;
That now most *Bairnes*, with Sheep, and ploughs are found,
Which makes so many *Ignorants* abound,
With Rustick Caryage; Manners harsh and rude,
And decent Comlynes, is quite seclude:
   For what makes Nature, civill myld and meek?
Kynd wyse, affable, gentle, slow to speek?
But good education: well bred, well taught.
In *Morall* Precepts, and divynely fraught,
With learned *Wisdome:* whence discretion flowes,
And Vnderstanding too, for Learning growes,
To bee the light of Nature; and I fynd,
Its the ornament, of a pregnant Mynd:
And though it were, but for to read, and wryte,
It is a needfull vse; and yeelds delyte,
To euery good *Conception;* giues direction,
To know aright, and so serues for correction,
And thus the *Ruther*, which behauiour rules,
Though graft in Nature, is refynd by *Schooles*.
So would to GOD, in tyme a course were tane.
That *Schooles*, and *Schoollers*, were repayrd agaíne,
   Another great abuse, is this that when,
Men runne in *Suretyship* for other Men;
Or els morgadgd in debt; yet will not pay.
Their *Creditors*, nor thy just Lawes obey:
But scorning, horning, Caption Rebells turne;
And in despight of Pow'r, all where sojourne.

                            Arm'd

The decay of Schooles.

Rebells.

Arm'd with *Rebellion, Pistols, Sword and Dagger,*
Threatning to kill, they roare it out, and swagger:
They boast their *Creditours,* and plague the Poore,
Even rambling through, best Townes, from doore to doore,
Whilst neither *Shrieue,* nor *Iustice* will lay hould,
Vpon these *Rebells:* nay; although they could,
They will not, why? some one respect or other,
Dryve in delayes, whilst they thy Lawes downe smother.
And thus this Land, is oure runne and crost,
With lawles *Bankerouts* and *Iustice* lost

 Some newly broke, as civill *Cheaters* doe,

Bankr-
routs.
Guard *Barwick,* and makes *Barwick* guard them too
It still keeps *Garrison,* all Men may see
In stead of *Souldiers,* now fled *Spendthrifts* bee:
This border Towne, lyke to that seat of *Rome,*
From Sword and Spoyle, to cousenage is come;
The one absolving sin: the other debt,
Though neither can nor could, such freedome get: '
Nay; *Barwick,* jumps with *Rome,* in more then this,
Slaughter, Adultry, Incest, whats amisse?
In ciuill Law, or *Church,* it will protect them,
Thou *Iustice Vengeance,* crying sins detect them,
Then who should curbe, this sheltring? or restrayne it?

The dis-
honest a-
buse of fu-
gitiue mar-
riages.
But thou gainst whom, and thy lawes they maintaine it.

 There's too of late a new eclipsd miscaryage,
But rather ane abuse, of honest marryage:
For now young persons, fauncyeing other loues,
Without consent of Parents thus it proues)
Or of their pastors approbation, neither
Of Towne nor Parish, nay, of Friend or Father;
Away they goe to *England;* there they're marryed,
And sometymes too, lyke Partyes turne miscaryed
Where fayling of Church rites, this yoke they draw,
That lawles Loue, may be made loueles Law.
For if the *English Preest,* be not *Palmestrat,*
He will not marry, they turne *Ambodextrat:*

          How

How can like Nuptialls stand, and stand with reason,
Although the preest conjoynes them : O ! what treason ?
Of fugitive deceat, is this to see.
When mine owne brood, from my kynd bowells flee,
From Parents loué, from lawfull Pastors pow'r,
For to be matchd by stealth : and would devoure,
Religion into shame ; whilst thou base Preist,
Turnes back from being Preacher, to a Beast ;
   What canst thou say, if such incestuous be ?
Els vyld Adultrers, brand with infamie,
Or els betrothd to others ; at which time,
Perhaps lyable to some criminall cryme ;
And dares thou brand thy selfe, and marryage stayne,
For one poore peece of gold, for three, or twayne,
Nay ; as by vnlawfullnes, they come to it,
Euen as vnlawfull, art thou call'd, to doe it,
O ! *Prelats* then, and *Iudges* of this *Land !*
Which both for *Church*, and *State* should justly stand,
Away with this, O let such Nuptialls bee !
Hel'd as injust, and punishd rigrously.

   Now for conceald Moneyes, I dare protest,
The searching of them, breeds a common Pest ;
The *Purcifant*, he goes abroad to summond,
Thome, *Will*, and *Dick* the heard scarce worth a *Dunmond*,
This *Ambodextrat* Villane, he warnes All,
Before the *Exchequer ;* and if they fayle,
A penaltye ensues ; els fill his hand
Or goe for *Edinburgh*, where come they stand,
Waiting, and waiting to be try'd and heard,
The *Messinger* he comes not ; they're debard.
From audience and dismissd : and thus they're crost,
With paynes great charges, and their labour lost,
Then judge great *Sir*, and yee my *Iudges*, judge,
If this and lyke, wracks not the Ploughing *Drudge*,
   For *Chamberlanes, Baillyes and Lairds Court Clarkes*,
I see the Projects, of their subtile warks :

Conceald moneys.

The

The first they fat themselues, by greed by stealth.
And out of ruyne, worke their *Mynes* of wealth,
Bringing most Lords to nought, els in such debt,
That they're not able, out of it to get:
The *Baillie* oft makes crooked the right causes,
Takes from both *Factions* brybes; with fals forgd clauses
will haue deceat calld trueth, if not the *Baillie*,
Will make the *Plaintives* part, a double Faillie:
The *Clarks* exact on all, they will haue feyes,
Payd and repayd for Acts, although but leyes,
Then help these faults, yee *Earles*, *Lords*, and *Knights*,
And let Domestick Servants, rule your rights,
Yea serious, bee your selues to take a count,
Of all your dewtyes, as your *Fathers* wount:
So shall your States, and Rents, encrease and stand,
And poore *Oppressd ones* freed from Factors hand,

Transpor-   As for my *Kyne* and *Cattell*, they're transported,
ting of   And *Sheep*, with *Gallowedian* Nages consorted,
Cattell.   To all the *English* quarters, heere and there,
Leauing my fields, halfe destitute, and bare,
Of their wont plenty and aboundance great,
Of all kind *Bestiall*; that content could get,
But see this droving, and this caryeing out,
Makes flesh both scarce and deare, all where about;
That now few houses great or small are kept,
As they were wont, being thus of *Cattell* stript:
And if it were not, for good store of fish,
There many mouths, would find an emptie *Dish*:
Then cause this (Sir) be helpd by straight restraint,
To quench the murmure, of a gen'rall plaint,

Now come I to my *Cornes* my *Wheat* and *Talloun*.
Myne *Yarne*, *Linning-Cloth*, *Oyle* many a galloun;
Salmon, *Salt*, *Herrings*, *Killing*, *Sethes*, and *Colle*,
With *Skin*, and *Hyde*, transported still to *Polle*:
Of which I grant there's some, might spared bee,
For mutuall *Commerce*, and *Commoditie*:

But

And Soueraigne *LORD*, KING CHARLES.

But for my *Wheat* my *Talloun* and my *Hyde*,
Let them be fenss'd, within my selfe to byde,
That *Leather* growing cheap, Woemen may weare,
More fyner Shoes, for *Leather* now is deare,
And so is tawning, Tawners haue such crosses,
With taxd *Gabelloes ;* miserable losses,
I will not here insist, although I could,
Lay open this infliction, as I should,
But since the maner, makes the meane so plaine,
I'le stryke no deeper, in a bleeding veyne.   *Transpor-*
    And should my Cornes be caryed to thy foes,   *ting of*
For foure or fyve Mens ends ; should gen'rall woes,   *Cornes.*
Be sowne abroad this *Kingdome ;* should Dearth, be rays'd ?
When wee haue equall plenty, *God bee prays'd :*
Fy, fy, on sinfull greed I O shameles blot !
That *Merchands,* would haue dearth, when GOD will not :
Nay they will pay before hand, rayse the pryce,
For which my *Lords,* approue them in their vyce :
And why ? because they gayne ; but ah alas ?
The *Tennents* left, into a woefull cace :
Thus *Pollicie* breads famine, and base greed,
Brings wealth to *Churles,* to my *Commouns* need,
Then (*Royall Sir*) prefer my *Commounweale,*
Aboue cursd *Misers,* never truely deale :
And for transporting Cornes, let Acts be made,
Hence forth they may at home, bee stopd, and stay'd.
    There other Towne-bred *Merchands* too, I know,   *Disembling*
Vnder a peeuish, *Puritanick* show,   *puritani-*
Of yea, and nay, forsooth its so, and ban not,   *call merch-*
Its good, the Pryce is small, cheaper I can not,   *ands.*
Would weigh a Mans purse, with his Lyfe and worse,
With fals *Hipocrisie,* themselves they curse .
When neither *Conscience, Religion,* nor *Trueth,*
They more respect, than *Harlotes,* do of Youth.
But serving *Tymes,* they serve their ends ; and why ?
For gayne they sell, and for to gayne they buy :

D

By

By hook, and Crook, they care not ; for deceat,
Is all the Mistresse, of their vpstart State,
Fals weights, fals measures, falshood eu'ry way,
Abound ; and Cousenage, turnes Merchand pay,
He's now the wisest Man, that can deceaue,
His *Nighbour*, though he play the errand Knave,
Fastning their wit, on guyle they make their drift,
Trayne fraudlent craft, to court, each *Catchpole* shift,
Whilst neither Law, nor Reason, they regard,
Till death transport them, to their last reward.

The spoyle   Now where are all my robust *Gallants?* where,
of Youth.   Are my *Bellona-Threatners*, doe, and dare?
Nay ; here's the very Quintissence, of trueth,
That Peace, and Idlenes, haue spoyld my Youth,
With *Cards* and *Drunkennesse*, lashiviuus *Lust :*
And all *Prophanenes*, swearing and distrust :
That now their Bodyes, are not half so strong,
As Nature lent them, to giue or free wrong :
And growne effeminat, weare *Woemens* loks,
Freize-hanging combd, o're Shoulders, Necks, and Cloks ;
That many doubt, if they bee *Mayds*, or Men,
Till that their *Beards* sprout foorth, and then they ken :
And yet their shame, hangs still about their *Heads*,
Whilst shaking Hayre, approue their foolish deeds,
Saint *Paul* forbids it, and hee tells them playne,
In doing which they're more, then shameles vayne ;
And *Absaloms Lyfe*, hayre-hung, betwene two Trees,
Might be a *Cauiat*, for such vanities :
For Manly exercise, is shreudly gone,
Foot-ball and Wrestling, throwing of the Stone :
Iumping and breathing, practises of Strength,
Which taught them to endure, hard things at length.
      And now *Tobacco*, that base stinking weed,
The abuse   That *Indian* witchcraft, smoaking in their head ;
of Tobacco. Turnes *Virile Acts*, and delicat discourse,
To Pot, and Pypes, reciprocall recourse :

Nay

Nay ; they're so bent, though when its spent to flashes,
They'le smoake it out, even Asses, sucking Ashes,
It was a damn'd devyce, a fatall curse,
To honesty, and health, and to the Purse,
It spoyles their *Memory*, and blinds their sight,
Dryes vp the moisture of the carnall *Wight :*
It smarts the brayne, and stupifiy'th the Wit,
Benumbes the sense, and here's the plague of it ;
Most brauest Mynds, turnes, *Coxcombs*, *Fooles* and *Sots.*
And now more slayne thereby, then my best *Scots,*
  For in a word, it is a drunken feast,
Depraving Man of senses, turnes him beast :
Some *Students* too, deserue to haue a dash,
For they can let it flee, smoake, flame, and flash,
And meanewhile wring out from Inventions brayne,
Some curious *Sermon*, in a whissing strayne,
And so can *Nobles*, *Gentry*, *Ploughmen* too,
Each glory to doe that, which others doe.
  Some take it for the fashion, some for Rheume,
Some for the Tooth-ach, others for the fleume :
Some for the Head-ake, some for Melancholy.
Some for to sharp their wits, and banish folly :
Some for their Pallet, in their warbling throt,
Some for good fellowship, to Pype and pot :
Some to quench Anger, some to put off tyme,
And some excessively, make vse a cryme,
Some *Rodomuntoes*, take it roaring downe,
And then rebelch it, lyke a spewing *Clowne :*
Some eate and chaw it, letting downe the juice,
And others steep it, for an open Sluce :
Some snuff, and sneize it, and convert in dust,
This greene *Negotian* leaf, in blak spent lust,
Some hungerbit, or Stomack-sick at least,
Convert *Tobacco*, in *Duke Vmphraes* feast :
Casting *Barmudoes*, in *Virginian* blocks,
They lock *Verinaes* in, with Venting Knocks,

And

And some when drunk, to make them sober mynded,
Till both their sense, and sobernes grow blinded :
   Then here's the slaurye, of this slabby sin,
Another Pype, another Pot, brings in :
The one bene spent, the other not they call,
For each of either, as their turnes may fall,
Whose *Strombolizing Nosethrills, Ætna* faces,
Makes halting *Vulcan*, change his *Lemnian* places,
To build his *Forge*, on foule *Cymberian* veynes,
Dying in blak, their Bowells, *Guts*, and braynes,
Whilst apprehension, makes their fond conceat,
To wast their bodyes, and exhaust their State.
   Some *Ladyes* too, haue head-akes in their Toes
And for remeed, takes *Phisick* at their Nose :
Some suck it stinkingly, and with distast,
And yet forsooth, they take it to liue chast,
Mixt with *Perfumes*, and Oyles, sweet Seeds, and snuff,
They swallow downe, in gluts this *Pagane* stuff,
Wresting another tast, then Nature can,
Lyke to their paynted *Cheekt*, deceauing Man ;
Some for the *Chollick ;* some for belly-ake,
And some do loue amayne, the *Pype* to take,
That now most female, *Ladyes* of each sort :
Doe make of *Pypes*, and *Vapour* but a sport.
Yet I confesse, its far more kyndlyer too,
For Woemen to suck *Pypes*, then men to do :
The one is Naturall, though oft abusd,
The other in neither, to bee excusd :
And last of all, *Tobacco*, I defyne,
To be the *Tuba Bachi, God*, of wyne,
Inviting *Drunkards*, clustring every where ?
To swagger, sweare, debosh, and revell care.

Against the wea-ring of Plaids.   And I could wish, that *Edinburgh* would mend !
This shameles custome, which none can commend :
Should *Woemen* walke lyke *Sprits ?* should *Woemen* weare,
Their *Winding-sheets* alyue ? wrapt vp I sweare,

                                        From

From head to foote in *Plads :* lyke *Zembrian Ghostes,*
Which haunt in Groaues, and *Shades ;* lyke *Fayry Hostes,*
Or winter wandring Wreaths : Base masked Whoores.
Buskd lyke *Callabrian Witches ; Skin-clungd Moores ;*
With fyre-scorching Tayles ; *Æthereall Wights,*
Or Nightly *Eremies,* that nev'r delights ;
But lyke cursd *Fiends* in darknes ; being the trick,
Of *Turkish Courtezans,* and to bee quick,
Of *Mercenary Harlots ;* Now base *Iads,*
Must Candle-light bee viewd ; O ! sin-worne *Plads,*
With *Drunkennes,* and *Whoredome :* who can avow ?
This beastly *Habit ; Towne,* I speeke to you.
   Looke to your Streets, at night see how they flock ?
Lyke buriall-busked *Bedlers ;* and provoke,
Good goers by to gaze, yea, often stand,
Till they invest them, with a Shouldring hand :
Where is their punishment ? where is good order ?
Where civill comelynes ? O to what border ?
Is honesty now fled ; When thus I see,
That richest, *Wyues,* with *Harlots* masked bee :
For in a word there's none, twixt both can judge,
In show, the *Matrone,* from the commoun Drudge :
Then as the *Hangman,* had late pow're to mend it,
The *Gallows* or the *Borrough-Loch* must end it.
   My Land is so surcharged, with cursing evill,
Diuell take the lears, the whole-ware still the Diuell ;
Fiend a bit, *Fiend* take you, the *Diuell,* an inch !
Diuell take them, *Soule* and *Body ;* there's a pinch :
How *Diuell* doe you ? the *Diuell* to you that speeres,
And some curse *Heaven,* and *Hell,* and by them sweare
Some cursing make, conditionall diversion,
Diuell take *Mee, God* saue all ; O ? there's reversion ?
That even the *Chyld,* the first word it can mumble,
Is *Diuell, Diuell, Diuell,* so *Babes* begin to stumble,
And why ? cause *Parents* ban ; the Servands tongue,
Spew curses forth corrupting, old and young,

The abuse of banning & cursing.

But

But ah ! poore *Wretches !* what a curse of euill ?
Is this at ev'ry word, to name the Diuell :
This, this, and lyke, makes now this *Ile* abound,
With *Hellish Snakes,* for Diuells allwhere are found :
There's nether *Russia Lituan,* or *Leif Land,*
Norway, North *Swaine,* my *North Iles,* nor *Lapland,*
Can yeeld moe *Witches, Warlocks, Charmers* too,
Then my *Mayne Lands,* even at this present do :
And though that some be brunt, there hundreths moe,
I hope ere long, shall through the fyre goe.
For tyme and tryall, earnest care may make,
The diuell to vanish, and his servants quake :
Then leaue your banning, and your cursing words ;
For *Yea,* and *Nay ;* the happyest speach affords.

Against Coles and Witches. But now belyke the *Colles,* this happy yeare,
By burning *Witches,* are growne wondrous deare,
And so they are, but sure the *Flemings* make it,
Although the *Commouns,* commounly mistake it :
But if my *Colles* to imposts, ones were put,
They soone would stay, the *Hollanders* were shut :
Yet *Colles* and *Witches* haue a nearer vnion,
First here by vse, then hence by dark communion :
Some *Colles* are fund, in Earths profoundest Cell,
Which *Colliers* hould adjacent neare to Hell :
And will not let, blynd *Limbus* ly betwene,
For *Colliers* haue in darknes, *Lynx* bred eyne :
Where sometymes they, with *Stygian* streames are crost,
Throwne downe to *Lethe,* in oblivion lost :
Whence *Colles,* bene Nyghbours next, to *Plutoes Pit,*
Are sent as *Messingers,* from gaping it :
To hurle downe below, with posting fyre,
These damn'd *Gehennists,* to their endles hyre :
Thus *Hell* and *Witches, Diuells,* and *Warloks* bee,
Linkd in with *Colles,* in hot affinitie :
Which GOD may grant ! long may their vnion stand,
Till *Witchcraft* quyte, be rooted from this *Land,*

For

For cheating *Brockers*, and cursd *Vsrers* they,
In eu'ry Towne, and Corner, beare great swey :
They're *Money-Mongers*, and they know tymes, slaurye
When need brings Vertue, halting to their knavery :
The *Brocker*, must haue Pawnes, and double Pawnd ;
And cares not for no caution, writ, nor Hand.
But quarterly, monthly, by week or day,
Must haue the *Gabelle*, of his cheating pay :
Els fayling of the Tyme, off goes the Pawne,
And thus is povertie, in bondage drawne.

Against
Brockers.

   The *Vsrer* will take suretye, Bonds, and Bills,
Or els *Morgadgement*, at disposers wills :
For fyftene a hundreth, yea, sometymes twenty,
And fills his *Coffers*, with such ill wonne Plenty :
Yea, lets it all runne on, till day and date,
Be long expyrd ; and to rayse his State,
Out flies horning, Caption, fensing Commands,
Imprisonment ; or els comprysing *Lands*.
Whilst the distressd *Debter*, rests pinchd, or slayne,
Vnder the crueltye, of this *Tigers* gayne :
O ! miserable wealth ! O ! wretched greed !
That eats the very bowells, out of need :
But for to mend this, whilst they're plaguing fangd,
The *Brocker* should be scourged, the *Vsrer* hangd.

Against
Vsurers.

   There's to a needfull *Cauiat*, I'le set forth,
For eu'ry *Noble Lord*, and *Man* of worth,
For *Bishops*, *Preachers*, euery towne, and place,
Where vagabounding *Greeks*, vse now to trace ;
Deluding and deceauing you, with leyes.
And *Testimonials* fals ; base forgeryes.
Of blynd inveiglings ; making you beleeue.
They must their wives, their Bairnes, or friends releiue ;
From slauerye, and from thraldome ; by *Turks* there tane,
Either in *Greece*, in *Asia*, *Iles*, or *Mayne*
Whom they would haue redeemd ; from bondage brought.
And Ransomes payd, for what dissembling wrought.

Concerning
vagabond-
ing Greeks.

But

But I assure Thee, as GOD liues in Heauen,
There's no such matter; nether are they driuen,
To any such distresse; my reason's here,
The *Greeks*, vnder the *Turke*, borne eu'ry where;
Haue freedome peace, and safety; liue as free,
As any Subjects heere, can, or may bee:
For now the *Turke*, being *Lord*, and they too sworne,
How can he thrall them, they his Subjects borne:
Nay; neither *Tythes* of Children, *Female Dote*,
They pay more now, for *Achmet*, rent that lot;
Yet when they payd them both, their lyues and Lands.
Were then as free, as ours are in our hands.

And far les for *Religion*, can they bee,
Exyld or thrald, or els where, forcd to flee:
Whilst there's libertie of *Conscience* giuen,
To *Greeks* and all kynd *Christianes* vnder Heaven,
Through all his large *Dominions:* want nought els,
Saue onely this, the vse of ringing Bells:
Nay I vow God; they liue more free of cares,
Vnder their Lords, then Myne do vnder theirs:
Then be no more deceau'd; recall tymes past!
How *Greeks*, haue gulld you, goulding them so fast,
But if you will bee fooles, when knaves thus passes?
Yee merit what they make you, *Dolts* and *Asses*.

The flatry of Hostill-cries. My *Hostes*, and *Hostesses*, in every house,
Can make their *Guests* so welcome they'le carrouse:
With merryment and laughter; tell a Tale,
Of *Robin Hood*, and *Wallace;* make their Ale,
Flee out of Pynts in Quarts: but being come,
To whats to pay? the *Hostesse* beats the *Drumme!*
Vp, vp, *Good-man;* away; there's one in haist!
Must speeke with you, Come? fy, he's almost past,
The *Hoste* thus gone, the honest *Guest* must stay,
And for *Thome Tratler*, all the reckning pay.

The scarci-ty of small Moncyes. So now, my Coyning-house, doth idle stand,
And there no Pictures, stampd with Irne nor hand:

There

And Soveraigne LORD, Kɪɴɢ Cʜᴀʀʟᴇꜱ.

There are no moneyes going, nor golden collours,
Saue *Dutch* and *Holland, Saxone, Austrian* dollours :
Now all are *Dollors ; Dollors* ought can doe,
And when they want them, they haue *Dollours* too :
For but them, with them, *Dollors* frequent be,
Dollors in want, and *Dollers* when they flee :
But worst, ther's no small money can bee had,
Nor change for gold or silver ; Men are made
Often for lack of change, to leaue, or losse
Whole, half, or part, of their twyse Dollourd drosse :
Men can not buy nor sell ; Men can not barter ;
And *Hostlaries* smart too in eu'ry quarter.
 So *Charity* is curbd ; Men can not giue
Their Almes, that would faine the poore relieue :
Then (Sir) there's *Copper, Copper* too is cheap,
Grieue not thy government, nor Moneyes keep,
Of so small valew, from thy *Commouns* hand,
Which still breeds wealth, and *Commerce* in my Land :
In this both *Spaine,* and *Italy* are blest,
With *France* and *Germany,* and *Holland* best ;
Where most part of their moneys are in brasse,
And freely too from hand to hand do passe :
Then (Sir) cause coyne, *Plaks, Achesons,* and *Turners ;*
Ought will suffice to stop the mouths of *Mourners.*
 Now eu'ry office beares the name of Lord,
And honour much injurd by wrong record :
First then, for Lords of Session, none should be
Call'd Lords for no respect, of what degree ;
Saue onely two, *Lord Chauncelor* for his place,
And the *Lord President ;* the rest I trace
But worshipfull and reverend, they're no more,
All *Europe* with the lyke, the lyke decore ;
And next my *Shrieue,* by heritage, or yeare,
Must be call'd Lordship, els he will not heare :
Then there's Lord *Provost* plac'd in eu'ry towne,
And *Iack* made Lord was yesterday a clowne ;

The abuses of diverse offices falsly intitulated Lords.

 E Yea

Yea, some-where there's Lord *Baillie*, and men must
Vpon his Sheep-drawne shaddow Lordship thrust :
So *Deanes of Gild* are Lords ; O Burges boords !
Whilst Towne and Church *Treasurers* too are Lords ;
And yet their Lordships in a commoun talc,
Can mixe their graue discourse with Pynts of Ale.
Some Kirks and Colledges afford I see
Lord *Rector*, Lord *Archdeane*, Lord how do yee ?
So also is Lord *Lyon* grauely Lorded,
Who more for worth than stile, is here recorded :
Next, there Lord *Doctor* of the shyting Potion,
Who for some *recipe*, (not for devotion)
Must be palmestrat, with red imag'd Ore,
For which his Lordship thanks the good *grandgore*.
  In comes Lord *Commisser*, and he protests
For *Clyents* and decreets, whilst yet, there rests
Some fatall Testments, which he must recall,
To be confirmed, then thanks death for all :
Then there's Lord *Constable* with his Nights Crue ;
Of frozen *Bussards*, that will call on you,
Come to the Lord *Constable*, come, or go
To prison ; speek, what say you ? yea ; or no ;
The *Passenger*, before his greatnesse come,
One single quart will stryke his Lordshcep dombe.
  And last, to Lord them all, there are *Trone Lords*,
Which beare sad *Burdens*, bund with rops and cords,
That sometimes serue the *Hangman*, Scaffolds make
For execution, and for justice sake :
All which are Lords ; of diverse ranks each Creature,
Even from the judges to the scume of Nature :
But if that any Kingdome can afford,
In all the world, the like name of a *Lord ;*
I'le be content to pawne my *Pilgrimes* lyfe,
For he best knowes how to decyde such stryfe :
Yet *anagram* me Lordes, O now take heed !
And yee shall find my Lords turne *drols* indeed :

                                              And

And so most are, (both *Colledges* exceptd)
And true *Lord Barons,* falsly interceptd
By *Russian* Fopperyes ; which corruption brings,
On Noble stiles, not given them of *Kings;*
Which if it be not help'd, whats more ado ?
But stile my *Pilgrime,* LORD TRAVELLER *too.*

As for my *Castles,* and my *Marine Ports,*
The first decay, the other, they want forts :
Would *Leith, Inchkeith,* and *May,* were sconsd and block'd,
As for *Dunbertane* it is strongly rock'd :
But more by *Nature,* than by *Airt* I see,
Whose mouldring walls brought low, defective be :
Which if thine eyes surveigh, Thou'll cause amend it,
And for its situat strength (doubtles) commend it :
Blaknes that Dungeon must be still kept dry,
Least with the levell ground it swaking ly :
Yet stately *Snadoun, Strivelings* Castelld beauty,
It still reserues for *Thee* a thankfull duety :
Yea ; if when need, a fort of great *Defence,*
Whence linking *Forth, Meander*-crook'd, runnes thence.

> *The ruyne of Castles and Sea Ports.*

As for thy *Pallace,* LITHGOVV, *Fawlkland* too,
And *Halyrude-house,* Mansions, when ado ;
Though now well kept, I feare long absence may,
Turne thine *Auncestors* Stations to decay :
And no great wonder, how can they abide ?
When *Thou* and *Thine* shall els where still resyde :
For *Edinburghs* fortresse it stoutely stands,
High-tip-toe rockd, o'relooking Sea and Lands :
Where *Iames* the Iust, of blest renowne, thy *Syre,*
Was borne, and got the Crowne of this *Empyre.*

Would *Soundbroughhead,* in *Zetland* were intrenchd,
And *Skalloway,* neare *Laxford* too reflanchd ;
And that *Orcadian Kirkwall,* eke rampierd,
With *Cafasound,* that harbour much admir'd :
Then would these Iles, Septentrion safer bee,
When made defensiue gainst the *Hostile Sea :*

E 2   But

But for most other parts, few can offend them,
Sea-sandy Shelfs, and Craggy Coasts defend them :
As for my westerne Iles, they need no hould ;
Each Ilander himselfe is Bulwark bould :
Yet (Sir) looke to it, least my *Forts* decay,
And these thy *Mansions* fall, and rot away.
 Now come I to *Land-passages*, and see,
I find defects, would GOD could helped bee :
Where are these *Bridges*, over Rivers plac'd ?
Which sometymes haue my *Body* maynely grac'd
Nay ; they're ruind, els vtterly decay'd
Whose vntectd *Arches*, spoil'd, are quite deray'd :
Most waters now haue neither *Bridge* nor *Boat*,
Which makes so many sink, or helplesse float.

The defect   What should I speake of *Perths* outragious *Tay ?*
of Bridges. That shortly twyse hath tane her *Bridge* away :
But wayle the losse, that *Towne* receav'd thereby ;
And for remeed to *Thee*, my *Sou'raigne* cry !
O Gracious Sir ! cause build that Bridge againe,
And flank each *Columne* with hornd *Arches* twaine :
The stones were long and larger than before,
The *Arches* wyder, doubling on each Shoare :
Which made more high and wyde, the strugling flood,
May calmely vent, and not proue half so rude :
For which, good work, the *Countrey* being easd,
Thou shalt be praisd, and GOD therein well pleasd.
 There many other *Rivers*, *Brookes*, and *Strands*,
Streames, *Rills*, and *Torrents*, march-divyding *Lands :*
Would faine be bridg'd, made passable and plank'd,
Men might find way, and *Benefactors* thank'd :
But where's the *Earle*, *Baron*, *Laird*, or *Knight ?*
Will prove so charitable, though he might :
Nay ; there's no *Commoun-wealth*, nor commoun works,
Most of them building Nests for Chimney *Storks :*
But to speake trueth, in times past, and of late,
When *Friers* and *Cloisters* had their swaggring state :

           These

These good and beneficial deeds abounded,
Which now by vs are ruind, rent, and wounded :
And yet my *Nobles,* brooke these *Tythes* and rents,
Supply'd this charge, which many one repents :
For them, what good they doe therewith, its knowne,
They sat themselues, then leaue it to their owne.
  Then to helpe this, cause eu'ry *Land-Lord,* lo !
Through whose just bounds, thy *Market Streets* do goe ;
To build, sustaine, repayre, whats in decay,
And over lets, to make free passage way.
But if this task may seeme to great for one,
Then let the *Shyre* helpe him where its done :
And as the work to modifie the meane,
Wherein the vulgars formost still are seene :
So shall this Nation blesse *Thee,* praise them too,
When *Landed Men* this *Christian* good shall do.
  Now for my losses, by the *Hostile Sea,*
These long fiue yeares, in numbers many be :
The *Divelish Dunkirker* ransacks my Ships,
And with the scourge of Pryde my fortune whips,
Along the shivring tops of rouzing billowes,
Menassing *Mars* and *Neptune ;* all he swallowes
Within the throat of *Hatred ;* and he fills
Their *Flandrian Ports* with *Masts* as high as Hills :
My Men are captiues, and their goods are lost
To them and theirs ; thy foe of too free cost,
Enjoyeth all, and then, at randon lets
Mens liues and freedome ; if he ransome gets :
And ly even as they please on *Ærmouths coast*
Or *Humber mouth,* where all my ships are lost :
Where then my *Cursars ?* Where thy Men of war ?
Nay, when they see them, hover off a far ;
And basely suffer thine *Enemies* to prey,
Vpon thy subjects, making no supply :
If this be right, or if warres be intended ?
I wish a better course, els they were ended.

*Incursary
Losses by
Sea.*

E 3

Besides

The misery of War.

Besides these Sea-bred griefs; ah ! now I see,
Through spatious *Europe* a deformitie :
What strange combustions, tumults, and vproares ?
Are here and there, alwhere the Sword it goares :
O wretched Tyme ! most barbarous and rude,
To see the *Christian World,* drunk dead with blood ;
And not one Kingdome left without cursd jarres,
So vniversall are these woefull warres :
Kings against *Kings, Nation* against *Nation,*
Perfites the Prophecy of *Desolation :*
The like deludge, reciprocating stryfe,
Was not, since last, *Rome* lost her *Tribune* lyfe :
   O woefull warre ! which lessens wealth and strength,
And brings the ruynes of ruine at length :
It doth dishonour *Honour,* and degrad
The mighty Man from what his greatnesse had :
Even like the rage of the impetuous flood,
Debording from his banks, leaues slyme and mood.
To choke the fertile plaines, supplants the rootes
Of *Hearbs* and *Trees,* defaceth quite the fruits
Of grapes and grayne ; and often breaks the walls
Of strongest *Townes,* whereon destruction falls.
   Even so the fury of the bloody *Warre !*
In breking downe the bonds of Peace, debarre
The links of *Loue* and *Alliance,* quite defaceth
The libertie of *Nature,* and disgraceth
The ornaments of *Tyme,* and cuts the throat
Of Martiall *Darlings ;* then casts vp the lot
Of desolation, which destroyeth all,
Which can to meane, or mighty Men befall :
What though to lyfe, we all but one way came ;
Yet diverse wayes we go out of the same :
So fatall *Sword* decrees *Deaths* worst and best ;
Mans Epilogue to be, *nunc mortuus est.*
Then heere's the *Catastrophe !* warfare brings,
For *Preter losse* the present thought of things.

As

And Soveraigne LORD, KING CHARLES.

As *Christendome* may curse that *Counte* of *Torne,*
The day that he was got, bred, breathd, or borne:
For diverse causes in *Matthias* tyme,
Which ah of late I turn'd to a vulgar cryme.
So may a lesser World, a greater curse
Impose on some, whose ruind drifts were worse:
But tush, let *Fortune* wag, the *Balls* runne on;
The *Wheele* in pieces chatter, all is One:
There is a day, when *Tyme* shall bring to dust,
There falshood and false honours most injust:
Let *Caperculian, Musick Nigromancers,*
French fidling playes, and blind dissembling *Dauncers,*
Enveigle heavie *Tymes,* and runne the *Snout*
Of trecherie vpon a sakeles rout:
There is a *Maskerat,* will ones discover
The length twixt *Reize* and *Calz,* from *Calz* to *Dover.*
   Take heed of *Sinons* teares, take heed of this
False-smyling *Clepho,* with a *Iudas* kisse:
Mongst sweetest flowres the link-layd Serpents ly,
And lurking sting, the harmelese goers by:
So vnder fairest words, the falsest heart
Doth pry, and dyue, to work some grievous smart:
For it is incident to Courteours still,
To speak one way and haue another will:
But much more in the *Minion,* who pretends
A Sou'raigne *Mateship* for his trechrous ends:
Which, though his greatnesse springs not from true merit,
But from the pow'r of loue, which *Kings* inherit:
Yet often, and too often, ah! I find,
That *Kingly* favours, breed a false, false mynd:
And seldome eu'r escapes without retort,
So doubtful are the dangers of a Court.
   So present tymes, may for example trade
On *Duke de Lerma,* whom *Don Phillip* made
His *Mineon,* and his *Oracle,* his guide;
The *King* being simple, meek, and mollify'd:

The tre-
chery of
Mineons.

This

This meane-borne gentle-man, now made a *Prince*,
Did swallow vp ambition ; and from thence,
The Dregs of Avarice, dishonest greed,
And from his *Prince* hee stole, not having need ;
In nyne yeares tyme, full eight *Millions* of gould,
Whilst *Phillips* Loue was dearer bought, than sould :
At last detect'd, and all his knaueries knowne,
His Spanish *Motto* in these words were showne :
El mayor ladron del Mondo ; Para non morir aorcado,
Vestiose de collorado, &c. and englishd thus,
The greatest Theefe, the oldest Knaue
That Hell, *the* Divell, *or* Spane *could haue ;*
To shunne the Gallowes, *hee with speed,*
Did cloth himselfe in collour red,
   For he turnd *Cardinall,* and gaue the *Pope,*
Two hundreth thousand Crownes to flee the rope :
So had this *Duke* his *Mineon,* eke a *Don,*
Made *Marques* too, call'd *Roderick Calderon ;*
Who following *Lermaes* footsteps, wax'd so bould,
That he stole too four *Millions* of pure gould :
Which being discouerd for his fellonie,
This courtly Theefe hee was condemn'd to dye :
The lyke and like againe I could produce,
But this may serue for to shut vp the sluce.

Admoniti-
ons for
Kings.   O ! if that Kings ! as they are Kings would look,
And read lyke records of as blak a book :
Sure they would see great errours they commit.
In giving trust to any *Parasit ;*
But thou blest King, thou art not cary'd so,
Thou canst discerne thy friend from secret foe :
And will not be the same that thou do'st seeme,
How fond soever vulgare censures deeme :
   Yet in times past, the like erronious errours,
Haue bred to *Kings* and *Kingdomes,* helples terrours :
Who from himselfe bequeaths himselfe, and *State.*
(And in his crowne would haue a rivall *Mate*)

                                  Vnto

And Soueraigne LORD, KING CHARLES.

Vnto anothers gouernment, and will ;
God knowes some *Puppy,* voyd of wit and skill
He is but half a Man, and not his owne,
Yea sometymes scarce, the half that I haue showne,
For he thats led, and ruld by others pleasure,
In judgement, nor in justice, keeps no measure.
   As KINGS are absolute, so, should they be,
As absolute, in sound dexteritie.
Saue in great matters, than to be advysd,
By *Counsells* graue, or they be interprysd :
If not and so, that one, must needs rule all,
Be't Lyf, or *Honour*, Liberty, or thrall :
Looke to the events, doubtfully confusd.
Whilst or the *Bird* be hatchd the *Egge* is bruisd :
What *Dauid* sayd of lyke ? I'le praysing tell,
He begd of GOD, to send them quick to Hell :
   So KINGS haue perishd, and their *Kingdomes* falne
In cruell bondage, and their *People* thralne :
Lyke made young *Osman*, loose his *Princely Lyfe,*
Which filld his *Kingdomes*, with intestine stryf,
So the last *Hungar King*, was crossd and sackt,
And by his *Minion*, fould, ruynd, and wrackt.
But why ? should I, examplify, so much,
Since thou hast deep experience of such :
Yet he is happy, makes anothers fall,
A warning to prevent vntymely thrall.
   Ah ! and thryse ah ! so *Germany* is layd,
Vnder the *Spanyards* foote ; and *Austria* made,
The head of that *Empyre :* greef beyond sorrow,
To see proud *Tirants*, from ten *Princes* burrow :
Such helples loanes ; that neither sword nor might,
Nor Law nor Reason, can recall their right.
O ! that one blow ! one *Tyme !* O ! angry fates !
Should ruyne both *Religion* there, and *States :*
Cursd be the spight of that vntymely doome,
Which *Spaine* divyseth, and confirmd by *Rome :*

The ruine of Germany.

F   *Spaine*

Spaine seekes dominion, and the *Popes* impart,
Them power to swallow all, so they haue part :
And *Thee*, and thy three *Kingdomes* too, they would,
Cast in the fornace, of a *Spanish Mould.*

The Span-
yards in-
satiable
greed of
dominion.

    Yet Tyme may lash, the force of thy prowd foe,
And make ambition, subject to lyke woe :
Who seeks *Kings* ruine, and would domineere
O're all the *Vniuerse*, yea, and vpreare,
The base record, of *Vandals Gothes*, and *Hunnes*,
Of whome they're come *Men, Daughters, Wyues*, and *Sonnes*,
Whose greed most *Indian* Soyles, can not contayne,
Nor large *Americk* the old, and new namd *Spaine :*
The Sea-coast *Affrick* Townes ; *Atlantick Iles ;*
Nor *Ballearen*, nor *Sardinian* Styles :
The fat *Sicilian* playnes, got by the blood,
Of murtherd *Gaules*, can not his pryde includ.
Nor the *Apulian, Callabrian* Lands, and more,
The Seate of *Naples*, the *Lavoreen* Shoare :
The *Millane Dutchy*, nor *Pavian* bounds ;
The racked *Belgia*, nor the high *Burgounds ;*
The *Pyrhenian Navarre*, the *Voltelyne ;*
Can not this *Monsters Monarchy*, confyne :
For if he could, he would, himselfe invest,
From *Pole*, to *Pole*, and so from East to West :
Yet doubtles Tyme, his pryde and greed shall dash,
And raze his might, for so can fortune lash.
    Thou mayst recall herein, that cruell payne.

Lithgows
iniust and
cruell tor-
turs inflict-
ed vpon
him in
Maloga.

And bloody Tortures, Lithgovv had in *Spaine*,
Which for CHRISTS sake, his Countrey and thy *Syre*
He patiently endur'd, O! thou mayst admyre :
His constancy for Trueth, and for that *Treason*,
Injustly layd on him, beyond all reason :
Being in tyme of Peace, and no suspect,
Of breach ; but what they falsly did detect :
And hauing too, thy *Fathers Seales*, and *Hand*,
For to protect him, to the *Æthiope Land :*

                                   Whose

Whose lyfe, the *English* factors seeing surgrieud,
By meanes of Noble *Aston* him relieud :
What Tongue ? what Pen ? what Mynd can well expresse ?
Or heart conceaue ? his Torments mercyles :
Nay ; none but thy late *Father*, rightly weighd,
And *Parliament ;* how they his Peace inveighd :
For which (deare royall IAMES,) had full regard,
His Suffrings, and his Trauells, to reward :
Yea, graciously maintaynd him, tooke delight,
To heare his rare discourse, of forraine sight :
Then (*Sir*) make fals, this Proverbe, turne his debter,
There seldome, comes (Men say) *a Father better,*
   Say though hee had not for thy *Crowne*, bene crost,
Rackd, bruisd, disjoynted, and his *Fortuncs* lost :
With all these moneyes, thy *Syre* did him gift,
And Thow Thy self, for to advance his drift :
With Papers, Observations, Patents, Seales,
Which now are lost, and lost for aye, he feeles :
Yet doe his Trauells merit, his rare adventers :
His wandring long, beyond the Earths full Centers :
His curious drifts, slighting wretched gaines :
His much-admyrd attempts ! his matchles paines,
His Fame hee wonne thereby, to Mee and Myne,
Leauing my stamp, on Earths remotest *Shryne :*
And where I was not knowne, did annalize,
My Name in records, of true *Sacrifice :*
   Yea did acquaint Mee, with each kynd of thing.
That pregnant Knowledge, could contentment bring ;
Strengths, Townes, Castles, *Cittadales* and *Forts*,
Distance of places, *Regions, Iles*, and *Ports*,
Their maners, too, and living, rites, and Lawes,
Customes and gouernment, Religious Sawes :
Of *Turke*, and *Iew*, *Arabian, Greek,* and *Moore*,
Sabunck, and *Coptic*, the *Egyptian* glore :
The *Cypriot, Tartyr, Creet*, and *Turcoman*,
The grosse *Armenian*, Sun-burnt *Affrican ;*

The

The *Abasine* and whyte *Moore* ; the *Nestorian*,
The *Chelfane, Iacobin, Syriack Georgian* ;
The *Amaronite, Lybian,* and *Nigroe* black,
Besydes all *Europe,* in a word to take :
All these and reasons, many hundreds moe,
Deserve that (*Sir*) thou shouldst appease his woe.

   For he's the first, of *Trauells*, ever wrot,
Since my all-Virgine Wombe, first bred a *Scot :*
The Prince of *Pilgrimes*, Father of them all,
And greatest *Traueller*, Earths circling Ball,
Can *Europs* eye affoord : O happy *Man !*
Whose mynd feasts, on rare sights ; which none els can ;
There Thousand Thousands, eu'ry where complayne,
That thy just bounty, should him not sustayne,
But hath imposd vpon him, a sore greef,
To make my Bowells, yeeld him now releef :
Where ah ! there's nought, but povertie and pryde.
And misregard to *Merit*, so wele try'd :
I could be more *Pathetick*, in his greef,
But that were too indulgent, I'le be breef,
Then (*Sir*) For my request, thy *Soyle*, thy *Nation*,
Help LITHGOVVS want, relieue his desolation.
Then shall thy bounty praise *Thee*, place thine *Heart*,
On merits Glory, gracious to desert.

Decayed   To speek of ruind *Churches*, vntectd, vnwalld,
Churches. Left vnprovyded, stipend-vnenstalld,
Into my Borders, *Iles,* and High-land parts, ⟩
Which deep experience, to my sight imparts.
It would too tedious be, and prolixe proue ;
So I'le desist, the helpe ly'th in thy Loue ;
Which euer yet, thou zealously exprest,
For GODS true Glory, in thy lyfe profest,
But true it is, the *Lairds* which owe the ground,
Are causes why, they thus abusd are found.

   But more than this, there *Preachers*, that are placd,
Within my *Maine*, and orderly imbracd

                                                    Yet

Yet can not get their stipends, and *Church* rent,
Without contestion, and great discontent.
The *Parish* Laird, or Lord, objects some clause,
Against the *Pastors*, Ministeriall cause,
Els thus in robbing, of his yearely fee,
To force him both, from Church and Parish flee :
   This done for law they goe, to plead it out,
Till slyding yeares, and months, runne thryse about,
Which now makes *Edinburgh*, each *Session* bee,
So full of Preachers, swarming as I see :
Whilst ah, their flocks at home, are evill taught,
And *Gods* blest *Sabboth*, too prophanely fraught,
With drunken Vyce, and lewd laschivious sin,
Which without Doctrine, soone comes creeping in :
Thus many Preists are plagud ; and vnrelieu'd,
The people perish, honest hearts are grieud,
The Lairds triumph, in their ambitious hate,
And care not for GODS worship, nor Mans state,
Which if it be not helpd, O grieuous crosse !
I feare *Religion*, shall haue the losse.
   So with this grieuance, I bequeath the rest,
To be reformd by *Thee*, and soone redrest :
Then weigh them right, into thy judgment just,
That these confusions may be brought to dust :
So shall this *Land* be happy, liue in rest,
By thy good *Gouernment ;* when Trueth thryse blest,
Shall Crowne thy Iustice ; and when Vyce shall be,
And errours grosse, repayrd in equitie.
   The *Parliament* done, now I must commend,
Some Nobles to thy Loue, and so I'le end :
Make much of *Hamilton*, my *Princely Peere ;*
Thy choysest Subject, and thy *Cousing Deare.*
Whose *Syre*, whose *Grandsyre*, whose *Pedegree*,
For faithfull service, to thy crowne and *Mee ;*
Deserve the *Mausolaeon Tombe ; Cariaes* wonder,
To blaze thereon, their fame ; and for to thunder.

*Ministers
wronged by
their Pa-
rish Lairds.*

*A recom-
mendation
of all the
Protestant
Nobles to
his Maie-
stie.*

To Tymes succeeding; in mem'rie of worth,
Their Noble actions: set so lyvely forth:
To each declyning Age: That even his part,
Their former Lyves, stamps in his hopefull Heart:
Whose greatnes is my Mirrour, and whose light,
Illuminats my *Westerne* bounds by right:
Whence gratefull Clyde, redounds from chearefull banks,
To that *Illustrious Youth*, ten thousand thanks.

The house of Mar.

To pen, and praise to *Thee*, that house of *Mar*,
In Mee were odious; since thou knowst how far;
It do'th surpasse most others: for that *Lord*,
Deserues my *Chronicle*, for to record,
His *Providence*, and *Wisdome;* whilst his deeds,
Do trample vpon Vertue; whence succeeds:
So many *Sonnes* and *Daughters:* O I rare birth!
Whome GOD may long blesse, and preserue on Earth:
That as their *Syre*, in his matchles fame,
So they them selues, may still retayne the same;
Whilst Glory, vpon Glory, shall redowne,
To Them and Theirs, an euer-fixd renowne:

Montrose.

As for that hopefull Youth, the young *Lord Grahame,*
Iames Earle of *Montrose;* whose war-lyke Name,
Sprung from redoubted worth, made Manhood try,
Their matchles deeds, in vnmatchd *Chiualry:*
I doe bequeath him, to thy gracious Loue,
Whose Noble Stocke, did euer faithfull proue:
To thyne old-agd *Auncestors;* and my bounds,
Were often freed, from thraldome, by their wounds:
Leauing their roote, the stamp of fidele trueth,
To be inherent, in this noble Youth:
Whose Hearts, whose Hands, whose Swords, whose Deeds, whose
Made *Mars* for valour, cannonize the *Grahame*.   (Fame

Munteith.

Wherein *Muntieth*, that auncient *Earle* may,
Plead for his part, whose right retaines it aye,
In *One*, and the same *Stock*, being branchd, and graft,
By discent in it, and whose Lawrell shaft:

                                                        Of

Of Honour aymes it, for his worth may clayme ;
The *Caledonean Mantle*, in the *Grahame*.
   To rouze the trueth, which still must passage find,   *Rothouse.*
Of worthy *Rothus*, and his learned Mynd ;
I doe admyre him, for his gifts most rare,
Which few can paralell, nor yet compare ;
With him for auncient Blood, nor present worth,
Which pregnant deeds, and Learned parts set forth.
   Now plead I for the Earle *Home*, and see,   *The Earle*
That *Martiall* Name, did much for Thyne, and Mee :   *Home.*
They were my *Bulwark*, in the easterne Border, ⌡
And keept my Nyghbour foes, in awfull order :
For *Home*, deryvd of *Homo*, is a *Man*,
And *Merse*, of *Mars*, so *Home*, and *Merse*, I scan :
Whose auncient services, and moderne Loue,
Deserve of *Thee* great thanks, rewards of *Ioue :*
Who by just merit, weare the *Sanguine Rose*,
Of all these Confynes, which my Lists, enclose.
  So paynt I foorth, with pensile-drawing hand,
That noble Mirrour, *Marshall* of my land :
   There's Noble *Cassells* too, and gallant *Mortoun*,   *The Earls*
Deserue, as they enjoy, Auspicuous Fortune,   *in generall.*
With *Murray, Ainzie, Sutherland*, and *Lorne*,
Lithgow, Eglintoun, Wigton, and *Kingorne :*
Buckcleuch, and *Buchan, Hadington, Glencarne ;*
Roxbrough, Galloway, Sea-Forth, Tillibarne !
Cathnes, Dumfermling, Kellie, Lawderdale ;
Perth, Louthian too ; *Crawfurd*, and *Annandale*,
And last, though first, so first, and last now looke,
Vpon thy blood and kinsman, *Lennox Duke*.
   All which are *Peeres*, by true *Religion* Crownd,
And Honour to, thy faithfull friends renownd.
Though here I place most, not as order growes,
But from my kyndnes, as affection flowes,
Let *Heraulds* rank them, its enough for Mee,
To show their Names, and keepe true Poesie

                          As

As for Lord *Barons, Lyndesay* and *CathCart,*

*Lord Ba-
rons.*

Boyd, Rosse, and *Yester, Forbus,* pious *Heart :*
Lord *Viscont Dupline, Chauncelor* of my *State,*
With *Marcheston,* as good, as now made great :
Sinclair, and *Saltoun ; Lowdon,* in the West,
With *Elphingston,* and *Burley,* I protest :
Borthwick, and *Dalyiell, Oglebie,* and *Skune,*
Cowper, and *Ramsay, Bruntilland,* Lord *Doune :*
Lovit, Halyrudehouse, Cranston, Blantyre,
Kinclevin, Balmarinoch, Lindores, Kintyre :
Madertie, Torphichen, and *Viscont Aire ;*
Carnagy, Drumlanerk, Weems, and *Traquaire :*
Desfurd, and *Iedbrugh, Colvin :* And how far,
May I, even with the best, bring *Lochinvar :*
With *Luce,* and *Waghton, Iohnson,* too and *Keire,*
Who know'th but they may *Lords* be the next yeare ?
Drum and *Glennorchy* too, I well may rank,
In way of Honour, sitting at their flank.

All these bee thyne, thy *Darlings,* and the knot,
Which tye my freedome, to each worthy *Scot ;*
Being religious Lords, and wele reformd,
From Superstition, and to trueth conformd :
And if some be not so, (dissemblers then)
They're scoffing Atheists irreligious Men :
For if the inward, with the outward show
Agree not; then they're *Hipocrits* I know,
But each and all of them, doe make profession,
Of CHRISTS reformed *Church,* by cleare confession,

*The Con-
dition of
Papist
Lords.*

As for my *Papist Lords,* its hard to say,
Whether the *Pope,* or *Thee,* they best obey,
For Mee, I will not count them, or make doubt,
But they may soone be tould, being here left out,
But this I may avouch, though they're enclynd,
In show to *Thee ; Rome* keeps their heart and mynd :
Contayning more, seven Hills within her walles,
And why, not too, their silly Hearts and Saules :

For

For there are holes and Caues, and ruind Pits,
And *Vineyards* too, to which my *Papist flits :*
Yea ; stinking Pudles, of *Sodomitick* lyues,
Where best the *Boy* with the *Cardinall* thryues.

   Yea ; and this *Pope Vrban,* ones my Protector,
To *Masculine* mis'rye was *Architector :*
Witnesse *Bullogne, Ravenna, Ferrare Torine,*
Ancona too, plac'd by the *Adrian Marine,*
What then *Romes Legat,* that's now *Pope* committed?
It were an odious thing to be omitted :
For when my Youths, he then surnamd my head
Came to him, seeking succour : O I then with speed I
If that the face was good, he soone calld in,
And gaue them Crownes, with blak *Gomorrahaes* sin :
Witnesse *Iack Ogelbie,* thou canst report,
What way this *Pope,* thy screeking *Bomb* did court?
For which this *Lad* beene grieu'd, in very spight,
He stole nyne hundreth Crownes, and took the flight,
From this same *Pope,* then *Card'nall Barbarino ;*
And came to *Venice,* crossd the *Alps* to *Rhino.*

   I could tell tyme and place, and how he vsd
This Youth with many moe, whom he abusd :
But now *Divell* fetch him, what should I reveale ?
He lou'd my *Lads* posteriour parts too wele :
In *Rome* and *Italy* was never seene,
A greater *Sodomit* than he hath beene :
He was my *Scots Protector,* and infectd them,
With beastly filthinesse, so he protectd them.

   Then heere's their *Pope,* his Holinesse indeed ;
CHRISTS *Viccar,* S*t. Peters* heyre, their *Churches head !*
O I *Monster* against *Nature ! O Desolation !*
O *filthy Wretch ! O vyld abomination !*
Downe stinking Sow, downe Beast to *Plutoes Cell,*
Instead of *Heaven,* keepe there the Ports of *Hell.*

   Now Priest haue with thee, for a single bout,
For well could I (if tyme seru'd) paynt thee out :

       G

What's now thy *Masse* ? (come tell me) nay its such ;
A foolish fopprie, that I dare avouch,
It is the sink of Sinne, the nest of errour ;
The gulfe of *Superstition ;* and the *Mirrour*
Of blinded *Ignorance ;* whose mumbling mood ;
Even in the action is not vnderstood.
 And there's the *Masse, Idolatrie* compleets !
The *Priest,* his owne *Creator* frames and eats :
But more thy *Blasphemy ;* O subtile foxe !
That dares to lock thy God within a *Boxe ;*
To be consum'd with *Mothes,* and wormish gnats,
Yea; worne with *Tyme,* and eaten vp with *Rats :*
As for thy *Miracles,* and penny-*pardons,*
Thy purging *Pit, Indulgences,* and *Guerdons :*
I know what thou confessd, thou touldst mee plaine,
They were but forged leyes, for getting gayne :
I could at length show hundreths of like errours :
Whose works, and wayes, of *Hell,* are meerest *Mirrours.*
O what delusions ? and what Divelish drifts ?
Of cursd suggestions, in the jugling shifts ;
Of false Opinion, intricat their braines
With blind diversion ; and with halting straynes,
Of bould Presumption ; thus dare cast the Mould,
Of their incestuous lust ; for now behould !
They trust in their owne labours, and degresse
From Gods true worship, in their mumbling *Masse,*

*The igno-
rance of
Papists.*   But for my Noble Brood, and crew of *Papists,*
They liue more by opinion, as do *Atheists,*
Than any sound construction ; for tradition
Is all they looke for in their superstition :
Yet when my *Church* threats excomunication,
As soone they find some wrested dispensation,
Or els forbearance : why ? Because they're Earles,
And court *Thy Court,* to beg *Thy* favour *Charles :*
Let this be help'd, for both to hould, and hunt,
Is more than ever sound *Religion* wont.

                                    And

And call to minde what *David* he would do.
First clenge his *house,* and then his *Kingdome* too ;
Say, if the Spring be sowre, how can the streame
Be sweet ; or how can light from darknesse gleame ?
For great *Ones* they are *Presidents,* and may
Bring good or bad into a commoun swey :
So People by example, more than *Loue,*
Are brought to follow what *Superiours* moue.
O ! if I might, as *Pastors* ought and should
GODS judgements show, and not for flattry hould :
I soone would show the cause why GODS offended,
And plagues vs so in all our drifts intended.
    But now allace ! Mens earthly mynded favour,
Can wound their zeale, and blind their sight for savour :
Yet of all *Preachers,* which my bounds contayne,
There's onely *Ramsay* of *Drumfreis* takes payne ;
To curb, and to convert, or els bring vnder
These stinging *Wasps* of ignorance the wonder ;
For he is placd in midst of the worst fry,
Of all these *Locusts,* which GODS word deny.
    But true it is, these *Idole-servers* may,   *Lack of*
Laugh at our coldnesse in good works this day :   *Charity.*
There is no Charity, nor true intent,
By the disposers of it, done, or meant ;
As ringing *Bells* cite others to the *Church,*
But they themselues neu'r enter at the *Porch :*
So many *Cymballs* sound through diverse throates,
And rayse their voyces contrare to their notes :
Whilst all their *Tunes* in such distracted mirth,
Are clog'd with clay, heart-grown vnto the Earth :
Which LITHGOVVS surveigh of my bounds, I know.
More amply shall in plainer tearmes show :
There's heere a mystery, which few can tell,
Vnles *Theology* the passage spell.
    Yet aboue all, let *Priests,* and *Papists* be,
Forc'd to convert, or banish'd quite from Mee :
        G 2   And

And show them no more ruth, then they show Myne,
In *Spaine*, and *Rome*, who strictly punish Thyne :
For it stands good, that lyke, for lyke againe,
Should be inflicted, lyke punishment, lyke paine.

Sir Willi-am Alex-ander Lord Secretary of Scotland.

    Now touch I *Menstrie*, fraught with crimson flames,
Of *Acedalian* fyre; whom *Hymen* frames,
The *Muses Darling ;* whilst *Appollo* vowes,
To sit betwene the *Temples* of his browes ;
And there knit *Garlands*, twist with *Delphian* bayes,
To crowne his sacred strayne, with divyne prayse :
Whence hee proclaymes him, *Prince*, of *Poets* all,
That ever *Albion* bred, or could enstall :
    But what I most admyre, and must commend,
Are these his rare adventures, he do'th send :
Hence t' *Americk ;* whence *Cannada* confynes,
His new layd limits : *Reason* too combynes,
A constant resolution, there to plant,
My *Noua Scotia ;* where nothing can want,
For grounds both fat, and fertile; their curling plaines,
Are cled with Woods; there wealth to Countrey *Swaines*,
May copiously aryse : Their *Rye* and *Wheat*,
With Cornes and grayne, might soone be brought compleet :
There *Pastorage* excells, their fish abound,
There flying Foule, and speedy *Cerfs* are found :
The Soyle a Climat cleare, the Seasons fayre,
Where fragrant fruits surpasse, Hearbs grow most rare.
    To which if that my Nobles, would but lend,
Their helping hands, and their provision send,
Of Folks and Bestiall, Seed, and euery thing.
O what encrease should this Plantation bring !
In doing which, they should enlarge my Name,
Making my bowells, famous in their fame :
And to which end, I vow, my *Pilgrime* would
Adventure too, provyding he had gould.
    There Christ shall be professd, the *Gospell* preachd,
And savage *Bruites* borne there, Salvation teachd :

And Soveraigne LORD, KING CHARLES.

From which braue *Menstrie,* in his matchles merit,
Shall prayse on *Earth,* reward from *Heaven* inherit :
Then *Alexander,* let that *Province* be,
Call'd *Alexandria,* from this name of *Thee ;*
That after Ages may the same record,
Thou was the first *Plantator* there, and *Lord ;*
Which simpathizeth well with that great King,
The *Macedonian Conqu'rour,* who did bring
The easterne World in bonds, made *Ganges* be,
The *Frontier* of his *fortunes ;* leaving *Thee,*
This *Patrimoniall.* place, the westmost *Mayne ;*
For to renew his memorie againe :
So *Menstrie, Thou,* with *Asiaes* great Commander,
Shall twise succeed, a second *Alexander.*

    Last plead I for my selfe, now my request,
Most Royall Sir, flowes from a prostrat brest ;
Even from the *Torrid Zone* of myne affection ;
I beg *Thy* deepest *Loue,* and deare *Protection :*
That twixt *Thy Heart* and *Soule,* two *Tropicks* great,
I vnder-plac'd, may find *Thy* radiant heat :
Whose tender Care, whose Deeds, whose Zeale Divyne,
May be *Heavens Æquinox* to Mee, and Mine :
That from *Thy Beames,* I frozen, may recoile,
As hot a flame, as Parcheth, *Æthiops* Soile :
So shall these *Circles, Hemi-spheares* of *Loue,*
And these fix'd *Planets,* which no storm can moue ;
Be my sole *Zodiack,* and the *Horizon,*
For to perfite, and crowne my glistring *Zone ;*
That *Thou* my *Worlds* great eye, and thy designes,
May happy be, through *Heavens Celestiall* signes :
So shall my *Faith,* and duety, be the *Polles,*
Whereon the *Axle-Tree,* of thy *Scepter* rolles :
Whence let these rayes *Antartick,* thy best glory
Reflexe on Mee, thine *Artick* Soile, growne hoary.

    And though my *Saturne Cape* salutes the *Starre,*
Which guides most Pilots, yet who can debarre ?

Scotlands recommendation to his Maiestie.

G 3   Mine

Mine *Iles*, and mayne dimensious bounds to yeeld
Thee, Martialists, the best on earth for field :
I am thine eldest *Daughter*, and my *Birth ;*
Thy nearest *Subjects* living vpon *Earth.*
    But why plead I so much ? Why paint I forth ?
My *Sonnes* in their illuminary worth :
Since thou art posting back to *Isis* banks,
And leaues me naked, onely cled with thanks.

Scotlands
sorrow for
his Maie-
sties quick
returne.

    Now must I spinne my long spunne web, and knit
Penelope, within the length of it :
Whilst *Memphis* groanes, to see sad *Sparta* mourne,
Twixt two arryvalls, and a quick returne :
Ah ! well I see the Sunne, when at the hight,
Must soone declyne to bring on darksome night :
And are my joyes fled, my *Darling* gone,
Like to the shaddow of some wandring *One ;*
I, I, thy stay to Mee, and Thy goodnight,
Seem'd but the glauncing of a *Faulcons* flight ;
Which makes my *Bowells* roare, my griefe resounds it,
There's none can heale my sore, but *Thow* who wounds it.

    That shearing Sword, which sharply stroke the *Heart,*
Of bleeding *Loue,* when *Æneas* did depart ;
Neu'r rent kynd *Dido* with a deeper wound,
Than thy departure makes my soul to stound ;
Even like *Palmeno,* paunting on his Bed,
Still wishing Death, or els his ayme to wed.

    But more kind *Turtle*-set, O Heart-growne-griefe !
To groane, till *Heavens* soone send my playnts reliefe,
I see ebbe foords, though shallow, bellowing roare,
Whilst deepest streames, in silence court the Shoare ;
So mighty Cares grow mute, when slender woes
Find choisest tearmes, slight sorrowes to disclose :
As deepest *Loue* is ever safest kept,
So is pale griefe more sadly closd, than weept :
What then, though woes get words, I'le deeply mourne
With sighs, salt teares, and sobs, till *Thy* returne.

                                        The

The wasting *Winter* of the *Sommers* gayne,
Neu'r wishd the *Spring*, the *Spring*, the *Harust* againe ;
With more celeritie, than I implore
Thy presence, were as oft renew'd, and more.
    Lyke to the Day-worne *Pilgrime*, shut from light ;
Closd with dark Coverts of the clowdie night,
Longs for the *Aurore* of the sequell Morne,
To see the face-blushd *Thetis* Sonne, new borne :
    So I wrapt vp, within the gloomy shade
Of sad oblivion, am a *Mourner* made ;
Till thy returne, (like to *Nocturnall* dew,)
Resume, refresh this flame, that burnes for you :
Which soone I wish might be reveiu'd and seene,
Cled with like glory, as *Thow* now hast beene :
Which if it were reciprocall, O well !
My Comforts could aboue my griefe excell :
Yet since *Thine* absence must my *Patience* proue ;
I'le cease to mourne, but never cease to loue.
    Then in a word, (though thousands ly in store)
I'le end, and this on my low knees implore ;
Yea *Heavens* which shaddow, and protect just KINGS,
With MIGHT and MERCY ; deoperculat wings,
Of LIGHT and GLORY, still saue, and defend
Mine happie MONARCH, both in Lyfe, and end,
With present BLESSINGS, future HOPES in IOVE,
PEACE heere on EARTH, and hence eternall LOVE.

F I N I S.

THE GUSHING
T E A R E S
OF GODLY
S O R R O W.

CONTAINING,

The Causes, Conditions, and
Remedies of Sinne,

Depending mainly upon Contrition
and Confession.

And they seconded, with Sacred and
Comfortable passages, under the mourning CANNOPIE of TEARES,
and REPENTANCE.

MATTH. 5. 4.
Blessed are they that mourne, for they shall be comforted.

PSAL. 126. 5.
They that sow in teares, shall reape in joy.

By WILLIAM LITHGOVV.

EDINBURGH,
Printed by ROBERT BRYSON,
ANNO DOM. 1640.
At the expences of the Authour.

TO THE

TRVLY NOBLE

MAGNANIMOVS

AND

ILLUSTRIOUS LORD,

IAMES,

EARLE OF MONTROSE,

Lord GRAHAME, Baron of

MURDOCK, &c.

Illustrious LORD,

F gratefull duetie, may be re-
puted the childe of reason,
then (doubtlesse) my choisest
wishes, and best Affection,
must here fall prostrate before your auspicuous and friendlie face, fast chayned, in
the fetters of obedience.   Flatterie and In-

A 2

gratitude

gratitude I disdayne as hell : And to court your Lo : with elegant phrases, were indeed as much as who would light a Candle, to light the Sunne : Your Noble and Heroicke Vertues light this Kingdome, and who can give them light : For, as the *Aurore*, of your honoured reputation, is become that *Constantinopolitan Hyppodrome*, to this our Northrene and virgine *Albion ;* so lykewise, the same singularitie of worth, hath raised your auspicuous selfe, to be the monumentall glorie of your famous, and valiant Predecessours, justly tearmed, THE SWORD OF SCOTLAND : Your morning of their Summers day hath fullie enlarged, the sacred Trophees of their matchlesse memorie ; best befitting the generositie of your magnanimous minde. That as the GRAHAME, from long antiquitie, being the most ancient surname, of this unconquerd Nation ; so they, your old aged Ancestors, have left a lineall construction of their Valour and Worthinesse, to bee inherent

herent in your most hopefull personage, which God may long continue to you, your Race, and your Posteritie. My humble request, pleads the continuance of your favour, that as your late renowned Grandfather and Father, were unto mee both friendlie and favourable (proceeding from their great goodnesse, not my deserts ;) so expect I the same from your tender bountie, which hitherto beyond my merit, hath beene exceeding kyndlie manifested. For the which, my prayse and prayers, the two sisters of myne Oblation, rest solidlie ingenochiated at the feete of your conspicuous Clemencie. This present worke in its secret Infancie, was both seene and perused by your Lo : but now enlarged, polished, and published : I have done my best, though not my uttermost : The discourse it selfe, runneth most on the causes, conditions, and remedies of sin, and they sharply linked in generalls and particulars :

The whole substance of my labours, sealing vp the happinesse of a sinners conversion to God, under the mourning Cannopie, of *Teares*, and *Repentance*. The lynes are plaine, yet pithie; and although the subject may carrie no loftie nor Poëticke style; yet the manner, the matter, the Man, and his Muse, are all, and only yours, and I left theirs, onlie to serve you, and your noble disposition. Accept therefore my good Lord, both the gift, and givers minde, with the same alacritie, as I offer them in Love and humilitie; which being shelterd under your pious and prudent Patronage, shall enforce mee to remaine, as I vow ever to be, whilst I have being,

Your Honours most obsequious
and most observant Oratour,

William Lithgovv.

The Prologue to the Reader.

Hou mayst peruse this worke, with kynde respect,
Cause ; none my good intention can controule ;
The style may (not the subject) beare defect,
Some Painter *will the fayrest face drawe foule :*
Excuse myne age, if faultie, blame my quill,
Defects may fall, and not fayle in goodwill.

My Muse declynes, downe slyde her loftie straynes
And hoarie growes, succumbing to the dust ;
Old wrung inventions, from industrious paynes
Draw to the grave, where death must feede his lust :
Flesh flye in ashes, bones returne to clay,
Whence I begunne, there must my substance stay.

Goe thou laborious pen, and challenge tyme,
For memorie, to all succeeding ages ;
In thy past workes, and high heroicke ryme,
And pregnant prose, in thryce three thousand pages :
Yet dye thou must, and Tyme shall weare thee out,
Ere seaven tymes seaven, worne ages goe about.

But Vertue claymes her place, and prostrate I
Must yeelde due honour, to her noble name :
Shee taught mee to take paynes, its done, and why ?
To make her famous, in her flying fame :
A Sculler, may transport, a royall Queene,
As well as Oares, and both their safeties seene.

Trust mee, my paynes, contend, for to bee playne
No style Poeticke, may this subject clayme :
Touch but Vermilion, *you shall see a stayne,*
No fiction, may averre, a sacred Theame :

Nor

The Prologue to the Reader.

Nor dare Panthoas, Cynthias *herball flowre*
Be seene, nor spread, till rolling Phœbus *lowre.*

Then read, misconster not, but wisely looke
If I divinely, keep a divine stile :
Which done, thou mayst, take pleasure in this booke,
An Infant, from devotion, bred the while :
Like treatise I, before neere wrote ; excuse
This new borne birth, from mine old aged Muse.

See ! here in generals, thou mayst observe
The cause of sinne, sinnes remedy, salt teares ;
Where sharpe particulars, for repentance serve
To blazon wickednesse, and wicked feares :
What here is done, to thee, to me, to all,
May be apply'd, as each one findes his fall.

Yet who can stop, base Critick *tongues to carpe,*
For Atheists *shall, and* Epicures *repine ;*
So scoffing fooles, on strings of scorne will harpe
To see this myte, a part of myne engyne :
But silly Gnats, worse bred then Berdoan *beasts,*
I slight their spight, my Muse in Sion *feasts.*

Would thou contend with me, who best should write
On choice of Theames, select'd between us twaine,
I could abide thy censure, take delite
In thy defects, to censure thee againe :
Since thou sits dumbe, and cannot bite, but barke,
Peace, hold thy peace, else show me thine owne wark.
But zealous eyes may come, come, and come soone,
To read this Task, if pleasd, Lo ! I have done.

To the godly and good Christian,
a fellow suppliant in Christ,

WILLIAM LITHGOVV.

THE
GVSHING TEARES
OF
GODLY SORROW.

Pring sweet cœlestial Muse, launch forth a flood,
Of brinish streams, in cristall melting woes ;
Rain-rill my plaints, then bath them in Christs blood
Let pearling drops, my pale remorse disclose :
  Sink sorrow in my soule, divulge my grief.
  Who mourns, and mourns in time, shall finde relief.

I can not reach, to what my soule would aime !
But help good God my weaknesse, and support
My bashfull quill : O ! teach me to disclaime
My self, and cleave, to thy all-saving Port :
  Touch thou my heart, so shall my lips recoile,
  Thine Altars praise, to sing sins utmost spoile.

Thrice blest is he who mournes, he shall rejoyce
Whilst godly sorrow, shall encrease his joy :
Lord heare my cryes, remarke my weeping voice !
Blesse thou this work, let grace my heart imploy ;
  That what these Tears aford, in this plain storie,
  May tend to my souls health, and thy great glorie.

                    Great

The gushing Teares

Great Son, of the great God, fulnesse of time !
Whom Heavens applaude, whom earth fals down before !
The promis'd Pledge, whom Prophets most sublime ;
Foretold to come, our Lord, the Son of glore :
    To thee knee-bowd, before thy face I fall,
    Come help, O help ! now I begin to call.

Most holy, mighty, high, and glorious God !
Most mercifull, most gracious, and kinde ;
Most Ancient, righteous, patient, and good,
Most wise, most just, most bountifull of minde ;
    Infuse thy grace, enlarge thy love in mine,
    Confirme my faith, conforme my will to thine.

Eternall One ! Beginner, unbegunne !
Thou first, and last ; Heavens founder, and Earths hall !
Container, uncontaind ! Father, and Sonne !
Thou All in All ! unruld, yet ruling All !
    Great Light, of lights ! who moves all things unmovd .
    Hearke, help, and heare ; for Christs sake thy belovd.

Sole Soveraigne Balme ! come heale my wounded soule !
Which fainting fals, under thine heavie hand ;
Regard my plaints, remit mine errours foule,
Let mercy far, above thy justice stand :
    Be thou my Heaven, place Heaven within mine heart,
    Thy presence can make Heaven, where e're thou art.

Come challenge me ! come claime me for thine owne !
Plead thou thy right, take place in my possession ;
Lord square my steps, thy goodnesse may be knowne,
In pard'ning each defect of my transgression :
    Arrest my sinnes, but let my soule goe free,
    Baile me from thrall, let sinne deaths subject die.

                                     Lord

of godlie sorrow.

Lord wing my love, with feather'd faith to flee,
To thy all-burning Throne, of endlesse glory ;
Mercie is thine, for mercy is with thee,
Lord write my name, in thine eternall story :
   O ! help my strength ! farre weaker than a reed !
   Accept my purpose, for the reall deed.

The good I would, alace ! I can not do,
The ill I would not, that I follow still ;
The more thou citst me, I grow stubborn too,
Preferring base corruption to thy will :
   For when thy Sprite, to serve Thee, doth perswade me,
   The World, the Flesh, and Satan they disswade me.

What should I say ? no gift in me is left
To doe, to speak, to think, one godly motion ;
Lord help my wants, for why ? my soule is reft,
'Twixt feare and hope, 'twixt sinne, and true devotion :
   Faine would I flighter, from this lust-lymd clay,
   But more I strive, the more I faster stay.

Lord, with the sonne forlorne, bring me againe,   Application, and invocation.
And cloth me, with the favour of thy face,
The swinish husks of sinne I loath, and faine
Would be thy childe (adopt'd) the childe of grace ;
   Thy Lambe was kill'd, for my conversions sake,
   Of which let me, some food and comfort take.

Thy glorious Hierarchy, and Martyres all,
Rejoyce, at the returne, of a lost sheep :
Lord, in that number, let my portion fall,
That I with them, like melodie may keep :
   So with thy Saints, my happynesse shall be,
   One, and the same, as they are blest in Thee.

The gushing Teares

Yet whilst I pause, and duely do consider,
Thy will, my wayes, thy righteousnesse, mine errours,
I cannot plead, to flie, I know not whidder,
So grievous, are, the mountains of my terrours :
  My sinnes so ugly, stand before thy face,
  That I dare hardly claime, or call for grace.

What am I in thine eyes ? if I could ponder ?
But brickle trash, compos'd of slyme and clay ;
A wretch-worne worme, erect'd for sinne a wonder,
Whilst my souls treason, is thy judgements prey :
  I have no health, nor truth, nor divine flashes,
  So wicked is this Masse, of dust and ashes.

Humble implorati-ons. Lord stretch thine arme, put Satan to the flight,
Exile the world from me, and me from it ;
Curbe thou my flesh, beat down my lusts delight,
Rule thou my heart, my will guide with thy Sprit ;
  Infuse, encrease, confirme here, from above,
  Thy feare, thy law, in me, thy light, thy love.

So shall I through Heavens merit onely rise,
And kisse thy soule-sought sonne, thy Lambe, thy Dove,
For whose sweet sake, I shall thy sight surprise,
And lift my hope, on his redeeming love :
  Blest be the price, of mine exalting good !
  Who payd my ransome, with his precious blood.

In Thee I trust, Lord help my wavering faith,
And with thy merits, my demerits cover ;
Dispell my weaknesse, strengthen my faint breath,
Renew my life, and my past sinnes, passe over :
  Be thou my Pilot, guide this barke of clay,
  Safe to the Port, of thy coelestiall stay.

                                                    Grant

of godlie sorrow.

Grant me obedience to thy blest desire,
Instruct my minde, environe me with ruth ;
Cleanse thou my heart, with flames of sacred fire,
Fraught with the fulnesse, of thy saving truth :
    Build up mine Altar, let mine offerings be
    Faith, feare, and hope, love, praise, and thanks to Thee.

Lord ! spare me for his sake, whom thou not spard,
For my sake ; even for him, from Thee above
Was sent downe here and slaine : O ! what regard
Bore thou to Man ; to send thy Sonne of Love,
    To suffer for my guilt, the fault being mine,
    But (ah !) good Lord, the punishment was thine.

Thy love great God, from everlasting flowes
To everlasting ; Mans reach onely brings
Forth the Creation ; but thy love forth showes
From all eternitie, eternall springs
    Of light unsearchable ; then praise we Thee,
    That ere time was, ordain'd our time to be.

God made all things, and God was made a Man,
All things he made of nothing ; but come see ?
Withoutten man, all things (the truth to scan)
Had turnd to nothing ; for from one degree
    God of himselfe, made all things : and what more ?
    He would not all things, without Man restore.

The Creators great love towards us his creatures.

He was of God begotten, all things made,
And borne of woman, all things did renew ;
For without man, all things had been a shade,
So nothing well, without a Virgin true :
    Thus God, and Man, conjoynd in one we feele,
    Life of our life, and soule of our souls weele.

B 3

What

The gushing Teares

What was he made? and what hath he made us?
I pause with joy, with silence I admire!
This mystery I adore! who can discusse?
That goodnesse great, sprung from so good a Syre:
   Can reason show, more reasonable way,
   Than leave to pry, where reason can not swey.

The Sonne of God, (behold!) was made a Man!
To make us men, th'adopted sonnes of God:
By which he made himself, our brother then,
For in all kindes, he keeps our brotherhood:
   Though Judge (save sinne) and Intercessour, see!
   He brothers us, we must his suppliants be.

With what assurance, then may we all hope,
What feare can force, despaire, or yet distrust?
Since our salvation, and our endlesse scope,
Hangs on our elder brother, Christ the Just:
   He'le give us all the good, which we desire,
   And pardon all the sinnes, on us engvre?

Christs inesteemable love. The burden of our miseries he bore,
And laid his merits weight, on our sick soules;
A kindnesse beyond reach; his goodnesse more,
Engross'd his name, for us, in shamefull scroules:
   O! wondrous love, that God should humble thus,
   Himself, and take Mans shape, to rescue us.

He who in heavens was admirable set,
Became for us, contemptible on earth;
And from the Towre, of his Imperiall state,
Imbrac'd a Dungeon, for angelick mirth;
   And chang'd the name, of Majestie in love,
   To shelter us, with mercy from above.

What

of godlie sorrow.

What eyes for grief, should not dissolve in floods ?
Whilst our vile sinnes, procur'd his woofull paine :
He sought our well (unsought) when we in woods
Of wickednesse, lay wallowing amaine ;
    And daily yet, by sinne, distrust, and strife,
    We crucifie againe, the Lord of life.

As irne in fire cast, takes fires nature,
And yet remaineth irne, though fram'd, what than ?
So he, who in Gods love doth burne, that creature
Partakes his holynesse, abiding man ;
    For love, seals up Gods counsels, ends the law,
    From which we sinners, cords of mercy draw.

Love, is the roote of vertue, and the childe
Of grace ; Truths mistresse, and religions glasse ;
The soule of goodnesse, in perfection milde,
The crowne of Saints, that conquer Paradise :
    The joy of Angels : O ! what springs of love !
    Flow from the Law, for us, and our behove.

Love con-
quers hea-
ven.

Ingratefull Man ! contemner of thy good,
Can thou not back-bestow, thy debt-bund love !
To him, for thee, did shed his precious blood,
And though rebuk'd, yet would he not reprove :
    Why did he fast, weep, watch, and labour take ?
    In basenesse and contempt, but for thy sake.

Then be not like, that plant *Ephemeron !*
Which springs, and growes, and fades, all in one day ·
But plead remorse, beg for contrition,
Mourne for thy sinnes, make haste, prevent delay :
    In this my self, shall to my selfe returne,
    He best can weep, that knowes the way to mourne.

I

The gushing Teares

Obsequious confessions.

I rather seem'd than been religious set.
Having *Jacobs* voice, and *Esau's* rough hands ;
I make profession, practise I forget,
My better zeale, hypocrisie commands ;
   I serpent like, do change my skinne, but not
   Disgorge the poison, lurkes within the throate.

Vice I have us'd, under a vertuous seeming,
And like the sea, though rivers in it fall ;
Yet not the sweeter ; or like *Pharaohs* dreaming,
The leane kine, yet were leane, when eaten all :
   Stay then dry soule, where are thy Teares ? what springs ?
   Should thy pale eyne cast out, when sorrow sings.

A distinction twixt worldly and godly teares.

I meane not childrens tears, when whipt for aw,
Nor mundane teares, for losse of trash or geare ;
Nor spightfull teares, which would revenge downe draw :
Nor teares of grief, for them concerne us neare ;
   Nor teares for death, nor teares for what disasters ;
   Nor teares for friends ; nor wives teares for men wasters.

Nor drunken teares, spent after sugred wine,
Which women waste, to colour imperfection ;
Nor *Dalilahs* fained teares, to undermine,
The strong mans strength, by way of fals detection :
   Nor *Sinons* teares, the *Trojane* state betrayde,
   With the wooden horse, *Ulysses* wit bewrayde.

Nor faigned teares, the *Crocadilean* sexe,
Do spend (I meane) their husbands to deceave ;
Nor these *Courtegian* teares, that love to vexe
Their sottish *Palliards*, and their meanes bereave :
   Nor teares of pitty, mercy beg from men,
   That's not the drift, of my obsequious pen.

                             Looke

of godlie sorrow.

Looke to thy lapses, and quotidian falling,
Then try thy conscience, if remorse creeps in ;
Which if it doe, thou art brought to this calling,
Of godly weeping, for the guilt of sinne !
    These tears are blest, and such mine eyes would borrow,
    But not these tears, which melt, for worldly sorrow.

Lord, strengthen me, wlth knowledge of thy word,
Square thou my judgment, I may walk upright ;
An intellective Heart, my soule aford,
Endue my sprite, with supernatrall light ;
    Faine would I slaughter sinne, that would me slay,
    And learne thy truth, Lord teach me thy right way.

Confound in me, this all-predominant sinne,
Which overrules my reason, sense and will ;
One head-strong vice, that lurkes, and lyth within
The inmost center, of mine utmost ill :
    Lord, curbe its force, and purifie my soule,
    From such uncleannesse, for its wondrous foule.

Grant ! grant remorse ! let godly sorrow show !
My full-swolne sight, my brinish tears, my sadnesse ;
Come sowre repentance, let sweet contrition know !
The mourning woes, of my rejoycing gladnesse :
    What though that grief, at morne worke me annoy,
    Yet long ere night, thou'le turne my grief in joy.

The best man lives, hath one predominant ill,   <small>The re-</small>
Oppos'd to the best good, he can effect ;   <small>pugnancie</small>
The worst man breaths, though curs'd, pervers'd of will,   <small>of ill and</small>
Hath some predominant good, he doth affect :   <small>good.</small>
    Even either answering, contrare to their kinde,
    Seeme to resemble, what they never finde.

C

Lord !

The gushing Teares

Lord! what am I, whose best is even accurst,
Who with thy Convert, is of sinners chief:
A sharde unsav'rie, of thy works the worst,
Unlesse thy grace, renew me with reliefe:
    Lord! will my well! prepare my heart, give eare,
    If faith can call, O! thou canst quickly heare.

The poore which almes seeks, he gets not aide
For any need, the giver hath of him;
But even because, he hath of us great need;
So we by faith, on Christian steps must clim:
    For God of his great love, he freely gives us,
    And without need of man, he still relieves us.

Contrary
extremi-
ties. A *Cynick* came, and ask'd the *Syrian* king,
Antigonus; a dram of silver coyne;
But he reply'd, it was too base a thing
For kings to give, or lend so small a loane:
    Said *Cynick* then, I would a talent crave,
    But thats too much, for thee (said he) to have.

Thus two extreams, were both extreamly met,
But its not so with God, and sinfull men;
The more we seeke, the more we're sure to get,
God of his bounty, is so good, that when
    We mercy crave, he grants it, gives us grace,
    Our wills and wayes, may in his precepts trace.

Lift up my falling minde, Lord! knit my heart
With cords of love, and chaines of grace to thee;
As *Jonathans* three arrows, did impart
To *Davids* woes, true signes of amitie:
    So rouze my sprite, let grace and goodnesse spell
    Mine Annagram, I LOVE ALMIGHTY WEL.

O!

of godlie sorrow.

O ! if I could, byte off the head of sinne !
As the shee Viper, doth the male confound ;
But not like her, whose brood conceiv'd within,
Cut forth her wombe, leave her dead on the ground :
    Lord ! grant, I sinne may slay, ere sinne slay me,
    The wounds are deep, my health consists in Thee.

Lord ! when I ponder on this worldly pride,
Vaine glory, riches, honour, noble birth,
Great lands, and rents, faire palaces beside,
Pastimes, and pleasures, fit-thought things on earth,
    Without thy love, and in regard of thee,
    They're nought but shaddows, of meere vanitie.

All under sunne, are emblems of deceit,
Link'd snares, to trap, blind man in ev'ry vice ;
They're feather'd baits, prest grines, that lye in wait,
To catch the buyer, unvaluing their pryce :
    Then carelesse soule, take heed, prevent this danger,
    Lay hold on Christ, and be no more a stranger.

The world is a mappe of evils.

Gods will allots, that my past curious sights,
In painfull prime, all where the world abroad ;
Should be repaid, with as darke cloudie nights
Of sorrows sad ; for now I finde the rod ;
    Sicknesse, and crosses, compasse me about,
    Whence none but Christ, can help or rid me out.

Listen to me, as to thy *Lazar* poore,
Thats overstamp'd with seals, of scabs, and sores ;
Both vile and wretch'd, lyth at thy mercies doore,
Begging for crummes of pitie ; and implores
    That thou wouldst open, with *Lydia* my heart,
    And make me *Sauls* dear second, thy Convert.

                           Thy

The gushing Teares

Thy lengthning hand, is now no more cut short,
Than in old times, of wonder-working dayes,
But thou canst turne, and safely bring to Port,
The wilsome Wandrer, from his sinfull wayes:
    O then great Sheepherd! pitie a lost sheep!
    And bring me home; safe in thy fold me keep.

Thou art the vine, I am the twisted branch,
Which on thy roote, my hopes must humbly twine;
For in thy sap, my sin-galld wounds, I'le quench,
No balme of *Gilead*, to that Balme of thine:
    O! better things, than *Abels* blood it speaks!
    It saves the world, and Mans salvation feeks.

Christs teares over Jerusalem. How sacred were these teares? fell from thine eyes:
When for *Jerusalem*, thou wept so sore:
Mercy did plead, deploring their disease,
For pitties sake, thou didst their well implore:
    A kindnesse passing love! when for thy foes
    Thou wept and cryde for; prophecying their woes.

That spikenard oyle, which on thy feet was spred!
Doth represent to me that bloody balme;
Which on the crosse, from thy left side was shed,
To slay the power of sinne, make Satan calme:
    O! let that oyle, by grace sinke in my soule,
    To heale my sores, and cleanse mine errours foule.

Breake downe the rock, of my hard flinty heart!
Let moisture thence, ascend to my two springs;
The head contains these Rills, let them impart,
Signes of contrition, godly sorrow brings:
    O! happy floods! of ever-springing joyes!
    That in the midst of weeping can rejoyce.

When

of godlie sorrow.

When pale remorse, strikes on my conscience sad,
Mov'd with the lapse, of my relapsing sinne;
Faith flees above, and bids my soule be glad,
Where mercy enters, judgement comes not in;
   One sigh in need, flowne from a mourning spirit,
   Thou'le not reject, being cast on Jesus merit.

We should
not despair
but hope
for mercy.

Come gracious God, infuse in me full grace!
Wrought by thy Sprite, my souls eternall good:
Let mercy plead 'gainst justice; Lord, give place?
The way is thine, my right, rests in Christs blood:
   Come pardon my misdeeds! release my smart!
   Then quicken me, with a relenting heart.

Whilst I conceive mans frailnesse, weake by nature,
How wretch'd he is? how prone to fall or sinke?
Of all thy works, the most rebellious creature:
Clog'd with ingratenesse, ever bent to shrinke.
   What thing is man (think I) thou shouldst regard him,
   And with a crowne of glory to reward him.

Thus pausing too, on long eternall rest,
That boundlesse time, which no time can containe;
How rich thinke I these soules be? and how blest?
In time strive here, that endlesse time to gaine:
   Strive then poore soule, to claime and climbe this Fort:
   For faith and violence, must force Heavens Port.

O Lord! how wondrous is thy powerfull love?
Whose mercies farre, above thy works excell!
Who can thy secret Cabine reach above?
Or sound these deeps, wherein thy counsels dwell?
   When thou for man, turnd man, and suffer'd death,
   To free slaine man, from thy fierce judgements wrath.

Impene-
trable
counsels.

C 3

Thy

The gushing Teares

Thy wayes are all inscrutable to Man,
For who can dyve, in thy profounding love;
Whose kindnesse is unspeakable; and whan
We would most comprehend, we least approve:
    Thy wayes, thy works, so farre excell us men,
    The more we strive to know, the lesse we ken.

The
works of
creation.

To look on Heavens, rich star-imbroidred coat,
That Cannopy, of silver-spangled skie;
The glorious firmament, clear without spot,
The Sphearick Planets, as their orders lye;
    The worlds two lamps, erect'd with mareveilous light,
    And Elements, which blinde our dazeling sight.

Darknesse, and light, all quarters, and their Climes,
The rolling Axletree, supporting All;
The Airts, and seasons, in their severall times,
This ovall Orbe, fenc'd with a glassie wall;
    These revolutions, from proud Planets fall,
    Poretnding Comets, Mans prodigious thrall.

The rolling seas, against the stars that swell,
Their reeling tides, their turnes and quiet rest:
These Creatures, and hudge Monsters therein dwell,
Nought here on earth, but that shape there's exprest:
    Their exhalations (earths concavities)
    And shoare-set bound, all wonders to our eyes.

Differen-
ces of man-
kinde.

These phisnomies of men, their variant faces,
Show the Creators wisedome, in creation;
Not one like other, in forme, nor in graces,
Manners, condition, qualitie, nor station:
    O strange! Mans frame, should thus all times be showne,
    By gifts and Vults divers'd, yet clearly knowne.

                      These

These birds ætheriall, glyding fowles that flee,
To court the clouds, alwhere the aire about;
Which nest the Rocks, steep walls, and springing tree,
Whose names, and kindes, none yet could all finde out:
   Each keep their office, set by natures stamp,
   And live, and die, within thy boundlesse Camp.

That influence, which man, beast, hearbs, and trees,
Draw from the silver *Phebe*, of the night:
The signes cœlestiall, aspectives to disease,
The Starres so different in their glorious light:
   Time, that was creat first, and last shall be,
   And ev'ry creature in their own degree.

How marveilous great, art thou almighty God!
Who by thy word, wrought all, and it was done:
Thou spreadst thy works, the Heavens, and earth abroad!
No part left vaste, that can creation shunne:
   O! what is foolish man, the childe of lust!
   That should not in, this great JEHOVAH trust.

Dull are my senses, any way to think,
My blind capacitie, can well conceave,
The supreame providence, by natures wink,
And bound his boundlesse pow'r, unlesse I rave:
   Like, who can once, exhaust the Occean dry?
   No more can I, in his great grandure pry.

A king command'd, a Philosophick man,
To shew him, what was God, and what his might?
He strove, and faild, and said, He could not scan
That greatnesse which excelld, best Natures light:
   The Pagan king admird, and yet this wretch
Confess'd, there was a God, in power rich.

                        To

The gushing Teares

Gods works shevv his Godhead.

To show us there's Deitie, all things ascend,
And mount aloft, as vapour, smoake, and fire,
The trees grow upward, waves when tost transcend,
All birds and fowles, ætherially aspire.
   So words, and voices, still their ecchoes raise,
   And man, whose face, is made on heaven to gaze.

There's nought but worms and beasts, which sight the ground,
But all denote, their great eternall Maker ;
Yet man, wretch'd man, is earth ty'd, and fast bound,
To things below, whereof he's still partaker ;
   Nay ; worse then beasts, he's choak'd with worldly cares,
   And kills his heart with greed, his soule with snares.

What are the humours, of our foggy braines ?
But stupid thoughts, conceiv'd of doubts and feare :
Best pregnant wits, suspition quells their straines ;
The wise, the worldlings, have their Emblemes here :
   A shadow without substance, I finde man,
   Nay worse ! than *Baalams* Asse, the truth to scan.

He sinne reprov'd, yet never sinn'd himselfe,
But wofull man, can both rebuke and sinne ;
That which his words most hate, becomes the shelf,
Whereon his inward lusts, fall deepest in :
   Mans lips are snares, his lips both false and double,
   His tongue, a sting, begets both shame and trouble.

Mans in-firmities.

O heavie lump ! the carcasse of disease ?
O Masse of ill ! the Chaos of corruption ;
O Microcosmos ! of infirmities !
O rotten slyme ! the pudle of inruption !
   I mean mans stinking flesh ; who can expresse ?
   The worst ; its best, is but base filthynesse.

A

# of godlie sorrow.

A plunge of carion clay, a prey for wormes,
A faggot (without mercy) for Hells fire ;
A gulf, where beats, sterne deadly boystrous stormes,
A whirlewinde, for Airts of each attire :
    Wherein combustion, sprung from contrare wills,
    Makes thoughts arise, like waves, surpassing hills.

And what's our beauty ? but a flash-showne show,
For when at best, its filthy, vile, and base :
The nose, the mouth, our excrements we know,
And breath stinke worse, than beasts of any race :
    Nay, sweetest things, than ever time made faire,
    They loathsome grow, unlesse the use be rare.

Mans
beauty,
summers
blossome.

The soule except'd, when I consider all
Gods workes and Creatures, Man is onely worst !
The rest sublunary, succumbent fall ;
Mans onely blest, or else for ever curst :
    All things as servile, serve for mediate ends,
    Save man, whose wage, on joy or woe depends.

Lord ! what am I, within this house of clay ?
But brickle trash, compos'd of slime and dust :
A rotten fabrick, subject to decay,
Which harbours nought, but crums of wretched lust :
    And if a guest, of one good thought, entreates me,
    I barre it out, to lodge the ill, that hates me.

Impietie, and custome, scale my Fort,
To rule my minde, like to their blinde desire :
Will, head-strong helpes ; corruption keeps the Port,
The hands and feet, set eye and tongue on fire :
    Then Eloquence breaks forth, a subtile foe,
    To trap the object, working me the woe.

D

Why ?

The gushing Teares

Self-love
rules the
world.
Why ? cause affection, begets opinion,
Opinion rules the world, in ev'ry minde :
Then sense submits, that pleasure should be Minion,
To base conceit, absurdly grosse, and blinde :
    Thus fond opinion, self loves halting daughter,
    Betrayes my scope, commits me to sinnes slaughter.

Then judgment falls, and fails, and reason flees,
To shelter Wisedome, in some solid breast :
They leave me both, left loaden with disease,
Whilst frailty fastens, sorrow on my creest :
    Delite contracts despite, despyte disdaine,
    Thus threefold chaind, their furies forge my paine.

My best companion, is my deadly foe,
Sin is my consort, and would seeme my friend ;
Yea ; walks with me, wherec're my footsteps goe,
And will not leave me, till my journeys end :
    The more I flee, the faster it cleaves to me,
    And makes corruption, labour to undoe me.

Sinne, and
the causes
of sin.
There six degrees of sinne, in man I finde,
Conception first, and then consent doth follow :
The thirds desire, that turns his judgement blinde :
The fourth is practise, ragged, rent, and hollow :
    The fift is flinty, keeps fast obduration,
    And last, the sixt, lulls him in reprobration.

Mans owne corruption is the seed of sinne,
And custome is, the pudle of corruption :
Swift head-strong habit, traitour-like creeps in,
And blows sinnes bellowes, to make more inruption:
    Nay ; the worlds example, sinnes strong secourse,
    Makes both the object, and the subject worse.

How

of godlie sorrow.

How many foes hath man ? within, without him ?
Within, lurks concupiscence, vertues foe ;
Without, the world, which waits, and hangs about him,
Both ghostly and humane, to worke his woe :
    Last comes the conscience, judge-set to accuse him,
    And verdict given, then terrour would confuse him.

Thus man is ev'ry way, tost to and fro,
Like Tunneise balls, when banded, still rebound :
All things have action, Nature rules it so,
The secret sprite of life, these motions bound :
    Their being honours God, who gave them being,
    But man fals back from him, gave reason seeing.

And yet to quench these fires, remorse creeps in,
And brings contrition, with confession crying :
Faith flees before, pleads pardon for our sin,
Then ragged rottennesse, fals down a dying :
    For repentance, and, remission of sinnes,
    Are two inseparable, sister twinnes.

Most have no teares for sinne, but tears of strife,
To plead malicious pleyes, and waste their meanes
On Lawyers tongues ; that love their envious life,
And what like party loose, the Cormant gleanes :
    Their cause, and charges lost ; O spightfull pride !
    They spend at last, the stock they had beside.

Like to the mouse, and frogge, which did contend,
Which of them should, enjoy the marish ground ;
The Kyte as Judge, discuss'd this cause in end,
And took them both, from what they could not bound :
    So Proctors seaze, on Clyants lands, and walls,
    And raise themselves, in their contentious falls.

Deceitfull
greed.

D 2

They're

The gushing Teares

They're like to *Æsops* dogge, who had a bone,
When through a flood he swim'd, fast in his head :
Where spying his shade, he lets it fall anone,
To catch the other, lost them both indeed :
   So spitefull men and greedy, (well its knowne)
   In seeking others state, they loose their owne.

Thrice blest is he, who knowes, and flyes, like men,
Since greed begets oppression, or debate :
And though Deceivers, play Politicks then,
To make their wrongs, a right, to raise their state :
   Yet forth it comes, no subtilitie can close it,
   For time, and truth, will certainly disclose it.

They thinke to hide their faults, by craft and plots,
To blynde Gods eyes, as they inveigle man :
O strange ! what villany their soule besots,
That dare 'gainst truth, the traitour play ; and than
   Deceive themselves, by a deceitfull way,
   Which tends to death, and make them Satans prey.

Then, there is nought, but once will come to light,
No sinne so close, but God will it discover ;
No policie can blinde Almighties sight,
Nor fault so hid, that he will once passe over :
   Unlesse repentance, draw his mercy downe,
   Thy darkest deeds, shall be disclos'd eft soone.

Jonah dis-
covered.

Behold *Jonah* ! from *Joppa* when he fled !
And would not stay, to do the Lords direction :
Clos'd in a ship, and hid ; yea, nothing dread,
Yet found he was, and swallowed for correction :

Paul con-
verted.

And *Paul* for *Damas* bound, to persecute
His Saints, was stroke, yet sav'd, his drifts refute.

Looke

of godlie sorrow.

Looke to *Cains* murder, how it was clear'd ?
And *Davids* blood-shed, with adultrie mixt :
Remarke the bush, whence *Adams* voice appear'd,
And *Israels* thoughts, when they their Maker vext :
   Then he who made thine eyes, and gave them sight,
   Can he not see, who gave thy seeing light.

It's not with God as men, Gods ev'ry where !   *Gods om-*
In Heaven, and earth, God's presence filleth all ;   *nipotency.*
In Hell below, his Justice ruleth there,
All things must, to, his omniscience fall :
   Man knows, but as he sees, and in a part,
   But God doth search the reynes, and try the heart.

How swinishly (alas) have I then liv'd :
Nay, who can say, that I have liv'd at all ;
Whilst buried else, in sleep, in sloth, or griev'd
With fals-forgd cares, conglutinating thrall :
   To tempt my loving, and most patient God,
   I have contemn'd his mercy, mock'd his rod.

There's nought so smooth and plaine, as calme-set seas,   *Repugnant*
And nought more rough, when rag'd, by stormy winde ;   *compari-*
The lead is cold as yce, or Winter freize ;   *sons.*
But when been firde, its scolding hote we finde :
   The irne is blunt, till toold, and edge be put,
   And then most sharpe, to stobbe, to shave, or cut.

So patient God, is loath, and slow to wrath,
His patience is as great, as great his love ;
Long suffring he, deferres to threaten death !
Till our grosse sinnes, his just drawn-judgements move,
   And then his anger stirr'd, it burnes like fire,
   Consuming man, and sinners in his ire.

The gushing Teares

Next ; pause I on, the momentany sight,
Of mans short life, that like a shadow flees ;
Much like the swiftnesse of a Faulcones flight,
Or like a bird, glydes by our glancing eyes :
    Then marvell I, how man can harbour pride ?
    Or wherein should, his vanitie confyde.

The weaknesse, and changes of our nature. To day he's stout, to morrow laid in grave,
His lookes alive, are plumd, like variant feathers :
Been throwne in dust, he turnes to earth a slave,
And as he breaths, the crummes of lust he gathers :
    But would he muse, on long eternitie,
    He would forsake himself, and learne to die.

To learne to die, that he may learne to live,
For in this course, his happinesse consists ;
Die to himself, that grace may vice survive,
In mortifying sinne, his blesse subsists :
    Come life, come death, thus dying so, he's blest,
    And doubtlesse shall, in peace of conscience rest.

O Jesu ! who redeemd us, being dead !
Whence could thy love, so farre to us extend ;
We had no merit, thou of us no need,
And yet thy grace our weeknesse doth defend ;
    For as man first, to be like God, condemn'd us,
    So God turned man, that God should not contemne us.

Farre better is a life unfortunate,
In end with honour, that yeelds up the breath ;
Than honourable life, and wealthy state,
With shame to perish, and untimely death :
    I rather wish, to be a sheepherd borne,
    Then live a Prince, and at my death forlorne.

Come

of godlie sorrow.

Come answer me, who would be undertaker,
Whether its best, to be a man or beast?
The beast dissolves, and not offends his Maker,
Nor makes no count, save to some carnall feast :
   But Godlesse Man, in grieving God, is worse,
   Throwne downe to Hell, and with that fall, his curse.

An objection between man and beast.

Who rightly weighs, the variable kindes,
Of Mortals all, in either death or life?
Shall see their bubling breath, tost with sharpe windes,
Of stagring doubts, ingorgd with timerous strife :
   Their conscience, and, their living disagreeing,
   In will or worke, most vanquish'd are in dying.

Nay, soule and body, at that dreadfull day,
Shall be conjoynd, and hurld downe to Hell :
This wretch thus damn'd, in tortring flames shall stay,
Chaind in that howling Radamanthan Cell :
   The beast he fals, and turnes to nought we see,
   But Man adjudgd, his worme shall never die.

The pangs of Hell.

As for the vertuous Saint, his happinesse,
Begins at death, which end all worldly noyes ;
He swarmes in pleasures, rich in blessednesse,
Death makes the passage, to his heavenly joyes :
   He feares no stop, nor stay, his faith instructs him,
   The way (though strait) his good Angel conducts him.

And wouldst thou learne whilst here, t'attaine that way,
Be humble first, and then religious set ;
Place heaven before Thee, make faith thereon to stay,
And then let zeale and love, fast setling get
   To grip Christs wounds ; then feare, then praise, then pray,
   Let earnest prayers, thy best devotion swey.

                                For

The gushing Teares

Prayer and meditation, two heavenly exercises.

For prayer is, the souls great sacrifice,
Which speaks to God ; and meditation,
Is Gods speech to the soule ; an exercise
Conjoyned together ; two revolv'd in one :
    The one invelopes the other, and speaks
    Reciprocall : Both our salvation seeks.

Which two, like *Hypocrates* twinnes are bred,
Who liv'd, fed, slept, joyd, wept, and dyed together ;
So can they not be separate indeed :
Though fasting doe prepare, their journey hither :
    This outward action, like t' a potion scoures,
    The other spirituall, are divinely ours.

Like to a paire of Turtles, truely set,
Whereof the one by death, been slaughter'd gone,
The other mournes, for losing of her Mate,
And languishing doth die ; No life alone.
    So meditation, gives matter to the minde,
    And without prayer, nothing shall we finde.

The effects of prayer.

For both bring reconcilement, and acceptance,
And makes thee, to thy father, a loving sonne ;
So by his Sonne, a brother of acquaintance,
And by the Sprite, a Temple ; squard, and done :
    Last in the Court of Heaven, thou art made free,
    A fellow, with th' Angelick hierarchie.

O joy of joyes ! O happy endlesse blesse !
Who can expresse, that glory there reveal'd ?
The eye, the minde, nor tongue can dascon this !
Since ravish'd *Paul*, amaz'd, hath it conceal'd :
    Then labour silly soule, this marke to aime,
    Which seen, and got, how great is thy good name ?

                                                            But

of godlie sorrow.

But (ah!) I stagger in the myres of sin,
And daily sinks, in pudles of defects:
The more I flee, the more I swallow in
The stinking marish, of absurd effects:
   The very boggy quagmyres of vice,
   I plunge them all, unvaluing weight, or price.

The price (alas!) is great, and I must pay it,
Unlesse Christs wounds, break open, plead for pitie;
O pledge divine! thy merits will defray it,
Thou art my surety, O prevent my dittie!
   Evert the sentence, least I lye in Jayle,
   Stand to thy mercy, Lord! be thou my bayle.

Christs
wounds
our health.

To square the lives, of godly men with mine,
How farre my selfe, fled from my self, I finde;
Thrice wretchd am I, to thinke me one of thine,
In whom corruption, rules the inward minde:
   It's more then strange, I should expect for good,
   Whilst still I trample, on my Saviours blood.

There is no sense in this, that I should slay
My silly soule, to crosse my crost desire:
Can head-strong passions, mine accounts defray?
When my just Judge, my reckning shall require:
   Nay, spare thy spurres, poore wretch, and call to minde
   A self-soule Murdrer, can no mercy finde.

That sinne which I hate worst, I follow most,
Yet faine would sift, the evil of deceit:
Loe! with repugnants, how my breast is tost,
Here lyes my safety, there the snaring bait;
   Sinne, like a Fowler, with a whistle takes me,
   And that good, which I would, it then forsakes me.

The in-
stabilitie of
man.

E   O!

The gushing Teares

O ! love ! and love it self ! Father of love !
And God of mercy, mercy is thy Name !
O King of pitie ! all my faults remove
Farre from before Thee, cover thou my shame :
    That here me to accuse, they never come,
    Nor hence to damne me, at the day of doome.

Ah ! wicked men ! they triumph in excesse !
To tempt thy patience, O long suffring God !
They glory to cast downe, the fatherlesse,
And on the Widows back, they lay their rod :
    They lose themselves, and so would lose their brother
    With them ; thy honour, in their pride to smother.

Unwise is he, and thrice unhappy too !
Who ill commits, that good thereon may follow :
He's like the Crocodile, that loves to wooe
The gray *Nyle* Rat, and eftsoone doth it swallow :
    Which, when enclos'd, it cuts his wombe, seeks breath,
    And with its freedome, workes the others death.

So haplesse man, in hurtfull wayes of sinne,
His hopelesse heart, he suffocats with lust ;
Till custome bring, sterne obduration in,
And then he turnes a Reprobate injust :
    The doore of grace is shut, his soule wants faith
    Then sinne leaves him, squard for eternall death

They gallop on, in dark-drawne pathes of Hell,
The glen is hollow, but the way is broad ;
In two extreames, the least they quite repell,
To shunne a fardell, they receive a load :
    The yoake of Christ is light, but ah ! they swallow
    The weight of sinne, which all their labours follow.

                               I crosse

of godlie sorrow.

I crosse my crossing armes, on my crost breast,
And musing lurks, to looke on humane state ;
How wretch'd it is ? how carelesse ? how deprest ?
To ev'ry snare, makes man unfortunate :
    That haplesse he ! for one small moments pleasure,
    Dare hazard (ah !) his souls eternall treasure.

Momental pleasures eternall paine.

The will, 'twixt reason, and sensualtie plac'd,
Is apt to be apply'd, to either side ;
But first, and firmest, Will by sense is trac'd,
Which is of youth, and childish age the guide !
    For seldome reason, can once conquer will,
    Cause ; sense presents for good, a pleasant ill.

Will overcomes reason.

And in that ill, a wofull sowre content,
Which frights itself, with shadows of despaire :
O ! miracle of madnesse ! what intent
Hath my cross'd soule ? to worke my grievous care :
    If mercy can not move me, to amend,
    Yet self-affection, might my good intend.

Why then sick soule ? dost thou not weep one teare ?
O ! that thy grief ! would windy sighes disclose !
Let mourning sorrow, melt in holy feare,
And pale remorse, dissolve, in watrie woes :
    For godly groanes, which deep contrition brings,
    They rent the clouds, and court the King of Kings.

Sighes and teares are holy sacrifices.

Whence pardon comes, and consolation too,
And strength to guard us, in worst stormy times ;
For what we would, the same he helps to doe,
And for one teare, he'le cover worlds of crymes :
    What though I faint ? cause, great is my transgression,
    Yet comfort comes, when there's a free confession.

E 2

Fraile

The gushing Teares

Fraile is the foolerie, of my fragile flesh,
Still prone to fall, but never prompt to stand :
I second causes, with a desperate dash,
Cares not for times to come, nor whats in hand :
    If I finde pleasure, in the worst of ill,
    I murder reason, with a fearlesse will.

How long shall wicked thoughts, in me remaine ?
To slay my soule, and bring thy judgements downe :
When wilt thou curbe my sinne, and it restraine,
Lest like a flood, it shall me helplesse drowne :
    Unlesse thy grace, support me, being fraile,
    There's nought with mee, that can with thee prevaile.

The godly sometime fall, and are recalld. Alas ! to number, what I should not speake,
Of holy ones, thy Prophets, and Apostles ;
How farre (too oft) from Thee, were they to seek,
Throwne downe, 'mongst thornie briers, and pricking thistles :
    Yet they were thine, thou suffer'd them to fall,
    That in thy mercy, thou might them recall.

Herein their weaknesse, and thy power was knowne,
That to thy glorious Fame, it might redound : ·
What though they straid, these wandrers were thine owne,
They knew at last thy voice, and trac'd the sound :
    Sometimes thy Saints would slip, and then repent them,
    With heart-swolne tears, which grief & grace had lent them.

Thy holy writs, bear of their names record !
To paternize my hopes, fixt on a Rock ;
How ev'r I faile, thou art a gracious Lord,
Full of redemption to thy chosen flock :
    For their examples, teach me to beleeve,
    Thou wilt protect me, and my faults forgive.

Gods

of godlie sorrow.

Gods Champion *Joshua*, when he *Jordan* crost,
And raz'd wall'd *Jericho*, downe to the ground:
Yet sav'd he *Rachab*, all the rest were lost,
Gratefull he was, this Woman mercy found ;
  Which towne lay waste, till *Hiel Bethelite*,
  In *Achabs* time, rebuilt its ancient seat.

Joshua's gratefulnes to *Rachab*.

This was that towne, which Christ so oft past by,
From *Galilee* to *Jebus*, *Sions* glore ;
Where throngd with folk, *Zacheus* could not spy
His sacred face, but run in haste before,
  And top'd a fig-tree trunck : Which seen by Christ,
  Come downe (said he) *Zacheus*, I'me thy guest.

Jesus at *Jericho* saved *Zacheus*.

This day salvation, to thy house is come,
I'le recompense thy curious carefull eye :
Select'd thou art, for my cœlestiall home !
Great is thy faith, though small thy stature be :
  By grace a Gyant, though a Dwarfe by nature,
  I am thy Lord, *Zacheus* is my Creature.

Thus *Joshua* and *Jesus*, sav'd two, here see !
A bordell Strumpet, and this Publican ;
To lesson us, what kinde soe're they be,
Turke, *Jew*, or *Arab*, *Moore*, or *Mussilman* ?
  Christ hath his own *Cornelius*, and his *Ruth*,
  The *Moabite*, *Centurions* fraught with truth.

For almes deeds and prayer, pierce the clouds !
Whence Rills of tears, do ever springing vent,
Remorsefull songs, explor'd by rusling flouds,
Bank'd with the willow, bondage still lament :
  Where Harpes lye mute, and hearts are fill'd with plaints,
  Deploring sore, stress'd *Sion*, and her Saints.

E 3   O !

The gushing Teares

O! if the Heavens! would now infuse in me!
Some divine rapt, to lay abroad her crosses:
But stay sad Soule! that is too much for thee,

Let Pastours plunge these deepths, and blaze her losses:
    Onely bewaile, her sorrows, and thy fall,
    Men may have tongues, and have no grace at all.

Not by compulsion, as by sense we see
Numbers do slide, each training one another;
Herod could speak, and yet with vermine die,
Curst *Cain* slew, the righteous man his brother:
    Saul he could prophecie, and yet he fell,
    The Witch at *Endor*, rang his passing bell.

Baalim could blesse, and *Baalim* he would curse,
And yet his Asse did check him, but come see!

Wise was *Achitophel*, his end was worse,
Proud *Absalom* was hair-hangd on a tree:
    Like be our foes, and like our Church now findes,
    We want but *Hushai*, to bewray false mindes.

Though *Ezra* wept, and mourn'd for *Judahs* faults,
Yet had he adversars, which sought to slay him;
Whilst rearing *Sions* walls, to barre assaults,
His threatning foes, sent *Bassads* to affray him:
    The people wrought, and built with dextrat hand,
    And in the left, their swords, for guard did stand.

So, so, and so, the state of Saints should be,
Resolvd to suffer, and resolv'd to fight:
Yea, for the faith, should not refuse to die,
Since truth averres, what we acclaime by right:
    But we have Wolves for lambes; their coat is all,
    If they get means, care not who stand or fall.

                  I scorne

I scorne their checks, but more their critick censures,
Whilst with an honest heart, I live, to live :
Whose sharp-edg'd calumnies, and scurrile tonsures,
Retort their breasts, but with more grief, to grieve :
  If Gods good sprite, by grace to blesse contract me,
  I care not, how, these turnecoat times detract me.

Their time is short, their sentence can not bide,
Like to opinion, so their verdicts follow ;
They're blinde in reason, malicious in pride,
Whose tongues are Tombs, their hearts both false and hollow.
  For whilst their craft, deceives them with deceeat,
  They swallow up the hooke, and misse the bait.

Themselves they slay, with the same dart they shoot,
And in the pit do fall, they digg'd for other ;
To stand for ill, they will not flee a foot,
Their evils, with a show of good they smother :
  But soone mischief, can overcrush their braines,
  Men swallow mounts, for execrable gaines,

Saikles en-
vie retorts
reply.

Alas ! what is the bubling breath of man ?
Whose life hangs on his nostrils ; like to dew
Falne from the humid clouds ; and no wayes can
Secure it selfe, from *Titans* scorching view :
  So mens conceit, in fond opinions flee,
  VVhiles this, whiles that, whiles naught their actions be.

Let *Davids* hymnes, discover all their drifts,
Till that their very eyes for fat leap out :
I love that soule surchargd with pious gifts,
Simple in life, and for his conscience stout :
  Say though his best were nought, his good intention,
  Cast on the Lord, begets a safe prevention.

                                            The

The gushing Teares

The malice of each snare, my thoughts imbrace,
But above all with darling sinnes I dandle ;
I pleasure take, wherein there's no solace,
And with the Butterflie, the flame I handle :
   The wings of lust I oyle, then sinne burnes me,
   And whilst I stand to live, I post to die.

Wormes are sepulchrall mates.

Wormes are my Mates, when I in grave am laid,
They'le feed on me, who lov'd to feed on dainties,
My senslesse Corps, shall with the senslesse spade
Be made a prey, to their devouring plenties :
   My bones shall rot, then turne in mouldring dust,
   This is the way of flesh, both bad and just.

And yet vaine Man, he little thinks or dreames,
Once of his death, nor what his end may be ?
His sense deludès him, and the world it seemes
A glasse to looke on, for his sensuall eye :
   He neither mournes for sinne, nor sinne forsakes,
   But from one ill, another worser takes.

What surging follies, overcloud my minde ?
With vain-wing'd fancies, and surmysing flashes ;
Such fleering thoughts, more lighter than the winde !
Breed nought but foolerie, which opinion dashes :
   My wish'd for wishes, straight conceiv'd and done,
   The care of carelesse dreams, I scarce can shunne.

Man headlong falls.

I posting runne, in wayes of naughty ends,
Lord ! crook, and stop my course, with streames of grace !
Which flood, can carry none that ill pretends,
Like *Jordan*, that, receives no barbarous face,
   Unlesse they swim : So, (*sans* remorse) they'le drowne,
   Who hazard here, quick sandie sins pull downe.

                          This

of godlie sorrow.

This saving grace, the soule guards with strong hand,
And if it slip, it can not fully fall:
Its like *Maronahs*, full disgorging strand,
Hembes in *Canaan*, from barbarian thrall:
    Like keeps the Lord his owne, and guards their wayes,
    They perish not; though chargd with fraile delayes.

The lake
Maronah
fathers
Jordan.

As *Jordan* circuits the holy land,
'Twixt *Liban*, and, that south-lake smoaking show;
From the *Petreian* soyle; joynd with a strand,
Which tribute payes, 'gainst *Jericho* I know,
    To famous *Jore:* One parts the *Midian* soyle,
    The other sackt, *Samarias* confynes coyle.

This is the march, girds *Canaans* south-east side,
But more the Lord preserves, and guards his owne
From ghostly ill, and from ætheriall pride,
From terrene sprites, from Hell, and what is knowne
    To plague the soule; he is a bulwark strong,
    Fens'd with good Angels, free all his from wrong.

Godly
teares, sa-
ving grace.

Then happy they, can creep within this Tent!
And sheltrage seek, under his mercies wings;
Sigh for thy sinnes, O! let thy soule repent!
Thy misdemeanour, to the King of kings:
    First grieve, then weep, last seeke thy Saviour's face,
    Let teares implore, for teares can plead for grace.

Kinde were these teares, which *Josephs* love had spent,
When with his brethren, he his brother saw:
His heart, surchargd with joy, it shrunke as shent,
To plunge that deep, which *Benjamin* did draw:
    But loe! moe teares! were shed one with another,
    When *Joseph* said, Behold, I am your brother.

F   Feare

The gushing Teares

Feare not (said he) the strict *Ægyptian* law,
Though to the *Ismaelites*, my life you sold:
For what was done, was done by God I knaw,
No spight of yours, his providence behold !
   Foresaw your need, and brought me here to be,
   A father to my Father's miserie.

There five yeares famine yet, shall worke your woe,
Wherein ag'd *Jacob*, and his race may starve,
Unlesse he flit ; then get you up and go
To fetch him downe, faile not in this, nor swerve :
   They went, he came, all met in melting joyes,
   For passions have extreames, as bairnes have toyes.

Since Nature then, in floods of teares can melt,
For joy of sight, to overjoy their love ;
Much more our teares, when we remorse have felt
For sinne ; shall glade, the powers in Heaven above :
   These tears are blest, and make us blest for ever,
   For godly grief, from grace, no crosse can sever.

Jobs patience and constancy.
Let patient *Job*, be paterne in like case,
Whose losse was such, as never yet was none :
Yet shrunk he not, sound steadfast love took place,
Faith forc'd his hope, and both proclaim'd in one :
   Sure my Redeemer lives, and he is just,
   Though he should kill me, yet in him I'le trust.

Mine eyes shall see him, and he will me save,
As I am confident, he will not faile :
Sterne rough calamitie, would me deceave,
But that's a shade, my purpose must prevaile :
   In God my soule is fixt, nought can dismay me,
   Nay death it selfe, nor Satan can betray me.

See

See ! here the Columne, of a lively faith !
The type of Christ, in meek and milde behaviour :
His friends they slight him, he contemnes his death,
And in his miserie, still avowd his Saviour :
   This was a love, excell'd all loves on earth,
   For Christ he lov'd, who lov'd him ere his birth.

Then how hate I my selfe, If I love not
My loving Lord, who lov'd me, from his love ;
He truely loves, who for thy sake I wot
Loves thee ; and himselfe for thee ; this we prove
   All kindes of love, without thy love, breed loathing,
   Unlesse we love them, for thy sake, they're nothing.

Love the Lord for his loves sake.

Great king of glory, all thy works invite !
Us to love thee, since thou first loved us :
As starres do from the Sunne, take light and heat,
For from that fulnesse, we the like discusse :
   How can our soules ? thine Jmage, want the sight,
   Of thy bright love, whose love is perfect light.

Lord ! we do all, depend upon thy love,
Because our being, had of thee beginning :
Next, thou preserves us, as we rest or move,
And art our end ; controlls us, when a sinning :
   All what we have, we have receiv'd from thee,
   And what we want, thou wilt the same supply.

O God of love ! thy nature is all love !
In love more glorious, than the sunne in light :
Thou art an infinite fire from above,
Which here enlightens, with its beames, each wight :
   A fire of love, a loving fire we finde,
   A light ! not burnes, a flame, not quels the minde.

Gods love our life.

F 2

O !

The gushing Teares

O Lord ! if thou thy tender love withdraw :
And from us slips one step, to turne thy back :
Are we not dead, in sloth and sleep ; no awe ;
But each temptation, shall presage our wracke :
    Then Lord uphold us ! since all worldly things
    Are ever changing, tyme their ruine brings.

The bre-
vitie of life. To day we live, the morne to grave we're sped,
We sight this world, as birds by gazers glyde ;
  As dreams evanish, so our dayes are fled ;
Like water bubles, as soone quelld as spyde :
    Thus heart-grown man, ingorgd with pryde and lust,
    He posts, and posts to death, then turnes in dust.

To argue on corruption, that subverts
The good we would, and choaks our best desires ;
It is a senselesse appetite, perverts
The light of reason, with entangling fires :
    A head-strong blinde irregulary ill,
    That captives wit, and wounds both sense and will.

Corrupti-
on cor-
rupteth all
things. Its strong in all infirmities injust,
Still fraile in goodnesse, weak in sound conception :
Its rull'd by nature, and her daughter lust,
Which blinds the light of knowledge, with deception :
    Like pitch, corruption, blacks the purest soule,
    And where it comes, makes ev'ry clean thing foule.

It takes best hold, on imbecillitie,
And where that fortitude, deficient is,
It dare not wrestle, with dexteritie,
Nor count with Temprance, one defective misse :
    Much like a Ruffian, or a Theefe by night,
    It loves, and lives in darknesse, more than light.
                                  Corruption,

Corruption, many wayes, may be defind,
To be a *Hydra*-neck'd *Herculian* snake ;
Stop'd at the eye, it compasseth the minde,
Barr'd from the soule, the heart it soone will take :
  Say, if the eare be deafe, the hand will feele,
  And if it smell not, it can taste too well.

Corruption, rules most states, and office places,
In Church and Common-wealth, it beares great swey :
It masks the Merchants, with *Gibeonitish* faces !
And with each trade, it can the harlot play :
  From mighty men to mean, see ! what I sought ?
  I finde them all corrupt'd, their wayes are nought.

Corruption, in their brybries, fraught with greed,
Corruption, in their flesh, subborn'd by lust,
Corruption, in their manners, full of need,
Corruption, in their sinne, and lives injust :
  Corruption, in their malice, flankd on pryde,
  Corruption, in their wills, blinde Natures guyde.

The power and varieties of corruption.

Corruption, in the treachrie of deceat,
Corruption, in false weights, and falser measures,
Corruption, in vile perjurie, and hate,
Corruption, in the hoording up of treasures :
  Corruption in hypocrisie and strife,
  Corruption in a base dissembling life.

Corruption, (ah !) in justice by the Judge,
Corruption, too, in partiall ends 'gainst reason ;
Corruption, in the traitour, that dare lodge
Corruption, fixt on murder, and high treason :
  Corruption, in oppression, and what then ?
  Corruption, in the lavishnesse of men.

F 3

Corruption,

The gushing Teares

Corruption, in forg'd tales, and false reports
Corruption, in fraile fleshly vile desires !
Corruption, in base taunts, and jeering torts,
Corruption, in despysing naturall Syres :
    Corruption, (ah !) in negligence and slouth,
    Corruption, from fond sports, in age or youth.

Corruption, in ambition, and high looks,
Corruption, in straind-selfe contract'd opinions.
Corruption, in best learneds, and best books,
Corruption, in great Princes, and their Minions :
    Corruption, in vaine courtly Courtiers stiles,
    Corruption, in sunk Worldlings greedy wiles.

Corruption, in abusing outward things,
Corruption, in vile drunkennesse, and swearing,
Corruption, in a Wranglers crafty wrings,
Corruption, in delay, and long forbearing :
    Corruption, in the ignorance of mindes,
    Corruption, in best knowledge of all kindes.

Corruption, in prest complements, and phrases,
Corruption, in bad cariage, mask'd with guile,
Corruption, in poore flattrers foolish praises,
Corruption, in most Pen-men, and their stile :
    Corruption, in a Sycophantick leyar,
    Corruption, in the Layers mouth and Pleyar.

Corruption, in Adultrie, and worse lust,
Corruption, in backbyters slandring tongue,
Corruption, in lost credit, without trust,
Corruption, in the gathering worldly dung :
    Corruption, in blinde filthy *Criticks* censures,
    Corruption, in mechanick glyding tonsures.

                      Corruption,

of godlie sorrow.

Corruption, in corruption, sinne afords,
And ev'ry way corrupt'd, corruption swallowes ;
Most grow absurd, corrupting deeds and words !
And in the pudle of corruption wallowes:
   The hollow heart of man, such venome vomites
   Of all corruptions, that they're fixt for Comets.

All which portend, some grievous dissolution,
In ev'ry state, a wofull alteration ;
Sprung from enormities of pollution.
This land is turnd, the face of desolation :
   Both great and small, the scourge of fortune feele,
   Whose fates are tost, still round about the Wheele.

To day a Lord, to morrow fled to warres,
To day a Laird, to morrow turnd a beggar ;
To day in wealth, to morrow closd with barres ;
To day in peace, to morrow swear and swagger :
   To day in farme, to morrow forcd to flee,
   To day puft, up, the morne, cast downe we see.

The vicissitude of fortune.

Sinne is the cause, which makes such judgements fall
On Land-lords now, who still oppresse the poore ;
They taxe and raxe them, keepe them under thrall,
That most are forcd, to leave both hold and doore :
   Whose grounds in end is sold, or else ly waste,
   Both Tyrants, and th' opprest, such changings taste.

Lord ! save me from this all-corrupted age,
Where craft joynes with extortion either hand ;
Blood, and oppression, may but passions swage,
Strict law and justice, quite forsake this land :
   Men now must gaze, like Souldiers battell broke,
   That looke for aide, else for the fatall stroke.

                   Nay,

The gushing Teares

Nay; we're corrupt'd, in thought, in word, and deed!
Yet of all sinnes, vile drunkennesse is worst :
It breeds all ill, and of all vice the seed,
It harbours lust, and makes the Actor curst ;
    And smothering shame, it wallows in despaire,
    Where spoiling vertue, seeks examples rare.

Noah first
set vines
and first
got drunk
with it.

Our Patriarch *Noah*, after the deludge,
Had shunn'd sommersing, of the first drownd World ;
He planted vines for man, healths sound refudge !
Yet made his toyle, the snare wherein he hurld :
    The grape was sweet and strong, see ! how he sunke ?
    He graft it first, and first with it was drunk.

This worlds sole Monarch, of the second age,
Who built the Arke, which sav'd him and his race
Undrown'd ; Behold ! was tane, and turnd the Page
Of glutting Bacchus, senslesse of his cace :
    Was it not strange ! this Columne could decline !
    That scaping waters, yet was drownd with wine.

But he, great he ! earths sov'raigne Lord and Father,
Had no intent, to foxe his sober senses ;
But tasted, touch'd, and drunk; then faild, or rather
He seald his fault, to shelter like offences :
    Not so; his slip, pleads o'resight unacquainted,
    And reason would, he tast'd the thing he planted.

Lots drun-
kennesse
begot in-
cest.

Like so, was *Lot*, ensnar'd, when fled for feare
From burning *Sodome*, and cavernd at night ;
Was by his daughters gull'd : They thinking there !
The world was gone ; sought to restore the right
    Of natures race : And he stark drunk imbrac'd them,
    But sure he griev'd, when th' action had defac'd them.

                                       But

But our grosse Drunkards, base pedestriat natures !
Will roare and quaffe, old houses, through strait windowes ;
Blaspheme their Maker, and abuse his Creatures,
And swear, they'le spend their bloud, and carve their sinnewes,
   To beard cold *Phebe;* then *Orlando* like,
   Rapt *Rodomunting* oathes, and *Cyclops* strike.

Whose red-ey'd sight, show faces fixt with Comets,
Through which (like *Vulcan*) they would seeme goodfellowes
O here he staggers ! and there he wallowing vomits,
And if mischiefe fall out, he courts the gallowes :
   Last, friends and meanes been lost, he's load with curses,
   Then bends his course to steale, or robbe mens purses.

The shame-
full effects
of drun-
kennesse.

What ill can Hell devise ? but Drunkards do it ?
All kindes of vice, all kinde of lusts they swallow : •
For why ? its drunkennesse that spurres them to it,
Satan suggests, and they his counsell follow :
   Then turne they frantick, mad distracted Sots,
   To clout their Conscience, with retorting Pots.

They lye and surfet, belch, and vomit blood,
Yea, ever rammage, brutish, and absurd ;
Their beastly manners, loathsome are and rude,
Deprav'd of senses, have their wits immurd,
   Benumb'd, debosh'd ; last sunke in beggars brats,
   Eate up with vermine, starve, and die like Rats.

Worlds of examples, I could here denote,
As well in ancient dayes, as moderne times :
What were these *Pagans* past ? what were they not ?
What are our present judgements ? for like crymes ?
   May not their *Alcoran,* serve to condemne us ?
   If we our selves, would from our selves exam'ne us.

G   May

The gushing Teares

Beasts and Philoso-phers con-demne ex-cesse. May not Philosophers? the light of nature?
Convince us, for like riot, and excesse?
Nay, even the beast (unreasonable creature)
Stand up and witnesse, of our sensualnesse:
   They will not once exceed their appetite,
   But man will surfet, with a deep delite.

In using, we abuse, Gods benefits,
And turne his blessings, to an heavie curse;
Surpassing temprance, we confound our wits,
No health for body, lesse for soule remorse:
   All things were made for us, and we for God,
   But being abus'd, they serve us for his rod.

Alas! where reason? when poore man misknowes
The life of knowledge, reason did infuse;
Shall understanding sleep? shall I suppose
That will is weaker, than a strong excuse:
   He knowes (I know) enough that can misknow
   The thing he knowes, its well, in knowing so.

No perfe-ction in humane knowledge. Well said *Alphonso*, (knowledge to expone)
That all what we could learne, by sight, or show;
By airts, by science, by books to study on,
Was the least part, of that we did not know:
   All what we know, we know but in a part,
   And that failes oft, corruption rules the heart.

What thou canst know, another doth know more,
And what he knowes, is but a glimpsing glance:
Who perfect is? nay none; who can deplore
His weaknesse, ruld by counsell, not by chance!
   Mans knowledge, like the shade, is swallowed soone,
   That hangs between its substance, and the Moone.

He

He knowes the ill, and in that knowledge rude,
And cleaves to vice, as wooll and briers are knit ;
Resolv'd to erre, misknowing what is good,
Rejects his soule ; then in a frantick fit,
    Neglecting God, neglects his owne salvation,
    And quaffing excesse, drinks his own damnation.

How Lord ! these faults behelpd ! teach me to mourne,
That being humbled, I may call for grace :
Let men presumptuous, 'gainst thy judgements spurne,
And in the pudle of their labours trace :
    Save thou my soule, for now my quivering heart,
    'Twixt feare and hope, stands trembling at sinnes smart.

A second *Jonah*, from thy voice I flee,
And with shrunke *Peter* I thy name deny :
I *Ahab*-like, keep spoiles of sinne for me,
And harbour lust, in *Lots* ebrietie :
    These lookes, that fell, from *Sion* on a Pond,
    Were not so foule as mine, nor halfe so fond.

Great defects in greatest Saints.

Unworthy I, to lift mine eyes above,
Or that the earth, should beare me, undevour'd :
Nay, nor my friends, on me to cast their love,
Nor saints pray for me, hath the truth deflourd :
    Yet, what God will, it needs must come to passe,
    He looks on what I am, not what I was.

Let grace take roome, that mercy soone may follow,
Renew my sprite, O cleanse my heart from ill !
Thy blood can purge me, though my guilt be hollow ;
Faith and repentance, have a piercing will :
    Infuse thy power, Lord strengthen me to turne
    Once to rejoyce, and never more to mourne.

                          As

The gushing Teares

Daniels dainties, poore mens plenties.

As *Daniel*, with thy servants three forsooke
To feed on *Babels* delicates, and wine :
But water, and poore pulse, they gladly tooke,
And yet their faces, did for beauty shine :
 Lord grant with them, all worldly snares I may
 Forsake, and learne, to trace thy law, thy way.

That kingly beast, or beastly king expos'd
Seven yeares to fields ; nev'r faild so much as I :
Nor these five kings, by *Joshua* enclos'd,
Brought forth, and foot-neckd, shamefully did die :
 Nev'r vex'd him more (for they their lands defended)
 Than I am griev'd, for having God offended.

That *Goshan* flight, to a desartuous soile,
Through uncouth way, deep seas, laid up in heaps !
Nev'r reft from *Egypt*, such a swallowed spoile,
With greater right (for now my soule it weeps)
 Then Gods just judgements, might on me befall,
 Unlesse his mercy soone prevent my fall.

These wandrings long, which *Israel* did recoyle,
Tost to and fro, in vast *Arabian* bounds ;
Full fourty yeares they spent, for twelve dayes toyle,
Starv'd, slaine, and quell'd, still galld by savage wounds :
 This crosse they bore, for grieving God so oft,
 But (ah !) my sinnes, for plagues do cry aloft.

Savages are better then bad christians.

Now having scene, rude *Lybians*, nak'd, and bare,
Sterne barbrous *Arabs*, savage *Sabuncks* od ;
Sword-sweying *Turkes*, and faithlesse *Jews* alwhere,
Base ruvid *Berdoans*, godlesse of a God :
 Yet when from me, on them I cast mine eye,
 My life I finde, farre worse, then theirs can be.

The

of godlie sorrow.

The rustick Moorish, sterne promiscuous sexe,
Nor *Garolines,* idolatrizing shame ;
The *Turcomans,* that even the Divell doe vexe !
In offring up, their first-borne, to his name:
    Nor *Jamnites,* with their foolish Garlick god,
    Are worse then I, nor more deserve thy rod.

Yet Lord ! with Thee, there's mercy ; and its true,
Thou art not wonne, with multitude of words,
Its force of tears from us, thy pitie sue,
Which thou regards, and pardon us afords :
    For words are formed, by the tongue, but tears,
    Speak from the heart, which thou most kindlie heares.

Use then few words (O silly soule) but weepe,
This is the heavenly language, and strong voice,
That calls to God ; for he our teares shall keep
Fast bottled in his pittie : Makes the choise
    Of teares ; few words, let sighs, and sobs display,
    Thine inward grief ; then tears beginne to pray.

In prayer use few words and many tears.

Lord ! thou wouldst not, to *Herod* speak, nor yet
Would answer *Pilat,* urgd by humane power ;
But soone thou spoke, when weeping women set
Their eyes on Thee ; and streames of teares did powre :
    These Judges sought, advantage for thy dittie,
    But *Sions* daughters, weept for Thee in pittie.

These great mens words, did reach but to thine eares,
But their warme drops, did pierce Thee to thine heart ;
Lord ! thou takes care on them, and on their teares,
Who mourne for others, when the righteous smart :
    But farre more pittie, on the sinfull soule,
    That mournes for sinne, and wailes her errours foule.

Christs silence, and patience.

G 3   Oh !

The gushing Teares

Oh ! that my head were waters ! and mine eyes !
A source of teares, to weep both day and night;
The peoples sinnes, with theirs, mine owne disease,
Which greater growes, than I beare have might :
    Such flouds of teares, would then my grief disclose !
    In airie vapours, flanck'd with watrie woes.

This worlds a valley, of perpetuall teares,
And what's the Scripture ? but a springing well
Of gushing teares ? flow'd from remorse and feares ;
For godly sorrow, must with Mourners dwell :
    And who can mourne, unlesse that grace begin
    To worke repentance ; this grief expiats sin.

Davids teares wet his couch. All night could *David*, wet with tears his couch,
And Prophets for the faults, of *Israel* mourne :
But (ah !) good God, when shall mine eyes avouch
Such happy teares, that may with Thee sojourne :
    If not thy judgements, yet thy gracious love,
    Might melt mine eyes, and Ponds of sorrow move.

Thou saidst, I will, compassion have on all,
That pleaseth me, compassion, for to show ;
Be pleas'd thy love, may me redeeme from thrall,
Free will to pardon, thine ; the debt I owe :
    How soone soev'r a sinner, should repent him,
    Thou swore in truth, thou wouldst no longer shent him.

Lord ! grant my minde, may second these my words,
And not invent, more than I practice can ;
If I deficient prove, good will afords
My sacrifice ; obedience is the man :
    Did not *Abraham*, this point paternize,
    Whose purpose, was, held for a sacrifice.

David

of godlie sorrow.

David resolv'd, on *Sions* lower flat,
To build a Temple, for the living Lord :
A daughter cloure, joynd with *Jehosophat*,
Benorthd, with *Moriahs*, squink devalling bord :
The Lord accept'd the minde, his thought was to it,
   And said, Thy sonne, but not thy selfe shall do it.

The widows myte, was thankfully receiv'd,
Good wills a sacrifice ; this seldome failes ;
The will, although the purpose be deceiv'd,
Is not to blame, the good intent prevailes :   <small>God ac-</small>
   The Lord accepts, even of the least desire   <small>cepts the</small>
   We have to serve him, though we faint or tire.   <small>will for</small>
                                                <small>the deed.</small>

When *Jacob* had, twice ten yeares *Laban* serv'd,
Yet *Laban*, would have sent him empty gone :
But he who serves the Lord, though he hath swerv'd,
Shall not misse his reward, nor go alone :
   The sprite of grace, shall second him, and love,
   Shall fill his soule, his faith shall mount above.

Then forward go, so runne you may obtaine,
Great is the prise, hold out the journeys end ;
Keep course, and runne, thou'le get a glorious gaine,
He who endures, shall onely there ascend :
   Rise eare, when young, and runne, betimes then do it,
   Who gets the start, and holds, shall first come to it.

The journeys long, the path is straight, and thornes
Ly in the way, to prick thee, on both sides :
Sinne like a Traitour, hourely thee subbornes,
To misse the marke, and blinde thee, with crosse guides :
   Yet constant runne, runne on, and be not sory,
   So rune thou mayst obtaine, a crowne of glory.

                                                       We

The gushing Teares

We see, for a light prise, a man will runne
His utmost speed ; and often loose his paines ;
That *Caledonian* hunter, never wonne
By strife of foote, a hare was all his gaines :
  But he who runs this course, shall earne a treasure,
  The butte of Heaven, must be his marke and measure.

Then blest is he ! keeps dyet, for this race !
And fits his soule, to take cœlestiall physick ;
Faith is the compound, and the potion grace,
Christ the Physician, mercy our soules musick :
  Then pardon seeks our suite, last, love crownes all,
  And raignes with glory, rivalls in one saule.

Christ is our Physician.

For this prepare thy selfe, since our short dayes
Are but a blast ; and yet our longest time
Is scarce a thought ; Looke ! what experience sayes,
That space, 'twixt wombe and Tombe, (O falling slyme !)
  Is but a point, then see ! and not suspend,
  A happy life, must have an happy end.

Our day of death, excells our day of birth,
And better wer't, with mourning folks to live,
Than like to fooles, that in the house of mirth
Would passe their time, and would that time survive :
  Relenting cryes, all times more needfull growes,
  Than laughing feasts : blest are all godly woes.

The insolencie of youth.

How vaine are frolick youths ? to spend their prime ?
In wantonnesse and slouth, lust galling joyes :
They quite forget, the substance of base slime,
Till rotten age, ramverse their masked toyes :
  And then diseases, hang about their bones,
  To plague their flesh with sores, their hearts with groanes.

The

of godlie sorrow.

The concupiscence, of youths sqink-laid eye,
Which lust begets, and inflamation brangles,
Is but the bait, invelops luxurie,
To follow practice, custome still entangles :
    The eye supports the thought, the thought desire,
    And then corruption, sets delight on fire.

Yet youth remember, in thy dayes of youth !
Thy sole Creator, remember thou must die !
Lest that these dayes may come, when helplesse ruth,
Shall say, No pleasure in them, thou canst see :
    Remember ! in thy youth ! O youth remember !
    Thy Christ and Maker, thou maist be his member.

Shall youth take pleasure, in vaine wantonnesse,
And with his fleshly lusts, go serve the Divell :
Then when growne old, in midst of rottennesse,
Would turne to God, and shunne his former evill :
    This cannot be, when thou canst sinne no more,
    Thou wouldst serve God, whom thou didst hate before.

Dare thou example take, of the good thief,
Nay, Christ was once, for all but sacrifiz'd :   Delay in
This can not ground thy faith, nor lend relief,   repentance
That one Thiefs mercy, thine is paterniz'd :   is dange-
    Can thou repent at will, choose time, and place,   rous.
    Nay, that falls short, its God who gives the grace.

Is any sure, when death shall call him hence,
Nothing more certaine, more uncertaine too ;
Time, place, and how, concernes Gods providence :
Then arme thy selfe, take heed, what thou shouldst do ?
    Bridle thy youth, amend thy life, repent,
    Such fruit is pleasant, from thy spring-tyde sent.

H

The

The gushing Teares

The morne is cooler, than the sun-scorch'd day,
The tender juice, more sweeter then old sap:
The flowry grasse, more fresh than withred hay?
The floorish fairer, than the Tronke, we trap:
   So dayes of youth, more sav'rie are to God,
   Than crooked age, all crooked wayes have trode.

Would thou live well, and live to live for aye,
Beginne at God, obey his word, and law:
Love, feare, and serve him, make him all thy stay,
Honour thy Parents, of the Judge stand awe:
   And neighbour love conserve: But ah! this age!
   Can show none such, but rot with lust and rage.

The sin-flowne *Dolphin*, after flying fish,
Nev'r swim'd so swift, as youth hunt after lust;
They dip presumption in a poysond dish,
And fearlesse tumble, in a fearfull gust:
   They wrestle not to wrest, but strives with strife
   To humour pleasures, in their head-strong life.

Its incident to youth, to mock old age,
And usuall too for age, to jeere at youth:
The one he dotes, the other playes the page,
A fondling foxd, with wantonnesse and slouth:
   Yet age is best, because experience schooles him,
   And youth is worst, 'cause vice and pleasure fooles him.

Youth and age are disagreeing.

Then 'twixt them both, the golden meane is best,
Neither too young, nor doting dayes are good:
Yet happy both, if faithfully they rest
With confidence, fixt on their Saviours bloud:
   For it can purge the old, of what is past,
   And cleanse the young, post after sinne so fast.

Both

of godlie sorrow.

Both *Timothie* and *Titus,* others moe,
Of rarest worth, though young, their youth-head chaind
In cords of temperance ; made vertue grow
In fortitude ; by which they glory gaind :
    Nay ; *Alexander,* in the prime of youth,
    Was wondrous chast, till strangers taught him slouth.

The *Persian* manners spoild him : But behold !
What good *Aurelius* said, the *Romane* King ?
If I were sure, that lust were not controld,
Nor punishd by the gods, above which ring :
    Yet for the fact it selfe, I will disprove it,
    'Cause why ? its filthy, base, and who can love it.

Continen-
cie by Pa-
gans com-
mended.

Would God ! that younglings, and the fry of nature,
Could so resolve, and play the Pagans part ;
Yea, old and young, and ev'ry humane Creature !
In this were blest, to take these words to heart :
    Then modestie should live, Religion flourish,
    And good example, one, another nourish.

A noble youth, been askd, whether he went ?
Reply'd ; he to the house of teares did go ;
To mourne with Mourners, that he might lament,
And learne to weep, when he did older groe :
    If hethnicks can show Christians such instruction.
    Our blind-set eyes, had need of their conduction.

Who sowe in teares, shall surely reape in joy,
For godly griefe, shall blessednesse inherit :
They who thus mourne, and thus their soules imploy,
Are firmely shelterd, under Jesus merit :
    Who shall transchange, their griefe, in glorious gladnesse,
    True happinesse expells, all sorrowing sadnesse.

     Blest

The gushing Teares

A brief
tract of
bitter re-
pentance. Blest were these teares, were spent, neare *Cajaphs* house !
By *Peter* griev'd, for imbecilitie,
Brought downe so low he was, nought could arrouze
His hope, for pardon, of infirmitie :
    Yard-closde alone, he weept, and wofull hee,
    With dolefull cryes, thus spoke, on flexed knee.

Have I (would he have said) deny'd my Lord,
With triple oathes, before the Cocke crew twice :
Which he foretold ; ah ! feare my faith had smord !
His looks accusd me, I had done it thrice :
    Was it not I, who vowd with him to die,
    And now forsworne, I from my Master flee.

Was I not *Cephas*, lately thought a Rock ?
And now the tongue, of a base serving maide,
Hath made me shrinke, and turne a stumbling block ;
We were but twelve, and one hath him betraide ;
    And I (as worst) have sworne, I knew him not,
    Mov'd by the voice, of a weake womans throat.

O ! that a Drudge ! should thus prevaile 'gainst me,
Who serves for wage, to him the Altar serv'd :
A slendrer weed, could no poore Hireling be,
And yet o're me shee triumphs ; I have swerv'd :
    This was Gods will, and now its come to passe,
    To show my weaknesse, with a weaker lasse.

Its strange ! two Drudges made me falter thrice,
With quivring oathes, and shivring words deny
The Lord of life : How could such hounds surprise
My stedfast love ? and not with him to die :
    No Judge controll'd me, yet two slavish snakes,
    Fill'd me with feare, with it, my Lord forsakes.

How

of godlie sorrow.

How fraile was I and fragile, to succumbe?
Mine hopes, unto such Wranglers void of grace;
I might have silence kept, and so sit dumbe,
Till *Cajaphas* had tryde me, having place:
    But I a Weakling, to a stragling sound,
    Forsooke my vow, and did my selfe confound.

Peters confession.

A silly fisher wretch, (no lesse he thought)
Was I, when God, from slaverie did me call;
And now to shrunke infirmitie am brought,
Worse then *Judaick* law, from Christ to fall:
    Who me select'd, to leave my nets, and when,
    He said, Thou shal'st, a fisher be of men.

How shall I answer make? what shall I doe?
His sighs, thus sobd, for groanes, and melting eyes,
Were all his words: Or whats my kindred too?
So base neare *Sydon* borne? that my degrees
    By birth were nought, but fisher men and fooles,
    The scumme of Nature, liv'd by warbling tooles.

Was I a chosen Vessel, thus to shrinke,
When erst in *Gethsemane*, my sword I drew:
And now beginnes, to flatter, lye, and winke,
Yea; failes and falls, with words, and oathes untrue:
    I might have with, my fellow flyers fled,
    But I would follow, and forsake my Head.

Love bade me venter, feare bade me stay back,
Faith forcelesse fled, a farre I followed on him;
Poore fainting I, though forward now falls slack,
I went to see, what doome, they gave upon him:
    Where courting *Cajaphs* fire (O snaring sinne!)
    Warming without, too cold I grew within.

H 3

I might

The gushing Teares

I might have fled, to hide me in some cave,
But curious I, would swallow shame and feare:
Could I sustaine his crosse, his death and grave?
To suffer that, which nature could not beare:
    All helpfull he! would he crave help unto it,
    Nay, fond was I, to thinke that man could do it.

Alone would he! O! all sufficient he!
Straight undergoe, his fathers hote displeasure:
Both God and Man, our Lord behovd to be,
So weighty was that wrath, laid up in treasure
    For sinfull man; but he all-conquering he!
    Triumph'd o're Hell, got us the victorie.

Peters reprehending himself. My Lord, but spoke, Whom seek ye? (O strong power!)
And backwards fell, the Sergeants on the ground;
He knew, confess'd, it was their time, his houre,
For so his love, to mankinde did abound:
    That as by Man, all flesh, accursd, should dye,
    Even so by man, all should redeemed bee.

Was I not witnes, to his word, and deed?
His miracles and mercies, workes of loue;
The Dumbe did speake, the Deaf did heare, the dead,
Hee raysd to lyfe; the Criples straight did moue;
    The Palseyes, Paraliticks, withred hands,
    Hee helpd, and heald; the blynd their sight commands.

Was hee not Christ, the Lambe, the sonne of God!
Whom I confessd, even face to face afore;
My soules Messias! who bore that heavy loade
Of Indignation; sinners to restore:
    Both sacrifice, and Sacrificer plight!
    A wondrous mercy, set before my sight.

For

of godlie sorrow.

For which ; vile worme, how could my lips deny ?
The Lord of glore, my life, my love, my light ;
VVas he not there ? and was not I hard by ?
VVhen that his looke, gave me this sorrowing night :
   Yet when my soules sharp eyne, saw what was done,
   My carnall eyes, in floods of teares did runne.

Faith wrought repentance, grace laid hold on grace,
My bitter streames, like brine, extreamly gush'd :
I wrung my hands, and knock'd my breast apace,
VVhilst sighes, sad sobs, from deep-fetchd groanings rushd :
   Then joy appeard, my conscience was assurd,
   The fault was pardond, and my soule securd.

Peters tears consummated in peace.

Thus *Peter* shrunke, his soule was humbled low,
(Not like to Popes, who his succession claime)
He sorrowing fell, and made contrition show
That he had faild : So did himself disclaime
   From first election, and from former grace,
   And causd remorse, give sad repentance place.

Then teares, O bitter teares ! relenting woes !
And airie vapours, from salt-raining eyes ;
Made windy sighes, and trembling groanes disclose
His lip-lost fall, the cause of his unease,
   Thus teares are blest, which godly sorrow brings,
   Each drop doth serve thy soule, to heaven for wings.

Though tears distill, and trickle downe thy cheeks,
So vanish quite, and seeme to thee as lost :
Their aire ascends, thy heart to God then speaks !
He harbours all, and is a gracious host :
   The Font he loves, and thats remorse for sinne,
   VVhich his grace works, before thou canst beginne.

The blessed fruits of godly tears.

                       Lord !

The gushing Teares

Lord ! frame my vvill to thine, and forme my heart,
To serve and feare thee, magnifie thy name ;
In this obedience, thou mayst grace impart,
For from thy favour, I must comfort claime ;
   Grant me thine invvard peace, refresh my minde, ·
   With sparkes of love, let sighs thy mercy finde.

All Mortals are, by nature miserable,
Then mourning is the habit, vve should vveare ;
Who sinne deplores, his case is comfortable,
Yet none can shunne, prest natures sorrovving feare :
   Flee vvhere thou vvilt, thou shalt not finde reliefe,
   Though thou changst place, thou canst not change thy grief.

Mortalitie is miser-able. This life is but a Font, of springing teares,
Weeping vvee come, into this vvorld, vvith cryes ;
And veeping vve go out, fraught full of feares,
There's nought but sorrovv, in our journey lyes :
   For vvhilst vvithin, this vaile of teares vve bide,
   We're load vvith mourning, griefe is Natures guide.

Jacob been ask'd, by *Pharo* of his age,
Reply'd, that fevv, and evill, vvere the dayes
Of his abode, in fleshly pilgrimage :
He gave this life, no better stile nor praise :
   Then sure vve're strangers, vvandring here and there,
   On this vvorlds stage, each acting lesse or mair.

Mans a pilgrime here. Nay, vve are pilgrimes here, tost to and fro,
There's no place permanent, on earth belovv :
Our dvvelling is above, then let us goe
To th' heavenly *Canaan*, vvhere all joyes flovv :
   Jerusalem, Jerusalems above,
   A glorious staunce, vvhere sits the King of love.

Its

of godlie sorrow.

Its not *Judeas* citie, built with hands,
The holy grave, and *Calvarie* containes;
With *Moriah*, where *Salmons* Temple stands,
Nor *Sions* seat, where *Davids* Towre remaines,
    Nor *Pilats* Hall, with farre moe relicks rare,
    This City is eternall, great, and faire.

Nor is it compass'd, with *Jehosophat*,
And on the south, with strait *Gehinnons* valley;
Nor on the north, with *Ennons* den halfe flat,
Nor wall'd about, lest *Arabs* it assaillie:
    This Citie is, impregnable, and more,
    Its fenc'd about, with everlasting power.

Indeed like *Olivet*, it overtops
This squink *Hebraick* citie; and excells   Our heavenly Jerusalem.
All earthly Mansions, which destruction lops
With fatall ruine: O what sounding knells?
    Fall from this fabrick, Angels singing musick!
    To lure our soules, to take cœlestiall physick.

Then come stress'd thou, who loaden is and weary,
And here refresh, thy fatigating soule:
Make haste, and come; and now no longer tarry!
Lest others barre Thee, from *Bethesdaes* Poole;
    When grace would touch thy sprite, thy heart is troubled
    But be not slow, lest losse on losse be doubled.

Consider Lord! these times wherein we live!
And harken to, thy chosen deare Elect;
Let *Israel* joy, and thine enemies grieve,
No time good God, their sacrifice neglect;
    But heare, and help them, guard them round about,
    With heavenly hosts, and thine Angelick rout.

The gushing Teares

Sions tears. Looke downe on thy stress'd *Sion*, and her teares,
And bottle up her woes, within the Urne
Of thy remembrance : Grievous grow her feares !
By Wolves in Lambskins, topsolturvie turne :
   Most fearfull seeme, these whirlewindes of time :
   Bred from the base, seditious dregs of slime.

Such wound her sides, but can not dimme her light,
The blood of Saints, is her espousall seed ;
When darkest stormes, would theat to bring downe night,
Thy spouse triumphs, in Christ her soveraigne head :
   No winde so high, nor wave so great, but grace,
   Can calme sterne blasts, when thou seest time and place.

When Man is snard by sinne, and seemes as lost,
Then God drawes neare, and makes his Sprite prepare
The soule for grace : So when forlorne or crost,
Christs Church appeares, that even her Saints despaire :
   Then comfort comes, the Lord will not exile her,
   Nor let the spight and craft, of men defile her.

Sions beauty. Pure like the gold is she, and christall cleare,
White as the snow, and sweeter than the hony ;
Thy virgine Spouse, most neare to Thee and deare !
Is farre more precious, than ten Worlds of money :
   The silver-fornace tryde, is not so fine,
   Nor halfe so sweet, tasts *Rethimosean* wine.

Sions crosses. Lord ! looke upon her crosses, and relieve
Her troubled Saints for Thee, and for thy Sonne :
She springs through briers, and 'mongst sharpe thorns doth live
Like to the Rose, in midst of thistles wonne :
   Her bloudy foes confound, protect her Saints,
   Erect, maintaine their zeale ; Lord heare their plaints.

Faire

Faire is thy sister, sweet thy Spousall love,
Her sent is bundled Myrrhe, fixt on her breasts :
She's thine cled with thy power, thine harmelesse Dove !
For in the Garden, of thy grace, she feasts :
  Come clasp her in thine armes ! come gracious Lord !
  And shew thy Virgin Queene, misericord.

Red shines the blush of *Sions* fragrant flowres,
Greene spring her boughs, like *Liban* Cedars tall ;
Swift flee her wings, to court her Paramours,
Knowne to her friends, but never knowne to all :
  Whose purple Roabes are pure, and finer farre,
  Then *Tyrians* wore, ere they were sackt by warre.

Like the Apple, in midst of Forrest trees,
Thy Welbeloveds so, 'mongst sonnes of Men :
The fairest 'mongst Women, with radiant eyes,
Would succour have, to save her from the Den
 · Of darknesse black : Lift up thy face and see !
  The spices, and ripe fruit of her fig-tree.

Whose breasts are like two twinnes, 'mongst Lillies fed,
Her rosie cheeks, more brighter than the Sunne :
One marke she beares, that in the soule is bred,
Another badge, lasts till our glasse be runne :
  The thirds a sparke, that mounts to Heaven above,
  The light of Saints, the love of endlesse Love.

Her richest garment, truth and righteousnesse,
And thats broudred, with mercy, grace, and peace ;
Faithfull in all, and patient in distresse ;
Constant to stand ; unchangeable of pace :
  And yet her beauty, Heavens no fairer fixe,
  Than mens tradition, would the same ecclipse.

She's

The gushing Teares

She's Catholick now, not ty'd to a place,
As *Jewrie* land, where God was onely knowne ;
Christs Church, points forth the Universe ; for grace,
Came with th'Evangel, peace to *Pagans* showne :
  The *Gentiles* then were call'd, as well as *Jews*,
  For mercy came with Jesus ; Gospell news.

And yet there many darknesse love, than light,
For sinne craves silence, and umbragious places ;
The clouds their covert, and their friend the night,
The day their foe, their Darling obscure faces :
  Thus blinde inveigling vice, turnes darknesse darke,
  For jet-black sin, can dim their foggy warke.

Too many darknesse love, so sinne provides,
That blinded eyes, must follow blinde tradition :
Blinde are they bred, but blinder far their guides,
Who maske poore Ignorants, with superstition :
  Whose Church maintaines, false miracles and treason,
  Blood, murther, incest, powder plots, and poyson.

Besides this Church idolatrous, and drunk
With indulgence and pardons, Policies,
At *Limbus* forgd : Absurd for gaine ; and sunk
In Purgatories, avarice, and lyes :
  There other orient Churches, erre, and fall,
  From Gospell truth ; they know it not at all.

The *Æthiopian*, *Abbasins*, the *Moore*,
Ægyptian Copties ; *Chelfanes*, *Georgians*, *Greeks*,
Nostrans, *Syriacks*, *Jacobines*, what more ?
Grosse *Armenians*, th' *Amaronite*, that seeks
  Talp-drawne ignorance : all of which do swerve,
  Tradition is the mistresse, whom they serve.

I could

of godlie sorrow.

I could dive here, in their distract'd conceit,
And blinde surmises, sowne these parts abroad:
But I suspend; yet here's a dangerous state,
To cast opinions, on the face of God:
   Their Patriarchs like themselves, do play the foole,
   That will not square Religion, with Christs rule.

O! if I could with *Jeremie* lament!
The worlds great errours, and my fallings too:.
And with grievd *Ninivie*, in time repent!
Lest with my slippings, justice me undo:
   Thrice happy were I, in this resolution,
   Ere death enhaunce my life, bring dissolution.

Yet soule despaire not, God is mercifull, Plenty of
mercy.
Long suffring, patient, full of kinde compassion:
His love to Man, is passing plentifull,
Whose grace and mercy, flow on our confession:
   For if one teare for sinne, fall from our eyes,
   He's pleas'd to pardon our infirmities.

How gracious then is God? how rich I say?
Is Christs redemption, fraught with saving bloud:
If we have faith in him, if we can pray?
And lift our eyes, fixt on the holy Rude:
   And then to suffer, in our zeale those pangs,
   Our Saviour thold, in this our welfare hangs.

My merit is thy mercy, that's the end!
Although good works, they are the way to heaven:
Yet not the cause, why I may there ascend,
That in thy love remaines, makes mine oddes eaven:
   For if thou hadst not dyed? what had I beene?
   And if not risen? what had my soule seen?

I 3

Thou

The gushing Teares

Thou wilt not gracions God, break the bruisde reed,
Nor quench the smoaking flaxe; for said thou hast,
That if our sinnes, were dy'd in scarlet red!
Thou'le make them white as snow, to let us taste
   Of grace and gladnesse: 'Cause the broken heart
   Thou'le not reject; contrition would convert.

Lord! thou ordaind, that death no flesh should shunne,
Cause why? it was, the doome and curse of sinne;
And so the punishment, of thy deare Sonne,
Which for our sakes, thy judgements cast him in:
   That as the Divell, prevailed by a Tree,
   So by a Tree, his power should vanquish'd be.

Then let the sight, of thy transgressions rude,
Draw drops of teares, from thine inunding eyes;
Since they did draw, so many drops of bloud
From thy Redeemers wounds; thy soule to ease:
   And looke what *David* said, in faith and feare,
   His sinnes were heavier, then his back could beare.

Then great was that sad burden Jesus bore,
In soule and body, to extirpe this curse;
His Father's wrath; our punishment therefore;
Our endlesse doome; eternall his secourse:
   His agonies, our happinesse implord,
   His bloody sweet, our detriments restord.

Christs passion our salvation.

As in a garden, first our sinne began,
So in a Garden, our redemption sprung:
That in like place, where *Adam*, the first Man
Was by the Serpents craft, exactly stung:
   So, so, in *Gethsemaine*, the Lord of light,
   Triumph'd q're sinne, put Satan to the flight.

Then

Then Christ is that pure glasse, wherein we spie
Our wants, our faults, or what amisse is done ;
Within, instruction, without, examples lye,
Here death proclaimd, and there salvation :
   The lists are set, then how can we come in,
   But by repentance, sorrowing for sin.

How precious were these tears of *Magdalen ?*
Who washt Christs feet, with eye-repenting drops ;   *Magdalens*
Yea, with her haire, did dry these feet agen,   *teares.*
And kiss'd them, with her lip-bepearled chops :
   Last, did anoint them, with a costly oyle,
   For which the Traitour *Judas,* checkd such spoile.

Thrice sacred worke ! but more blest oyle and teares,
Spent in the presence, of her soules Redeemer,
To expiat sinne : Whom now the dead endeares
To be a Saint ; for so did Christ esteeme her :
   And for which love, its memorie should last,
   From age to age, till all ages be past.

Besides her owne salvation, she became,
A dayly follower, to her Lord and Master ;
Yea, ministred things needfull ; fed zeales flame
With heavenly food, whereof she was a taster :
   Nay, to his death and grave, she never left him,
   And witnesse bore, how thence his Godhead reft him.

Came not kinde *Mary ?* weeping to his grave ?
To looke for Christ, but could not finde him there ;
The Angell spoke, and ask'd, Whom would you have ?
Said she, To see my Lord, is all my care,
   But he's not here ! (alas !) he's stolne away !
   And where he's laid, I know not, nor what way.
                              The

The gushing Teares

The winding-sheet she found, clos'd at both ends,
And close by the Tombe side, she sate her downe :
She sought, she felt, she search'd, and still suspends,
He was, and was not there : back to the towne
    She bends her face, yet staid, and cry'd, and wept,
    My Lord is stolne, whom souldiers watch'd, and kept.

The heavie stone roll'd back, which fourty men,
Could scarce advance ; yet where's my loving Lord ?
I'le runne and tell, let the Apostles ken !
What villanies this night, the *Jews* afford :
    Yet gone, she soone turnd back, love masterd heart,
    For from the Sepulchre, she would not part.

Nor did darke midnight fright her, nor the sight
Of two bright Angels, set at either end
Of his interrement ; nor their words afright
Her mourning zeale ; whose scope did deeper tend,
    To seeke the Lord, who gave her light and grace,
    And till she found him, would not leave the place.

At last Christ, in, a humane shape appear'd,
Whom she mistooke, and for a Gardner deemd :
Said he, Why wepst thou ? whom seekst thou ? she feard,
Said, Tell me, if, thou stole him, us redeemd :
    Then Jesus nam'd *Mary ;* she turnes about,
    And cry'd *Rabboni,* with a joyfull shout.

Christ reveals himself to Mary Magdalen.

This lessons us, that when we fast or pray,
We should not faint, but hope our suite shall speed :
He'le come, and come in time, though he delay,
Our suite he'le grant, thou we mistake the deed :
    Then *Mary*-like, let faith, charge hope, and do it,
    Faile not, be instant, grace shall bring thee to it.

Christ,

of godlie sorrow.

Christ, from the worldly wise and great, kept back
These mysteries, which silly ones did see :
And why ? his will, did this poore woman take,
To witnesse that he rose, and rose on hie :
    That by his resurrection, we might rise,
    To cut the clouds, and rent the azure skies.

As mines of gold and silver, still are found
On barren Hills, and scurrile fruitlesse parts :
So faith, so feare, so zeale, Religion sound !
Are chiefly plac'd, and fixt, in poore mens hearts :
    Did not Christs wisedome, this foresee, and choosd
    The scummes of Nature, whom the world refusd.

Lord ! grant with *Magdalen,* I spend my teares !
With sighing sadnesse, to implore thy pittie ;
That when my conscience, shall be void of feares,
I then may know, thou hast destroy'd my dittie :
    Speake peace, I pray thee, to this soule of mine,
    Since what I have, is all, and onely thine.

As fire reserves, two properties well mixt,
The one to warme, the other light to shoe :
So mercy hath two branches, better fixt,
Love to give peace, and pardon to forgoe :
    For pittie rules the helme, and Mans distresse
    Craves calme, in midst, of stormie wickednesse.

Fire hath two properties.

Like so, are troubles, th' whetstone that doth square
Stress'd hearts with prayer ; humble them most low :
Why ? cause adversities, they still prepare
The soule with patience, to sustaine the blow :
    All crosses to the just, their well intend,
    The cause being Christs, their suffrings in him end.

          K   Thou

The gushing Teares

Thou Joy of joyes, sweeter farre than sweetnesse,
Thy mercy is that balme, which heales my sores :
Thou peace, and pittie, oynt my wounds with wetnesse,
No drouth of sinne, can chink, my weeping gores :
  Why ? cause each sinne, begets a source of teares,
  When sinne evapourats, then grace appeares.

Then pardon, fraught with pittie, stops the Font,
Let sorrow melt the soule, in anxious sadnesse :
Deep sobs, and windy sighes, above they mount !
Whence they returne, surchargd with godly gladnesse :
  No sinne so sterne, but mercy can suppresse it,
  If with repenting grief, we but confesse it.

Lord save me from presumptuous sinnes, and save
My soule from sinnes desert ; mercy is thine !
All my transgressions, kinde remission crave,
They lye before thee (though the fault is mine)
  Begging for pardon, pardon they implore,
  And in my frailnesse, guiltinesse deplore.

A wounded conscience, who can beare that load ?
O racking sting ! that galles the quivring soule :
All sweet chastisements, of thy gentle rod,
Are cleansers, for, to purge our errours foule :
  But this mad grief, contracts a gnawing worme,
  Tempestuous whirlewindes, of an endlesse storme.

Ther'si
no flying
from Gods
presence. What quick evasion ? shall my flight contrive ?
To hide me from thy face, what way ? or where ?
If in the depths I drench, lo ! thou canst dive :
If to the utmost coasts ? lo ! thou art there !
  What umbrage, Cell, or Cave, the world about,
  Can men ascond, but thou wilt finde me out.

Above

Above, else deep beneath, or here below,
Thy presence is: Then whither shall I flee?
There is no point, but that point thou dost know,
Though smaller, than, the smallest haire can bee:
  No rocks, nor hills, nor darknesse can me night,
  Nor blacknesse vaile, from thy all-seeing sight.

Then in a word, there's no refuge for me,
But flye to thee, whose sight I can not shunne:
To beg for peace, and grace to mortifie
My sinfull lusts; before my glasse be runne:
  Lord! let mine eyes distill, like melting sleet!
  Or *Marie*-like, who washd with teares thy feet.

It is the minde, and not the Masse thou seeks,
My sprit is thine, and longs to be refinde:
By it thou knowst, my secreet wayes and creeks,
Whether I be, to good or ill inclinde:
  My soule's the Ruther, of my journey here,
  Be thou my Pilot, safely loofe, and steere.

God craves the heart.

Conduct me straight, to thy Cœlestiall Port,
That in the Sabboth, of eternall rest,
My soule may reigne: And with the Angels court
Thy face, with joyes, that cannot be exprest:
  Where all content, in fulnesse of rich pleasures,
  Shall them attend, in overjoying measures.

Who here within, this Domicile of dust?
And boggy baggage, of a stinking lump?
Would stay to eat, the excrements of lust,
And feed on filthinesse, that rotten stump:
  Nay, none but Abjects; holy Ones rejoyce,
  To be dissolvd, make happynesse their choice.

K 2

But

The gushing Teares

But some heart-sunke, in worldly greed and cares,
Would build their Paradise, in this base life :
And by extreames, involve them selves in snares,
Hating the truth, in falshood spend their strife :
   And what envy, can not accomplish ? they
   Will make extortion, all their hatred swey.

Can thou forgivenesse crave, for thy misdeeds ?
And will not first, forgive anothers wrongs :
How can thou pray, or thinke thy prayer speeds ?
When in thy heart, thou malice keeps ; and longs
   To be revengde : This is no Christian life,
   To pray and praise, when sunke in spite and strife.

Away with envy, malice, pride and hate,
Let not the Sunne go downe, upon thy wrath :
Live to the Lord, and live in holy state,
Love one another, there's the marke of faith !
   Live, and live holy, whom thou serves regard !
   He'le come, and come in haste, with thy reward.

Greed breeds envie.

Then be not Spider-like, that doth exhaust
It selfe, in workes, of little use, and time :
Nor like the *Indians* rude, absurd, devast,
That will give gold, for glasse, rich gemmes for slime :
   And precious stones, for toyes, and trifling things,
   Which strangers bring; knives, whistles, beeds, brasse rings.

All smell of greed, though not of perfect wit,
Then hang not downe thy head, for lack of trash :
Let *Crœsus* be, thy *Lydian* Mappe ! he'le fit
Thy greedy humours, with a falling dash :
   All which are shades, of floating vanities,
   Mans onely constant, in unconstancies.

                                           Shall

of godlie sorrow.

Shall rich *Saturnia*, with her cramming gold ?
Deceive my heart, and move my minde to swell :
Or with false lookes, vaine hopes to me unfold ?
To snare my thoughts, which vertue may expell :
   A figge for worldly baits ; a tush for greed !
   For being poore, Ime rich in having need.

A contempt of riches.

And why ? cause povertie, that is so light,
As being weigh'd, in ballance with the winde,
Doth hang aloft : Then can not seeme no weight !
Nor dare to sit, as sad, on my free minde :
   Say, if it should, it were some fainting thought
   Would me deject ; for povertie is nought.

Then all my riches, is content I see,
A stock more sure, than Wealth can Worldlings lend :
Poore was I borne, and as poore must I die,
Unlesse good luck, a chest, to death extend :
   Get I a sheet, to wrappe up my dead bones,
   I'me richer far than gold, or precious stones.

Seven foot of ground, and three foot deep I crave,
The passing bell, to sound mine obsequie :
Gold, lands, and rents, the living world I leave,
Else if I smart, by streames, by flouds, or sea :
   Then shall some fishes belly, be my grave,
   No winding sheet, my Corps shall need to have.

But stay ! what passion, thus diverts my minde ?
Dust shall to dust, and earth to earth returne ;
If I can here, true peace of conscience finde,
What losse ? what trash ? what crosse ? can make me mourne :
   For when laid low, and having lost this frame,
   My soule shall mount to Heaven, from whence it came.

        The

The gushing Teares

The im-
mortall
substance
of the soul. The soule it is, of heavenly substance fram'd,
Breathd in at man's nostrils, by his Maker ;
A sprit invisible, Gods image nam'd,
With whom of Essence, infinite partaker :
    Will, mem'rie, knowledge, faculties divine,
    Are my soules socialls, reason do confyne.

Will, is to rule, and knowledge to conceave,
And memorie, a locall power assumes ;
Knowledge, as chief, makes understanding crave
A league with love, whose worke true blesse resumes :
    Lo ! there's the fruit, of this cœlestiall mould !
    Which never here shall rot, nor hence grow old.

Then teach me, Lord ! to count my slyding dayes,
That I to wisedome, may my heart apply :
So shall thy statutes, guyde my slipprie wayes,
And circumspection, all my actions try :
    Who knew his date of life ? and might attaine it ?
    Would learne to live well, else he would disdaine it.

We're apt to note, the lives of other men,
But not our owne ; selfe-love, our sense divides ;
Like two ships, under saile, and one course, ken ?
Both sailers think, each other swifter glides
    Than their owne ship : So we can check and show
    The lives of others, and our owne misknow :

Our haires growne gray, our desires then grow greene,
And after earthly things, we hunt amaine ;
We love this world so well, as oft its seene !
That we are dead with grief, ere death hath slaine
    Us with destruction : Age would faine be young,
    To nurse the serpent, that his soule hath stung.

                                 Man

of godlie sorrow.

Man lives like him, who fell into a pit,
Yet caught a grippe, by a branch'd tree, and hung
Above his head, a hony Combe did sit,
Whence his deep appetite, delight had wrung :
   Below two gnawing wormes, razing its roote,
   The tree fals downe, and greed devourd the fruit.

The pit our grave, the Tree, this mortall life,
This hony combe, vaine pleasures of the world ;
Two gnawing wormes, the speedy thiftu'ous strife,
Of night and day, wherein our dayes are hurld :
   Time clouds our light, the glasse is runne, we fall,
   Downe to the dust, where death triumphs o're all.

The mi-
sery and
shortnesse
of life.

Then darknesse covers Man, he mouldring rots,
Earth gluts him in her wombe, away he goes !
His better part, resumes one, of two lots,
No shade, nor sepulchre, can it enclose :
   It either mounts above, or falls beneath,
   There is no midst, can stop, or stay its path.

Each course is violent, faith conquers Heaven,
By force and wrestling, in the way of light ;
VVhich strait is, and few enter : Most are driven
Downe to the gulfe, of ever-sorrowing night :
   That way is broad, where numbers, numberlesse,
   Fall in earths Cell, plungd in cursd wofullnesse.

Such as the life's, so frequently the death,
The Divels deceit, prolongs us in delay :
Then wouldst thou flee that pestilence ? set faith
Against temptation : Runne the happy way
   That leads to life : Make thy confession cleare !
   And beg for peace, then mercy will draw neare.

Yet

The gushing Teares

Yet ah ! how fraile am I ? how weak ? how wretchd ?
That even my conscience, trembles at my cace :
Alas ! poore sleeping soule ! how art thou stretchd ?
In drousie dulnesse, void of good, and grace :
   Pluck up thy selfe, condole, confesse, convert,
   And strive to stand, although thy steps divert.

The Compasse stands not, solide to the Pole,
Though with the Loadstone, any point is touchd ;
But hath some variation, we controle,
To the East or West, as hourely is avouchd :
   So none of our best deeds, though touchd with grace,
   Points God amaine, deflection marres our pace.

Frailtie
and falling
follovv
man.

Which made Saint *Paul*, ingenuously confesse,
That by himselfe, he nothing knew, nor could
Be thereby justify'd ; 'cause his digresse
Was judg'd by God ; the Loadstone true that would
   Point forth each point ; and yet forget, forgive,
   The least, the maine, the guilt, for which we grieve.

The Woman for adultrie, been accusde,
Was brought to be adjudgd before our Lord :
Their thoughts he saw, and what deceit they usde ;
They fled, she stood, and found misericord :
   Woman (said he) thine adversars are gone,
   Ile not condemne thee, mercy is my Throne.

How good and gracious, was the light of grace,
That purgd, and pardond, this Woman unrequested :
She's gone, and freed, the law could take no place,
No roome for *Moses*, when his Master feasted :
   For why ? from double death, he set her free,
   The Judge was pleader, he discuss'd the pleye.

                                        Alas !

of godlie sorrow.

Alas! when I recall, preteriat times,
What losse finde I, in my lost dayes and deeds:
For morall slips, a world of weightier crimes,
And to condemne me, justice, judgement pleads:
    Yet stay sad soule, conceive, confesse, condole,
      With me my sinnes, my frailties Ile controule.

What frivole fancies, flow from my flowne minde?
Which often blinde my judgement; and divert
My better aimes; whilst reason can not finde
The cause of such delusions; for I smart
    In their velocitie; abusing will,
      They thrall combustion, to assist their ill.

What foolish prancks, in gesture, deed, or word?
What fond conceits, in flash-flowne merryments?
What scoffing squibs, which taunting mocks afford?
What idle straines, in vaine spent complements?
    Have I not done; and in such actions quick,
      To foole my fellows, with a jeering trick.

The va-
rieties of
vanitie.

This thought, that surmise, this flash, that reglance,
Of suddaine, motions, else of flowne conceats:
More voluble they were, than wide-wingd chance!
Which tops all things, all where, and at all dates:
    There's nought more swift than fancie, nought more fond.
      More light than winde, which flees, and is not found.

Then, Lord, ingraft in me, a constant heart,
Sound, grave, and solid, holy, wise, and just:
Prudent in much, and provident in part,
That all, my all, may in thy mercies trust:
    Rule thou the Ruther of my foggy minde,
      Lest in dark mists I wander, and turne blinde.

Bring

The gushing Teares

Bring me unto my selfe, from outward things,
And from my selfe, even to thy selfe, bring me ;
That I in chast will, and pure desirings,
May be like Thee, as I'me in nature : see ?
   Lord set me wholly, on fire with thy love,
   That my lights, and delights, in Thee may move.

This Worlds a Mappe, of transitorie toyes !
Which to expostulate, were labour lost ;
A shaddow mask'd, with hypocritick joyes,
Fals in the face, and hollow in the cost :
   And whats our love, or life ? when dead, ere rotten ?
   Our short stay here, is presently forgotten.

Man like to vapour melts, wealth as the winde,
Doth flee away ; and honour like fond dreames,
Dissolves to nought ; so Parentage we finde
Unnaturall oft : Yea, children by extreames,
   Rebellious grow : So mighty men grow meane,
   And meane men great ; this change is daily seene.

Would God mens sonnes, could learne how Storks they do
Who, when their old growne weake, diseasde, distrest,
Their young ones beare them, on their backs ; and lo !
They flee with them all where, from nest, to nest ;
   With care they keep them, bring them what they need,
   Though they themselves, have their owne young to feed.

Its strange ætheriall love, should passe humane !
For our young brood, would have their Parents die ;
Ingratefull That they might get their goods, and thereby gaine,
children to If poore, so want, they will them straight denie :
aged pa-
rents.   Nay, slight them, scorne them, raile on their distresse,
   Thus they decline, and here their wretchednesse.

                                  O love-

O lovelesse age ! you might this fault amend !
And pittie Nature, gave you life to live ;
Be not like Vipers, for to make an end
Of these, who did, your blood and beeing give ;
   If not the Turtle, play the Eagles part,
   Since Parents are, your Pelicanes in heart.

All thinges runne contrare, in a head-strong change,
The world growes grim, mens hearts grow false and double ;
Twixt sonne and father, this is nowayes strange,
To see each one, forsake anothers trouble :
   Nay, friends, familiars, blood, kinred, mother,
   Live most in strife, no love 'twixt one another.

So elements are changd, in part from nature,
But above all, the earth growes bare and old ;
The Moones prest influence, failes in some Creature,
Short falls her force : The Sunne growes tyrde and cold,
   And seasons frozen ; the airie clouds convert
   In boistrous windes : most Climes ! like tributes part.

Most grounds grow barren, and their fruits are blasted,
And bestiall perish, by depressing stormes :
The aire's, intemperate, and the fields ly wasted
With nipping frosts, and canker spoiling wormes :   Elemental
   Nay, mens conditions change, and Christian love   changes.
   Growes worse than barbarous, we hourely prove.

Mercy, good Lord ! grant mercy, for thy Name
Is Mercy, mercy, Lord of kinde compunction :
Father of pittie, compassion we claime,
Lover of love, thou life of loves conjunction :
   Come patient Syre ! O thou long suffring God !
   And slow to anger ; come ! spare thy threatning rod.

The gushing Teares

The present miseries of Christendome.

Looke downe on Christendome, this Westerne world,
Whose lands, (with fatall sword) are drunk with blood :
Where Kings and kingdomes, in combustions hurld !
Turne spectacles of scorne, to Pagans rude :
    There is no Nation, within Christian bounds,
    That suffers not disasters, threats, or wounds.

The *Infidell* beholds, and swearing sayes,
That our Religion, is a bare profession :
For Christs dishonourd, in our ambitious wayes,
No faith we show, farre lesse of truth confession :
    Pryde, puft with malice, is our Christian marke,
    Deceit, despight, our daylie divelish wark.

Here wounds, there bloud, here death, and there disasters,
Here Mothers mourning, for their slaughterd sonnes :
There Widdows weeping, servants for their Masters :
Here helplesse Orphanes, bursting forth starv'd groanes :
    There sisters for their brothers, sorrowing sore,
    Last fatall framelings, one another gore.

This universall scourge, is grievous great,
For kinred, nor alliance, nought can swage :
Faith, for performance, breeds but greater hate :
Deep words and seales, turne reason ragg'd in rage,
    Kinde honesty is fled, true love exyld,
    And conscience with deceitfulnesse defyld.

Looke on this halfe *Europian* angry face !
And thou shalst see, the mother of mischiefe !
Point forth at *Rome*, that hollow hellish place,
Eye but her Prelats, hatchers of our grief !
    And thou shalst finde, that Antichristian Whoore !
    Would nought but Millions, for one life devoure.

                              She

of godlie sorrow.

She hunts her hounds abroad, and they obey,
Some worke, some runne, some plot, some poyson Nobles;
Some treason hatch, some murder! what they say,
Is fac'd with Sophistrie; perjurie doubles
   Their mentall muttrings: The *Jesuites* their Trumpet!
   Must sound the cruelties, of that *Babell* Strumpet.

At home, we have at home! at home, alace!
A world of woes, and rogueries of like kinde:
I could, I would, I should, bewray this cace!
I dare, but dare not, signifie my minde:
   That faction is so strong, and I so weake,
   That thrice the Prison, they my lodging make.

They bragge like Butchers, of their beastly deeds,
And laugh at cruelty, as at a play?
Their hornes they push, and policie them leads,
Nought but mischief, their head-strong course can stay:
   And glutting gape, to have old rotten *Rome*
   Erect'd our Mistresse, else themselves consume.

What kinred can they claime, to *Tybers* banks,
(The river shallow, and in Summer dry)
We have Gods word, and they posternall blanks,
The light here shines, with them doth darknesse lye:
   Or shall the truth, in foppish relicks rest,
   That were to *Britaine*, an *Egyptian* pest.

But stay, O stay! long have I liv'd, and liv'd
To see their blindlesse, in dejections fall;
I know their wayes, and at their lives have griev'd
They pierce our wills, and we their projects thrall:
   Is any under Sunne, so well acquainted,
   VVith them, as I, whose body they tormented.

L 3
                              They

The gushing Teares

They wish that *Malaga* had burnt me quick,
As doom'd I was so, by *Spaines* Inquisition :
Whose tortures (ah !) fast to my bones doe stick,
And vexe me sore, with pangs of requisition :
    Great God avenge't, confound them ; and restore
    Me to my health ; for Ile debord no more.

Lord, give me grace, of all things to praise Thee,
Who never leaves thine owne, left in distresse :
Thou first discoverd, then deliver'd me,
A worke of love, beyond my hopefulnesse,
    I sought, thou wrought, then did enlarge my life,
    Free from destruction, last, from Papall strife.

Now to observe my method, Ile returne
To square construction, with deploring Saints :
Then here's my rule, Ile both rejoyce and mourne,
For teares bring joy, when mercy crownes complaints :
    The just man sinnes, seven times a day ; and I
    Full seventy seven times, may each houre descry.

Oh ! if mine eyes ! like *Arathusean* Springs,
(Fled *Greece* to *Syracuse*) could yeeld three Fonts :
One to bewaile originall sinne, stings
The life of nature ; the other (ah !) amounts
    To actuall trespasse ; the last, and worst comes in,
    To consuetude, a deadly dangerous sinne.

Compari-
sons of
freedome
from sin.

Yet as the Malefactour, when set free
From death and pardond ; his heart is overjoyed ;
Or as the Prisner, set at libertie,
Which long before, he never had enjoyed :
    So Man, when freed from sinne, and Satans clawes,
    His soule triumphs, and loves religious lawes.

A

of godlie sorrow.

A shipwrackt man, cast on some planke to seeke,
The safe set land ; which got, how glad is he?
So shipbroke sinners, in some stormie creek,
Of sinfull seas, and sterne iniquitie :
   Beene free to coast the shoare of grace, and landed,
   More greater joy, than theirs, nev'r soule commanded.

A wandring sonne, long forraniz'd abroad,
In Parents hopes, left desolate, or slaine :
Yet when returnd, and shaken off the load
Of strangers rites ; how they rejoyce amaine?
   So Saints, so Heavens, so Angels joy, when changd,
   One sinner turnes, who long from God hath rangd !

These teares at *Babell* spent, on *Tigris* banks,
Where *Euphrates* salutes, that stately station :
Sowre-set *Hebraick* plaints, powr'd forth by ranks,
Of mourning Captives, banishd from their Nation,
   And *Sions* face : O sad *Judaick* songs !
   Wailing for sinne, and sterne *Chaldean* wrongs.

The Jewish tears on Babilons banks.

None of their teares were lost, they pierc'd the heavens,
Whence kinde compassion, free deliv'rance sprung,
God from his deoperculate Cherubins !
Imbracd these feares, his chosen flock had stung :
   Then *Mordecais* sackcloth, Queene *Esthers* woes,
   Wrought *Hamans* death, made *Israel* to rejoise.

Thus teares, and pale repentance, brought reliefe,
Though once exyld, see now, they're back-reclaimd :
The least construction, bred from godly griefe,
Begets like mercy, mercy stands proclaimd :
   At Heavens court gate : for Christ the trumpet sounds !
   And bids all sinners come, he'le heale their wounds.

Who

The gushing Teares

VVho pleads for peace, shall mercie finde with God,
The oyle of grace, shall oyle their stinking gores ;
All fatigating soules, griev'd with the load
Of sinne, may come, whose case remorse deplores :
   For sanctify'd crosses, all just Mens troubles,
   Are not prest sorrows ; Mercy ! comfort doubles.

I never finde affliction, fall on me,
VVithout desert; for God is true and just :
Nor shall it come, and without profit be,
For God is good, as mercifull I trust :
   Then welcome all afflictions sent from God,
   He whom he loves, he chastens with his rod.

Correcti-
on begets
awe.VVho loves his childe, administers correction,
And keeps him under awe, cause of complainers ;
Yet notwithholds, kinde Natures best affection,
But curbes his will, to rectifie his manners :
   Much more Gods love abounds, cause we are fraile,
   And playes the Jayler, then becomes our baile.

He lets us fall, that he may raise us up,
And though we sinke, we cannot headlong drowne,
By gentle stripes, he represents the cup
VVhich Christ drunk of ; our patience for to crowne :
   As *Peter* sunke, then shrunke, was twice recall'd,
   So if we sinke, or slyde, we are not thralld,

The love of God it free, his mercy gracious,
There's no constraint, binds God, to pittie man,
But of free will, would make our soules solacious,
To glorifie his goodnesse ; if we can
   But apprehend by faith, what he hath done.
   For us, through Christ, his onely righteous Sonne.

Man

of godlie sorrow.

Man pondring on his momentany dayes,
May well conceive, the brevetie of time :
From which extract, he should contract the praise
Of him, who hastes, to short the sense of slime :
  And if it were not, for his owne Elect,
  He would prolong the day, and speed neglect.

What is this age of ours ? much like a span ;
Yea ; like the water buble, shent, as swelld ;
Even as the glyding shade, so fadeth Man,
Or like the morning grasse, soone sprung, soone quelld :   Short and
  Nay, like the flowre which falls, then rots ere noone,   evil are
  So melt our dayes, and so our dayes are done.   our dayes.

And yet what are our dayes, the longest liver ?
As one man once, I saw, seven score yeares old :
Nay, diverse six score, health was such a giver
Of lengthning time, ere they returnd to mould :
  And yet a dreame, whose larger halfe of life,
  Was spent in sleep, the rest in toile and strife.

Oh ! if ambitious men ! their ends were showne !
That like the froth, do beat on rocks of death :
That shadow short, from a fled substance flowne,
Much like a dreame, so vanisheth their breath :
  Then would their deeds, forbeare to tyranize,
  The Just might live, and offer sacrifice.

But (ah !) their thundring spight ! like t'a storme thuds !
And boasting men, would thereby God upbraid ;
The light they scorne, and in Infernall clouds,
Would smother vertue, with a sanguine spade ;
  Is not this Christian world, with bloud o'rewhelmde !
  Their swords with strife, their heads with hatred helmde.

      M   See !

The gushing Teares

See! godlesse Tyrants, tyrannizing still,
And scourging Saints, themselves they scourge with shame:
Like *Nimrod* they, 'gainst Heaven will have their will!
Though justice, in sad judgements plague the same:
    At last, behold! where they themselves sojourne,
    Their threatning swords, back in their bosome turne.

When *Dionisus* for tyranny had fled,
He kept a schoole, in *Calabria*, eight yeares:
At *Montecilion*, opposite indeed
To *Sicilie*; which he at last endeares:
    A king to turne a schoolemaster, was strange!
    But back to turne a King, a rarer change.

In this our age, what kings have beene dis-thrond,
Detect'd, cast downe, last banish'd from their bounds:
I could recite, and where th' injust were crownd,
And Princes headlong, hurled from their grounds:
    Pryde fosterd spight, with them the Ulcer brecks,
    Which gored the harmelesse, broke ambitious necks.

Would God mens choler, could with patience lurke!
To blunt the edge of anger, and to curbe
With *Job* their passion; let forbearance worke
The stress'd *Athenian* suffring: Not disturbe
    Times meek-fac'd calmenesse, prosperous in peace.
    With which no soile, more blest was, once than *Greece*.

Athens made the mother and mirour of miseries.

Have I, said *Athens*, beene the mother nurse!
Of lib'rall Airts, and science, Natures light;
And now my Carcase, beares the vulgar curse,
Of *Spartaes* scorne; and *Lacedemon* spight:
    Shall malice tread on virtue? shall disgrace?
    Of neighbours hate, on my gold tresses trace.

                        Though

of godlie sorrow.

Though thirty one Invaders on me prey,
Each one triumphing, in anothers ill :
Yet flexe I not, though forc'd for to obey,
No pride shall presse my patience ; nor good will,
  Gaine me to flatter : Nor puft Tyrants shall
  Bruise me in pieces, though I suffer thrall.

Yet was her Virgine body, made a Whoore
To ev'ry proud Insulter ; and her fame
A Strumpets voice : Whom *Mars* did once defloure,
And turning Harlot, robd her Vestall name :
  The Victors glutting, on her vanquishd spoyles,
  Made griefe guide sorrow ; Fortune fixt her foyles.

In this digression, take a morall note,
From slaughterd *Athens*, now a village left ;
That all beginnings, (not their endings) quote,
Have floorishd faces, from their spring-tyde reft :
  Their *Medium* is not long, the morne is all,
  And then their end, in lumps of fragments fall.

What once was *Ilium* ? *Tyrus* now calld *Sur* ?
And *Ninivie*, whose ruines are ruind :
Seven ported *Thebes*, rich in silks and Furre,
And *Carthage*, *Africks* glory, now declind :
  Nay, save of three, some monuments are showne,
  The other two, their seats, are hardly knowne.

The inconstancie of vvorldly pride.

So *Antioch*, whence sprung the Christian name,
And *Sions* Dame, *Judeas* sacred citie :
Yea, *Alexandria*, famous in her fame.
With *Babylon*, the remaindure of pittie :
  Though not like *Jericho*, a lumpe of stones,
  They're but rent relicks, of their former ones.

M 2

A

The gushing Teares

A wondrous thing of Nature, I observe,
When *Xerxes* cross'd, the *Hellespontick* sea:
In greatest Grandure, then begunne to swerve
From Princely courage, staid dexteritie:
    Where when the Pontick waves, with troups were cled,
    Of numbers, numberlesse, and he the head.

Ambiti-
ous *Xerx-
es*, bevvail-
ing the
brevitie of
life. Then burst he forth in teares, and wept amaine,
(Gazing on thousands, which his puissance brought)
And said, This sight, and all this glorious traine!
Within an hundred yeares, shall come to nought:
    I weep (said he) 'cause nothing here can stay,
    But like full streames, they slide, and steale away.

My horse, my Chariots, Engynes, men of warre,
And Souldiers strong, shall all dissolve in dust;
My spight 'gainst *Greice*, and their imperious jarre,
My greed of honour, their revenge injust,
    Which *Sardis* bore: Shall eftsoone be as they,
    Had never beene, so mortall things decay.

Thus mournd this Pagan King, whose rule may learne
Most moderne Tymes, to waile like consequence:
For in which Mappe, true judgement may discerne,
That ancient dayes, had full experience
    Of natures frailtie, changings, mortals being,
    Whose restlesse course, was sight-lost shadows flying.

So day and night, on two extreames depend,
Either to lengthen, or to shorten prest:
The restlesse tides, like alterations spend,
By *Cynthias* waxing, waining is exprest:
    The seasons runne, foure times the yeare about,
    And are renewd ay, as their times go out.

No

of godlie sorrow.

No state doth solide stand ; Man most mutable !
In fortune, or himselfe, each leaving other :
He carelesse fled from meanes : If disputable ?
His meanes are fled from him, to court another :
    Whats mine to day, to morrow may be thine,
    And whats thine now, next day, it may be mine.

Nor is their health in beauty, nor in strength,
Of body soundnesse : Subject to disease,
Is ev'ry creature ; young and old at length,
Shall feele infirmities ; Natures worst unease,
    Graft in corruption : None can sicknesse shunne,
    But he must suffer, ere his glasse be runne,

Such sowre flagelloes, are the rods of nature,
To whippe the childe of lust, with sound correction :
Cause why ? they're Moulds, where grace renews each creature,
And makes chastisements, signifie affection :
    Nay, they're preparatives, against sterne death,
    Beene fenc'd with patience, flankd about with faith.

All which denote, men should not fixe their hearts,
On transitorie things, or trash below :
All under sunne, in whole, in rest, or parts,
Are Emblemes of inconstancie I know :
    Man, Beast, and Tree, Wealth, Honour, Health, and Fame,
    Are but crost Changelings, of this changing Frame.

Whats heere (beholde !) but toyle, and worldlie losses ?
Sinne, shame, and sorrow, trouble, griefe, and scorne,
Spight, strife, and malice, ignorance, and crosses,
Adversities sterne face ; friendship forlorne :
    Pryde flankd with povertie, Tyrants infliction,
    Of gall'd oppression, to adde distresse affliction,

This life is loaden with crosses.

M 3

Such

The gushing Teares

Such passive moods, are frequent growne, that now
Old crazd calamitie, begins to quiver :
Both rich and poore, live timerous, and how ?
The one to keep whats got : The others feaver,
  Burnes for to get, the first, fears losse, and trembles,
  The seconds patience, with content dissembles.

The flat-
tery of
Courts.
In Citie, Court, and Countrey, here's their fall,
Deceit, deceives them, with deceitfull stings ;
But most in royall Mansions ! there's the gall !
Where Sophistrie, speaks two contrary things :
  And neither thinks to do : Here flattrie stands,
  To blinde the truth, there ambodextrate hands.

Then blest are they ! who live at home in rest,
And neither follow Court, nor courtly toyes :
That life is sweet, and of all lives the best,
For homely Houlds, are chargd with privat joyes :
  Most Courtiers mouthes. seeme kind, with hearts as hollow
  As derne *Sybillas* Hall, which few can follow.

To day they smile, and promise what you would,
And fill stress'd suppliants, with inunding hopes :
To morrow as unkinde, and frozen cold,
And tramp in dust, their suiters sad-sought scopes :
  Unlesse their palmes, you oynt, with sov'raigne ore,
  Your suite is lost, and you left to deplore.

The very Dunse, that yesterday was base,
When having got an office, looks as hie
As skie-set clouds, then will cast downe his face,
And squinke acquaintance, to have courtesie :
  This Ruffian, who did homage thee before,
  Now thou must beck to him, and him implore.

                                        Tell

of godlie sorrow.

Tell Courtiers of repentance, they will mock !
And turne their teares in taunts, and scoffing jests ;
He who feares God, they hold him as a block,
Its vice and foolerie, their conceit digests :
    They never dreame of judgement, nor of death,
    But spend in complements, their flattering breath.

Let none mistake, nor misconstruct my minde,
I meane of Courts, in generall all where ;
There's good and bad, in any hollow kinde,
Both men and beasts, in this may claime their share :
    A Savage, I have found, as kinde in part,
    As best thought Christians, save the noble heart.

All I desire, and what my soule can wish !
Is that the truth may stand, and vertue flourish ;
Lo ! there's the daintie, of an holy dish !
To feed poore soules, and humble ones to nourish :
    And for this cause, each one should pray with other,
    Gods word may prosper, and his Church our mother.

Sions prosperitie prayed for.

Lord spread the Mantle, of thy mercy round
About the borders, of her glorious shrine ;
Enlarge her power ; let earths remotest bound,
Stand for the limits, of her light divine :
    That thou who on bright Cherubins doth ride,
    May guide, and guard, the beauty of thy Bride.

I'le dive no more in sinne, and crooked wayes
Of rotten nature, which corruption brings :
Nor from the worlds example, draw these strayes
Of th' head-strong multitude ; confusion stings :
    Ile lay about the Ruther of my minde,
    To keep a safer loofe, and thirle the winde.

What

The gushing Teares

What rapt cœlestiall, forceth my desire ?
To be dissolv'd ; my soule may mount aboue,
To see these joyes, that blesse, that glorious hyre :
Which Saints enjoy ; life's ever-springing love !
  My hope resumes, I might as happy rest,
  In pleasures there, as they are happy blest.

Now I returne (good God turne thou to me)
As Travellers, who have been long abroad ;
Are forc'd by love, their soile and friends to see,
No rest, till then, their hearts, the way have trode :
  So I'me estrangd, my Countrie is above,
  Heaven is the place, thou Lord, my light, my love.

Great is the glory, of thy glorious face !
Enstall'd with Angels ; Saints, and Martyres gone :
Set fore the Throne, with legions of each race,
Singing applauses, to that blessed One,
  The Lambe of Love ; our Advocate, thy Sonne,
  Who by his death wrought our Salvation.

Fixe fast my thoughts, to the tree of thy crosse,
Draw all the forces of my soule to Thee :
Lift up my heart, let me renounce the drosse,
And dregs of ill ; let me aspire on hie !
  And walke 'twixt feare and love, in all my deeds,
  As thou 'twixt justice, and mercy proceeds.

The sun shines on the good and bad. Thy vertues are for us, sufficient great,
Like as the Sunne it shines, the World all where ;
Yet ev'ry man, enjoyeth so much heat,
As if it shinde to him, in proper share :
  So are thy graces, infinite, and we
  Enjoy the fruits of their felicitie.

                                        But

But what ? our lives are short, so are our dayes !
Except in troubles ! miseries, alace !
Our continuance certaine, in uncertaine wayes,
No time of death is knowne, to us nor place :
 Gods will is so, to have us still prepard,
 An set on watch, lest that our steps be snard.

Each minutes life, steps forward to sterne death,
And ev'ry act, robs some part of our life ;
Like him who sailes in ships, and action hath
In toylesome paines, yet forward flees his strife :
 We cannot twice returne in Natures state,
 'Cause time runs post, and can make no retreat.

My Sunne of life, hath his Meridian past,
And plung'd I am, in th'after-noone of age;
The night of Nature, fastens on me fast !
And death waits closse, to pull me from this stage :
 But Lord, thou wilt not, leave my soule in grave,
 Let ly the Corps, they'le once conjunction have.

Our dayes
nor time
can never
returne.

Now having sung, of deep remorse, and teares,
Lord ! save me from these weeping teares of Hell ;
Which grief declares, and ever-gnashing feares !
For losse of joy ; and sense of horrours fell :
 Who would not here, a few spent teares disclose,
 Shall there bewaile, in floods of bitter woes.

As sea-bred fishes, never saltnesse wed,
But still their bodies, stay both sweet and fresh :
So grant my soule, thats with corruption cled,
May live as pure, not medling with the flesh
 But sinne begins first, in the sillie soule,
 And ends into the body, base and foule.
N

What

The gushing Teares

Christ is
our Phy-
sitian.

What shall I say ? when mans rot in disease,
And ulserd sore, the Phisitian draws neare,
To give him pills and potions, worke his ease,
And lets him blood, he may his health endure :
   Much more Christ's bloud, can purge and cleanse the soule,
   Of all uncleannesse, pardon what is foule.

Then to great *Jove*, the mighty King of kings,
Ile prostrate fall, on my low bended knees ;
To beg for mercy, mercy comfort brings,
And joy of sprit, works peace from gushing eyes :
   So Lord of Lords ! sweet Christ, what I would have ?
   Is knowne, and showne, I call, I cry, I crave.

Now by these words, whom seek you, and confession,
By thy breath, made the Sergeants backward fall ;
By that care rouzd thine, slumbring in digression,
By thy pangs in *Gethsemane*, one, and all :
   By that power and patience, fore *Anne* exprest,
   By that prophecie, of *Cajaphas* the Priest.

By that deep agony, of bloud and sweat,
By these sore scourgings, spittings on thy face,
By these rough nailes, piercd thy hands and feet,
By all these mockings, done thee for disgrace :
   By that sharpe speare, which smote thy tender heart,
   By that Viniger thou drunk, and gall of smart.

By that crowne of thornes, thrust on thy bare head,
By these blood sprinklings, downe thy face that fell :
By that heavy Crosse, on thy shoulders spread,
By thy descending downe, in earths dark Cell ;
   By that great power, of thy great resurrection,
   By thine ascension : O profound election !

By

By thy five bleeding wounds, I thee implore,
And by the vertue, of thy death and passion ;
By that purple Roabe, forc'd in scorne thou wore,
By all these taunts, these Ruffians spent for fashion :
  Nay, by that superscription, wrote for news,
  Jesus of Nazareth, King of the Jews.

The suffe-
rings and
passion of
Christ.

By thy nativitie, and incarnation,
Yea, by these words, *Mother behold thy Sonne,*
And Sonne, Behold there, thy consolation !
Go live, and live in peace, live both as one :
  Nay, by this moode, for heavie was thy load,
  Why thus forsakst thou me, my God my God.

By thy baptisme, 'fasting, humiliation,
By all thy miracles, and wonders done :
By these teares thou shed, and transfiguration
On *Tabor* seene ; As thou art Christ, Gods sonne :
  Save, shield, and shelter, my designes, my wayes,
  For my souls health, and thine eternall praise.

Nay, by, and for, and from, thy self I beg,
For pittie, grace, and pardon, free remission
Of all my sinnes : O cleanse me the least dreg,
That lurkes within my Temple ; thy possession :
  Let all be cleane, Lo ! there's the totall summe !
  My soule implores, come now, Lord Jesus come.

Great King of ages ! Monarch, of all times !
Thou first, and last, is, was, and ever blest !
Redeemer, unredeemd ! Purger of Crymes !
Thou Light, of lights, thou Mans sole-soveraigne rest :
  Encrease, in me thy Sprit, infuse thy grace !
  Confirme my heart, show forth thy loving face.

N 2

Sweeter

The gushing Teares

Sweeter than hony ! or the hony Combe !
Life, light, and love, all goodnesse, peace, and grace !
Sonne of Mercy ! that in blest *Maries* wombe
Incarnate was ; left Heaven thy mansion place ;
   Where now thou art, and art all where ; Come see !
   My heart, my help, my health, depend on Thee.

In Thee I rest, Lord ! sanctifie my hope,
In Thee I trust, Lord ! fortifie my faith ;
In Thee I grow, Lord ! fructifie my scope,
In Thee I walk, Lord ! rectifie my path :
   In Thee I stay, in Thee I live, and die :
   In Thee I move, in Thee above I flie.

Lord ! grant thy grace may make these TEARES so blest ?
(And blesse them all, shall them peruse for blis)
That godly griefe, may in their blessings rest,
Remorsefull soules, whose teares implore for this :
   LORD ! pittie me, LORD ! pardon my TRANSGRESSION,
   Lord ! cleanse my HEART ; Lord blesse thou this CONFESSION.

FINIS.

A
Briefe and summarie
discourse upon that lamen-

table and dreadfull disaster

at D u n g l a s s e.

Anno 1640. the penult

of August.

Collected from the soundest
and best instructions,

That time and place could certainly
affoord, the serious enquirie of the

painfull and industrious Author.

By W i l l i a m L i t h g o v v.

EDINBURGH,
Printed by R o b e r t B r y s o n.

The Argument.

WHat mean you Poets now? where are your verse?
Shall Gallants die? will you forget their Herse?
Shall after times be robbd, of what disasters
Have now falne out? fye on you Poetasters
Why sit you dumb? or can you not performe
So sad a task, on such a grievous storme?
Else gape you for reward, whilst there is none
Left to requite you, save your selves alone:
This perhaps may stop you, why? without gains,
Prest Penmen shrink, its true, gifts sweeten pains
But most men think, pathetick stiles seem hard
For some to do, the like hath numbers marrde:
Shall I grown old then write? nay, I must to it,
Since you, and your young straines refuse to do it.
This work ten months ago, had seen the light,
But unperformde promises, bred o'resight.
At London, and at home: Should I conceale
For blandements, what I'me bound to reveale,
And at my cost dischargde: No, that were rare,
To see mee court (Camelion like) the aire.
VVould God like subject, heavens from earth had closde,
Then friends nor foes, had grievd, nor yet rejoicde.

A 2

But

The argument.

But all Monarchick Tyme must seal this blow,
What we construct, that sequel times may know:
Deeds smotherd, lye intombd, thoughts without words,
Are dumb mens signes, what our prime light affoords,
Is utterance from knowledge; though now dark times,
Shut murder up, closde with perfidious crymes:
Nay, whats not now? hands, seals, oathes, writs, & vows,
Are cancelld, or forsworne; deceit allows
Base falshood, for best truth: (O treacherous hearts!)
How shall the heavens revenge us! on your parts
Yet patience crowns our suffrings, and none such
But they who can the marke of conscience touch.
Then since its so; that words and woes agree,
Let silence sleep, Ile mourne where mourners be.

Times

Times sorrovvfull disaster
at *Dunglasse*, containing infallible
grounds and reasons, how that most
exccrable and parracidiall deed
was committed.

Et melting flouds, sad silent groaves, and winds
Bank-falling brooks, & shril woods that blinds
Prest Nymphall lists ; let frowning time, & all
The Elements admyre, this monstrous fall,
And marveilous mishape, done under tract
Of homicide, by an abortive fact :
Come let them roare, and rent the azure skies,
(Lamenting this lament) with shrinking cries,
And agitat reports : let ecchoing hills,
From their wide sighted tops, rebounding fills,
The solitarie plains, with trembling sounds,
Of dreadfull Massacres ; gorging stressd bounds,
With laborinths of fears ; come spend their time,
To siste the Traitour, and that treacherous cryme :
Which this black herse averrs : let heavens, and all,
That move, and live, within earths massie ball ;
Adhere, and witnesse bear, of these disasters,
And by their kindes, turne prodigall, worne wasters,
Of watrie woes : let darkned dens and caves,
Steep rocks sunk glens, dead creatures from their graves
Shout forth their plaints, sowre stormy showres of grief
To plead our pleading losse.   And to be brief ;
Come soul-set mourners, for untimely death,
That can expresse your sighes, and panting breath

                                                With

Times sorrowfull disaster

With hollow groanes, come shed with me salt teares,
And plunging sobs, for mourning now appeares:
Say, if deep sorrow, may from passive mood,
Turn watrie woes, in a *Palmenian* floud:
Its more then time, Cœpartners had their share,
Grim grief is easde, when care reforgeth care,
For if the minde (like to a soul tormented)
Make passion speak, melancholy is vented.
   What shaking terrour stroke me to the heart,
Whilst I conceivd the fact, and saw the part
Left desolate and spoild, and so confounded
That my forcd cryes, from Ecchoes twice rebounded,
Fell flatlings down, where they and I lay so,
Alive or dead, I knew not, if, or no:
For passion (like to rapsodies) subverts
The vitall sense, extreames construct our smarts.
And none so shallow, but they may conceave
That sudden news, if bad, our souls do leave,
Laid in a litargie, of sensllesse sleep,
Till rouzd, and then pale eyne begin to weep:
Such pearling drops, with windy sighs and sobs
Heart groaning grief, and *Cataphalion* blobs,
When brust, begets a voice, that voice sad words
Which now my self; to my sought self affords.
   O fatall stroke! O dolefull day and houre!
What raging hate, made time to lurk and loure,
To murder such brave sparks, (beside all others)
A noble Lord, two Knights, and two kinde brothers,
All *Hammiltons* of note? with many moe,
Which in a Catalogue, I will thee show,
Placd here at the conclusion, for direction
So far by tryall, as I got inspection,
VVith cost and toylsome paines: who can deplore
Their tragick end? else who can keep in store

                                     Their

Their fatall names ? full threescore young and old,
Were killd and quelld, in that unhappie hould ;
And smotherd down with stones : like fearfull end
Was ne'er heard of : what ? did a cloud portend
That blustring blow, which rose on sunday morne,
Forth from the sea, and to *Dunglasse* was borne.
O pitifull presage ! which they did see,
Yet had no luck, from that hard luck to flee.
But what ? who can expresse this grievous act ?
Hearts may conceive, what no pen can extract :
Some few of all were safe, and onely nine,
Of which there two, this mem'rie I propyne ;
Young *Dalmahoy* and happie *Prestongrange*,
Who by heavens marv'lous mercy, in this change
Did wondrously escape ; and yet both wounded,
Have in that harme, their health again refounded,
All thanks to *Jove :* Lord make them wise to know
Their lives sweet safetie, in that dreadfull blow.
For in the twinkling of a rolling eye,
Their friends and they were severd : But come see,
How all the rest lye shent, some undiscoverd
Are there shut up, with heaps of fragments coverd,
And bodies torne and crushd : what shall I say ?
But curse th'accident, of that dismall day.
 What, had the destinies, or angrie fates,
Crossde constellations, deaths prodigious Mates,
Or ominous aspects, self-bloudy Comets,
That like prest whirlewindes, their furie vomits,
With anxious threats on man, decreed this wonder !
That dye they must, and dye with such a thunder.
O sterne mortalitie ! that with their death,
Reft blind posteritie, of lookd for breath,
And natures tract, for they thryce hopefull Syres,
Might have had children to their full desires :

                                                    Which

Which' now we want, whilst they themselves are laid
As low as dust, by deaths predom'nant spade.
   But stay sad soul, what means these heaps of stones,
And lumps of walls, spread as confused ones ;
Trace here and there : where, when I went a spying,
My heart it faild me, and I fell a crying :
O Heavens ! (said I) how came this deed to passe ?
So many Worthies slain, in sackt *Dunglasse* :
For what ? by whom ? what evill had they done ?
That one black sudden blast, they could not shun :
Wast their Ancestors fault ? their owne much worse ?
Their kinreds guilt or friends ? their childrens curse ?
Or hyrelings scourge ? O Heavens will ye conceal
This stratagem, and not the truth reveal :
If mortall men were angels, we should know
The cause, the sin, the Wretch, the hand the blow :
But this combustion, ah ! confused tort,
Was but a crack : and now to make it short,
There's one suspect'd, and that suspitions true,
Actor he was, if done of spight, judge you,
As after you shall hear : But I'le proceed
In method and in matter, so take heed.
   Lo, I have searchd, and tryde, and seen the place,
And spoke with some alive ; but for the cace
And manner how, they know no more, then they
Who never saw't, so sudden was the fray :
That even the thought, of that prepostrous fit,
VVas sensible, to have robbd them of their wit,
If deeply weighd : as who would from a rock,
Leap headlong in the sea, such was that knock,
These Innocents receivd : a Lyons heart
VVould shake in pieces, to conceive their smart,
And short farewell. So quick was their goodnight,
Like to a Faulcon in his hungrie flight.

                                         That

at Dunglasse.

That lends the eye a glance, that heart nor minde
Can show the like, except the rushing winde.
Which forceth me, (if melting woes may mourne)
Backwards to look, and to my plaints returne :
O sad disaster ! so monstrous and cruel,
As if hells mouth, had lent the action fewell,
Is more then admirable : what flesh can
Dascon the fault, and that short fury scan.
  Afore the floud and after, the like blow
Was never heard of, nor no time can show
So foule a tragick act : done, and undone,
Was both the deed, and dead ; the glimpsing Moone
VVas in the wayning hushd, as if the night
That followd on, had lost its borrowd light
From curling *Thetis* : Like crack, nor like smoake
Made never *Strombolo*, that burning rock
In the *Eufemian* gulf ; nor *Vulcans* shop
In the *Æolian* Iles, can this o'retop,
Nor no like furious flame ; nor *Ætnaes* fire
In three set parts, may with this crack aspire,
For all its force : was malice so incensde,
That neither space nor favour, was propensde
To harmelesse honestie. O dreadfull doome !
That with a clap, did threescore lives consume.
Or was it so, that flesh and bloud may shrink,
To ruminat on them ? or shall we think
But our deserts are worse ; the good with bad
Do suffer oft, for destinie is mad.
  Me thinks that hell broke loose, and that the Divell
Had got his reynes, the actor of this evill :
O divine providence ! how could this be ?
VVhen he thats kept in chains, was now set free
Is he not limitd, and thy mighty power
Set to controle him, else he vvould devoure

Thy

Times sorrowfull disaster

Thy Saints, and choicelings, but belike its so
Thou lets him smite, yet saves thy people tho :
He could not torture *Job*, without commission
Nor yet work here, without thy large permission :
Was there no way to death, but by the rage
Of a tempestuous sound ? could nought asswage
Thine angrie face, O God ! but dye they must,
And with a violent rapt, be throwne to dust,
As Doomesday had been set, to raze the world
With twinckling speed, so were they from us hurld.
If done in field or battell, it had been
No cause of sorrow, lesse of weeping eyne.
For *Mars* conceives no sturt, nor will allow
His Darlings should, to peevish wayling bow,
Which we must yeeld to : yet if we compare
Acts past, with present, this fact must be rare.
   How Kings were murderd, & their Kingdoms thrown
Downe to destruction, is distinctly known
By pen and pensile ; and preceeding times
Have left to us the reason, and their crymes.
Proud *Pyrhus* with a stone, from a weak hand
Lost life and Kingdome, and his great command
And *Agamemnon*, after ten yeares warres,
Returnd ; when done, were vanquisht *Phrigian* jarres,
Was by his page transactd, (with a back thrust)
From high bred honour, to disdainfull dust.
VVhat bloud was shed, in the *Pharsalian* field,
Where *Cæsar* fought with *Pompey;* both did weild
The accidents of fortune, for they strove
To lord the earth, next to imperiall *Jove ;*
Cæsar was victor, and that *Romane* floure
Lost all the world, within one dismall houre :
Yet *Cæsar* smarts, (the Fates his doome extend)
He rose with bloud, and made a bloudy end.

1 will

at Dunglasse.

I will not speak, of *Tamberlanes* great fight
Five hundred thousands, put to death and flight :
Nor from the *Thebane* Captaines will I bring
Their bloudy Trophees, nor of *Carthage* sing,
And her subverted Champion ; nor sackt *Tyre*,
Nor *Ilions* doome, shall my pen set on fire :
Nor siege I *Jebus*, (*Josephs* sacred storie)
Where vanquishd Jews, lost with themselves their glory
Nor of the eastern Monarchy Ile sing,
How *Philips* son, was made a *Persian* King,
And spread his wings to *Ganges ;* whence returnde,
To *Babels* delicates ; where fortune spurnd,
Against his pride, and by a slave (made slave)
Was reft, of what he reft, nay, worse the grave.
  Like instances, I many could produce,
But these may serve, for to shut up the sluce :
Yet what of all, can all these paralell
This horrid murder : No, I will thee tell
Like villany and fact, read never man,
If with the matter, you the manner scan.
Traitours to Castles fled, fraught with despaire,
Have blown themselves, and fortunes in the aire
But that was madnesse : Voluntarie acts
Are murders, the Devil constructs such facts :
But this *malheure*, ah ! unexpectd disdain,
Came thundring forth, and with its crack they're slaine,
A ravishd thing, like to a thought or gleame
Of fancies fled ; so was this deed a dream,
To sight and swift conceit : O wondrous wonder !
And fearfull blacknesse, of a boystrous thunder,
Which rent the clouds : Oh ! what shall I report,
To correspond this all-predominant tort :
But stay and muse, on accidents have been,
Or voluntary deeds, too often seen ;

Crossd

Times sorrowfull disaster

Crossd ships at sea misled, by chance, or spight,
Or for revenge, been vanquishd by strong fight
Have blown themselves aloft.   Looke for the nones,
How men were burnt, and slaine, and drownde at ones :
Take here the Popes *armado*, lately shrunk,
Where seas with Papists bloud, were soundly drunk
Along the *Kentish* shoare, till *Neptune* staggerd,
Whilst hyrelings on, his tumbling sides they swaggerd :
We thank thee *Martin Trump*, thou playd a spring
On thy great Trumpes, made *Tritons* dancers sing
Spaine and *Romes* overthrow ; and set us free
From their damnd plots, perfidious policie.
I will not here insist, although I can
Discusse their projects, subject, craft, and man.
    Then to illustrate all, take Eighty Eight,
Take merchant sights, take Pirats, & more slight
Take *Tartarets* and Frigots, you shall see
When stressd and clasped, how desperatly they die :
This word, Give fire, transcends them through the aire
Where with themselves, their foes the like doe share,
And seldome failes, unlesse a distance be,
The one been sackt, the other back doth flee.
VVhat of like accidents, they're but extreames
Forcd on revenge, self-murder crownes their names
VVith endlesse torture : But ah ! this deed now done,
Can not be matchd, with nought beneath the Sunne.
Yet some Ile point, to let you see what wounds
Depend on Climats, and their sun-scorchd bounds.
    Then I to Earthquakes come, and deafning thunder,
VVhere Ile touch three grosse accidents of wonder,
At *Berat* near *Castras* in *Languedock*,
A thunder-bolt upon thee steeple broke
(The folk been fled for safetie to the Church)
Full sixteen hundreds, closd within its Porch)

The

at Dunglasse.

The steeple (stroke) fell down, and with its fall
Down came the Church, the tecture, roof, and al
VVhich smotherd the whole people : Never one
Escapd that roaring shot, save twelve alone
That kept at home, been sicklie, agd, and lame,
And had no strength, to court this falling frame,
This stone-walld town laid waste, the sequel day
I came to view it, fearfull was the fray :
This thundring blow fell out, on fryday morne
One thousand, six hundred, and thirteen worne.
From thence to *Lombardie,* Ile quicklie trace,
To *Pearie,* that incorprat haplesse place,
Set on the river *Ladishae,* and closd
Between two hills, the Alpes are here disclosde
VVhich bend to *Rhetiaes* land : this citie crownd
For Orenge, Fig, and Lemmon, was renownd :
The tenth of August, and on sunday night,
At eight a clock, appeard a fearfull sight :
An earthquake shook the hill, above, and under :
The town streets trembled, like quagmyres asunder :
The rock falls from above, the towne it sunk
Ingulfd within earths bosome : as it shrunk,
There was none savd, not woman, man, nor childe,
Nor gold, nor goods, (the truth been here instyld)
Except a bell, that from the steeple brust,
When it was swallowd, with a counter-thrust :
The river followd on, and in it run
Long five houres space, till all was full, and done
Returnd to its own course : the Bell was found
On th'other side of *Ladish,* dasht on ground :
Three thousand lives were lost, and ly interrd,
VVithin one grave : behold, how fortune errd.
  Last to *Bizantium,* I amazed come,
To reckon on mishaps, and there's the summe,

Times sorrowfull disaster

In winter (not in Harv'st the usuall time,
When *Terramoti* court, each parched clyme)
An earthquake movd, and in the town it fals,
Near *Bosphores* side, and razd a myle of wals,
Which fencd the place ; and in that glutting downe
Three thousand houses, land, and sea did drowne,
Which held ten thousand people : but its true,
There were few *Greeks*, the most were *Turke* and *Jew*,
And so the lesser losse : I will not stand
Here to expostulate (from hand to hand)
How that ground was recoverd ; but it cost
The great *Turke* more, than all was drownd and lost :
But for their sepulchre, I daring swear,
I never saw the like, as I saw here.
Lo, this great judgement fell, in dark December,
One thousand six hundred, ten, as I remember.
   Yet to comment on this, these incidents,
Arise as *Bassads*, from their elements,
Of fire, and aire : the one through clouds it brusts,
The other choaks it, with retorting gusts :
Composde of contraries, lightning, and raine,
The former forcd, the sequell addes the straine.
The last as reinvestd, in earth is found,
When hollow sun-scorchd chinks, divide the ground :
The winde rushd in, begets a monstrous birth,
That can transplant, or raze mountaines of earth.
Townes, forts, or Cittadales, transforme a lake,
In heaps of sand ; so, so, the earth can quake :
Not done by airt nor hand, or hellish plots,
As this abortive deed (exposd on *Scots*)
Was by the Devill devisde, he actd his part
And causd distress, with groaning Patients smart
Done by *Ned Paris*, arraignd at the Court
Of Heaven, and Earth, for this tremenduous tort

                                      Enforcd

at Dunglasse.

Enforcd on death.   Come let thy ghost appear,
To answer for thy fact, thats sifted here :
Wast done of malice ? or of negligence ?
If not of purpose, lesse was thine offence, ?
And yet no oversight, nor carelesse minde,
Can thee excuse, for that would judgement blind ;
No, its not so, thy bloudy oathes and curses
Bewrayd thy drift ; thy foure times mounting horses,
That after noon : and still would flee, yet stayd,
The train was laid, but thou the fact delayd,
Till thy Lords comming back, with knights and gentry
VVherein the inner Court, just at the entrie,
To mount the stairs, there, there, thou smote thy maister
And many Gallants with that damnd disaster :
VVhich in thy looks was seen, ere it was done,
Mischief hung in thy face, that afternoone,
With railing, swearing, cursing, boasting some,
(VVhom thou affectd) to haste soon to their home :
And yet one scapd, whom thy menacing throat
Did spur away, the greater his good lot,
The stable keeper there, *Will Paterson*,
That did attend thee then, set me this down.
But Ile come near, and try more strict conclusions,
Base mindes ill set, are fosters of confusions ;
Then what meant that irne ladle in thine hand
Tane from the Kitchin hot (O hels fyrebrand !)
VVhence to the *magazin*, thou kept thy way,
VVhere eighteen hundred weight of powder lay,
Of which thou hadst the charge, and onely thou
Came onely there : what ? did thy Lord bestow
On thee that trust, and durst thou play the knave
To kill thy Maister : Vile opprobious slave,
Mad were thy brains, and still were known for madnesse
All times absurd, and rammage in thy badnesse :

A great

Times sorrowfull disaster

A great blasphemer of Gods name, and more
Thy proverb was, Devill damne me, there's the gore,
That slew thee with that slaughter : O cursde wretch !
And wicked drudge how could thou this way stretch
Thy cruel hands, was there no pittie left
To save the saiklesse ? was thou so far reft,
(O senslesse sot) from reason and respect
Of men and Master, that thou wouldst infect
The earth and aire with murder : Oft I said
To thine and my consorts, this *English* blade
Is neither sound nor civil : O ! how can
His Lord give trust, to such a frantick man :
A daily drunkard, sotting here and there,
Led with deboshrie, and infernall care.
  Another thing condemnes thee, that same night,
An houre before the deed, in deep despight,
Thou wouldst not give to souldiers, match, nor ball,
Nor powder, save two shots : And worst of all
These Carabines thou chargd, and didst deliver
To *Troupers* were half chargd : nor seldome ever
Had half of them flint stones : their bals were choakd
Half raches downe, and could not be revokd,
Nor shot undread, though time and place cravd aid,
Bred from that *Barwick* fray, was there defrayd.
Thy speech disclosd thy spight, thy rammage looke
And glooming browes, gave signes (if not mistook)
Of unafronted drifts : Thy grumbling words,
And chattring lips, were sharper far then swords,
Which erst had been more calme : this tale was thine,
Some *Scots* ere long should smart, as they at *Tine*,
Which wore the Papall badge : vvhich thou performd,
Whē that brave house, with thy cursd hāds thou stormd,
VVhich vvas made knovvn to some three dayes before
The deed vvas done, it vvould be done, and more

These

at Dunglasse.

These news from *Barwick* came, and many heare it,
But could not know the manner how to feare it:
Which shows it was devisd, and sought, and wrought
By Traitours in both lands, ere it was brought
To such a dreadfull passe.   How this Wretch livd,
Doubtlesse some had, in both the Kingdomes grievd,
And lost their *Hydra* necks: Now Ile returne
To cavell with the Traitour, and this turne.
Thy body in three parts, sore torne was found
And one of them thy legge, which on the ground,
Lay twelve weeks hid 'mongst stones, and this I saw
Two swyne its flesh, from thy cursde bones did gnaw
A just and loathsome sight: In thy left hand
The irne ladle stuck fast; the grip and band
Was hard and sure, that scarce one man could throw
The ladle from thy fingers; there's a blow.
Would God before *Breda*, that thou hadst died
Three yeares ago, where thou wast vilifyed
With every souldier; then this wofull deed
Had not been done, nor such deep grievance spread
In honest hearts, O vyle barbarian barbour,
And son of a poore Porter, could thou harbour
So deadly damnd disdain, as for to kill
All kinde of sex, in thy most scelerat ill:
Nay, could not spare thy self; had thou no wit
To save thy self and flee, when time thought fit.
   Away unhappie beast, what shall I conster?
But curse thy birth, bred for a murdring monster:
Did not thy Maister cloath thee, like a Knight,
And stuff thy purse with gold: O thanklesse wight!
His love thy life abusde, whilst drunken snake,
The Tavern turnd thy Church; did thou forsake
The law of duetie, but curst *Malandrine*,
Thy brain-sickpate, must run on his ruine.

Might not seven yeares twice o're command thy part.
To honour his familiar noble heart:
Were ever any knew him, but admyrd
How his rich minde, was with great gifts inspyrd,
And hardinesse of Heart; Lord *W.W.* may,
Recall that combat, of his vanquishd day:
And could this Ruffian, th' abject of a Traitour,
Injure so high a sprite, so kynde a Nature.
And yet he lives, (so great was his good name)
Christs Martyr, truths mirrour, faiths soul-plight fame
The cause was good he dyed for, but the fact
And parracide, was hatefull, here's the tract.
  O inhumane! most execrable deed!
So barbrous neckt, with a *Cyclopian* head,
Framd like *Enceladus;* that thrice me thinks,
He's worse than Villane, at this murder winks.
What heathnick, or what Pagane? savage bloud
What infidel? could have provd half so rude
As this cursde cative, *Englands* Monster borne,
That with the fact, left life and soul forlorne.
What *Jamnite?* or what *Sabunck?* garlick slaves
Would not to nature stoupe? whose light conceaves
A tender kindnesse, to conserve the race
Of mankinde, Vertue, having the first place:
But this *Cerberian* snake, had no regard
To great nor small, like doome was never heard
As he decreed: ah! I want words and breath
For to detect this *Charon*, and their death.
But he like *Erostratus* would aspire,
That set *Dianas* Temple in a fire,
To purchase flying fame: So frantick he
In this *Catastrophe*, would living be,
Which I adhere to, and for longer time,
Ile fix on brasse, his filthy fact and cryme.

If

If any be suspectd, more than this wretch,
Let justice, and sound judgement to it stretch,
And let our Parliament, sift and search out
The plot, the man, the guilt, if there be doubt.
For common fame I leave't, and for like torts,
Of tortring tongues, Ile not build on reports.
Why ? thats absurd to follow flying fame,
Its deep experience, reares up truth a Name.
   Now Ile return to my Pathetick style,
And mourne with mourning Ladies grievd the while,
For losse of their dear husbands ; O pale woe !
When two made one, the knot dissolves in two,
Rent by the Fates, egregious whirling rage,
And not by frequent death, done by a Page,
And quintiscencd Saltpeter : O who can !
Their melancholy mindes, in sadnes scan !
Each soul reserves its grief, each hath like losse,
For life there's death, for comfort sorrows cross
A common woe ; peculiar to each one
Graft, and engraves, a sympathizing moane :
First, thou great Dame, thryce noble by thy birth,
Sprung from a princely stock : what tongue on earth
With words can swage thy woes ? thy sorrows show,
From heart-grown grief, that foule pernicious blow,
Attachd fore thee : thy face, thy food, thy rest,
And sleep denote, how thy sad soul's opprest
With helplesse care : whilst scarcely half a year
Did thou enjoy this dearest Jewell, thy Dear :
Great was that love, thy loving *Hadington*
Bore to thy soul : thy love again did crowne
His fixt respect : By which your tender hearts
Knit up in one, made love act both your parts :
That *Hymen* blushd (the god of sacred rites)
To see how love involvd in one, two sprites :

C 2

And

And why ? no wonder, both alike excelld,
The one the other, in goodnesse paralelld,
He spoke, you smild, he winkd, & you conceivd
His mentall scope, what great content receivd
Your mutuall intents, whilst demonstration
Reciprocat, brought *Paphos* one oblation :
And yet he left thee, not to live alone,
But left thee his fair Phenix, being gone.
A pledge of comfort, representing still
His face, thy stamp, his heart, thy love, his will.
    O like *Penolope !* if thou couldst spinne
A daily threed, and that same threed untwinne,
Till he turnd back, so that the fates had sworne
Thy pennance should be, twentie winters borne,
And he redeemd : But stay sad Muse returne,
Galld grief and love, can not together mourne.
Two passions, two extreams, and here I finde,
They're violent rapts, in either of each kinde.
Away with *Didoes* stroke, *Lucretiaes* smart,
Faire *Hieroes* thrust, *Palmeniaes* fatall dart,
Which grim despaire (not love) forcd them to act
Their self sought murder, in a tragick fact :
Call, call to mind ! Gods providence, and see
Nought comes to passe, without heavens high decree,
Which mortals must embrace : then Lady spare
Thy ruthlesse grief, lay on the Lord thy care.
    And ye the rest, deare Ladies in your kindes,
Let sorrow smart, take comfort, lift your mindes
Above all worldly crosses ; you shall see,
The length of dayes ; hence soules eternitie
In endlesse peace : Cast all your griefe on God,
He can release, and chasten, bruise the rod.
Lo, deepest streames, in smoothest silence slyde,
Whilst Channels roar, so shallow mourners glyde,

With

at Dunglasse.

With words at will, but mighty cares sit dumbe,
Like livelesse corps, laid in a livelesse Tombe :
Whence moistned vapours, forcd from humid woes
Lye in oblivion terrd.   And now to close,
As quickly went their soules to heaven, we hope,
As their lives quickly fled : the traitours scope
Was set on murder : but their Angels watchd
And caught their sprites, as with a twinkling catchd
To Paradise : Where now thrice blest they be,
With glorie crownde ; heires of eternitie,
And endlesse joyes : for they as Martyres died,
And now sweet souls, with triumphs dignified :
Set up' mongst Hierarchies, of sacred sprites,
That to their blest societie, them invites,
To seale their Martyredome, in Jesus hand
Cled with his righteousnesse : Who can demand
A better state ? then face for face, to face,
The face of faces, in that glorious place ;
Where Saints and Martyres, environing round,
The old Eternall, with the joyfull sound
Of Aleluhiaes, sing before the throne
Holy, holy, Lord, to Heavens holy One,
The Lambe of God, hembd in with burning glore,
Praise, might, dominion, Majestie, and power :
Where they (thrice hopefull happie) ever blest,
Are crownd and raigne, in long eternall rest.
   So, so forbear, ye who keep grief in store,
    Take up your crosse, and for them mourne no more.

And now followeth the names of the moſt part of them that died at *Dun-glaſſe*, the penult of Auguſt, 1640. ſo farre as poſſibly the Author could collect by ſerious inſtruction, and diverſe informations, both of the vulgars, and better ſort.

T*Homas Earle of Hadington.*
Robert Hammilton of *Binny* his brother.
Master *Patrick Hammilton*, his naturall brother.
Sir *Alexander Hammilton* of *Lawfield.*
Sir *John Hammilton* of *Redhouse.*
Colonel *Erskine*, son to *John* late Earl of *Mar.*
John Keith, son to *George* late earle *Marshall.*
Sir *Gideon Baillie* of *Lochend.*
Laird of *Ingilstoun* elder.
Laird of *Gogor* elder.
Alexander Moore, heritour of *Skimmer.*
John Gate Minister at *Bunckle.*
Niniane Chirneside in *Aberladie.*
James Sterling Lieutenant.
Alexander Cuningham Lieutenant.
David Pringle Barbour Chirurgion.
Robert Faulconer, Sergeant.
George Vach, Haddingtons Purveyer.
John White Plaistrer, an *English* man.
William Symington, Lochends servant.
George Neilson in *Alhamstocks.*
James Cuningham in *Hadington.*

John

at Dunglasse.

John Manderstoun.
Matthew Forrest.
Patrick Batie.
Alaster Drummond, alias *Gundamore*
John Campbell.
John Idington.
James Foord, John Arnots post boy.
John Orre.
Andrew Braidie.
John Tillidaff.
John Keith, a childe.

Women five.

Margaret Arnot, daughter to the Postmaister at Cock-
    burnspeth.
Marjorie Dikson, John Keiths servant.
Marion Carnecrosse.
Aleison Gray.

With twelve bore armes, whose names I could not ken,
Souldiers for time, not mercenary men :
The rest (unfound) ly terrd, corps, clothes, and bones
Under huge heaps of glutinated stones.
    Lo, I have done, as much as lay in me,
To try the truth, and blaze it, likes it thee,
Ime pleasde : if not, a figge for Carpers checks,
Whose chattring spight, the rule of reason brecks.
And now to close, let Cricks of all ranks,
Convince their censures, and yeeld me kinde thanks
    For what gain I, save labour, pains, and cost,
    To show the living, how the dead were lost.

FINIS.

SCOTLANDS

PARÆNESIS

To Her Dread Soveraign,

KING

CHARLES

THE SECOND.

Mens Scotiæ.

All Presbyterians, pure, sincere and true,
Afflicted by that Independent crue,
Are here untouch'd, and are declar'd to be
Joyn'd in the League and Covenant with me.

Printed in the Year, 1660.

SCOTLANDS *PARÆNESIS*

To her dread Soveraign,

KING CHARLES

The Second.

COme to thy Land, my long'd for Soveraign,
And here in safety and in honour raign :
Come to these bounds, where, of thy royal Stem,
Ten and One hundred wore the Diadem :
Disperse griefs cloudy frowns, to me restore
Those Halcion dayes which I enjoy'd before,
When by his presence, my late gracious King,
Transcending pleasure to my coasts did bring,
And all my minions joyntly did expresse
Their boundlesse comfort, and my joyes excesse.

   Raign with those joy'd enduments from above,
Th'Almighties blessing, and thy Subjects love.
Raign and live long, Thou period of my pleasure
My joyes triumph, the sum of all my treasure,
Best of my thoughts, center of my delight
Raign, as a beam of beauty shining bright
From heavens aspect : Raign in all Royal parts
A King of men, a conquerour of hearts.
Raign, let *Jehova's* will model'd in heaven
In gold characters, on thy Throne be graven,
Of Piety and Justice ; to enable
Thee to defend the one and other Table.
Raign, *Scotland's* Lyon to the worlds end out,
Who dare presume to call thy Power in doubt.

First,
In the Authors
Poeme, inti-
tuled, Scot-
lands *welcome*
to KING
GHARLES
in Anno,
1633.

A 2

Raign,

Raign, and triumph throughout great *Britans* soyle
In spight of all envenom'd breasts that boyle
With hell-hatch'd malice, in that neighbour ground,
Wherein excesse of raigning sins abound,
Raign, and that Land from vipers venome clenge,
So shall that motto hold, *Raign* and *Revenge.*

A guard from heaven have hedg'd thee so about,
That thee to harme all furies stand in doubt :
For why ? That All-sufficient hath prepard,
Emplumed squadrons for thy surest guard.

But that thy Throne unmoved still may stand,
Let true Religion flourish in thy Land,
Pure and sincere, in freedome and in truth,
Redrest, reform'd, from Gods own Heraulds mouth,

Let King *Josias*, and thy Grandsire be,
Examplare types and speaking maps to thee :
He with his Royall Robes his heart did rent,
For the neglect of Gods blest Covenant,
Then caus'd the same be read, and sworn to all,
Who in the limits of this Land did dwell :

1581. So from the year our blessed Lord was born,
Our Covenant by good King *James* was sworn,

1584. And was confirmed after some few years
To all his Household, and his noble Peers :
And now of late, Seign'd and redintegrate,
By all the loyall Subjects of our State :
Let Head and Body then in one accord,
To Seign, Swear, keep our Covenant with the Lord :
And as my *Patriots* dear, of each degree,
Are sworn to maintain Authoritie,
So shall they joyn, and strive even all as one
To re-install thee in thy Fathers Throne ;
Of Vipers brood th'infected soyle to clenge,
And make that antheme sound, *Raign* and *Revenge.*

The great Avenger shall revenge my cause,
And make these Monsters feel the Lyons pause,
Who by one fact the worst of acts have done,
Unparallel'd as yet beneath the Moon,

Yet

Yet palliate with Justice cloak that so,
Those men by Justice, Justice should ov'rthrow.
   With raigning sins all *Israels* Kings were stain'd,
Even from the time that *Jeroboam* raign'd,
With Rapine, Violence, Murther, Sorcery,
And all did act accurs'd Idolatry :
Yet none of them by Statute were depos'd,
Or to a publike censure once expos'd,
Arraign'd, condemn'd, or struke by Justice hands,
Within the Cities of these bordering Lands :
But when their vicious raigns and lives were ended,
Their sons or kins-men to their thrones ascended.
Raign and *Revenge* the breach of faith by those
My feigned friends, but most pernicious foes :
Base skurrill rogues, by Satans angels sent,
To swear and scorn the League and Covenant :
Camel'on Monsters, mingling truth with lies :
Stain'd with these colours of repugnancies,
Proud *Babels* tenents seeming first to hate,
But now like *Babel* ruling Kirk and State :
Bishops Hierachies sworn to suppresse,
Now like *Erastus* Anarchy professe ;
My Presbyterial Church-government,
Though seeming to maintain, They disassent :
They seem'd t'extirpate Schisms and Sectaries,
But now they tolerate old coyn'd Heresies :
And worst of all, if any worse can be,
They strive to break the neck of Monarchie,
And trample on their Princes, whom before
They seem'd with Civil Worship to adore :
And *Englands* Peers they levell with the ground
Of locusts base born swarms, which there abound
A swarme of *Brownists*, fond *Separatists*,
Proud *Antinomians*, wilfull *Erastists*,
Old *Levellers*, monsters Inhabitants,
Last worst of all, that crue of *Independants*,
In whose infected souls these tares are sown,
And to a full perfection lately grown,

In Church-Government.

As

As Superstition, Schism, Heresie,
Tyrannie, Profainnesse, and Idolatrie,
Hypocrisie, a sin the last on earth,
Matth. 7. 22. Which shall revive in Judgement after death.
    O then how many plagues have they deserv'd ?
What grievous torments are to them reserv'd ?
Who in a desprat way, have hatch'd such evils,
As are of new suggested by the devils,
Who first, damn'd Atheists, trampled have upon
The sacred Statutes of the holy One.
Next in a furious, but a fond conceate,
Englands time scorning Lawes have abrogate :
And strive if they had power as will, to wound
Even Nature's frame, and all the world confound.
    The King of Kings first Monarch's did install,
And daign'd them by the name of Gods to call,
To show that earthly Powers Sovereign,
Have all their power from him, by whom Kings raign ;
Moses the meek, from Heaven, and not by chance,
Had rule in chief ov'r Gods Inheritance,
And was als absolute, in all degrees
As any that bear rule in Monarchies :
Witnesse rebellious *Korah,* with his mates,
And many murmurers their Confederates :
The first by a miraculous sort of death,
Were quick up-swallowed in the opening earth ;
Then fourteen thousand, and seven hundreth mo,
To *Pluto's* boures did in a moment go,
And for all hatching treason in their breast
Against their *Prince,* and Gods anointed *Priest.*
    Revenge, The Lord shall from his store-house bring
More grievous plagues on those that kill's a *King.*
Arise, O Lord, stretch forth thy powerfull hand,
Against the Justice-Juglers of that Land.
    Joshua to *Moses* for his valourous deeds,
As *Israels* Monarch, by Gods will succeeds ;
Who from his sacred mouth that choise did breath,
Menacing rebels with assured death.

Next

Next after *Joshua*, Judges were sole Princes,
Who did govern all *Palestines* provinces,
Till that unconstant *Israel* then neglected
And crav'd a King, was not then *Saul* elected
By Gods appointment and expresse command ?
And then anointed by the Prophets hand :
Young *David* next, Gods Minion, was install'd,
And from a sheep crook to a Scepter call'd ;
That from his loynes, a Virgin and a Mother
Should bear her Son, her Father, and her Brother.
Now give me leave a little to digresse,
And of that Plant this Antithese expresse :
Though call'd the Father of Eternitie ;
That we Gods sons the Son of man would be :
He daign'd 'mongst beasts, be born low in a cell,
That high in Heav'n men might with Angels dwell :
And though the word, yet child-like stammer would,
That to their Gods men might speak uncontroul'd :
The glorious Monarch of the World was poor,
That heavens rich store he might to man procure ;
Hungry he was, this with his Man-hood stood,
That men might feed on heaven descending food :
The precious Spring of Life for ever blest,
That we should drink his streames would suffer thirst ;
In end, the Life, th'eternall *King* would die,
That we should live and raign eternally.
  But to our purpose, Monarch's here below,
Can neither Chartor, Seal, nor Seasing show
Of their demaines, the Scepter, Sword and Crown,
And sacred oyl which from the heaven came down
Are symbols of their holdings from above,
Joyn'd with Gods blessing, and their peoples love,
Together with a Line of long succession,
And benefit of many years possession,
They are, and were of all Endictments free,
And Judged by their Peers they cannot be,
As Gods Vice-gerents answering to none,
But to that *King* who rules and raigns alone.

But

But if it be their fate to be detain'd
In firmance long, and in a Court araign'd ;
It is the will of God that so should be,

Psal. 107, 40. Who poureth down contempt on Majesty :
Job. 12, 21. 'Tis for our sins the Lord will have it so,
That strength curb Law, force Justice overthrow.

    Try Times, Records, which to our knowledge brings,
The reverence and respect we owe to Kings ;
David from dales to rockie deserts mounted,
By cruel *Saul* was like a Partridge hunted,
And had no time to rest, nor scarce to breath,
Affrighted with the fear of present death :
And though he had him twise caught in a snare,
Was counsell'd twise, his life no more to spare ;
Yet said, who dares stretch forth his murthering hand,
Against the Lords Anointed of the Land
And guiltlesse be, though branded with the crimes
Of Tyrants, who have liv'd in worst of Times ;
'Tis better far a Tyrant known should raign.
In any soil, nor want a lawfull King.

vide The new Yea though an Infidel, we should obey,
Confession of And for his honour and his safety pray :
Faith, c. 23 : The Jews, both Priest and People, all as one,
Are bidden serve the King of *Babylon ;*
Pray for that Cities peace, though there they be
Detain'd and kept in long captivitie.
So in our Lord and his Apostles time,

Tiberius. Four Tyrants rul'd in all the *Syrian* clime,
Caligula. He bids give *Cæsar* what is *Cæsars* own,
Claudius. And being tax'd, have by example shown
Nero. That due obedience should to *Kings* be given,
Who are though Tyrants, authoriz'd from heaven.

    Saint *Paul* what's due to higher Powers preacheth,
Obedience to Kings Saint *Peter* teacheth,
To Masters all, and froward though they prove,
They should be serv'd with due respect and love,

    A prosperous, fortunate, and happy crime,
Was call'd a glorious vertue for the time ;

O

O but suspend your judgment for a space,
And ye shall find a change in fortunes face,
Which shall ov'rcloud these flatterings rayes of light,
And turn them to a sad tempestuous night ;
Of treacherous Traitours such shall be the chance,
Who though at first they seem to have some glance
Of Halcion dayes, from fortunes raying face :
But sist a while ; ye shall not find the place
Of their abode, all but repentance shall
Here be confounded, and condemn'd in hell :
Revenge, good Lord, and such black sorrowes bring
On those vile Traitours who have killed a King.

    Great *Cæsar* did subvert the *Roman* State,
And to himself th'Empire did mancipate,
Who would but think that *Brute* and *Cassius* part
With all the rest that stob'd him to the heart
Was just, since that by fraud and policie,
He did ov'rturn *Romes* ancient liberty ;
O ! but behold, that Senats tragick cace,
They all were slain, within a three years space,
And some themself, with that self blade did kill,
Wherewith they lately *Cæsars* blood did spill.

    A modern Divine, glossing on this act,
Confest that *Cæsars* proud ambitious fact
Was first unjust, but when the Senate call'd him
Romes great Dictatour, and had once install'd him,
It was high Treason, to stretch forth their hand
Against that man who did in Chief command
Now as a Monarch, so that all the blood
Of those was justly shed, who him withstood.

    Then doth God favour Ethnick Princes cace,
Though alians from the Covenant of Grace,
Redresse their wrongs, confound their enemies,
Detect and punish lewd conspiracies
Hatch'd and fomented in a Trait'rous brain,
And shall he not the fire of vengeance rain
On that damn'd race ? Who in a tracherous mood,
Hath dyed their hands in Gods Vice-gerents blood.

        B   And

And then by show of Justice trampled down
Englands old Lawes ; have taken Head and Crown
From my blest *Charles*, who now in Glory sings
Unceasing Pœans to the King of Kings ;
Whose life a mirrour was of these blest three,
Religion, Justice, and Sobrietie
To God, to Man, and to himself, three Graces
Which now are heard, seen, shining in all places,
And shall remain transcending and entire
Till this great Fabrick be consum'd with fire,
   Now since that Monarch's are by God elected,
Let no man deem, that people dis-affected
Can loose the reins of their Government,
Or from their Line the Crown and Kingdom rent,
Excepting few, for Europes Monarchies
Are now subsisting of these four degrees,
Kings absolute, By Conquest, by Election,
Conditionall for favour and protection,
The first two branches meerly Soverain,
By wavering subjects can no change sustain.
The latter two not being of my strain,
It suites not here, nor can I now explain
The first two Powers, as their prerogative,
The Father dead do in the Son survive.
For now what State being parallel'd with mine,
Hath so stand, out against the waves of time.

Alexander.   For whiles that *Grecian* had subdu'd the East
And Monarch like in *Babylon* was plac'd,
The raign of my first Valiant *Fergus* than,
From God, and not by chance of War began,
Three hundreth years and fourty past and gone
Before our Lord took humane Nature on.
England from *William's* Stock of many Kings,
Us-ward in Line, to *Charles* the Second springs :
Ireland, in like sort, by a Conquest long
Deriv'd, doth to their Lord and King belong :
Though Commons acting on a tragick Stage,
A thing unheard in any former age,

                           Under

Under pretext of Jugling-Justice hands,
Have put to death the Soveraign of those Lands,
And in that Burley Court, would change the frame
Of *Englands* Statutes, would root out the steme
Of former Kings, and have without consent
Of King or Peers, acted a Parliament.

   A Parliament is model'd by the figure
Of a strong man, standing in force and vigoure
With sword in hand, menacing death to those
Who dare Gods will, or Subjects well oppose :
Whereof the King is head : the Peers the heart :
The Commons Members, and th'inferiour part :
How comes it then, shall such a monster made
Of basest parts, rule without heart or head ?

   God will stir up all Christians, Kings, and States,
In my revenge to be confederates,
And with me joyn, this dismal case is theirs,
Which may befal to them or to their heirs.
Crowns are in play, a Monarch is become,
The pannel'd Subject of base Commons doome.

   Up, let your Navies, and your Royal Hoasts,
Strike sail, land, vapour on the English Coasts,
Display your Ensignes, Princely Standards rear :
First strike with terrour, and a panick fear
Those bloudy Gemsters, who have trampled down
The Head, and made a stage play of the Crown.
Then shall we find them out forth from their dens,
From mountains, plains, from dales, and moorish fens,
Or where that Crue of Traitours may be found ;
We shall their rampiers level with the ground :
Their Strengths and Forts, since levelling they crave
From strong engines, let them such level have
As we impart : Let Justice then have place,
Till shee have quite cut off that cursed race.

   But if incens'd with fury they defie us,
And rang'd in squadrons have resolv'd to try us,
The worlds great Judge, no doubt in whom we trust,
Shall be our safeguard as our cause is just :

Thus

Thus shall our courage taught by wit and skill,
Skill arm'd by courage, both by power and will,
Make English ground incrimson'd with the blood,
Of that Schismatick *Independant* brood :
So what once *Cæsar*, we may say the same
Truely, we came, we saw, we overcame
And routed all, none shall escape our wrath,
But all shall die a just deserved death :
And Peace shall be proclaim'd in all those Lands,
Which now are purg'd by our victorious hands :
Then shall I still my King, young *Charles* Maigne,
And change that motto, thus *Triumph* and *Raigne.*

Epilogus.

ANd thou great King of Kings who rules above,
By whom Kings raign, by whom they live and move,
Moisten my soveraigns soul with showrs of grace,
That with him we may breath the aire of Peace
Raying with Truth ; that here he may secure,
Thy Divine Worship true, sincere and pure :
So shall we praise Thee, who for ever raigns,
And whose transcending Power all Power sustains.

FINIS.

www.ingramcontent.com/pod-product-compliance
Lightning Source LLC
Chambersburg PA
CBHW060519030726
47498CB00004B/998